Reckoning

WHAT READERS ARE SAYING

"What a ride I got! Love, action, excitement, crime families—heck, what more could you ask??"—Amazon reader "cedarblue," 5 stars (on *Malavita*)

"This story truly exceeded my expectations. *Revenge* is action-packed, and when the pace picks up, it does not slow down.... I cannot wait to read the next book."
—*The Romance Reviews (TRR)* site, 5 stars, Top Pick (on *Revenge*)

"Here is to a WHOOPING 5 stars. If I had to describe this book in about four words, it would be action-packed, sexy, romantic, and adrenaline-rushing.... This would make a kick-butt movie! There were times when I was fanning myself, sitting on the edge of my seat, and so mad I had to put it down. The steamy scenes were oh so delicious!"
—*Reading on the Wild Side* blog, 5 stars (on *Revenge*)

"The suspense keeps the pages moving quickly in book two of the Blood and Honor series. A fast pace, credible characters and a complex plot guarantee hours of entertainment."
—*RT Book Reviews* magazine, 4 stars (on *Retribution*)

"*Redemption* knocks it out of the PARK!!! This is the novel I was waiting for!!! ...I was blown out of the water on this one."
—*Steph's Book Retreat* blog, 5 stars (on *Redemption*)

"This series is awesome!!! If this series was ever made into a movie, it would put *The Godfather* to shame! ... I VERY HIGHLY RECOMMEND THIS BOOK. I WANT TO GIVE IT MORE THAN 5 STARS."
—*Julie's Book Reviews* blog, 5 stars (on *Redemption*)

"Hallelujah!!! I got the ending I needed and bonus happiness with Ruggero's story. With a title like *Reckoning*, I knew WHO I hoped was going to face their final reckoning. However, Delamar has proven time and time again, that no character within the Blood and Honor series is guaranteed a life and that its members can die at any time... The final showdown – The Reckoning – was unreal and full of surprises I wasn't expecting. ... I have loved this series from the first novella, *Malavita*, to this one and I'm not ready to say goodbye."
—Angela S. Goodrich for *Crystal's Many Reviewers* blog, 5 stars (on *Reckoning*)

"I burned Thanksgiving dinner because I couldn't stop reading this book! Once again, Dana Delamar has delivered gold! ... The characters are developed, honest, complex and HOT!!"
—Amazon reader Amy, 5 stars (on *Reckoning*)

ALSO BY DANA DELAMAR

Blood and Honor Series: Mafia Romance

Malavita (Prequel)
Revenge (Book One)
Retribution (Book Two)
Redemption (Book Three)
Reckoning (Book Four)

Writing with Kristine Cayne

Total Indulgence Series: MMF Ménage Romance

Her Two Men in London (Book One)
Her Two Men in Tahiti (Book Two)
Her Two Men in Sonoma (Book Three) – coming 2018

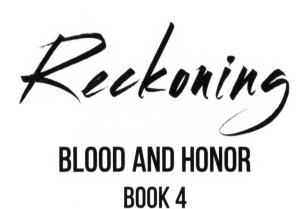

Reckoning

BLOOD AND HONOR
BOOK 4

DANA DELAMAR

ACKNOWLEDGMENTS

Many people contributed to the creation of this book. No writer goes it alone, and I am certainly no exception.

Once again, I am indebted to my wonderful critique partner, Kristine Cayne. She devoted countless hours of her time and attention to this book, helped me through some major stuck points, and cheered me on through a series of health issues. This book wouldn't exist without her support and contributions. A thousand thanks!

I'd also like to thank my fabulous beta readers, Kim, Stephanie, Trish, and Ninia, for their insights, comments, and catches. You all pitched in at the last minute, and you all made this book better than it was!

Mille grazie to Luigia Tella for answering my numerous and sometimes strange questions about Italy. Any errors are my own.

I owe a great debt to Romance Writers of America® and specifically my hometown RWA® chapters, Eastside RWA and Greater Seattle RWA, for providing inspiration, support, guidance, friendship, real-world craft advice, industry contacts, and knowledge that proved invaluable. Thank you all.

Last but not least, I'd like to thank my family, my friends, and most of all, my ever-patient husband, James Davis, for putting up with my many hours in the writer cave, making me scrumptious meals, and rubbing my shoulders when I'm tired. You put all my romance heroes to shame.

CAST OF CHARACTERS

The Lucchesis

Enrico Lucchesi (LOO kay zee) – *capo* (head) of the Lucchesi *cosca* (crime family)

Kate Lucchesi – wife of Enrico Lucchesi

Antonio Lucchesi (formerly Legato) – *capo di società* (second in command) of the Lucchesi *cosca*

Bianca Lucchesi – wife of Antonio Lucchesi and mother to Luca Lucchesi

Francesca Lucchesi – mother to Fedele, Sandro, Bianca, and Matteo Lucchesi; widow of Domenico Lucchesi

Ruggero (rooj JAIR oh) **Vela** – bodyguard to Enrico Lucchesi

Nick Clarkston – illegitimate son of Enrico Lucchesi; Interpol agent

Delfina Clarkston (née Andretti) – daughter of Dario Andretti; married to Nick Clarkston

Rinaldo Lucchesi – deceased; Enrico Lucchesi's father; former *capo*

Domenico (Dom) Lucchesi – deceased; first cousin to Enrico Lucchesi and former *capo di società* of the Lucchesi *cosca*

Fedele (feh DAY lay) **Lucchesi** (deceased), **Alessandro (Sandro) Lucchesi** (deceased), **Matteo Lucchesi** – brothers of Bianca Lucchesi and sons of Domenico Lucchesi

Antonella (Toni) Lucchesi (née Andretti) – deceased; Enrico's first wife; daughter to Carlo Andretti and sister to Dario Andretti

CAST OF CHARACTERS (cont.)

The Andrettis

Dario Andretti – *capo* of the Andretti *cosca* (Milan branch)

Ilaria (ee LAR ee ah) **Andretti** – wife to Dario Andretti

Lorenzo Andretti – grandfather of Dario Andretti; *capo* of the Andretti *cosca* (Calabrian branch); head of La Provincia (ruling commission of the 'Ndrangheta, the Calabrian Mafia)

Salvatore (Sal) Ruscino – brother-in-law to Benedetto Andretti; *capo di società* of the Andretti *cosca* (Calabrian branch)

Cristoforo (Cris) Andretti – deceased; son of Dario Andretti and *capo di società* of the Andretti *cosca* (Milan branch)

Benedetto Andretti – deceased; son of Lorenzo Andretti; former *capo di società* of the Andretti *cosca* (Calabrian branch) and head of La Provincia

Carlo Andretti – deceased; son of Lorenzo Andretti; former *capo* of the Andretti *cosca* (Milan branch)

Other Characters

Loredana (lor ay DAH nah) **Montisi** – a fervent anti-Mafia judge

Nora Montisi – Loredana's mother, former judge

Elena Farnese – sister of Ruggero Vela

Orlando Farnese – nephew of Ruggero Vela

Silvio Fuente – officer of the *carabinieri*

Vittorio Battista – godfather to Enrico Lucchesi and *capo* of the Battista *cosca*

Giovanna (joh VAN ah) **(Gio)** (Joh) **d'Imperio** – daughter of Gianluca d'Imperio

Gianluca (jon LOO kah) **d'Imperio** – *capo* of the d'Imperio *cosca*

GLOSSARY OF TERMS

avvocato (ahv voh CAH toh) – lawyer, attorney, advocate

bambina/bambino (bam BEE nah/bam BEE noh) – baby, child

basta (BAHS tah) – enough (as in "I've had enough!" or "Stop!")

bella/bello, bellissima (BEHL lah/BEHL loh, behl LEE see mah) – beautiful

bene (BEN ay) – good

bisnonno (beez NOH noh) – great-grandfather

capisci (KAH pee shee) – you see, you understand

capo (KAH poh) – head (don) of a crime family (*cosca*); plural *capi* (KAH pee)

capo di società (KAH poh DEE so cheh TAH) – second in command of a *cosca*

cara (CAR ah), *caro* (CAR oh) – dear, sweetheart

carabinieri (car ah bin YAIR ee) – Italy's national police force; a single member of this force is a *carabiniere* (car ah bin YAIR ay)

ciao (CHOW) – informal hello and goodbye

colpo di fulmine (KOHL poh DEE ful MEE nay) – love at first sight; literally "bolt of lightning"

comparaggio (cohm pah RAH joe) – the Southern Italian institution of co-parenthood, whereby the person making this vow swears to be as a parent to the child. A co-father is referred to as *compare*; the "parent" and "child" are *compari*. The vow is thought of as indissoluble and incorruptible. Within the Mafia, *compari* will not betray each other.

contabile (cone TAH bee lay) – accountant; treasurer for a *cosca*

corte (KOR tay) – court

cosca (KOHS kah) – a crime family; plural is *cosche* (KOHS kay)

Cristo (KREES toe) – Christ

culo (COO loh) – ass

davvero (dahv VAIR oh) – really, seriously

Dio mio (DEE oh MEE oh) – my God

GLOSSARY OF TERMS (cont.)

figlio (FEEL yoh) – son

giudice (JOO dee chay) – judge

grazie (GRAHTZ yeh) – thanks. *Mille* (MEE lay) *grazie* means "Many thanks."

idiota (ee dee OH tah) – idiot

Madonna (ma DOEN nah) – the Virgin Mary; Mother of God

malavita (mah lah VEE tah) – the criminal underworld, the criminal life

mandamento (MAHN de men toh) – district, region; plural is *mandamenti*

merda (MARE dah) – shit

mi dispiace (MEE dees pee YAH chay) – I'm sorry

minchia (MEEN kee ah) – holy shit, fuck

'Ndrangheta (en DRAHNG eh tah) – the Calabrian Mafia, or "the Honored Society." Members are *'Ndranghetisti* (en DRAHNG eh tees tee), or "men of honor." A single member is an *'Ndranghetista.*

nonna (NOHN nah), *nonnina* (nohn NEE nah) – grandmother, granny

nonno (NOHN noh) – grandfather

padrino (pah DREE noh) – godfather

papà (pah PAH) – dad

pasticceria (pah stee chah REE ah) – pastry shop, bakery

per favore (PAIR fah VOR ay) – please

perfetto (pair FEHT toe) – perfect

polizia (poh leet TZEE ah) – Italian police

porco Dio (POR koh DEE oh) – literally "pig God"; *very* vulgar religious curse

porca miseria (POR kah mee ZAIR ee ah) – literally "pig misery"; means "damn" or "bloody hell"

porca vacca (POR kah VAHK kah) – fuck, shit; literally "pig cow"

prego (PRAY go) – welcome

GLOSSARY OF TERMS (cont.)

principessa, principe (prin chee PESS ah, PRIN chee pay) – princess, prince

puttana (poot TAH nah) – whore, prostitute

pubblico ministero (POOB blee koh minis TAIR oh) – public prosecutor

sì (CEE) – yes

sicario (see CAR yoh) – assassin, hitman, enforcer

signore, signora, signorina (seen YOR ay, seen YOR ah, seen yor REEN ah) – sir, madam, miss; the "e" is dropped from *signore* when used with a last name

soldati (sole DAH tee) – soldiers

Sottotenente (soh toh teh NEN tay) – Second Lieutenant

stronzo (STRON tzoh) – shit, turd, bastard

ti amo (TEE AH moe) – I love you

ti voglio bene (TEE VOHL yo BEN ay) – I care for you / I love you (nonromantic)

troppo (TROHP poh) – too much

vaffanculo (vahf fahn COO loh) – go fuck yourself

vincolo di sangue (VIN coh loh DEE SAHN gway) – blood bond

zio (TZEE oh) – uncle

PROLOGUE

Twenty years ago
Rome, Italy

Scanning the street again, Ruggero Vela leaned against one of the columns that flanked the massive double doors of the bank behind him. It was half past noon, and hot for early May. Sweat gathered beneath his leather shoulder holster, and the Beretta under his left armpit no longer felt cool. He wished he could remove his suit jacket, but that wasn't possible, not with the hardware it concealed.

His stomach rumbled, and he lit up his third cigarette of the day. Tapping the ashes on the stone steps and shifting a bit more into the shade, he turned to his father standing at the column across from him. "Papà, how much longer?"

His father took a drag on his own cigarette, squinting against the smoke rising around his face. "Don Lucchesi will be done when he's done."

The hit of nicotine should have been soothing, but it wasn't. "When do you think it will happen?" The "it" Ruggero had promised not to mention again. But it was all he could think about, what with the recent hit on the Bove family.

"Stop obsessing. You're ready."

I wish I believed you. "What's it like?"

He got the stare, the one Livio Vela was famous for among his fellow 'Ndranghetisti. "Don't be so eager."

"I'm not. Just curious." *And not sure I can do this.*

His father crossed over to him, placed a hand on his shoulder. "Listen. I'm only going to say this once. You think killing a man is like in the movies. It's not."

"I know. That's what I'm... nervous about." Ruggero wanted to tell the truth, but a *sicario*, an assassin, was never afraid. He was the sharp blade that his *capo* would send against his enemies, the shadow in the night, the man other men would fear. The one who would be the very last thing many men would ever see.

Livio's eyes narrowed again into their famous squint, as if he were taking his son's measure. Then he patted Ruggero's cheek. "I was like you once. We all were.

1

Taking a man's life is a hard thing to do. And it's a hard thing to know about yourself. It's like a serpent coiled around your heart."

Ruggero rubbed his sternum, and Livio laughed. It was good seeing his father smile; he didn't do it often. And Ruggero knew just what to say to make him laugh again. "I hope we have lunch soon."

His father let out a dry chuckle and tousled Ruggero's hair. "You're always hungry."

With a tap to his chest, which had filled out considerably with muscle during the half-year since he'd turned sixteen, Ruggero returned the smile. "I'm a growing boy."

Motioning with his chin, his father indicated the *pasticceria* across the street. "Run over and grab yourself a pastry. Make it quick."

Ruggero tossed his cigarette and hurried through the people thronging the sidewalk, then dodged between Vespas and cars that rarely stopped for other vehicles, much less pedestrians. He made it safely to the other side before realizing he had only a few coins in his pocket—probably not enough to get anything. Turning around, he glanced over at his father, who had straightened up and ground out his cigarette, his eyes trained on their *capo* stepping through the double doors.

Damn. He needed to hustle. Ruggero started into the street, and the sharp blare of a Fiat's horn sent him back up on the curb, his heart pounding in his chest. *Cristo*, that had been close.

He flicked his eyes back to his father and the don again, and a sudden movement caught his attention—two men, dressed in dark colors, were advancing on his father and the don from opposite directions. Both men wore the intent focus of predators, and their sharp, quick movements as they dodged around obstacles marked them as professionals.

Papà! He almost screamed the word aloud, but at the last second bit down on his tongue and drew blood. Calling attention to himself and alerting the hitmen was a bad idea. Ruggero plunged into the street, his feet slipping on cobblestones slick with water from the *pasticceria* owner's efforts to keep the sidewalk clean. He flicked open the switchblade he kept in his pocket and held it pointed down, against his leg, where it wouldn't attract much notice.

He'd reached the other side just as the man on the right was coming up behind his father. This time he couldn't help shouting. Livio turned toward Ruggero's voice, and Ruggero motioned frantically, trying to make his father aware of the *sicario* that stalked him. But his father yelled "Look out!" instead of dealing with the threat that was upon him.

Pain seared across the left side of Ruggero's face, from just beside his eye and down across his cheekbone, then a massive weight slammed into him and knocked him almost off his feet. Without thinking, he stabbed upward, catching his assailant in the abdomen. As he'd been taught, he twisted the knife and dragged it hard across the man's belly, gutting him like a fish. The man gaped at him for a moment, then tried to grab for the bloody mess of intestines that bulged from the wound.

Acid rose up the back of Ruggero's throat, but he inhaled deeply and focused on his target—the man's carotid artery. With a quick slice, he severed the vessel, then shoved the man out of the way, leaving him to teeter on the sidewalk, blood spurting from his neck, as people screamed and ran.

Ruggero charged over to his father and the don. His father was bleeding heavily from a wound to the upper belly and his face looked pale. His knife was out though, and blood dripped from it as he squared off with his opponent, a young darkly tanned man with close-cropped hair. The man said something, his accent Calabrian—Ruggero couldn't hear his words over the rush of blood in his ears. Then the man lunged for the don.

"No!" Ruggero shouted, and the assailant did what he'd expected: he turned from his quarry to confront Ruggero instead. He met Ruggero's first thrust with a quick one of his own. The Calabrian's knife slashed through the light wool of Ruggero's suit coat, the tip of the knife skimming across his ribs and leaving fire in its wake.

Ruggero danced back, and his father's voice rang in his head. *Watch his eyes; they'll tell you where he's going to strike.* The man glanced up at Ruggero's neck, and Ruggero made sure he was ready to block the strike and to deliver one of his own. The attacker closed in, clearly not expecting the sudden blow to his chin when Ruggero snapped up his left elbow to block. He followed the move with a stab into the Calabrian's windpipe. Plunging the blade in, he ripped it to the right, tearing the throat open. The man let out a gurgle.

Just as Ruggero was about to relax, a flicker in his peripheral vision alerted him to another threat: a third *sicario*, who'd already reached his weakened father.

"Papà!" This time the word came out, but it was too late. The man slid up behind his father and drew his blade neatly across Livio's throat.

Ruggero pulled his Beretta, tears blurring his vision as he took aim and squeezed the trigger. He had to save his *capo*; that was their number one job. Protecting the man they served. Protecting the man who'd saved his father from a life in prison.

The bullet found its mark; the assassin stumbled, then fell. Ruggero advanced on him, his attention narrowed to one single focus: making sure the *sicario* was dead. He reached the downed man and pumped two more bullets into his head. He would have fired again, but the don laid a hand on his shoulder. "*Basta.*" Enough.

Heaving in a breath, Ruggero looked his don in the eye. Rinaldo Lucchesi stared at him, pity written in every line of his face.

Ruggero had saved his *capo*. But he'd gotten his father killed.

Falling to his knees, Ruggero took his father's hand, but the light had already left his eyes. Again, he heard his father's words. *Taking a man's life is a hard thing to do. And it's a hard thing to know about yourself. It's like a serpent coiled around your heart.*

Something squeezed in his chest, and tears flooded his eyes. The serpent was there; he could feel it. It owned him now.

CHAPTER 1

Present day
Como, Italy

Ruggero Vela tugged at the bow tie around his neck and grimaced. *Damn penguin suit.* Why had he ever said yes when Antonio had asked him to be best man? He surveyed the church again, all the rows of guests waiting for the appearance of the bride, then glanced at Antonio Lucchesi, the groom, standing beside him in front of the altar. Tonio looked nervous and excited in equal measure. Ruggero wished he shared Tonio's excitement.

But all Ruggero could focus on was his speech as the best man. He worried the folded-up paper in his pocket. Telling funny stories and being heartfelt in front of a crowd?

Not his thing. At all.

Maybe he should have asked Don Lucchesi for help. But he hadn't wanted to bother the don over such a small thing. Over something that any man should be able to do without blinking. Any normal man.

Ruggero knew a hundred ways to kill someone. But not much else. Not how to be a friend, for example. Or a husband or a father. Not that he ever expected to be either of the latter two, but he should know how to be a friend.

Of all the lessons his father had imparted before his death, none had included something as simple, as basic, as that. How to be someone's friend, when all you knew was how to end lives. Not how to live one.

He'd just have to muddle through and hope he hit the mark. He had known one thing though: you didn't turn down an invitation to be someone's best man. He'd never have insulted Tonio that way. Not after everything he'd been through during these last few months.

The music for the bride started up, and Bianca Lucchesi came down the aisle on the arm of Don Enrico Lucchesi, her godfather and the adopted father of the groom. She'd always been quite a stunner, but today she wasn't merely beautiful;

she was radiant, like an angel. If you believed in that sort of thing. Which Ruggero didn't.

Still, he could barely look at Bianca without a lump forming in his throat. What the hell was happening to him? He coughed and glanced away, and that's when he saw it: movement in the shadows near the vestibule of the church.

The hairs prickled at the nape of his neck, and he reached across his chest for his gun... which he didn't have. *Minchia!*

Bianca and the don reached the altar, and the don embraced her and kissed her on each cheek before handing her off to Antonio.

Ruggero started to lunge forward, to get himself between the don and the unknown danger that lurked in the shadows, but the man who stepped out of the gloom brought him up short. Sottotenente Silvio Fuente, of the *carabinieri*. He was flanked by four other officers.

The don also saw the intruders. He stared at Fuente for a moment, and the man shrugged, then nodded, and the don took his seat. Ruggero tried to read his *capo*'s face, but the don seemed untroubled. Though surely he wasn't. His eyes flicked to Ruggero, then to Antonio and Bianca, and he gave Ruggero a pointed nod.

Yes. He needed to focus on the task at hand. On the ring in his pocket. He made eye contact with Tommaso, the senior guard nearest him, and shook his head slightly. They were not to interfere with the officers.

Fortunately, the bride and groom didn't seem to have noticed Fuente or his colleagues. Tonio and Bianca were holding hands and grinning at each other as the bishop spoke to those assembled. The man droned on and on about love and commitment and the special joy of two people joining as one, while Ruggero twirled Bianca's wedding ring around and around the tip of his little finger. *Come on, man, can't you see the don is going to be arrested? They won't wait forever.*

At last the bishop addressed Antonio directly, and recited the vow Tonio was to repeat. Ruggero handed the ring to Tonio, who cleared his throat, then said, the slightest tremor in his voice, "I, Antonio, take you, Bianca, as my wife and promise to be faithful to you always, in joy and in pain, in health and in sickness, and to love you and every day honor you, for the rest of my life." He slid the ring onto her finger as he said the words, and a tear spilled down Bianca's cheek.

She reached up and wiped her face, and Ruggero had to look away. It was insane to think that she and Antonio had both nearly been killed just six weeks ago, while rescuing their son, Luca. And now, here they were, on Valentine's Day, taking their vows.

Life was short, crazy, and unpredictable. None of them would ever have guessed they'd be here today, much less that the *carabinieri* would be crashing Antonio and Bianca's wedding. Fortunately, Fuente and his men hadn't advanced, presumably out of respect for the bride.

Bianca took a deep breath and blew out, then she shot a smile at Tonio that made Ruggero happier than ever for his friend. She was one hell of a woman; she'd shot her own brother to save Tonio's life. Her voice shaking, she repeated her vow after the bishop as she slid a simple gold band onto Antonio's finger. "I, Bianca, take you, Antonio, as my husband and promise to be faithful to you always, in joy and in pain, in health and in sickness, and to love you and every day honor you, for the rest of my life."

There was that lump again—right smack in Ruggero's throat. *Dio*, was he turning into a woman? He'd been to a dozen weddings, and they'd never been more to him than occasions where he'd had to watch his *capo*'s back. Even his sister's wedding hadn't meant that much to him—then again, he'd been only six at the time. He'd missed Elena terribly afterward, sure, but he hadn't registered then, or in all the time since then, what a wedding truly was: a joining of two people. The start of a family, of something new. A beginning. A chance to start over.

And if any two people had earned that chance, they were Antonio and Bianca, who'd risked everything to save the son they'd created when they were teens, a son no one other than Bianca had known existed until recently.

Six-year-old Luca Lucchesi sat in the front row snuggled up to Kate, the don's wife. He was dressed in a miniature tuxedo, and he beamed up at his parents as Kate ruffled his blond hair and whispered something to him.

Even Ruggero had to admit that Luca was a cute kid. Though Luca was still a little intimidated by him—perhaps it was the scar that sliced across Ruggero's left cheekbone—something made Ruggero want to put the boy at ease. He'd shown Luca how to teach his new puppy some tricks, and that had gone a long way toward relaxing Luca, though some lingering tentativeness remained.

But that was a problem for another day. Fuente and his men had come forward as the bishop concluded the ceremony, and now they were approaching Don Lucchesi.

This wasn't good; Fuente had belonged to them at one point. Now, he obviously belonged to another. And Ruggero didn't have to guess who that person was.

Lorenzo Andretti. The man everyone in the Lucchesi *cosca* wanted dead.

———— ◆ ————

His heart beating a little faster than normal, Enrico Lucchesi rose from his seat in the church and met the *carabinieri* officers before they'd reached him and his wife. Silvio Fuente was in the lead, of course, and his black mustache curved up as he gave Enrico a broad smile. "The day has come at last," Fuente said.

"What day is that?"

Fuente held up a pair of handcuffs. "The day when the great Enrico Lucchesi is exposed for what he truly is: a Mafioso."

It was Enrico's turn to smile, though it was the last thing he felt like doing. "Signor Fuente, you know as well as I do that an arrest does not make an allegation true." He deliberately left off the officer's title, a thing that would rankle Fuente and remind him that the title was Enrico's doing.

Fuente's lips pursed before his smile resurfaced. "You may have slipped from the law's grasp before, but you won't this time."

Enrico leaned down to whisper in Fuente's ear. "Put on a show for your colleagues all you want, but you and I both know what I can do."

Fuente huffed with laughter, but this time kept his voice low, for Enrico's ears only. "And we both know what your enemies are capable of."

So this was Lorenzo's doing. Was Fuente being paid, or threatened? "May we have a word?"

Fuente waved Enrico over to a spot several meters from his fellow officers. Enrico positioned himself so that he could see Kate, and he offered her a grin that was far more confident than he felt. Her features didn't relax, and she clutched Luca to her side. *Madonna.* He didn't want her fretting about him, not on top of the pregnancy. She'd had every possible test, checking for damage to the child after Carlo Andretti had drugged her, and she didn't need to add Enrico to her list of worries.

"What is this about?" Enrico asked.

"The Dinelli case. We have the gun."

Enrico's gut went cold. They had him at last. Fuente had hinted before that he knew where the gun was, but Enrico hadn't known whether he was bluffing until now. "And you've found Grantini?"

Fuente held his eyes. "No. But you already knew that."

"I wouldn't have asked if I'd known." Though of course he had. Sergio Grantini was nothing but bones now, somewhere in the depths of Lake Como. Sergio had betrayed Enrico; he'd gone to work for Carlo Andretti. And he'd helped Andretti frame Enrico for the murder of Judge Federico Dinelli.

Holding up the cuffs, Fuente said, "Put out your hands."

"May I have a few minutes with my wife?" When Fuente hesitated, Enrico pressed him. "She's got a lot on her mind with the pregnancy. I'd like to reassure her. I won't fight you."

Fuente sighed, then tapped the face of his fancy watch. "Five minutes. No more."

Enrico didn't thank him; he probably should have, but he couldn't bring himself to do it when what he really wanted was to punch the man. Hadn't Enrico paid him enough? Though maybe he should be feeling sorry for Fuente. If Lorenzo was applying pressure, Fuente was in an exceedingly tight spot.

Much like Enrico himself.

He quickly reached Kate's side and the knot of concerned people around her: Tonio and Bianca, Nico and Delfi, and of course Ruggero. They'd all want a word, but the one who mattered most was Kate, and he had to concentrate on her. He asked Bianca to take Luca off Kate's hands, then he escorted Kate a few meters away, his hand at her elbow.

She trembled beside him, and his stomach grew tight. This was so far from the life of comfort and ease that he'd wanted for her. Turning, he faced her and placed a hand on each of her shoulders. He held her at arm's length for a moment, then pulled her close and whispered in her ear, using his English to make sure she didn't miss a word. "*Cara*, I have to go with them. It is about the Dinelli case. They have found the missing evidence."

"The gun?"

He nodded.

"What about Grantini?" She knew as well as he did that Grantini was dead. But if anyone could hear… He suppressed a smile. She was a sharp one, his Kate.

"No. But the gun is enough to hold me. For a while." He kissed her cheek and lowered his voice so it was little more than a breath. "Call Trapani. He will know what to do. Antonio will be in charge, Ruggero his second."

She stiffened in his arms, and he tightened his grip on her. "This is only temporary. You know where the bag is?" The bag that contained their false IDs, credit cards in those names, stacks of cash, and a list of banks and account numbers. The bag that was hidden on their property.

Kate nodded. "I know."

"*Bene*. If something happens, you take it and run."

She stifled a sob. "I can't leave you."

"You may have to, *cara*. Lorenzo…"

She shifted in his arms and placed a finger on his lips. "I'm *not* leaving you."

He placed a hand on her belly and was rewarded with a kick from their son. "You have to protect him. If Lorenzo makes a move, you run."

"Where would I go?"

"Anywhere you want. The IDs will protect you."

"And who made them?"

He frowned. Of course Kate would think of the major point of vulnerability. "It is no one that Lorenzo can get to."

"You're sure?"

Enrico stroked her cheek and pressed a kiss to her lush mouth. "I would not risk your life on anything I was not certain of."

She held his eyes, her own brimming with tears. "*Ti amo*," she whispered, her voice breaking.

"*Ti amo, cara*." Somehow he kept his voice steady, firm. He kissed her once more as Fuente drew near, the heels of his neatly polished boots thudding on the cathedral's marble floor. Then Enrico turned from the woman he loved more than anything else in the world and held out his hands.

The steel cuffs snapped over his wrists, and it was done. Patches of red mottling his cheeks, Antonio tried to stop Fuente, but Enrico shook his head. "It's all right, Tonio. I won't be gone long."

Now who was bluffing? Enrico caught Ruggero's eye and motioned toward Kate with his head. Ruggero nodded once, and the determination on his face was the only thing that made Enrico relax in the slightest. Ruggero would keep her safe.

The officers escorted him outside. It was the first time in many years that Ruggero hadn't been with him, always slightly ahead, shielding him from being a direct target, gun at the ready.

Now Enrico had no one between him and death. Any one of these officers could be in Andretti's pay. If he was going to survive, Enrico would have to rely on himself alone.

The thought provided little comfort. He was on his own, without a gun or a knife. A defenseless deer among a pack of sharp-toothed wolves.

———◆———

Everyone convened at Enrico and Kate's villa for the wedding reception as planned, but no one felt like celebrating. Kate tried to get people to eat, drink, and dance, but no one was fooled by the smile plastered on her face. Don Vittorio Battista, Enrico's godfather, approached Antonio and Ruggero soon after they arrived. "We should have a family meeting," the old don suggested, and the tension in Ruggero's belly unwound ever so slightly. Yes, they needed to make a plan.

Ruggero and Antonio sent everyone who wasn't needed home. Gianluca d'Imperio and his family were the last to leave. He came over to Antonio, Ruggero, and Don Battista standing by the fireplace in the large drawing room. "You have my full support, of course," Gianluca said to them, his eyes on Antonio.

"*Mille grazie*, Don d'Imperio," Antonio said.

Gianluca laughed. "You *can* call me Gianluca, you know."

Tonio reddened. "Someday I will get used to this."

D'Imperio clapped Antonio on the back. "You weren't born to it, but you need to start acting like you've been a Lucchesi your whole life. *Capisci?*"

"I know."

Gianluca's daughter Giovanna raced up and threw her arms around Antonio in a quick hug. Then she whispered, of course loud enough for everyone to hear, "If you break the bed on your wedding night, I've heard it's good luck."

That made everyone smile and Antonio laugh, and then the d'Imperios were gone, and it was only the family left. The only problem was Tonio's sister, Violetta. She wasn't part of the business, and Tonio wanted to keep it that way. Bianca's mother, Francesca, came to the rescue. "Violetta, how about you and I take Luca and Cocco out back?"

Luca clapped his hands at the suggestion. "Cocco wants me to bring the ball!" The fluffy white pup yipped when he heard the word, his tail wagging furiously.

"Let's get you changed first," Francesca said, taking Luca's hand. She and Violetta led him upstairs where they had a bag for him. It had been a good day so far; Luca hadn't asked for Tonio's blue scarf, which he'd carried around with him nonstop since the night his adoptive parents had been killed. Ruggero hoped it remained that way; with Enrico gone, Tonio didn't need any more worries.

The rest of them headed into the spacious dining room and gathered around the long, highly polished mahogany table: Ruggero; Don Battista; Kate; Antonio and Bianca; Orlando Farnese, Ruggero's nephew and the *cosca*'s treasurer; and Enrico's other son, Nick, and his wife, Delfina. The fact that Delfina was Dario Andretti's daughter made Ruggero a bit wary, even now. She'd proved again and again that she could be trusted, but still, she was an Andretti by birth. And here they were, including her in their plans.

Then again, Enrico's late wife, Antonella, had been an Andretti too. And she'd never betrayed him, as far as Ruggero knew. There was always a first time, however. But he kept his concerns to himself. The last thing they needed right now was strife within the family.

Don Battista turned to Kate and put a hand on her forearm, speaking in English for her and Nick's benefit. "Caterina, what did Rico say to you before he left?"

She put her hand over his and gave him a tight smile. Then she looked at Antonio and Ruggero. "He said that Antonio was to be *capo*. And Ruggero *capo di società*."

An icy sensation flitted through Ruggero's midsection. "That should be Orlando's job."

"He said you. And you know why." She held his gaze; did she truly know? He'd thought that had been between him and Don Lucchesi, and he wasn't about to blurt it out in front of Antonio, who was giving him a quizzical look.

Damn her for putting him on the spot, but did he really expect any less? Kate wasn't one to tiptoe around. She said what she meant, and she meant what she said. It was one of her most admirable qualities, when it wasn't making him uncomfortable. "Well"—he flicked a glance at Orlando—"yes, Orlando is quite new to this."

"As is Antonio. No offense," she said.

Tonio smiled. "It's the truth. And I do need help."

"It is settled then," Don Battista said.

Nick leaned forward. "I'll see what I can find out about the case through Interpol."

"You would do that?" Ruggero asked. Ever since Enrico had extricated his son from the mess he'd gotten into with Dario Andretti, Nick had been quite clear that he wanted nothing to do with the inner workings of the family. He'd wanted to stay in Interpol, at the London bureau, and as far out of the family business as possible. As possible as it was, considering that he was the son of one Mafia don and son-in-law to another.

"He's my dad. I have to help him. Whatever it takes." Nick looked around the table. "It's not like I'm not already compromised."

"As long as we have that clear," Ruggero said. He didn't bother to mask his irritation with Nick. The boy wanted to have it both ways, and that was impossible. But neither Nick nor his father could see that. Either you were in the 'Ndrangheta, or you were out.

But that was the story of Enrico Lucchesi, wasn't it? The man who didn't want to be a don, but was. And his firstborn was more of the same.

And yet there wasn't another man Ruggero would rather have followed. He trusted Enrico Lucchesi with his life. He'd sworn it, but it was more than a mere vow. The don had called him friend, and meant it. He'd offered to make Ruggero his right hand before, to make him *capo di società*. And Ruggero had turned it down, had insisted that Antonio was the better choice.

But that wasn't the real reason he'd refused the job.

In his heart of hearts, Ruggero knew he was unworthy. And like a coward, he hadn't wanted to admit that aloud. For the only time in his life, he hadn't been completely truthful with his don. But some things were better left unsaid.

Antonio interrupted his thoughts. "That bastard Fuente. I know why he flipped."

"Why?" Ruggero asked.

"After Cris was killed, Fuente was looking through the bank statements we'd been showing the others to prove that I hadn't stolen the money. Fuente must have pieced together how much Lorenzo and Sandro had stolen from Enrico. He must think us weak."

"Well, we're not at our strongest," Orlando said. "That infusion of cash from the d'Imperios has gone a long way toward making us less vulnerable, but we still have a huge hole in our balance sheet."

Don Battista stroked the abundant steel-gray mustache that bristled above his upper lip. "I can help in that regard. Why didn't Enrico ask?"

No one said anything. Then Kate sighed. "Pride, I'm sure."

Antonio tapped the table. "I might be thinking about this all wrong. Fuente wanted information about Lorenzo."

"What did you tell him?" Don Battista asked.

"That he had ties to Italo Baldassare. And possibly the Russians. But I didn't mention the Vilanoviches."

"Those fuckers." Nick put an arm around Delfina and hugged her close. None of them had any love for the Vilanoviches, but Nick had nearly lost his wife because of them.

"I'm sure Fuente believes he can use that information somehow," Antonio said.

Ruggero snorted. "If Fuente thinks that gives him any leverage over Lorenzo, he's an idiot."

"We ought to talk to Fuente. Find out what he knows," Antonio said.

"As if he'd be honest." Ruggero doubted anything less than a gun in the mouth would get him anywhere close to the truth with Fuente. Not that he was about to go after an officer of the law, especially the one who'd just arrested his boss. Fuente was a double-crossing prick, but an assault on an officer would rally the *carabinieri*, and the *cosca* didn't need more trouble. Certainly not with Don Lucchesi in jail.

"We've got to try." Antonio held Ruggero's gaze. "Think you can intimidate it out of him—*without* breaking anything?"

Ruggero cracked his knuckles. "I'll restrain myself." Fuente was a turncoat of the worst sort; he'd not only broken his oath to the *carabinieri*, but he'd also spit on the man he'd turned traitor for. A man had to have some principles, but apparently Fuente didn't understand the concept. There was really only one way to deal with men like that. But that way was denied Ruggero. He'd have to be creative.

"Okay then," Antonio said. He turned to Delfina. "Delfi, do you have any idea what your father is thinking? How closely is he working with Lorenzo?"

She shook her head. "I don't know. He says very little around me. He's still upset that I didn't leave Nico."

"And the baby?"

Her eyes filled with tears, and she shook her head again. "We've been trying, but it hasn't happened. I lied to Papà. I told him I was pregnant, but it has to happen soon, or he'll realize what I've done."

"We've been trying for only six weeks, honey. It'll happen," Nick said and kissed her cheek.

"And if it doesn't? That pretend baby is the only thing keeping him from attacking this family."

"Stop worrying. The stress isn't good for you."

"How can I *not* worry? At this rate, Mamma might get pregnant before I do!"

"They're really trying again?" Kate asked.

Delfina nodded. "Papà needs a new heir now that—" Her breath hitched before she said the rest. "Now that Cris is dead. Mamma's still young enough to try."

Cristoforo Andretti had been an admirable boy. The only Andretti Ruggero would ever say that about. Cris had worked hard to help strengthen the ties between the families, and he'd actually defied his father and great-grandfather to help Antonio and Don Lucchesi try to avert a crisis in their own *cosca*. But Lorenzo Andretti had made sure his great-grandson hadn't drawn breath for long afterward. Too bad they hadn't been able to prove that to Dario Andretti. He hadn't accepted the proof Antonio had offered, that Lorenzo had ordered Cris's death.

Then again, Dario had long hated Enrico, and that hatred had blinded him to the truth more than once. Now the tentative alliance forged through Nick and Delfina's marriage hung on by mere tatters. If Dario found out the truth, he'd be sure to sever the alliance altogether. As it was, he could be working against them anyway. They had to assume so.

Ruggero leaned forward. "Baby or no baby, I don't trust Dario not to attack us." He looked at Nick and Delfina. "For everyone's safety, I think we need to make some changes. Move everyone into this house. With all the security upgrades, it's the safest place to be. And we can concentrate the guards here." Not only had Enrico upgraded the security systems and electronic surveillance, he'd also had bulletproof glass installed in much of the house, though the renovations to the solarium were still underway.

"All of us?" Antonio asked. He, Bianca, and Luca had moved in with her mother rather than leave Francesca on her own in the large villa next door.

"Yes." Ruggero turned to Orlando. "Your mother too. I don't like her alone in Calabria. She's too close to Lorenzo. Between you being *contabile* and me being *capo di società*, he's bound to go after her."

"Good luck convincing her," Orlando said. "She hates it up here."

No. Elena had hated it here after their father had died. After Ruggero's mistake. With Papà gone, she hadn't seen a reason to stay around. She'd packed up her family and gone back south to be with their cousins. That's what she'd said. But Ruggero was quite certain that Elena actually hadn't wanted to see his scar every day, to be reminded that it was his carelessness that had gotten their father killed.

Well, she'd have to be reminded now. He wasn't going to lose her too. "I'll make her see that it's for the best."

"Do you need more men?" Don Battista asked.

"We could use some experienced guards for the house," Ruggero said. "We've lost quite a few these last several months, and we're behind on training replacements."

"Weapons?"

"We're well-stocked there."

Don Battista nodded. "Anything you need, you ask. Don't stand on pride. If the Lucchesis fall, I'll be Lorenzo's next target."

"Aside from you and the d'Imperios, who else can we count on?" Antonio asked, and Ruggero almost smiled. He'd been about to ask the same question. The boy was learning.

"I've been speaking to several families who have bad blood with the Andrettis. They're not happy with Lorenzo being in charge. Even though he won the vote to run La Provincia, it wasn't the landslide he'd thought."

"Can you secure their help, should it come to war?" Ruggero asked.

"I believe so. Now that Lorenzo has fired the first shot, I'll see who's willing to join forces with us."

Kate squeezed the old man's arm. "*Mille grazie*, Vittorio," she said, her voice wavering.

He leaned forward and kissed her cheek. "Caterina, do not worry. We will protect your family. I am Rico's *compare*; he is not alone. He's as much my son as any of my boys."

Tears slipped down her cheeks, and she wiped at them and took a deep breath. "I'm sorry I'm losing it. This day started out so well, and now Rico's in jail, and the wedding's been ruined—"

"No, it wasn't," Bianca said. "The wedding was fine. We'll just have a big party after Zio Enrico is back home."

Nick chuckled. "It turned out a lot better than when Delfi and I got engaged. At least no bullets were fired."

The table fell silent for a moment, then Tonio started laughing. "And I didn't end up in the hospital like I did after your engagement party. That *really* would have put a damper on the wedding."

Kate put a hand to her mouth, and for a moment Ruggero thought she was struggling not to cry. Then she let a giggle burst out before smothering it. "I shouldn't be laughing. It's not funny."

"It kind of is," Tonio said. "We're all still here, aren't we? The Andrettis have tried and tried, but they keep missing."

"Bad aim," Nick said, his voice light.

"*Really* bad aim," Tonio added.

"Colossally bad," Delfina said. "And I never thought I'd say this, but thank goodness my father is so angry he can't see straight."

Even Ruggero smiled at that. But they couldn't rely on the Andrettis to keep making mistakes. Even a blind man would eventually kill something, as long as he had enough bullets.

———— ♦ ————

After the family meeting broke up, Don Battista approached Ruggero. "Take a walk with me."

Ruggero couldn't help raising a brow, but he put on his coat and accompanied the old don outside into the barren garden. Dusk had fallen, and the air was crisp and cutting, making their breath into great clouds of smoke as they strolled along the path that led down to the lake. What business could the don have with him?

Don Battista said nothing for a while, not until they reached the edge of the dock. There he stopped and looked out across the lake, the insistent lapping of the water the only sound. Finally he turned to Ruggero. "We are at war. Make no mistake about it." Ruggero nodded, and waited for more. Don Battista put a gloved hand on Ruggero's shoulder. "Tonio is a good boy. I have no doubt he'll make a fine *capo* someday. But he is not ready for this war."

"He might surprise us."

"He might. But we can't rely on 'might' or 'maybe.' We need certainty."

What was the old man saying? "*Sì.*"

"You will have to be prepared to step in. You will have to be prepared to make the difficult decisions."

"It's not my place."

Don Battista turned to him, his eyes hard. "You are *capo di società*. Rico offered you this job once before. That's what Caterina was referring to, yes?"

The don may have been old, but nothing got past him. "Yes."

"And you refused it because…?"

"Tonio is the better choice."

"Is he?"

Ruggero clasped his hands behind his back and looked away. "It is done. What does this matter?"

"It matters very much. You may think yourself a mere soldier. A guard. Rico's *sicario*. But you are capable of much more."

His throat tight, Ruggero said nothing. He shifted his weight, wanting to walk away, to not hear another word.

"I knew your father well; he was a good man. What happened to him was a tragedy."

The old anger welled in Ruggero's chest. "It was my fault."

"You were a boy."

Ruggero met his gaze. "I was a man. I'd taken the vows. I knew the consequences. I had a job to do, and I failed."

"We all make mistakes, every one of us."

"My father paid the price for mine. Don Lucchesi nearly did as well."

"You kept Rinaldo alive."

"I probably wouldn't be standing here otherwise."

The don squeezed his shoulder. "It is time to forgive yourself. It is time to be the man this family needs you to be."

Ruggero took a deep breath, the words on his tongue, nearly choking him. *What if I fail?* He opened his mouth, but didn't trust himself to speak.

He didn't have to. Don Battista clapped him on the back. "You are ready. Trust me. I am counting on you. When the time comes, you must act, even if Tonio or Rico will not. You may have to defy them. You must be ready to save this family."

"You mean killing Lorenzo Andretti."

"Exactly." Don Battista held his gaze. "While this trial hangs over Enrico, we must be careful, but when it no longer does…"

Ruggero nodded. Once a hitman, always a hitman. He'd known it, in his bones. Lorenzo Andretti must die. And it was Ruggero's job to ensure Andretti's demise.

CHAPTER 2

Milan, Italy

Judge Loredana Montisi surveyed the half-full courtroom before letting her gaze rest briefly on the defendant: Enrico Lucchesi, owner of the Banca di Falcone, upstanding businessman, and philanthropist. At least, that was the official story. Lucchesi was so much more than that. According to the reports from the Direzione Investigativa Antimafia (DIA), Enrico Lucchesi was a Mafia don, a tax evader, and the mastermind of a criminal enterprise with tentacles that stretched from Lake Como to Rome.

But most importantly, Lucchesi was the man responsible for the murders of Judge Federico Dinelli and his family.

Loredana's pulse quickened. She couldn't avenge her own father's death at the hands of Mafia assassins, but she could ensure that Dinelli and his family received justice at last.

The defendant stood before her, flanked by his lawyers, Agostino Trapani and Ulisse Adimari. Both men were sharp and shrewd. Lucchesi had chosen well. But she hadn't expected any less.

Lucchesi was finely dressed, not a hair out of place. If she hadn't known better, she'd have sworn he'd come from his home instead of the bowels of San Vittore prison. Lucchesi's very pretty and obviously pregnant wife sat behind him, ringed by assorted family and friends.

A handsome black-haired man to the right of Lucchesi's wife caught Loredana's eye. His dark gaze met hers, and the hostility she saw in it chilled her. The man looked as if he were thinking of shooting her where she sat, and the menacing scar that snaked down the left side of his face only added to his aura of danger.

Well, if Signor Sinister thought he could intimidate her, he was flat-out wrong. And if Enrico Lucchesi thought that bringing his poster boy for Mafia thugs was a good idea, he'd sorely miscalculated. Everyone knew Loredana Montisi didn't back down from a threat. It was in her blood, her heritage. The legacy she'd received from her parents—the judge who'd been killed, and the judge who'd been maimed in the same attack.

She'd see Lucchesi rot in jail if it was literally the last thing she did. No judge-killer was going free on her watch. And the sooner Lucchesi was locked up for good, the better.

Speaking of soon, where the hell was Corvi? Loredana checked the clock on the wall. They couldn't start until the prosecutor appeared, and the man was already ten minutes late. She was taking a sip of her espresso, the steaming liquid warm in her throat, when she nearly choked. What if Lucchesi's men—maybe led by Signor Sinister—had killed Corvi to derail the case? She picked up her mobile phone to call the prosecutor's office when it buzzed in her hand. A text from Corvi: *Almost there!* She exhaled in relief.

"Pubblico Ministero Corvi has been delayed and will be here momentarily," she announced and let her gaze rest on Signor Sinister, giving him just a trace of a smile. *Your boss is going to jail. And there's nothing you can do about it.*

The man held her stare and crossed his arms, making his shoulders look even broader and his biceps strain against his suit jacket. Like his boss, he was well-dressed, but many Mafiosi looked slick and respectable. Or tried. This one would never succeed. Nothing could mask the man's intensity, his sharp, predatory air. The wolf in the sheepfold, that's what he was.

The courtroom door burst open, and Pubblico Ministero Patrizio Corvi bustled up the aisle, his coat slung over one arm, an espresso in the same hand, his fine leather briefcase in the other. He placed his things down at his table and gave her a slight bow. "*Scusa*, Giudice Montisi. The metro stop nearest me was closed, and I had to run to the next one."

"I see you still had time to pick up espresso." She allowed a little amusement in her tone.

Corvi smiled. "Of course. An Italian doesn't run on tea."

Someone laughed, but Loredana tried not to. "Next time, give yourself an extra fifteen minutes. Everything else may be on Italian time, but not my courtroom."

Corvi cocked his head and gave her a sheepish nod. Most judges wouldn't have minded starting fifteen minutes late; she wasn't one of them. She'd always prided herself on her punctuality. Her mother said it was the German in their background coming out in her. Though it wasn't that at all. Loredana just disliked chaos and disorder. The more orderly things were, the better. And part of establishing order was keeping track of time. Couldn't people see that?

She took a breath and let it out. *Dio mio*, she was turning into Mussolini. "Pubblico Ministero Corvi, are you ready to start?"

Corvi rose. "The prosecution will show that the defendant should be indicted for the following crimes: murder, tax evasion, obstruction, and evidence tampering. And with your permission, Giudice Montisi, we'd like to look into the workings of the Banca di Falcone. Last night, we received a tip that the FIU is investigating possible money laundering."

Money laundering? So the Financial Intelligence Unit had finally caught up to Lucchesi. She shouldn't be surprised. "By all means, please consult with the FIU and bring back your findings."

"I'll have something by next Monday."

"*Bene.* Have you a recommendation regarding precautionary measures to be taken in this case?"

"Considering the severity of the charges and the means available to the defendant, we're recommending the defendant remain in custody for the duration of the preliminary hearing."

Lucchesi's wife gasped, and Lucchesi turned in his seat to comfort her. Tears streamed down her face, and Loredana felt a twinge of sympathy for the woman. Then again, Signora Lucchesi shouldn't have married a Mafioso. Loredana turned to Lucchesi's lawyers. "What is your response to these charges?"

Trapani stood up and smoothed a hand down the front of his black robe. "Firstly, we will show that there is no merit to these allegations. Our client is the victim of a well-orchestrated conspiracy, involving members of the *carabinieri* and a business rival. The recent investigation being undertaken by the FIU is merely a precaution; the Banca di Falcone suffered an internal attack by a rogue employee intent on besmirching Signor Lucchesi's good name and sabotaging his business."

Conspiracy? Rogue employees? At least Trapani was going to make this case entertaining. "Regarding the prosecution's recommendation of provisional custody, how do you answer?"

"Our client is a highly respected businessman with strong ties to the community; he's not a flight risk. He will voluntarily surrender his passport."

Corvi cut in. "The defendant stands accused of four counts of murder, not to mention evidence tampering. There is a high probability that he will resort to either or both again to avoid imprisonment."

Trapani addressed her. "Giudice Montisi, these allegations are unfounded. Our client is being accused of murder through the most tenuous of ties; no one has alleged that he himself committed these murders. He has an airtight alibi. Moreover, what the prosecution alleges to be 'evidence tampering' is more properly construed as blatant incompetence on the part of the *carabinieri*. The so-called 'evidence' against our client has been missing for nearly three years. Now it miraculously appears. The *carabinieri* cannot establish an unbroken chain of custody; therefore, this evidence is inadmissible. It would be inhumane to hold Signor Lucchesi in custody under such a flimsy pretext. The tax-evasion charges against our client have already been dismissed once before for lack of evidence, and this matter involving the Banca di Falcone has no bearing on the rest of the case."

Trapani did have an excellent point about the evidence. "We will address the chain of custody first thing. I share your concerns." Let that be a warning to Corvi; the prosecution had better have that matter thoroughly sorted. She wanted to indict Lucchesi, and she didn't want any future conviction to be overturned on appeal. She glanced at Corvi. "Your response?"

"Giudice Montisi, where there's smoke, there's fire. Would a truly upstanding businessman, as the defendant claims to be, have many encounters with the law? A few months ago, the defendant's wife killed her prior husband in the defendant's bedroom. Even more recently, a young man was killed at the Banca di Falcone by the defendant's godson. Clearly, the Lucchesis are violent people willing to murder to solve their problems."

Trapani looked like he'd swallowed a porcupine. "Objection! These matters have no bearing upon this case. And neither one involves any violent actions on our client's part."

"The defendant's associates and family members have a nasty habit of 'disappearing' or turning up dead. Or killing people who get in their way." Corvi sniffed loudly. "If it smells like the Mafia, it *is* the Mafia."

Trapani's face darkened, and Lucchesi slowly shook his head. "There is no proof of Mafia association; this is mere slander on the part of the prosecution." When Trapani seemed about to go on, Loredana raised her hand.

"Save it for the preliminary hearing. It would seem that there is enough merit for serious concern about the defendant's likelihood to resort to violence."

Trapani took a deep breath. "Giudice Montisi, have some compassion. As you can see, our client's wife is pregnant with her first child. She is American, alone in a foreign land, with only her husband for company. This hearing could stretch on for many months. You would deny her the only source of comfort she has during this difficult time?"

The twinge came back. On the other hand, if Lucchesi remained free, who knew what might happen, given his history? "I sympathize with Signora Lucchesi. However, I must sympathize with the interests of the citizens of this land more. The defendant shall remain in the custody of the state."

Corvi smiled and Trapani rubbed his forehead. He conferred with Lucchesi and Adimari for a moment, then turned back to her. "In that event, Giudice Montisi, we'd like to request an immediate trial."

Interesting. And risky. Both sides would have less time to prepare, since there would be no indictment phase, only the trial itself. "Pubblico Ministero Corvi, any objections?"

The prosecutor shook his head. "As long as I have a week to look into the matter with the FIU first."

"*Bene.*" She was about to dismiss them when Trapani spoke up.

"Giudice Montisi, we'd like to request that Signor Lucchesi be kept in solitary confinement. He is no hardened criminal, and considering his wealth and position, he is likely to be the target of others in the prison population."

And keeping Lucchesi separated from the general prison population would restrict his ability to communicate with any associates he might have behind bars. "Granted." She consulted her calendar. "We will reconvene next Monday."

Signor Sinister gave her another dark look before following his boss and the others out of the courtroom. She could barely restrain herself from smiling at him. *Enrico Lucchesi, upstanding businessman? My ass.*

———◆———

Ruggero gave Judge Loredana Montisi one last glance before he left the courtroom and followed the lawyers and family into a conference room. *Dio mio,* the judge was a real looker. Just the type he'd go for, if he allowed himself to date: long dark hair, the face of Botticelli's Venus, and so smart she practically radiated intelligence. And he was willing to bet she had a perfect body to go along with those classic features.

Too bad she was a complete ball-breaker. At least she seemed willing to listen when it came to Grantini's gun; if they could knock it out of play, the rest would fall apart. However, he'd feel much better about their chances if she had let Don Lucchesi remain at home.

The group of them entered a windowless conference room: Don Lucchesi, Kate, Antonio, Trapani, Adimari, and himself. They settled themselves around the table in the cramped room while the officers assigned to Don Lucchesi stood guard outside the door.

Kate clutched Enrico's hand. She'd stopped crying, but misery was etched on her face. The don tenderly stroked her hair and kissed her, murmuring something Ruggero couldn't hear.

Trapani cleared his throat and looked around at them. "Please be aware that we are not guaranteed privacy." That was a nice way of saying that the room was probably bugged. "Despite what happened today, I feel good about our chances of an acquittal. However, aside from the faulty chain of custody, the issue of greatest concern right now is the FIU. Should they find evidence of possible wrongdoing, that would expand the scope of this case and cast doubt on Signor Lucchesi's innocence."

Focusing on Enrico, Trapani continued. "Rico, your friend tells me there is nothing more that can be done on his part. Matters at the FIU have taken on a life of their own. They are demanding a meeting within the next seventy-two hours."

So, Demetrio Ricci, Don Lucchesi's friend at the Banca d'Italia, and director of the FIU, couldn't hold off the investigation any longer. The timing couldn't have been worse. With Enrico unable to attend the meeting, it would be in Antonio's hands. And unfortunately, Tonio was the target of the investigation.

"I can handle it," Antonio said, even though he looked less than confident.

"What about Orlando taking the lead?" Ruggero asked. "He knows the numbers and the details backwards and forwards, and he wasn't a bank employee at the time, so he seems more neutral."

Antonio looked at Enrico. "What do you think?"

"It's an excellent idea. Just don't let him bore the investigators."

Ruggero chuckled. "That's exactly what we need. No one loves the details like Orlando."

"True." The don nodded. "Give him free rein." He turned to Trapani. "Keep this trial moving. I want to be home in time to see my son born." He kissed the back of Kate's hand. Then he leaned over and whispered something to Trapani and motioned with his head to Ruggero. Trapani nodded, and Ruggero could almost guess what Enrico had said. It had to be about the evidence. Aside from Enrico, Ruggero was the only man alive who knew what had happened. And it had to stay that way.

One of the guards knocked on the door and stuck his head in. "Two minutes."

They said their goodbyes. Ruggero wished he could slip the don a weapon. Even though Don Lucchesi would be in solitary confinement, that was little comfort. Andretti could easily buy off a guard. But it was better than nothing. And Enrico wasn't stupid. He could handle himself, but it would require constant vigilance, and every man had to sleep sometime.

They had to get the case dismissed as soon as possible. And there was only one thing Ruggero could do to help: determine what Silvio Fuente knew about the evidence he'd "discovered." Somehow Ruggero had to get the truth. And this time he couldn't resort to blows.

———— ◆ ————

Breaking his once-a-week cigar rule, Lorenzo Andretti lit up a second one, inhaling with great satisfaction. The newspaper in his lap blared the headline: "Scandal Brewing at the Banca di Falcone." The subtitle read: "Embattled CEO Enrico Lucchesi Facing Murder Charges in Unrelated Case." Lorenzo picked up the phone and dialed Salvatore Ruscino, his most trusted man—though Lorenzo kept even Sal at arm's length. No one deserved anything more.

Sal was watching over Lorenzo's grandson Dario. Now that Lorenzo had successfully blown apart the alliance between Lucchesi and Dario, Dario might possibly have come around to Lorenzo's side. Provided he didn't believe Antonio Lucchesi's accusations. That blond bastard somehow had gotten Sandro to confess before he died, and Sandro had apparently been eager to drag Lorenzo down with him. It figured. Sandro had betrayed his own *cosca* for his own gain; of course he'd betray Lorenzo too. But it was the orphan's word against Lorenzo's, and Dario was so poisoned by hatred for all things Lucchesi that he seemed to have dismissed everything Antonio had said.

And that was for the best. Should Dario ever come to believe that Lorenzo had ordered the death of Dario's son, Cristoforo, the war would be infinitely harder to win.

"Enzo," Salvatore said, his cigarette-roughened voice greeting him. He skipped the respectful title he'd normally have used, in case the line was tapped.

"Sal. I trust you've seen the papers?"

"*Sì.* It's all happening, just like you said."

"We'll be pounding the nails in his coffin any day now."

Sal laughed. "I'll swing the hammer myself."

As always, Sal's eagerness and brutality were great assets. "How's my grandson?"

"The same. He says little. Leaves most of the day-to-day management to me."

"Has there been any thawing?"

"No. But his daughter claims to be pregnant."

That would not be good; a Lucchesi-Andretti grandchild could ruin everything. "You think she's lying?"

"I think it's awfully convenient."

Sal was right about that. "Even if it's true, keep Dario wondering about it."

"Will do. What did you hear from the courthouse?"

"The judge is concerned about the gun. But she kept him in custody."

"As expected."

Loredana Montisi's family history was exactly why they'd picked her. All it had taken was a call to Italo Baldassare, Lorenzo's favorite corrupt politician, to make the selection of a judge in the Lucchesi trial less than random. "She granted an immediate trial and put him in solitary confinement though. You've made the arrangements?"

"Still working on it, but I should have it settled within the week," Sal said.

"Don't take too long. If she tosses the gun, he could be out in less than two weeks."

"Do not worry yourself, Enzo. You can count on me."

"*Bene*." He said goodbye to Sal. Just in case Sal couldn't find a guard to take care of Lucchesi, Lorenzo would arrange a little nudge for Loredana Montisi. She needed to know her place in all this.

And should they fail to get Lucchesi while he was in jail, the next phase of Lorenzo's plan was about to unfold. It was time for Alexei Vilanovich to make himself worth all those euros Lorenzo had paid.

———— ◆ ————

Loredana climbed the stone steps to her apartment building, followed by Brigadiere Stefano Gaspare, the *carabinieri* officer who'd been assigned to her as a bodyguard. She'd argued repeatedly that she didn't need one, but ever since she'd been shot at five years ago, she'd had one or more guards assigned to her at all times. This one, Stefano, was at least easy on the eyes.

They reached the secured entrance, and she pulled out her key to unlock the door. "See you tomorrow, Stefano."

The sergeant major moved a little closer, looming over her, and casually placed a hand on the door frame above her head. He was considerably taller than she was, making her feel her femininity all the more. "I'm supposed to make sure you get safely inside," he murmured, bending down so his lips hovered near her ear.

She looked up. Shut him down, or say yes? It had been quite a while since she'd indulged herself in a little no-strings fun. Stefano was a year or two younger than she was, but at least he was over thirty. Anything younger would have made her feel old.

He gave her a lazy smile, displaying perfect white teeth, and his hazel eyes sparkled with mischief. *You only live once.* Her mother was visiting Loredana's sister Allegra, and the apartment would be quiet. Lonely.

"I suppose you ought to be thorough," she said and gave him a coy smile before inserting her key in the lock. He opened the door for her and held it so that she could duck inside.

The door shut behind them with a clang, and Stefano placed a hand on the small of her back as they walked through the lobby, her heels clicking on the marble. Enjoying the warmth of his hand, she smiled. She liked a man who wasn't afraid to stake a claim. They walked over to the elevator, a rickety wire-frame contraption. Every time she stepped inside it, she wondered if she'd be the one it died on. At least she wouldn't be trapped for long if that happened. The open design of the elevator and its shaft would make her predicament readily visible.

The elevator door slowly creaked open, and Stefano followed her inside, his hand slipping down to grip her ass. Her mouth dropped open. Anyone could see them! But he just smirked at her and left his hand where it was. Well, two could play that game.

Without looking at him, she brushed a hand over his crotch. When her fingers traced the swell of his cock, already half-hard beneath the fine cloth of his black uniform trousers, a nervous thrill zinged through her and settled low in her belly. She let her fingers linger on him for a moment, then she started to withdraw, but he clamped a hand around her wrist. "Don't stop," he said, the words low and rasping.

"I'll stop if I want to." She tugged on her wrist, holding his eyes until he relented and released her. Then she closed her hand over his cock again, tightening her grip and digging in her nails until he grunted. "Got that?" she whispered.

The elevator jerked to a halt at her floor, then the door opened with a buzz. Stefano followed her out and tipped his black officer's cap at her. "I hear you."

"*Bene*. Just so we're clear."

"We are." She unlocked the door to her apartment, and he crowded her inside, then pushed her up against the door as it swung shut. He claimed her mouth in a bruising kiss, and she knocked off his cap and fisted his short brown hair, tugging on it mercilessly.

Stefano shoved a hand between her legs, groping her through the thin material of her skirt, then he rucked the fabric up to her waist and slipped his fingers in her panties. She'd been wet since he'd touched her in the lobby, and she moaned into his mouth.

"Loredana, is that you?" her mother called out.

Loredana froze, her eyes going wide. Stefano pulled back and looked at her. She put a finger on his lips, then shook her head. He licked the finger she was pressing to his mouth and rubbed his own against her aching clit, then he released her.

She eased the door open and pushed him out while answering her mother and scooping up his cap. She shoved the hat at him, but before she could close the door, he leaned back in and kissed her. Then he waggled an eyebrow at her and stuck his fingers in his mouth. The ones that had been between her legs. "You taste like heaven," he murmured.

"Go!" she hissed, her cheeks hot as burning coals.

"*Ciao*." He winked and tipped his cap at her again before wheeling about on his heel.

She checked out his ass as he headed back to the elevator. Damn. What the hell was Mamma doing home?

"What's taking you so long?" her mother yelled, and Loredana shut the door. She smoothed down her skirt and checked her appearance in the mirror by the door. Her lipstick was smeared, and she scrubbed at it with her fingertips, her lips still tingling. Oh, that would have been fun. Stefano was cocky, but from what she could tell, he'd earned the right. *Some other time.*

"Coming," she called. *I wish.* She slipped off her heels and headed down the hallway to the spacious living room. It still looked much the same as it had before her father had been killed. With a little start, Loredana realized it had already been twenty-two years. He'd been gone for nearly two-thirds of her life, and still she missed him.

Her mother, Nora Montisi, sat in her favorite chair, reading glasses perched at the end of her nose, peering at one of her endless crossword puzzles.

"Mamma, I thought you weren't going to be home for another two days."

Her mother looked up and presented her cheek for a kiss. Just the left one though. She didn't like to be kissed on the right.

That side still bore an ugly white scar that bisected her cheek. Her doctors had urged her to have plastic surgery, but she'd always insisted there was no need. She'd never remarry after Ludovico, and getting rid of her scar would be like erasing him from her life too. He'd died in her arms on the very steps outside their apartment building. Right in front of Loredana and her sisters.

Loredana tried to shove the memory away. She hadn't thought about it in years, so what had brought that on?

An image of Signor Sinister glaring at her in the courtroom flashed through her head. Okay, so maybe he *had* gotten to her. A bit.

"Allegra was driving me crazy. And I forgot how noisy the kids can be when they're cooped up during the winter."

Loredana took the chair across from her mother. The chair had been her father's, and the fine leather creaked as she eased into it. Sometimes it still felt strange to be in his chair, but Mamma had insisted someone use it, and neither Allegra nor Gisella had wanted to. And now both of them were gone, off raising families of their own.

The way Loredana ought to be. Would have been, if Daniele, her fiancé, hadn't turned tail the minute they'd been shot at. Was that why she'd said yes to Stefano? Was she subconsciously looking for a man who wouldn't desert her if Signor Sinister did come calling?

"Are you all right?" her mother asked. "You seem preoccupied."

"It's nothing. Just thinking about a case."

"Which one?" Her mother gestured to the paper. "The one involving Baldassare, or the one involving that banker?"

"The banker." She'd hardly given a thought to the Baldassare case. This would be Baldassare's first appeal of the election-fraud case, but his third brush with her. Sure, he was the prime minister, but he didn't scare her. Since judges had lifetime appointments, he couldn't touch her job. And he could make all the noise he wanted about not getting a fair trial and getting tried in the press, but it was all just talk. "What does the paper say about the Lucchesi case?" Loredana asked.

"Just that it might expand into money laundering." Nora smiled and tapped the newsprint. "Your papà would be so proud of you. The paper says you're as tough on Mafia scum as your father was. Maybe tougher."

"I try." But she'd grown a little troubled in the time since the hearing that morning. Both sides had handed her their briefs, and the details of the missing evidence—and its suspicious reappearance on the eve of Lucchesi running into trouble with the FIU—made her intuition tingle.

Something was just a bit too convenient about it all. Setting aside the possible tax evasion and the current charges, Lucchesi's record had been more or less spotless, other than an alleged drunk-driving accident almost a year ago. And now there were two huge stains on that record. What were the odds of that happening at the same time?

"What's bothering you?"

Loredana shook her head. "You know I don't like to discuss cases with you."

"Your father and I used to do it all the time."

"Well, you shouldn't have."

Her mother looked at her over the top of her glasses. "I hadn't realized I'd raised such a stickler for the rules."

"Mamma."

Her mother snorted. "Gisella's right. You're such a prissy *principessa*. Never want to get your hands dirty."

Loredana's stomach tightened. "What does that mean?"

"You heard me."

"No. I want to know what you meant."

"Nothing. It's just that you could remove that stick from your *culo* every now and then."

"Look, I can't afford to make a single mistake. If those thugs ever thought they could bribe me or extort me, it'd be all over. They'd own me. And I couldn't live with that."

"*Dolcezza*, I fear for you."

"There's no need, Mamma. I have my guard."

Her mother raised a brow. "Ah, yes, the handsome Stefano."

Loredana ducked her head and studied the tiles below her feet. "Don't talk about him like that."

"I'm not stupid." Nora laughed. "I've seen how he looks at you."

"It's not like that."

"And why not? You're a beautiful woman. He's a beautiful man. Besides, it's good to get one a few years younger. Then you might not spend so many years alone at the end."

"Mamma, I'm not looking for a man right now."

"Loredana, you're thirty-four. How much longer are you going to let Daniele hurt you?"

And just like that, there was a lump in her throat. She didn't trust herself to speak.

"How long, *dolcezza*?" Her mother's voice was soft, tender, but the words sliced like knives.

Daniele had cut her to the bone, the way he'd broken off with her. All he'd said was, "I can't do this." He hadn't even begged her to quit the judiciary. Not that she would have, but his lack of effort spoke volumes. How could she have been so stupid? She'd believed he'd love her forever, that he'd be the man she'd grow old with. But in a matter of months he'd replaced her with a pretty society wife, the daughter of Milan's mayor, and that had been that.

Loredana rubbed a hand over her eyes and sighed. "I don't know, Mamma."

Her mother pursed her lips and shook her head. "Sometimes I worry that I made a mistake with you."

"What do you mean?"

"I pushed you into the law. I'm not sure it makes you happy. And you'd be married by now if I hadn't."

"To Daniele? No thanks." The shooting had done her a favor, in a roundabout way.

"That was an extreme situation."

"Not really. If he'd actually loved me, he'd have stood by me and fought for me. And he did neither. I don't need that kind of 'commitment' from a man. Good times *and* bad. That's the vow."

"You're being a little harsh."

Loredana shook her head. "And you're making it sound like my life is ruined, all because I don't have a man."

"Well, if your gorgeous guard grows a pair and asks, give him a chance."

Loredana suppressed a laugh. *He had his hand in my panties just a few minutes ago. And it's your fault we're not in bed right now.* "Okay, Mamma."

"At least you know he's not afraid of a little gunfire."

No, he wasn't. Once again, Signor Sinister popped into her mind. Though a man like that probably wouldn't miss.

CHAPTER 3

Enrico flipped over the plastic toothbrush to rub the right edge of the handle against the rough cinder-block wall of his cell. He'd already worn down the other side in preparation for forming a sharp point at the end. He needed a weapon of some sort, and this would have to do until he could find something else.

Judge Montisi had proved to be every bit the ball-breaker she was reputed to be, but her concern about the *carabinieri* having no clear chain of custody was very promising. If she was as by the book as she appeared, she was his only chance of getting a fair trial.

And had she been in Andretti's pay, she certainly would have shrugged off the entire issue.

He'd turned the TV on to mask the scrape of the plastic against the cement, but he stopped anyway the second he heard a footstep at the end of the hall outside his cell. He quickly pocketed the toothbrush and lay back on the bed, putting his hands behind his head and pretending to be engrossed in a show about the plight of the black rhino.

The footsteps stopped outside his cell, and he looked over at the *agente* standing outside his door. "Come here," the officer said, beckoning him closer. The man glanced around, and the hairs rose on the back of Enrico's neck.

"What do you want?" he asked, sitting up, but making no move to approach the door.

"I'm a friend."

"I have no friends in here."

The *agente* frowned and beckoned Enrico closer. "I have a message. From Trapani."

Enrico approached the bars, but kept himself out of arm's reach. "Go on."

"He hired me. To look out for you."

Enrico crossed his arms. "And I would trust you just because you say so."

The *agente* broke protocol and stuck his hand through the bars. A folded-up paper was in his palm. "Because of this."

Enrico took the paper and unfolded it. It was one line, written on Trapani's letterhead. "Trust this man." Those were the only words on it.

It could be legitimate. But Agostino hadn't signed it. Plausible deniability, perhaps, if the guard were caught.

"So maybe he sent you."

"He did. Is there anything you need?"

"Besides a gun and a get-out-of-jail-free card?"

The officer huffed in amusement. "Anything else?"

Pens made decent weapons. "A pen and paper. I'd like to write to my wife. And some books." He motioned to the TV. "I need something besides that."

"What kind of books?"

"Contact Trapani. He can get a list from my wife." There, that would prove whether the man was who he said he was. Kate would include the book he'd been reading. The one that was still sitting on his nightstand. A biography of Julius Caesar.

He pictured their bedroom, Kate alone in the bed, her hands on her rounded belly. He wanted to be with her, to hold her close. To kiss her. To feel their son kicking. They hadn't picked a name yet, but he was thinking of Rinaldo, after his father. He hoped she would agree. His throat constricted. He'd promised to protect her, to be with her always, and he was breaking that promise.

The *agente* was starting to turn away when Enrico stopped him. "What's your name?"

"Abramo." First name only.

"Could I make a phone call?"

The man grinned. "You know it's after hours."

"I thought you were my friend."

The *agente* motioned for him to turn around and place his hands through the opening in the bars. Steel bands snapped around his wrists, and Enrico resisted trying to pull them apart. He didn't need any reminders of how helpless he was. Even more so, now that his hands were cuffed behind his back.

His heart rate spiked as the *agente* unlocked the door and opened it. What if the man hadn't been sent by Trapani? "Do you know if anyone associated with the Andrettis is in this prison?"

"I think there are two or three men here, yes."

"Can you make sure they get nowhere near me?"

"I'll do my best." The *agente* put a hand on Enrico's shoulder and steered him toward the telephone area. It was late, but Kate would be happy to hear from him. Just as he'd be happy to hear her voice. She'd become his home, his everything. He just hoped to get back to her soon.

The half-sharpened toothbrush moved against his leg as they walked. It, and the guard who walked beside him, a guard he wasn't sure he could trust, seemed like the thinnest protection. In fact, they seemed like no protection at all.

———— ◆ ————

Ruggero paced around his room at the Lucchesi villa and listened to his sister's number ring. And ring. *Come on, pick up. I know you're mad at me, but—*

"Yes?" Elena answered, her tone crisp.

"It's me. Again," he said. Could he sound any lamer?

"I have caller ID."

"I'm glad you answered then." He winced at his sarcasm. He needed to tone it down.

Silence fell between them, the seconds ticking by with excruciating slowness. "I don't know what more there is to say," she finally said.

He sighed and rubbed his forehead. She was going to make him beg. He'd exhausted everything else during their earlier conversation. The one she'd ended by hanging up on him. "Elena, *per favore.* Not to make me rest easy. But for Orlando. He's worried about you."

"Then *he* can call me." The phone went dead again.

Fuck! He tossed the mobile phone on the bed and stuck both hands in his hair, pulling at the strands until his scalp hurt. He wanted to punch something. He hated the turmoil in his gut, the feeling that she was in danger and he couldn't do a damn thing.

He wanted to just drive down there and force her in the car. But the trip was about twelve hours one way, and he couldn't leave the don's wife and son—sons— unprotected. Not that he was supposed to be guarding them, but still… he couldn't shut off the urge to look out for them. Or his sister. Any minute now, Lorenzo could pounce on her.

He could take the jet. But he'd still be gone at least half a day. And right now, he didn't want to be gone for a minute. Maybe he should send Tommaso down? But what good would that do? Tommaso couldn't force Elena to leave.

Damn it. What the hell would work on her? Guilt? Maybe he could have Orlando try again. Get the kid to do some acting, talk about how worried he was. Which he was; Orlando just kept it bottled up. He could be a pretty cool customer when he wanted, and he'd gotten better at masking his feelings during the weeks he'd been in the *cosca.* He'd even asked Ruggero to teach him to shoot. And Orlando hated guns.

Ruggero picked up the phone and left his room to look for Orlando. His nephew was often in the library, where he'd set up a desk he could work from.

Just as Ruggero was nearing the library, a ball of pastel blue yarn rolled out of the drawing room, followed by a curse from Kate. He picked up the ball and carried it into the room.

The don's wife was sitting on one of the sofas, a basket of yarn beside her, a half-finished knitting project in her lap. Tears rolled down her cheeks.

Ruggero hastily looked away and placed the ball on the table in front of her. "Here," he said, then started to withdraw.

"Thanks. Can you help me with something?" she asked, sniffing back tears and wiping her eyes.

He hesitated, then shrugged. "Of course."

She held up her knitting. "I screwed this up, and I need to unravel it. It'd help if you'd wind it up as I pull it off." She patted the sofa beside her.

"Bianca or Francesca would be better at this," he said, still standing.

"They're gone. They took Luca and Cocco out. Tonio went with them."

"Orlando?"

She snorted with laughter and patted the sofa again. "Are you afraid of a little yarn?"

"No. I just need to talk to him."

"He went with them. He's too pale, you know. I insisted."

Ruggero sat beside her and took the end of the yarn she extended to him. He started winding it around two of his fingers.

"That's too small," she said. "Wind it around your palm."

He freed his fingers and did as she asked. They worked in silence for a moment, then he asked the question he probably shouldn't. But he'd promised Enrico he'd take care of her. And that meant more than just physically. She needed to stay well. "Why didn't you go with them?"

She stilled for a second, then resumed her work. "I wanted to be by myself."

Maybe that was true. Maybe not. "What did Don Lucchesi say when he called last night?"

"Just that he's okay." Her eyes welled again and she wiped them. "He picked a name for the baby."

"What?"

"Rinaldo."

"It's a good choice. He was an honorable man."

"I know. I met him before he died. When we went to Capri." Her voice thickened, and Ruggero tried to think what to say. So much had happened since then—the attempt on Kate and Enrico, Rinaldo's death, Kate's abduction—but that trip had been a honeymoon of sorts for her and Enrico. Well, at least it had started out that way.

"He'll be back soon," he offered. The words sounded inadequate. Empty.

"I worry about him so much," she sobbed. "And I can hardly stand to be around Tonio and Bianca. I mean, I'm happy for them—overjoyed, really, but it hurts to see them together. It reminds me that Rico isn't here and that he's in danger." She covered her face with her hands and swore. "I *need* to stop crying. I want to. What is *wrong* with me?"

"It's the pregnancy. The hormones. My sister was that way with Orlando. Our aunt said it meant she was having a boy, an early warning of how much heartache he'd bring." He paused. *Dio*, he was babbling. And why was he talking about heartache? "Not that he'll make you sad, just that…" He trailed off. *Just stop talking.*

"Just that he'll be a pain in the *culo*?" she asked, humor tinting her voice.

"*Sì*." She went back to unraveling her project. "What are you making?" he asked.

"Booties for the baby. And before you say anything, yes, they *are* going to be better than that scarf I made for Tonio."

Ruggero let out a snort of laughter. "Luca loves that scarf."

"Well, he's the only one."

"It kept him warm that night." The night his adoptive parents had been murdered. The night that Antonio and Bianca had almost gotten themselves killed as well while trying to rescue Luca.

Kate smiled. "It did. Though Enrico still loves to tease me about it."

"Maybe you should make him one."

Her hands stilled. "You don't think he's jealous?"

Dio mio. He so did not want to get mixed up in that tangle. "No. He might like to have it with him. While he's gone."

She sighed. "You think he's going to be gone for a long time."

"No. But a while. Maybe longer than he thinks. We have to prepare ourselves for the possibility."

"I don't want to. I don't want to think about—" She gasped and pressed a hand to her swollen belly.

"Did he kick?"

She shook her head, her lips mashed together, her eyes widening. His pulse quickened, and he scraped the yarn off his hand. "What is it?"

"I don't know. I just—" She gasped again. "Something's wrong."

"Contractions?"

She nodded, then shook her head. "I don't know. It hurts."

He pulled out his mobile phone and dialed Beppe, telling the guard to bring a car up to the house immediately. He ended the call and turned to Kate. "Can you walk?"

"I think so." He helped her up, hovering beside her. She stopped on another gasp, and that was when he decided to take over.

"I'll carry you." He scooped her off her feet before she could protest.

She felt surprisingly light in his arms. He'd have to talk to Francesca and Bianca about making sure Kate was eating enough.

They passed Maddalena, the maid, in the hall. "Get *la signora*'s coat," he said. She scrambled up the stairs and returned with a jacket as Ruggero was putting Kate in the back of the car. Beppe was in the driver's seat. Ruggero took the coat and placed it over Kate, then climbed in beside her. "Drive," he said to Beppe.

Kate gasped again as they took off, and she reached for his hand. He gave it to her and willed them to go faster. She had to be okay.

They finally got Kate to the hospital, and she was quickly taken to an exam room. Ruggero paced around the waiting area, unsure whether to call the prison or to wait until he had news. His mobile phone rang. It was Elena. "You didn't call me back," she said.

"You were mad at me. Remember?"

"I expected you to try again."

An urgent page went over the hospital's PA, and Ruggero looked around, hoping the nurses and doctors weren't rushing to Kate.

"Are you in a hospital?" Elena asked.

"Yes. Signora Lucchesi is having some problems."

"What's wrong with her?"

Ruggero ran a hand through his hair. "I don't know. She's pregnant and her husband's in jail. I don't think she's eating enough."

"And *you're* the one taking care of her?"

"I was the only one who was home."

Elena sighed, and he could almost see the roll of her eyes. "You truly think I'm in danger?"

"I do. Yes." He paused. "Orlando misses you." *I miss you.*

"Obviously, you could use someone to watch out for Signora Lucchesi."

"Definitely." No need to mention that Francesca and Bianca were trying to do just that.

"Okay then, I'll come."

"I'll send the jet."

"You'll send the *jet?*" She laughed. "Listen to you."

"Elena, please. Don't fight it."

"You think I'd refuse a private jet?"

"I don't know."

"I'm stubborn. Not stupid."

He allowed himself a tiny smile. "No argument here. It will be there in a few hours. I'm sending a man down with it. Tommaso. He'll get you at the house."

"I'll be ready."

"*Grazie.*" He hung up and called Tommaso. As he was wrapping up the call, a doctor approached.

"Signor Vela?" she asked.

"*Sì.*" He studied the doctor carefully but couldn't read her face. His gut tightened. Was it that bad?

"Signora Lucchesi is fine. She just had some contractions. False labor."

"Isn't it too early for that kind of thing?"

The doctor nodded. "It is. But stress can bring it on. And exhaustion."

"She's been sleeping, as far as I know."

The doctor shook her head. "She stated that she hasn't. Not for a couple days."

Damn. "What can we do?"

"I don't want to prescribe anything, because of the baby. Warm milk, warm baths. A calm environment..."

He nodded. What she needed was her husband back. "We'll figure something out." What, he didn't know.

He hoped his sister knew what to do, because he was lost.

———◆———

Antonio looked through his papers one more time and tried to quell his nerves. He'd successfully defended himself before. But that had been to fellow 'Ndranghetisti—this time he had to do so to the Financial Intelligence Unit, which meant he couldn't be as frank as he wished. In fact, he had to reveal as little as possible about what had actually happened when Sandro Lucchesi had stolen his password and tried to frame him.

He looked around the massive conference room in the heart of the FIU's headquarters. Every millimeter of the room was designed to impress, from the frescoes on the walls and ceiling, to the inlaid marble accents around the windows and doors, to the gleaming expanse of the walnut table that he, Trapani, Orlando, Ruggero, and Gavino Idoni, the bank's head of IT, and Max Strasser, the bank's physical security expert, were gathered around. The clock on the wall—an ornate affair, not the utilitarian sort one would expect—said that they were fifteen minutes past the expected start time of the meeting.

Of course. The FIU investigators wanted them to sweat.

At last the door swung open, and a secretary carrying a tray of cold cuts and pastries entered, followed by another with a tray of cups filled with steaming espresso. She handed them each one, then placed others around the desk as the first man came through the door. The only one Antonio recognized was Demetrio Ricci. The rest were unknown to him. But somewhere in their midst was undeniably a man in Lorenzo Andretti's employ. Ricci had done his best to suppress and delay an investigation, but even though he was the director of the FIU, he wasn't able to make the matter just disappear. Especially not once details of the case had been leaked to the press.

Antonio was certain that leak had been Lorenzo's doing.

Ricci started the meeting by introducing his staff. The only one Antonio took notice of was Casimiro Parodi, the head of the Suspicious Transactions Directorate. He was studying Antonio with great interest, and something about Parodi's manner caught his attention. It took Antonio a while to realize what it was. Parodi was smiling—a smug, self-satisfied smile, as if he had the winning hand in a game of cards. Was he Lorenzo's man?

After the introductions, Trapani spoke first. "What would you gentlemen like to know? We've provided all of our records."

Ricci turned to Parodi. "Casimiro, I believe you have a list of concerns?"

Parodi straightened up in his seat and pulled a sheet of paper toward him. Donning a pair of reading glasses, he focused on Antonio. "Signor Legato—"

"It's Lucchesi now," Antonio corrected him.

Parodi stared at him over his glasses. "How interesting. Would you care to explain?"

"Signor Lucchesi recently adopted me."

Parodi smiled as if he'd known what Antonio was going to say all along. "So, Sandro Lucchesi did in fact have reason to be concerned about your behavior at the bank?"

"What are you talking about?" Antonio asked.

"He sent us a statement."

Ice flooded Antonio's veins. "What?"

Trapani put a hand on Antonio's arm. "We are unaware of such a statement." He held out his hand. "May we examine it?"

"Certainly." Parodi handed over a document that detailed Sandro's suspicions regarding Antonio's behavior and how Antonio was trying to frame him so that he could push Sandro out of the bank and the family.

"This is bad," Antonio muttered.

Trapani touched Antonio's forearm and whispered, "Calm yourself. Let me answer." To the rest, Trapani said, "This is baseless. Sandro Lucchesi had a personal grudge against Antonio."

"Is that so?" Parodi asked. "Aside from Signor Legato's—excuse me, Signor *Lucchesi's*—obviously successful attempt to insinuate himself into the Lucchesi family, why would Sandro have had a grudge against him?"

"It was a family dispute involving Antonio's involvement with Sandro's sister."

Parodi smiled. "He did not feel Antonio was good enough for her?"

Trapani looked at Antonio before he spoke, and Antonio nodded. They had to reveal it, or else the FIU wouldn't believe the story. "Antonio and Sandro's sister were involved as teens, and she had a child out of wedlock."

Parodi raised a brow. "Is that so? Perhaps that is why your *client*"—he stressed the word as if Antonio were on trial—"shot and killed Sandro Lucchesi a month and a half ago?"

"You've done your homework, Signor Parodi," Trapani said, and when Parodi smiled, Antonio wanted to punch him in the face. Parodi *was* Lorenzo's man. Antonio had not an iota of doubt.

Antonio leaned forward, ignoring Trapani's restraining hand on his arm. "Sandro Lucchesi kidnapped my son, murdered my son's adoptive parents, injured his own sister, and damn near killed me. I only did what I had to do to protect my family and myself."

"And now you are married to Sandro's sister and have custody of your son, yes?" So Parodi did, in fact, know the entire story. He'd just wanted the rest of his colleagues to hear Antonio's "confession." *That fucker.* When Antonio nodded, Parodi continued. "You seem to be the winner in all this."

"My son was severely traumatized. I'm not sure he'll ever be the same. I would rather not have him if I could've spared him that night. My wife still has nightmares."

"But you sleep untroubled."

How dare Parodi accuse him like this? Antonio almost swore aloud, but Trapani squeezed his arm, so Antonio took a breath and collected himself. "I have nightmares too."

"Do you?" Parodi asked, but it might as well have been Lorenzo Andretti sitting across from him. Lorenzo had obviously given Parodi a script to follow, and Antonio had played his part perfectly.

"Yes." He turned to Ricci. "I was unaware this meeting would turn into a dissection of my personal life."

Ricci looked at Parodi. "Casimiro, what other concerns do you have?"

"Many." He turned back to his papers. "The numerous transfers in question were all executed from Antonio's user account. Where is the evidence that Sandro Lucchesi was even involved?"

Strasser jumped in at that point and showed the video of Sandro entering the bank. He also explained that someone had requested a replacement keycard by impersonating Antonio and claiming that Antonio's had been lost.

"Was this extra card ever traced back to Sandro Lucchesi?"

"No," Strasser said. "But Sandro gained entry to the bank at the same time that the replacement card was used, and he did not use his own card. The video we have is from the jeweler's next door. The bank's own cameras had been disabled prior to Sandro's arrival."

"So all you have is a coincidence?"

Trapani leaned forward. "Antonio was in Cernobbio at the time. He was nowhere near the bank."

"He has witnesses to his whereabouts?"

"That witness is dead."

"How convenient."

"Sandro is the one who killed him," Antonio said.

Parodi smiled. "Again, how convenient."

Antonio threw up his hands. "You've obviously made up your mind."

"I am merely trying to safeguard the Italian public and the Italian banking system. And I will do so to the full extent of my power." Parodi straightened his papers. "Your account was used. How?"

"Sandro stole my password."

"So you admit that your security is lax? You can't keep your account secure, your security team issues keycards in response to interoffice memos without additional verification, your cameras were disabled without your security team being aware. How can we be expected to trust the Banca di Falcone with the public's money?"

Strasser's face reddened. "We've implemented several safeguards to address those issues. In addition, it should be noted that none of this would've been possible without insider participation."

Idoni spoke up. "One of my employees in IT was working with Sandro."

"Excellent," Parodi said. "And has he confessed?"

Idoni looked to Trapani before answering. "Unfortunately, no. He was found dead shortly after the break-in."

"Ah." Parodi shook his head. "The dastardly handiwork of Sandro Lucchesi, I suppose?"

"That is what we believe," Trapani said.

"Again, how convenient."

If he could've gotten away with it, Antonio would've strangled the man. Lorenzo had chosen well. Unfortunately.

Orlando spoke up. "All of this is irrelevant. The transactions were reversed to the extent that it was possible, and when it wasn't, the account holders were reimbursed. No lasting harm to the public or the banking system was allowed to happen. We've addressed the problems by changing security measures and procedures. The Banca di Falcone has operated for many years without fault. This was a well-orchestrated internal attack perpetrated by a rogue employee. I can account for every cent of money involved. We have nothing to hide."

Orlando was so convincing, Antonio almost believed him. Orlando brandished his own stack of papers. "Shall we review the particulars to ensure we have satisfied your concerns?"

"I'd be delighted to do so," Parodi said.

Ricci interrupted. "Is such a review absolutely necessary for this meeting? I do believe you've had adequate time to review the facts, Casimiro. Do you have any specific questions?"

It was Antonio's turn to smile. "Perhaps you'd like to focus on the transactions that we were unable to reverse?" The ones that involved the money Sandro had stolen on Lorenzo's order and transferred to Lorenzo's account at a bank in Liechtenstein—a bank that had been stubbornly uncooperative, giving Lorenzo time to transfer the stolen funds so that they could no longer be recovered.

Parodi shook his head. "Signor Ricci is right. There's no need to dig through those records."

Because you don't want your boss's dirty laundry exposed. "Are you certain?" Antonio asked. "If you have any lingering doubts, surely they must center on those transactions and that bank? We certainly wondered why they were so uncooperative in this matter. It's as if that bank manager were complicit in this crime."

"The bank at issue is the Banca di Falcone."

Antonio smiled. "We would relish an inquiry from the FIU regarding the behavior of the bank in Liechtenstein."

Parodi shook his head. "Your attempt to distract us from the problems in your own bank is rather transparent."

"And your reluctance to inquire further is rather suspicious."

For the first time, Parodi looked uncomfortable.

Orlando jumped in. "Certainly we can take a few minutes to review." He handed out papers and walked through each transfer in detail, step by step, Parodi interjecting several times that there was no need, but Orlando just kept going until everyone's eyes were glazed. He probably would have continued, but Ricci finally brought the meeting to a close.

"*Mille grazie*, Signor Farnese, for such a detailed and meticulous overview. We will discuss the case among ourselves and contact you with the results of our investigation within two weeks."

As they were filing out of the conference room, Parodi waited for Antonio to reach him. "I have my eye on you," he hissed.

Antonio fixed the man with a stare that contained every thought he'd been having about Parodi's demise. "And mine is on you."

"If you're trying to threaten me—"

"I'm not trying."

Parodi took off his glasses. "I'm not so easy to get rid of. I am not Sandro Lucchesi."

"And yet you serve the same man he did. Beware becoming another casualty."

"You cannot intimidate me."

Antonio smiled. "You would do well to note who's alive, who's dead, and how much protection Andretti gives his minions."

"If you touch me, they'll know who did it."

"Unfortunate accidents happen all the time."

Parodi held his gaze for a few moments, then left without another word. Antonio had scored a hit, but would it end the inquiry?

Or was this merely Lorenzo's opening salvo?

CHAPTER 4

Ruggero sat next to Kate in the courtroom, his sister Elena on her other side. They were in the first row of seats behind the defendant's table, and Kate was seated directly behind Enrico. The two of them were whispering to each other and holding hands. She seemed a little better.

Elena's no-nonsense, take-charge demeanor had helped. As soon as she'd arrived, she had very quickly convinced Kate to get out of the house and walk the grounds with her, on the pretext of showing her around, and had otherwise made herself indispensable.

But Elena had still said little to Ruggero. Rather, he hadn't given her the opportunity. He didn't want to hear it. He knew he'd failed Papà; he knew he'd failed her. He didn't need anyone else to point that out.

"*La corte*," a clerk announced, and Judge Montisi, followed by the co-judge for the trial and the six lay judges, filed in. The two judges were in the shapeless black and white robes of their office, and the lay judges wore sashes with the colors of the Italian flag.

"Are those the jurors?" Kate asked while the two judges conferred with each other.

Enrico answered. "Sort of. It's not the same as in the United States. They're townspeople, chosen at random."

"So the next part is questioning them to see if they've heard about the case in the news?" she asked.

He shook his head. "We don't do that here."

"But won't they be prejudiced about the case?"

He shrugged. "Maybe. That's why this FIU investigation couldn't have come at a worse time. It just casts more doubt on me."

"They'll be sequestered though."

He shook his head again. "No."

"But that's ridiculous!" she said. "How can they possibly be expected to be impartial?"

36

"Sequestering them is just not practical, *cara*. Trials here can drag on for years."

"Years?"

"Mine won't. I asked for an immediate trial for that reason."

Kate inhaled deeply. "You're not going to be home for the birth, are you?"

"I will. We'll get the evidence tossed out. You'll see."

She nodded, and Enrico glanced at Ruggero, concern in his eyes. If Ruggero could've spoken freely, he'd have told him everything Elena was doing. But all he could do was nod: message received.

Judge Montisi called the court to order, and once again, Ruggero allowed himself to study her, his eyes drinking her in—the way she brushed the hair out of her face, the flick of her hand as she paged through a stack of papers, the way she licked her lips after taking a sip of espresso.

Several times she met his eyes, her own slightly narrowed, as if she'd love to put him in jail too. No doubt she'd be all too happy to do just that.

Dio, why did she have to fascinate him? He should hate her. But he knew her history—the press delighted in reciting it again and again—how her father had been killed by Mafia assassins, how her mother had been disfigured. How Loredana had risen quickly in the judicial ranks, how she'd earned her reputation as a fearless crusader against the Mafia, despite numerous threats and a serious attempt on her life some years ago. Her fiancé had deserted her over it.

What a coward. But then, most men were. It was the whole reason the Mafia flourished. Most people wouldn't dare stand against them. Most men didn't have the balls Loredana Montisi did.

And that just added to her allure.

At least he'd never have to worry about getting entangled with her. They might as well be living on neighboring planets—their worlds would never collide. They might observe each other from a distance, but that was all. And that was how things had to be.

Besides, he didn't have relationships, much less with a judge, of all people. He had an arrangement with a call girl in Milan. He could get what he needed without worrying about any attachments. Attachments he couldn't afford to have.

"Pubblico Ministero Corvi, have you met with the FIU?" Judge Montisi asked.

Corvi rose. "I have, Giudice. However, based on their meeting with representatives of the Banca di Falcone, the FIU has decided to conduct some additional investigations, and they've asked me to wait another week, possibly ten days, for their ruling."

Perhaps Antonio's and Orlando's statements at the FIU meeting had sunk in. If the FIU were pursuing the Liechtenstein bank and discovered a connection to Lorenzo Andretti and the Russian *Mafiya*, that would bolster their case. However, it was a risky strategy. Andretti was a Banca di Falcone client, and that rodent Parodi could try to claim that the bank had insight into Andretti's dirty dealings and hadn't done anything about them. After all, Don Lucchesi had been married to one of Lorenzo's granddaughters at one point.

Or perhaps the FIU was digging into something else. Orlando had assured him that they'd find nothing incriminating—Don Lucchesi had a foolproof system for funneling money into and out of the bank, using a complicated series of trusts, charitable foundations, and dummy corporations set up on behalf of the family and their clients. All of it entirely legal, of course.

How much 'Ndrangheta money winds up in the pockets of our lawyers? Ruggero eyed Trapani and Adimari. He'd never liked having to depend on such men to cover their dealings. They knew far too much and did not have a blood vow to bind them to the *cosca*. Yet Enrico trusted them, perhaps because both men had families, and they'd both seen what happened to traitors and those they loved.

"Did the FIU give you any indication of what new angle they were pursuing?" Judge Montisi asked Corvi.

"None. I should be ready to report back next Wednesday or Friday."

"*Bene.*" She flicked another page in the stack of papers in front of her. "Moving on to the chain of custody. Has the *carabinieri* been able to account for the whereabouts of the gun in question?"

Corvi scratched his chin and cleared his throat. "A review of the computer records shows the gun being scanned in on 7 January 2008. There is no record of it being removed from the evidence vault."

"And yet it could not be located for almost three years?"

"That is correct, Giudice."

"How can this be?"

"Apparently it was misfiled."

"For three years?"

Corvi nodded. "Yes, Giudice."

"And then it was found?"

"Yes. By Sottotenente Silvio Fuente."

"He found it by accident? Just stumbled upon it?"

"That is not my understanding."

Trapani rose. "Giudice Montisi, the defense wishes to question Silvio Fuente. However, the prosecution has insisted that such a measure is unnecessary."

Her gaze lasered in on Corvi. "I should like to hear from this man as well."

"Giudice, I did not wish to call an officer of the law from his duties over such a trivial matter."

Judge Montisi leaned forward. "You think the matter before us is trivial?"

"I meant no offense. Merely that this is a minor clerical error. Moreover, Sottotenente Fuente would doubtless know nothing about what happened beyond what the computer records show."

"Which is damnably little."

A few of the lay judges snickered, and Ruggero suppressed his own smile. She was like a hound who'd cornered a boar—not letting up for a moment.

"I want Fuente in court this week. And I want the person in charge of the evidence vault here as well." She waited a beat, then added, "I want *answers*, Pubblico Ministero Corvi. I want assurances regarding this evidence and the integrity of the chain of custody. Without these, the gun is worthless."

Could it be that easy? Ruggero risked a glance at Enrico, but nothing in the don's manner gave his thoughts away.

"You will have them, Giudice." Corvi shuffled his papers. "If I may, Giudice Montisi, I would like to state that should the gun be rendered inadmissible, there is still plenty of reason to hold the defendant in custody. The man who wielded the gun, Sergio Grantini, is missing; in fact, the last time he was seen was twenty-four hours prior to the attack on Giudice Dinelli and his family. I would also like to remind the court that Carlo Andretti, the man who was Signor Lucchesi's co-defendant in the tax-evasion case before Giudice Dinelli, is dead. He was murdered and the body discovered at the site of a house fire last year."

Trapani raised a hand. "Objection. Relevance?"

Corvi turned to Trapani. "I am merely pointing out that the two men we *should* be putting on the stand can't be here today. Or ever. And that surely benefits your client."

"Signor Grantini's whereabouts are unknown. He could still appear before the court."

"Can you produce him?" the judge asked.

"Not as yet. We're still trying to locate him," Trapani said.

As the lawyers argued back and forth, with Trapani asking again for an immediate dismissal or at the least, house arrest, Ruggero felt a strange prickle at the back of his neck. He turned, seeking the eyes that no doubt were locked on him. At first, he saw no one beyond the reporters who lined the back of the courtroom. But then he spotted him: a fellow 'Ndranghetista, from the looks of him. A young, hard-looking man in a gray tracksuit jacket. His hair was carefully slicked back, his gaze unflinching as Ruggero's eyes caught his. Ruggero didn't recognize him, but he'd bet good money that the man worked for Lorenzo Andretti.

But the question was: Why was he here? Had he smuggled in a weapon? Did he plan to gun down Don Lucchesi when the day's hearing was over? Or had he merely been sent to keep tabs on the proceedings?

Ruggero had managed to hide a ceramic folding knife in a compartment in the heel of his right wingtip. He leaned down and slipped the weapon out, palming it and moving it to his pocket. It wasn't much, and if the other had somehow smuggled in a gun, it might not be enough.

Judge Montisi dismissed the court, and Ruggero leaned over to Kate. "There's something I need to do. Stay with Beppe and Elena."

She searched his face. "What's wrong?"

"It may be nothing."

He turned from her, then glanced at Beppe before motioning with his eyes at the man in question, who had risen, but made no move to leave the courtroom just yet. Probably because Enrico was still conferring with Trapani and Adimari.

Beppe nodded and moved closer to the women. His pulse quickening, Ruggero slipped out of the row of chairs and headed for the back of the courtroom.

Tracksuit ignored his approach. *Stupid punk.* If he thought Ruggero was harmless, he was an idiot. Even bare handed, Ruggero could easily kill a grown man. Give him a ballpoint pen, and the job was even easier. Give him a knife, and it could be over in an eye blink.

He circled behind Tracksuit, and the guy crossed his arms, but didn't follow Ruggero with his eyes. *Arrogant little* stronzo.

At last Tracksuit headed for the exit, and Ruggero shadowed him, careful to stay within a few paces. If Tracksuit was paying attention, he wasn't making it obvious. Could he have actually failed to recognize Ruggero for what he was?

Impossible. Tracksuit might be an idiot, but he'd have to be blind. Besides, Ruggero had been sitting with the family. Tracksuit *had* to know who he was. *What* he was, despite the fine suit.

Tracksuit entered the crowded outer hallway, but instead of moving toward Enrico and the crush of reporters surrounding him, he headed the other way. Ruggero scanned the hallway, looking for Tracksuit's target. Was it Kate?

No, she and Elena were with Beppe near Enrico. There was no one else in the family nearby, no one of note, other than Judge Montisi, who was strutting away from the courtroom, her long hair swinging between her shoulder blades. Tracksuit headed in her direction, and Ruggero's heart sped up. What was he up to?

The judge walked down the corridor and took a right. Probably headed for the restrooms. And that would be the perfect place to kill her. Was Andretti concerned that she was going to throw out the gun?

Ruggero quickened his stride and rounded the corner right behind Tracksuit. The man reached for something in his pocket and called out to the judge, who turned just in time to see Ruggero tackle Tracksuit to the ground.

They hit the marble hard, and Tracksuit writhed under Ruggero like an eel. Then he stopped moving and held up the object in his hand. An envelope. "Protecting the enemy, I see," the man sneered at him in Calabrian.

"Give me that." Ruggero ripped the envelope from the man's grasp. He let Tracksuit up, and the punk made a show of dusting himself off.

"Make sure she gets it," he tossed over his shoulder as he turned to go.

There was something hard inside the envelope, and Ruggero started to stuff it in his pocket, his eyes anywhere but on the judge.

"You're Calabrian, aren't you?" she asked, approaching him. "I couldn't follow what he said, but I recognized the accent."

Ruggero looked at her then, taking in the hands on her hips, her flashing eyes, but he didn't respond.

"Give me the envelope." She held out a hand.

He hesitated. "It could be dangerous."

She crossed her arms. "What are you hiding? Drugs?"

———— ◆ ————

Loredana stared directly into the dark eyes of Signor Sinister. His heavy brows popped up slightly at her question, then a smile tugged at his lips.

"Drugs? No." His voice was softer when he spoke to her than it had been when he'd barked at the man he'd tackled. His Italian was good, the accent marking him as a Northerner. Yet he spoke fluent Calabrian as well. And didn't that just confirm all her suspicions about Enrico Lucchesi?

She held out her hand again. "Then give me the envelope."

"There's something hard inside. I don't know what it is."

"Everyone is screened."

She heard a soft click, and a switchblade appeared in his hand. Her blood turned to ice, but just like that the knife was gone. For a second, she questioned whether she'd seen it at all.

"I'm not going to hurt you," he said, and she realized she was breathing hard. To mask it, she snapped her fingers. "Now." When he made no move to hand her the envelope, she added, "*Per favore*," then regretted it. She didn't need to be polite. Not to a man like him.

He stepped closer, and it took everything she had not to retreat. The man moved with the coiled, precise grace of a jungle cat, his eyes locked on hers. He held out the envelope, his thick fingers brushing hers as she took it.

A shiver ran up her arm at the contact. He was within easy reach of her. And he was armed.

"How did you get that knife in here?" she asked as casually as she could.

He shrugged, his eyes not leaving hers. "It's not important."

"I beg to differ."

"Beg all you want." He gave her a half-smile then, and she was startled by how much his features changed. The stony menace of his face was gone. There was someone in there, someone warm. Someone who was… flirting with her?

She almost returned the smile, then suppressed it. No matter how handsome he was, she couldn't let her guard down with him. Not for a minute. *Dio* only knew what he was capable of. She ought to call the *carabinieri* and have him arrested for bringing that knife in here. But he was making no move to hurt her.

He motioned to the envelope in her hand. "Want me to open it?"

She shook her head, though her pulse was racing. It was too small to be explosive, wasn't it? She flipped it over and slid her finger under the seal. A single sheet of paper with a typed note was folded up inside, along with something that slid around the envelope as she moved it. She dumped the item into her palm. A bullet. Her mouth went dry and she looked up at him.

His lips had flattened out again, and his black brows were drawn together. "What does it say?" he asked, his voice a soft rasp.

She read it aloud. "The evidence speaks for itself. Lucchesi deserves to rot. He does, or you do." A chill swept through her, and her hands trembled. A sudden weakness almost buckled her knees. It was happening again. Last time, the men who wanted her dead had missed; who could say she'd be so lucky again?

"You are in serious danger," he said. "There are men who want Enrico Lucchesi dead or locked up in prison, and they want you to put him there."

"No shit," she said, then almost laughed at her lack of decorum. She fumbled her mobile phone out of her purse and shakily dialed Stefano and asked him to meet her.

"Who did you call?" the man asked when she was finished.

"One of my guards."

"*Carabiniere?*"

She nodded. She shouldn't be talking to him. But she couldn't seem to stop.

He advanced on her, and she backed up half a step. He put a little distance between them in response. "Listen to me. Trust no one. None of them."

"Why?"

"How many cases have you seen where the *carabinieri* is in bed with the Mafia?"

He had a point. But she trusted Stefano. "And *you* wouldn't slit my throat?"

"I'm not sure who you think I am. I'm just someone hired to protect Signor Lucchesi."

"And I wonder how far you'd go to ensure his safety."

"As far as is necessary."

"That's hardly reassuring to someone like me."

"It wasn't meant to be." His silver-gray eyes bored into hers. How many men had stared into those eyes during their last moments on earth?

"Is that a threat?" she asked.

"It's a warning. What you do next in this case is of great importance to a great many powerful men."

"What are you saying?"

That half-smile appeared again, but it didn't reach his eyes this time. "You aren't stupid. And I don't think I need to spell it out."

He moved closer again, and this time she jumped away, her back hitting the wall. Trapped. Blood pounded in her ears, and his smile widened. He placed one hand on the wall beside her head and leaned in, just centimeters from her. He smelled of espresso, cigarettes, and a light cologne. Something lemony. "I wasn't going to hurt you. I've never hurt a woman, and I'm not about to start."

"Then what are you doing?"

"Reassuring you."

"I thought you didn't do that."

He chuckled, low and deep, and his other hand met the wall on the other side of her head. He had her caged in quite effectively, but his gaze was what held her captive. She struggled not to squirm, to meet his eyes, to keep him from knowing how desperately she wanted to run.

He leaned in, his voice dropping, his words a whisper. "I want you to remember how you're feeling now: heart beating fast, every cell excruciatingly alert, ready to jump out of your skin. Remember this, and don't forget. You are in danger, Giudice Montisi, and remembering that is what's going to keep you alive."

He was so close his lips brushed her hair, and she couldn't suppress a full-body shiver. He lifted a hand from the wall and brought it close to her face, almost as if he were going to touch her, then he dropped it to his side.

The rapid tap of footsteps signaled someone's approach, but the man didn't move. He just stared at her, and when Stefano rounded the corner, relief practically swamped her.

"Who are you and what are you doing?" Stefano growled, his hand moving to the gun holstered at his hip.

The man raised his hands and backed away from her. "My name is Ruggero Vela. And I mean no harm. Just the opposite."

Stefano stepped forward as if to confront the man, and Loredana suddenly found her voice. "It's fine, Stefano."

"You sounded upset on the phone," he said, keeping his eyes on Vela.

Vela moved farther away from them, then dropped his hands and wheeled around.

"Wait a minute!" Stefano barked.

"It's fine. Truly," she said and waved at Vela to go.

Once Vela was around the corner, Stefano came closer and cupped her jaw. "You're sure?"

"I'm sure. Someone—a man he tackled—gave me this." She handed Stefano the note and the bullet.

He scanned it quickly, his eyebrows rising then falling. "Damn Mafiosi," he muttered. "I'd better call this in."

Porca miseria! Stefano could ruin everything. She clutched his arm. "You didn't see that man talking to me."

"What?"

"You didn't see him. *Capisci?*"

"Who is he?"

She lowered her voice. "He provides security for the defendant in my latest case."

"Lucchesi?" Stefano asked.

She nodded. "I can't be seen talking to him, or I'll have to recuse myself. What he said to me—it's immaterial."

Stefano pursed his lips and stared at her for a moment. Then he nodded. "If you say so." He brushed the hair off her forehead and pulled her into his arms, but didn't try to kiss her. He just rubbed his hands up and down her back, his touch soothing, warm. "You're still shaking," he murmured.

"I'll be okay."

He planted a kiss on the crown of her head. "You will be. I'll keep you safe."

She nodded against him, but she couldn't relax. If Vela was part of this, if he wanted her dead, she was sure he'd achieve his goal, Stefano or no. But the man had made no attempt to hurt her. And that note—the writer wanted Lucchesi in jail. Vela didn't. Unless that had all been a setup.

Could Vela be telling the truth? Or was this some elaborate game to make her sympathetic to Lucchesi?

CHAPTER 5

Loredana Montisi smelled better than the finest whiskey: a complex bouquet of something floral, a trace of sandalwood, and a hint of vanilla. Ruggero would never forget that scent as long as he lived. But right now, he had to. He had to focus; so much depended on it.

He'd consulted with Trapani immediately after the confrontation with Tracksuit and updated the lawyer on the threat against Loredana Montisi. A couple hours later, Trapani had given him a message from Don Lucchesi: Protect the judge, above all else. She was the key to Enrico's freedom.

Ruggero arrived at the crowded bistro in downtown Milan where he'd arranged to meet Silvio Fuente. It was one of those touristy places on a public square, stuffed to bursting with chattering people. No one would take notice of them.

He chose a table outside and tapped a cigarette out of the pack and lit it. When the waiter frowned at him, Ruggero placed a twenty euro note on the table beside his plate and the man pocketed it and took his order. Espresso, *doppio*, with prosciutto, cheese, and olives. Something light. He wasn't going to be there long. He finished the cigarette and was considering having another when Fuente strolled up. Thankfully the officer was out of uniform. He took a seat and motioned to the half-full pack, and Ruggero extended it to him.

"How kind," Fuente said around a cigarette as he lit it. The waiter came back and frowned at Fuente, who flashed his badge in response. If the waiter hoped to make another twenty euros, he'd have better luck elsewhere. "So why am I here?" Fuente asked after ordering.

"This case. Is Lorenzo Andretti leaning on you?"

Fuente picked a fleck of tobacco off his tongue, then took another drag. "What difference does it make?"

Ruggero snatched the cigarette from Fuente's fingers and snapped it in half before stabbing it out on his espresso plate. "Tell me."

Fuente chuckled. "I would've thought you'd show more finesse."

"And I would've thought we could count on you. Considering how much money my employer has sent your way."

Fuente clasped his hands together and leaned back. "Money can't buy everything."

Ruggero leaned forward. "But it did buy your position and that nice promotion, Sottotenente."

The waiter brought Ruggero's food and Fuente's espresso. Fuente raised his cup and motioned to Ruggero's plate. "Let's not be unpleasant."

Ruggero fingered the knife still in his pocket. If he had Fuente alone, he'd have his answers in a matter of heartbeats. Instead, he reached for the food, eating slowly while Fuente sipped his espresso and watched him.

"It's funny," Fuente said.

"What?"

"Seeing you eat. You always seemed half machine to me." He tapped his own chest. "Not human."

Ruggero resisted the urge to smash Fuente's face into the ceramic tabletop. *He's playing with me.* He counted silently to ten, making great work of removing the pit of an olive with his teeth. "And you've seemed half devil to me."

Fuente smiled and stroked his dark mustache. "So, have we misjudged one another?"

Ruggero rolled a piece of prosciutto around a stick of pecorino cheese. "We can help you, if that's what you need."

The twinkle left Fuente's eyes and his mouth tightened. "What I need—" He abruptly stopped speaking.

So he was right. "Tell me."

Fuente tapped a finger on the table's edge, for once not meeting Ruggero's eyes. Then he swallowed visibly and looked up. "I need nothing."

All at once, Ruggero understood. "He has one of your children." Fuente's eyes dropped to the tabletop. "We can help, in exchange—"

With a slice of his hand, Fuente cut Ruggero off. "I'm done with games. I've played too many. I can't afford to play another."

"Is it a son or a daughter?" Ruggero kept his voice soft, his words calm, as if he were trying to soothe a spooked horse.

Fuente closed his eyes for a moment and a sigh escaped him. "My son. Nino. I received his ear yesterday."

"You know where he's being held?"

The officer shook his head. "He's promised to release him. As soon as I testify."

"And what are you going to say?"

"Whatever he tells me to."

Time to gamble. "You could tell the judge privately what's happening."

Fuente snorted. "You're that naïve? Anything I tell her would be in front of the prosecutor. And Corvi is in Andretti's pocket."

Damn. "We'll find your boy."

"Well, you've got two days to do it. Then I testify." He pulled out his wallet, and Ruggero waved his money away.

"We'll find him."

Fuente shook his head. "No, you won't. Not unless Andretti wants him found." He rose and walked away across the piazza.

Ruggero pulled out his mobile and called Beppe. They'd start looking. But Fuente was probably right. The odds of finding the boy were slim. Ruggero's stomach tightened, and he pushed the plate of food away. He'd gained the truth from Fuente without touching the man, but he was still failing his don, and he saw no way to win this round.

The only thing left to do was the newest part of his mission: protect Judge Loredana Montisi. At all costs.

——— ◆ ———

Ruggero had no trouble finding Loredana's apartment building. He had enough contacts to ensure that he could find just about anyone—at least anyone who played by the rules. And the judge certainly did. If Lorenzo was threatening her, that meant she couldn't be bribed, a rarity in these times. Most people found it far easier to take the Mafia's money, do what they asked, and look the other way.

Lighting up a cigarette, Ruggero took a post on a doorstep across the street from Loredana's building. He'd already rounded up several men to assist him in keeping watch over her. It was unlikely anything would happen today—the threat had just been made. Lorenzo would most likely wait for her response. She had two days before she'd make a ruling on the evidence; two days to sweat and shake over her decision. Lorenzo's was an ancient strategy, but it was effective.

Ruggero's main purpose tonight was to assess the situation—how many *carabinieri* she had with her, and how experienced they were. He worked his way through half a pack of cigarettes as he studied the comings and goings at her building. She had three guards with her now, on staggered shifts. Between what he'd observed and what the first man he'd posted had reported, he'd determined that every four hours, a new guard came and an old one left. It was a good plan; it kept them fresh and didn't let any one of them get bored.

He had noticed something disturbing, however; most of the guards were very young and certainly inexperienced. Did Lorenzo have a hold on the man in charge of assigning her guards? Or was the *carabinieri* just doing what was easiest— assigning young men without families and excuses for having to be home in the evening?

Around eight, as Ruggero was growing stiff from hours in the late February chill, a somewhat older man arrived. The one she'd called at the courthouse. Stefano.

There had been something about the way she'd talked to the guard, the way he'd looked at her, that spoke of a connection. Perhaps an intimate one. Ruggero studied the man. He hadn't really looked at him before, but he scrutinized him now as he strode up to the building. Tall, broad-shouldered, a little too sure of himself, but certainly what Ruggero assumed women considered good-looking. No scars on this one. Stefano tipped his cap at two women who were leaving the building, and they both rewarded him with wide smiles.

Ruggero's fingers tightened on the cigarette he was holding, nearly crushing it.

He didn't want Stefano around Loredana, didn't want him smiling at her or tipping his cap and looking at her. And he certainly didn't want him touching her.

He tossed the cigarette on the ground and stamped it out. Taking in a lungful of crisp air, he pulled out his mobile and called his replacement. He gave the man directions, then hung up. A light went on in Loredana's living room, allowing him to see her and Stefano by the window, talking. She reached up and smoothed her hair back, and something in Ruggero's stomach curdled. She wanted Stefano; he could see it. She wanted him in a way she'd never want a man like Ruggero. As far as Loredana Montisi was concerned, Ruggero was a worm to be scraped off her shoe.

When his replacement arrived, Ruggero almost cursed him out for being late, but he checked his watch first and stayed his tongue. The man was five minutes early.

Then why had the wait seemed an eternity?

Ruggero stalked off to his car. He pulled out his mobile again and placed a call to a number he knew well. There was only one cure for how he was feeling: he needed to get laid.

———— ◆ ————

Dario Andretti took another sip of Scotch and eased back into his leather desk chair. Delfina and Nick had just left the house, and it was quiet again. He hadn't realized, until Cris was killed, how much life his two children had brought to the house. Delfina with her constant industry, Cris with his laughter and high spirits.

Now Delfina was listless and weepy, and Nick a silent shadow never more than arm's length from her. And Ilaria—he took a deep breath—she still accused him with her eyes, even when they lay in bed together, even when he was inside her, even when they tried to make another child. They never would replace Cris; her eyes said it, and his heart knew it.

And yet what else could they do but try? Delfina and Nick had no interest in the *cosca*, so a new heir was necessary. Vital. If something should happen to Dario, the last thing he wanted was for Ilaria to be at another's mercy—not Lorenzo's, or any of Lorenzo's grandsons', and not any of Dario's underbosses'. The underbosses might treat her well as the widow, or they might discard her and take what she had. Certainly Lorenzo or any of his progeny would think nothing of putting her out of the house.

Delfina and Nick would take care of her, he had no doubt. But they would want her to go to London, a place where she knew no one. This was her home. The home she and Dario had shared for many years.

Their married life hadn't been all roses, especially while Dario's father Carlo had been alive, but they'd had many good years, and that brief time, between Carlo's death and Cris's, that had been wonderful. No more trying to avoid Carlo when he was on a tear, no more fighting, no more anger reverberating through the halls.

Now those halls lay silent, under a pall of darkness.

His throat tightened, and he took another pull on the Scotch, then pushed it away. He'd been drinking too much, but it was the only thing that dulled the pain, the only thing that allowed him to join Ilaria in their bed.

He blinked away the tears that had gathered in his eyes. He'd thought losing his sister Toni had been bad; losing his son was infinitely worse.

Cris had been part of him—the best part. They may have fought at times, but Dario had been proud of him. Cris had truly embodied the meaning of honor: he'd done well by those he loved, he'd worked hard to achieve peace.

That bastard Lorenzo had destroyed him. He'd snuffed out Cris's life as if he'd been nothing more than an insect. And why?

Because Cris had dared defy him.

Oh, Dario had been angry too at what Cris had done, but he'd seen the wisdom in it, the necessity of it in terms of forging a true alliance with Enrico Lucchesi.

Though now—now he'd love to have back his leverage over Lucchesi. He'd love to crush him. Lorenzo may have ordered Cris's death, but he'd used Enrico's good-for-nothing godson to do it, and that never would've been possible if Enrico hadn't broken 'Ndrangheta law, if he hadn't tried to salvage his family at the later expense of Dario's.

True, Lucchesi couldn't have known where his actions would lead, but even a fool could have predicted there'd be trouble. You couldn't execute a traitor and spare his sons, no matter how well you thought you'd covered up the truth. Sooner or later, the worms would surface. That was the nature of things. And 'Ndrangheta law was designed with the nature of men in mind.

Again and again, Lucchesi had bent their laws or broken them, and again and again, he'd managed to escape justice. After Cris's actions—turning over to Lucchesi the recordings that proved Enrico had suffered a traitor's sons to live— Dario had no way to prove Enrico's guilt. He knew, and Enrico knew, the truth, but Dario couldn't take that to La Provincia. Likewise, he could never prove Lorenzo's guilt in Cris's death.

If he wanted justice—a reckoning—he'd have to obtain it himself.

Dario scrubbed his hands over his face. It had been a little over seven weeks since Cris's funeral. Seven weeks of mourning, of inaction on his part. Seven weeks of allowing Lorenzo to proceed unimpeded.

But that ended today. If he hoped to destroy Lorenzo and Lucchesi both, he had to tamp down his grief and start putting his plans in motion. And step one in his plan was to divide and conquer. Lorenzo had given him Salvatore Ruscino as a second, now that Cris was gone, but Dario knew Sal remained Lorenzo's right hand. No doubt Sal would be ready to knife Dario in the back when it suited Lorenzo.

There was only one reason Dario wasn't already dead, and that must be because Lorenzo didn't yet feel entirely secure in his control of the 'Ndrangheta. Once he did, he'd be able to act with impunity.

Therefore Dario had to split Lorenzo from his major ally. If Lorenzo didn't have Sal, he'd be forced to be more cautious, and he'd be that much more vulnerable.

Still, killing Lorenzo would be difficult. Lorenzo's men feared him more than they feared death, and he kept himself well-guarded at all times. Moreover, the old man had a network of spies and informants to rival that of many governments.

The only thing Dario still had were the recordings from the bugs Toni had planted years ago around Lorenzo's home. Most of them had stopped transmitting, but a few still worked. They gave him snatches of Lorenzo's thinking now and then, but mostly there was nothing of value. Lorenzo wasn't in the habit of saying much, particularly about his plans. Apparently he clung as much as possible to the old habits of speaking outdoors and saying as little as possible on the phone. Dario would keep monitoring him, but it wasn't easy with Sal around. If Lorenzo ever knew about the bugs, he wouldn't hesitate to strike Dario dead.

So Dario would have to concentrate on Sal and hope he could turn him away from Lorenzo. Picking up the phone, he called Sal, told him they needed to talk. Sal promised to be there within minutes.

Dario could hardly wait. He paced around his office, ordered some espresso from the kitchen, and determined his opening move.

Sal was true to his word and arrived ten minutes later. He strode into Dario's office, his imposing bulk gracelessly filling one of the chairs in front of Dario's desk.

Sal was in his early fifties, and his years in prison had left their mark. His face and hands bore the evidence of countless battles, and the endless cigarettes he'd consoled himself with had etched deep lines around his mouth. Still, his eyes were hard flecks of slate, and his body thick with cords of muscle. The lump of a gun was clearly visible under his left armpit.

Despite his current rank, Sal had never forgotten his time as a bodyguard and hitman for Lorenzo. It was one of those many kills that had earned him a twenty-year stint in prison. To his credit, the man had never complained or turned on his *capo*. No doubt that was why Lorenzo had rewarded him now. And Sal had the added benefit of his sister having married Lorenzo's late son, Benedetto, and thus becoming part of the Andretti family. Just as Sal himself had done. Too bad his catch hadn't been as good as his sister Pia's.

Angelica Andretti was young, yes, and attractive. But she was a widow with an unexpected bit of baggage—a three-year-old son. A son that Sal was now forced to raise and embrace as his own.

Dario had known about the son before the wedding; he doubted, however, that Sal had. There was only one way to find out.

Dario pasted on a smile and chose his opening shot. "How's married life?" He added a wink and a slight leer to the smile, one Sal couldn't ignore.

Sal shifted in his seat, his eyes flicking away from Dario's. He shrugged. "As well as can be expected."

"Oh?" Dario raised a brow. "Is she having trouble adjusting to Italy?" Angelica had been raised in the United States.

Sal nodded. "A bit. Her Italian is rusty and my English isn't what it could be."

"And maybe the age difference isn't helping?" Angelica was less than half Sal's age.

Again Sal shrugged. "She says her boy doesn't like it here."

Her boy. Yes, that was definitely a sore spot. "It must be nice for you though.

You already know you have a boy to take over when you die."

Sal's fingers tightened on the armrests of his chair, but he said nothing.

Time to act concerned. "You *did* know about the boy beforehand?"

Sal's jaw worked. "The day of the ceremony, yes."

Dario made a *tsk*ing noise. "Well, I suppose Lorenzo didn't want to put you off a good match."

"I don't mind the boy. I do mind—" He slammed his mouth shut and said nothing more.

"You wish Lorenzo hadn't required you to make him your heir." Dario said the words softly, carefully.

Sal met his eyes. "You knew about the boy?"

Dario nodded. "Of course. He's my cousin. But I didn't know that Lorenzo would ask you to take him as your heir."

Sal shook his head. "You know that he's refused my sister's sons their proper places in the *cosca*?"

Dario suppressed a smile. "I think that's more a reflection on Benedetto's behavior than anything to do with Pia."

"Lorenzo took good care of Remo's boy though. And Remo clearly betrayed him. Whether Benedetto did is unclear—"

"Oh, it's clear to me," Dario said. "Benedetto nearly got Cris killed with that Russian coke deal he engineered behind my back."

"Well, then. Lorenzo shouldn't be grooming Marcello as his second in case something happens to me. If he thinks Remo and Benedetto betrayed him, he ought to treat their sons the same."

Dario affected a sigh. "Pietro and Severino may be your nephews, and I know you're trying to look out for them. But even you have to admit that they are..." He trailed off, trying to think of the perfect word. "A bit unpredictable." Which wasn't entirely true. The one thing you could count on with Pietro and Severino was that they'd stab you the minute your back was turned. In that way, they were perfectly predictable.

Sal's mouth tightened. "So they've had some problems. If Lorenzo took them in hand, they'd behave themselves."

"Maybe he has his hands full with Marcello."

"That's just it. Marcello is everything Remo was. Stubborn, willful, defiant."

Dario gave him a genuine smile this time. "I'm sure that's how Lorenzo describes me."

A grin tugged at the corner of Sal's mouth. "Well, those are the nicer things he's said about you."

Dario clasped his hands together and leaned forward. "I am well aware of how my grandfather views me. And I know why you're here."

"To support you."

"To keep me in line. And to keep an eye on me." Sal said nothing, just held Dario's gaze. "I don't have anything against you, Sal." *Except that you're an obstacle.* "In fact, I think we should be friends."

A sharp bark of laughter left Sal's lips. "You think I'm stupid."

"No. But Lorenzo does."

Sal thrust his chin forward. "I'm his second, and he made me a *mandamento* head. He has more regard for me than he does you. You could have been head of Lombardy. Instead he chose Lucchesi."

"You know why you're his second? Because you're loyal. You could've turned on him when you got nabbed for killing that *carabiniere*. But you didn't. He figures you won't turn on him. That doesn't mean he respects you."

"Of course he does."

"You're a peasant to Lorenzo. A strong back, a pair of fists. Muscle. Not brains. Not family. And certainly not Andretti royalty."

"I'm married to his granddaughter."

"Only because no one else would take her with a boy in tow. And no one else would agree to Lorenzo's terms. You want so badly to be part of the family, and he knows it."

"I'm already part of the family."

"An uncle to his most useless grandsons."

Sal reddened. "Just because you don't like me being here—"

"I'm saying this to open your eyes. Think about how he's treated you. How he let you rot in jail."

"He got me a good lawyer, got the sentence cut in half."

"He's *used* you. As my babysitter. As a convenient husband for Angelica. He's cutting *your* blood out of succession."

"My sons will have their place—"

"After *her* boy."

Sal straightened in his seat. "*Basta.* I've heard enough."

Dario shook his head. "What's your gut telling you? Did Lorenzo treat you with respect when it came to your marriage?"

"I know what you're trying to do."

Dario spread his hands. "I could be your friend, Sal. We could help each other. I'm just trying to get you to see the possibilities."

Sal started to rise. "If we're done—"

"All I'm saying is think about it. And no, we're not done. I'll be taking a more active hand in things from now on."

"And that means?"

"You can take a break, Sal. Be with your wife and her boy."

As Sal left the room, Dario relaxed back into his chair again. He took another sip of Scotch. The first seed had been planted. Now to see what sprouted in its place.

CHAPTER 6

Ruggero pulled up outside the familiar apartment building in downtown Como. No one would guess that a call girl lived there; the address was relatively exclusive. Few clients ever visited her at home, but Ruggero had been seeing her since his early twenties, so he was an exception. He paused, his hand on the car door's handle. Fifteen years. He'd been seeing Chiara for fifteen years. And yet she knew little about him, other than his first name. And how to get him off.

He knew her full name of course—her real one, not the one she gave to clients—and how much money she made and where it went. He'd had to make sure Chiara wasn't secretly working for law enforcement—or a rival family. And when she'd had a tangle with the *polizia* a number of years ago, he'd interceded on her behalf and made the problem go away with a well-placed bribe.

Fortunately, she'd had the good sense to understand his intercession for what it was—a gesture of goodwill, nothing more. *Una mano lava l'altra*. One hand washes the other. She'd expressed her gratitude with a lengthy blow job, and then it had gone back to business as usual between them—just how he liked it.

He pressed the button beside her last name and paused for the buzz that granted him entry. He didn't have to wait long.

Chiara greeted him at the door, from head to toe as coiffed and poised as the society matrons that lived around her. That was one of the things he liked best about her—she never looked cheap. Her golden-brown hair had been swept up on her head, her riotous curls tamed and sleek. In her black beaded dress, cut just below the knee, she could have been hosting a fundraiser or a black-tie dinner party, instead of playing private hostess to a hitman.

She motioned him inside and pressed kisses to his cheeks. Her light floral perfume teased his nose, and he inhaled deeply, hoping to drown out the memory of Loredana Montisi's luscious scent.

It didn't work. He'd liked Chiara's perfume before; now he wished she wasn't wearing any.

She led him into the living room and poured him his favorite drink—Galliano on the rocks—while he took a seat on the high-backed brown leather sofa, the soft buttery hide squeaking as he shifted. He'd been in her apartment many, many times, but he let his eyes roam the space anyway, taking in a change or two since his last visit, a month ago. Had it really been that long? He used to visit her at least two to three times a week.

She pressed the glass of Galliano into his hand, then sat beside him and clasped his knee. "I wasn't sure I'd see you again," she said. "It's been so long."

He shrugged. "Been busy."

A smile played along her lips. "I'd hate to think my talents have worn thin."

He took a sip of the Galliano, its vanilla top note reminding him again of Loredana's scent, and eyed Chiara over the rim. This was where he should have reassured her. But the words died in his throat. Instead he shook his head. She could take that however she wished.

Chiara reached up and ran a hand through his hair, her fingers gliding over his scalp. It was a gesture he usually found soothing. He closed his eyes and let himself relax for a moment. His time with her had always been something apart from his routine, his normal state of vigilance. With Chiara, he could just feel, just dissolve under her hands.

She moved closer, the leather protesting beneath her. Her other hand moved up his thigh, stroking the muscles, making them twitch, making his cock jump to attention. Yes, this was what he needed. This would get his mind off Loredana Montisi. It had been a month since the last time he'd seen Chiara. He was sexually frustrated, that was all.

Chiara's hand closed around him through the thin fabric of his suit trousers, her talented fingers promising him a world of pleasure he'd denied himself for too long. Setting down his drink, he pulled her atop him and slid her dress up to her waist, his hands cupping her ass. The G-string panties she wore were the only hint of what she truly was, underneath her mask of wealth and privilege.

She lowered her lips to his, but he twisted so that he kissed her neck instead. He mouthed the satiny skin and nipped at it. The gasp that slipped from her might have been genuine. It was hard to tell with Chiara. He reached down between her legs and caressed her *figa*. He fingered her lightly, teasing her, studying her face as she writhed against him.

It all seemed real, but was it? Did he truly excite her?

That had never mattered to him before; he'd never given her desires a second's thought. He'd always accepted that he was a job to her. That sex was something to be purchased and enjoyed. An exchange of money for pleasure, nothing more.

"You like that?" he asked. She said nothing, just pressed his fingers harder against herself. He slid two fingers inside her, pumping them in and out. She was slick, her internal muscles clamping around him, and he yearned to feel their grip on his cock. But he had to know first. Did she actually want this?

"You want me inside you?" he asked. She moaned in answer. He repeated the question. He wanted a yes, wanted to see desire in her eyes. When she didn't answer, he took her chin in his hand and tilted her face so she had to look at him. "Do you?"

Her brown eyes met his, a slight crease between her graceful brows. "Of course."

"*Davvero?*"

The crease deepened. "Are you all right?" she asked, growing still.

He said nothing, just stared at her, his chest rising and falling, his heart beating, his *cazzo* crying for release.

This was what he thought he'd wanted. This neat, easy exchange. This tidy, no-fuss, no-muss fuck. A simple answer to a simple need.

But what he needed now, what he wanted most, was anything but simple.

She cupped his face, her fingers tracing his scar before they rasped against his heavy stubble. "Everything okay?"

Something tightened in his throat. He pulled her hand from his face and shoved it against his crotch, his fingers urging her to touch him there, to take him out of his head, to making him stop thinking.

Stop feeling.

She stroked him firmly, then started unzipping his trousers, her fingers finally reaching his bare flesh. He closed his eyes, tried to let go. Tried to just be.

"I know what you need," she whispered, then glided down his body until she was kneeling between his legs. She pulled his *cazzo* out, her warm breath washing over the tip, and a vision of Loredana Montisi between his legs, kneeling at his feet, flashed into his head.

Porca vacca. He roughly tucked himself back into his trousers, and Chiara sat back on her heels. "What's wrong?"

He pulled out his wallet and peeled off a thick stack of euros, double the usual amount. He set them on the table and rose.

She snagged his sleeve. "Just tell me what you want, and I'll do it."

He shook his head. "What I want, you can't give me. Unfortunately."

A few curls had come loose from her sleek updo, and she smoothed them back as she rose, her dress sliding back down over her hips. "You've met someone." She gave him a smile he could only interpret as sad.

"It's not like that."

"That's how it looks." She crossed her arms, but it wasn't an angry gesture.

"She's never going to see me as anything other than what I am."

"Which is?"

"A thug."

Chiara shook her head. "And when you look at me, do you see a whore?"

That tightness in his throat came back, and he shook his head, not trusting himself to speak, but she must have seen something on his face. She moved close, barring his path to the door, and took hold of his lapels. "You know what I see when I look at you?"

He didn't dare say a word, and for once he could hardly meet her eyes.

"I see a man who's forced to be hard. A man who's ready to crack. Who's afraid to be more than he is."

He stiffened at her words, wanting to be angry, wanting to deny them. His right hand flexed into a fist, his default response to any threat. He forced the fingers to straighten. He'd never hit a woman in his life, and he wasn't going to start now.

He stepped past her and reached the door before she spoke again. "Wait." He paused, then turned to look at her. She smiled, her eyes glittering. "The first time I saw you, you scared me half to death. And for a long time, I didn't know what to make of you. But I finally learned something."

"What?" His voice creaked like an unoiled hinge.

"There's a person in there. A good one."

He snorted. "I didn't think you were a romantic."

"I'm not." She paused. "If she's worth it, she'll see it too."

He opened the door and left, his feet pounding against the stairs until he hit the street. He started the Maserati and swung out onto the road with a brutal twist, barely glancing for traffic first. Blood thundered in his ears and his hands gripped the wheel so tightly they ached.

Chiara was wrong. Loredana Montisi would never see him as anything other than what he was.

A savage.

———◆———

When Ruggero Vela walked into her courtroom on Friday, Loredana breathed in deep against the fluttering in her belly. Vela took a seat behind his charge, Enrico Lucchesi, then looked up, his wolf's eyes finding hers. Those eyes were back to flat and stony today, and that flutter of unease rippled through her again. She should have him frisked, but that would only let him know how much he'd rattled her.

And with what? A cheap bit of theatrics, designed to make her think Lucchesi was innocent, the victim of some conspiracy. Well, it wasn't working. Not entirely. Though she was very interested to hear from Sottotenente Silvio Fuente, the prosecution's first witness, regarding the gun.

The man himself was sworn in a short while later. In his early forties, his second lieutenant's dress uniform perfectly pressed, his black mustache neatly trimmed, Silvio Fuente presented the puffed-up façade of a striver, a man so concerned with climbing the ladder that it didn't matter if he had to lop it in half to do so.

She'd examined Fuente's *carabinieri* record carefully, noting how he'd risen from nothing and received a mysterious promotion that had catapulted him well beyond the level a man of his background could normally expect. Even more interestingly, Fuente had been the lead investigator in a number of questionable events involving the defendant. Events from which Lucchesi and his associates had walked away uncharged.

Corvi was taking Fuente through the history of how he'd discovered Sergio Grantini's missing gun. "So, Sottotenente, you found the gun on 6 February 2011. Is that correct?"

Fuente nodded, holding his black officer's cap in his lap. He tapped it against his knees, and she frowned. Was he just nervous about testifying in court? Or was he preparing to tell a lie?

"Please make sure your responses are verbal in nature," Loredana said.

"*Sì*. My apologies," Fuente said.

"This gun had been missing since 3 March 2008," Corvi said. "How did you come to find it?"

Fuente hesitated, then smiled. "It was quite simple, really. Once I put my mind to the problem."

"How so?"

"I knew the gun had to be somewhere in the evidence vault. It had been logged; it had been present at the initial hearing. And then it had been logged back in."

"But it was not with the other evidence in the Dinelli case."

"No. First I searched the files surrounding that one in the vault, in case someone had just made a simple filing error. But it was not in any of those." Fuente paused and stroked his mustache, his dark eyes gleaming. Everyone was riveted to his testimony, and he knew it.

"How then did you determine where it was?" Corvi asked.

"I took another direction. All evidence is logged according to the case, and a name, such as 'Dinelli,' is associated with the case. However, each item is also tagged with various information. It occurred to me that perhaps someone had filed the gun away based on one of those tags, instead of the case name and number. You know how it is—everything gets taken at the evidence desk, and then some poor clerk—usually a trainee—has to put it back."

"I can picture what you're saying, Sottotenente," Corvi said.

"So you see how a mistake could be made."

Loredana suppressed the urge to roll her eyes. "You've explained that quite well, Sottotenente."

He shrugged and smiled. "I only wanted to be thorough."

"How then had the gun been misfiled?" Corvi asked.

"Objection." Adimari rose. "The evidence was missing, not misfiled. We don't know that it was even in the evidence vault."

Loredana peered over her glasses at Adimari. "So noted. Pubblico Ministero Corvi, please choose your words more carefully."

Corvi reddened, but he pressed on. "Sottotenente, where did you find the gun?"

"It was in a file for a case involving a man named Grantini. Not the case involving the disappearance of Sergio Grantini, the man who pulled the trigger in the Dinelli case, but another Grantini altogether. 'Grantini' was one of the tags on the gun. I merely searched all the files with that name attached."

"And it was that simple?"

Fuente nodded, then remembered himself and spoke into the microphone. "Personally, I'm shocked no one thought of it earlier."

"So it was a simple clerical error."

"Yes. A mistake, nothing more."

Corvi turned to Loredana. "We have no more questions for this witness."

She signaled Adimari to speak. He stood, his bulk not at all disguised by his voluminous black robe. "This Grantini file you've mentioned, Sottotenente. Was it among the active files?"

Fuente fiddled with the hat. "No. It was in the inactive section."

"So the gun—the *lone* gun recovered with prints—in the murder of an anti-Mafia judge just accidentally got filed away among the inactive cases?"

"I can only speculate." Fuente raised his hands out to the sides to express his uncertainty.

Adimari addressed Loredana. "Giudice Montisi, the witness has just admitted that much of his testimony is mere supposition and speculation. I ask that his testimony be stricken from the record."

"That is over-reaching, Avvocato Adimari."

"Sottotenente Fuente has given us no reason to believe his speculation has any merit to it."

Corvi broke in. "It's no coincidence that the same name popped up twice: Grantini."

"Granted. Motion denied," Loredana said. "Have you additional questions for this witness, Avvocato Adimari?"

"Yes, one." He addressed Fuente. "The timing of your finding this evidence is quite curious. Signor Lucchesi has a blameless record, and yet the minute an issue is raised about the Banca di Falcone, you suddenly find evidence in the defunct Dinelli case. That seems... strange, does it not?"

Fuente frowned and smoothed his mustache. "Seeing his name in the paper renewed my determination to find that gun."

"So it's mere coincidence? Just as the gun's disappearance was a mere clerical error?"

"Yes."

"I believe little in coincidences."

As do I. Loredana addressed Adimari. "Have you any further questions for this witness?"

"No."

"Next witness," Loredana said. Cesare Casseri, the head of the evidence vault, strode into the courtroom. Like Fuente, he too wore a nicely pressed dress uniform, but he was far more nervous than the second lieutenant. Was he trying to hide something?

Casseri walked them through how evidence was tagged, bagged, and filed, including how many times it was scanned in and when. He painted a picture of an office that did its best, but sometimes faced staff shortages.

Adimari's turn came again to address Casseri. "Can you prove that item number 14B, a Beretta 92S allegedly used in the murder of Giudice Federico Dinelli, never left that evidence vault during the almost three years that it was unaccounted for?"

Casseri swallowed visibly. "I cannot."

"Moreover, can you assure the court that your staff has been immune to bribery?"

"My staff?"

"They are the only ones allowed in the evidence vault, are they not?"

"Well, no. Sometimes officers need evidence quickly, and we don't have the staff to retrieve the file at the moment."

"So in all truth, any officer could have been in the vault, unsupervised, for any length of time?"

"Yes."

"And is it not also the case that you have, from time to time, employed civilian contractors and trainees in the evidence vault?"

"Well, yes..."

"Is every millimeter of the vault under video surveillance?"

"Yes." Casseri seemed relieved.

"And can you produce the video that shows item number 14B, the Beretta in question, being placed in the wrong file?"

"No."

"And why not?"

"The recordings go back only one month."

"A month? Does that seem like adequate backup to you?"

"We're talking about terabytes of data. We simply haven't the funds…" Casseri trailed off, looking miserable.

"So, it is entirely possible that the Beretta could have been removed from the vault and tampered with at any time?"

"It is not likely, no."

"That was not the question. I asked whether such a thing was possible."

"That's like asking if it could snow in July. Anything is possible."

Adimari looked at Loredana. "The *carabinieri* cannot provide any proof of an unbroken chain of custody, and their security measures are a farce. Moreover, the timing and nature of the 'rediscovery' of this evidence is highly suspect. Giudice Montisi, I humbly submit that this evidence is inadmissible."

Here it was: the moment of truth. If she threw out the gun, would the threat against her materialize? Or was it merely a bit of theater, as she believed? She took a deep breath to calm her roiling stomach.

Either way, could she live with herself if she allowed such shoddy police work to pass muster? She still had plenty to hold Lucchesi on. Corvi needed to work harder, that was all. And she needed to call the bluff of whoever had threatened her. "I agree, Avvocato Adimari. Item number 14B, the Beretta 92S, is inadmissible."

A whoop of joy went up from the family members and associates behind Lucchesi's table. "However," Loredana continued, "the case shall proceed. The suspicious activity at the Banca di Falcone could be linked to the original tax-evasion case being tried by Giudice Dinelli, and thus could provide the motive for his murder."

Trapani rose. "Giudice Montisi, the only piece of evidence that in any way— however tenuous—linked our client to the unfortunate death of Giudice Dinelli has been ruled inadmissible. Therefore, we respectfully request that our client be released from custody."

"Denied."

Trapani was undeterred. "Surely you cannot object then to house arrest? Our client's wife was admitted to the hospital eight days ago. She needs her husband at home to reduce her stress level and ensure a healthy baby."

Again Loredana felt that sympathetic twinge, but what if Signora Lucchesi had exaggerated her symptoms? House arrest was too risky for a man of Lucchesi's means. "Denied. The defendant shall remain in the custody of the state."

Signora Lucchesi leaned over the railing and grabbed onto her husband, her shoulders shaking.

Loredana's chest tightened. And what if it *hadn't* been playacting?

Her eyes came to rest on Ruggero Vela. He was still staring at her, his arms crossed. Was that disappointment on his face?

Too bad. Your plan didn't work on me. She held his gaze until he turned away.

Rising to leave the courtroom, she couldn't help scanning it one last time, looking for the young Calabrian in the tracksuit. Signor Vela's accomplice. Finally she saw him. He too was watching her, his face grim. He nodded when their eyes met, and a shudder rippled down her back.

Had she just signed her own death warrant?

CHAPTER 7

Enrico had been in jail for just shy of two weeks. Although having a cell to himself was a luxury most prisoners would kill for, he was beginning to hate the isolation, the lack of contact with other people. The brief times he was in court were his only chance to speak to Kate in person; visits from his family were not permitted.

At least Abramo had proved himself, delivering everything Enrico asked for, including several items that could only have come from Kate, such as the biography of Caesar.

Enrico read the books Kate had sent, wrote her letters every day he couldn't call, and engaged in what exercise he could, but he itched for more. He could barely restrain himself from babbling at Abramo, the *agente* in Trapani's pocket. Even though the man had taken money from Trapani, it wasn't wise to say too much to him. Who knew where his loyalties truly lay?

Between the isolation and the constant need for vigilance and discretion, Enrico looked forward to his daily shower more than a little. Those few minutes of bliss, of forgetfulness, were everything—just the sensation of hot water on his skin, the scent of the soap Kate had sent reminding him of home enough that if he just kept his eyes closed, he could imagine himself there. Instead of where he was—in the bowels of San Vittore prison.

A daily shower—alone—was another luxury most prisoners didn't get either. Enrico had to count his blessings, though they seemed damn few, especially on a Saturday like today, when two long days of solitary confinement loomed, with little to break the monotony.

He checked the simple digital alarm clock in his cell. Five minutes after nine. Abramo was late. Enrico checked over the bundle he'd prepared—towel, washcloth, soap, shampoo—again, just to have something to do. Finally he heard footsteps.

But it wasn't Abramo who greeted him. It was another *agente*, one he didn't know. "Where's Abramo?" he asked.

"Sick." When Enrico made no move to turn his back and present his hands for cuffing, the guard sighed. "You want a shower or not?"

Enrico studied the *agente*. The man looked bored, and his sleepy eyes and sudden yawn decided the matter. Even so, Enrico patted his right pocket before turning around—one last confirmation that his sharpened toothbrush was with him. Though it was very little, it was better than nothing.

The guard silently escorted Enrico through the corridors to the tile-lined communal shower. As usual, it was empty—this was the time when the prisoners in solitary were brought in, one by one. They each had ten minutes to undress, shower, and get dressed again. Like the improvised toothbrush weapon, the scant time wasn't much, but it was something, and it helped break up the day. Counting the walk, it used up an entire fifteen minutes.

Sleepy Eyes motioned Enrico to turn around, then uncuffed him. Enrico stripped down quickly, taking care to leave the pocket with the toothbrush easily accessible. One never knew what could happen. He'd just stepped under the spray when another prisoner was brought in.

Enrico froze and looked at Sleepy Eyes, who didn't react. Was that good or bad? Then Enrico studied the other *agente* and the prisoner.

The prisoner was in his mid-thirties, tall and athletic, lean as a swimmer, a dirty blond with blue eyes like chips of ice. The high, well-defined cheekbones and pale skin further marked him as a foreigner. And as the man stripped down, revealing the distinctive tattoos of the *vory v zakone*—the eight-pointed stars on his shoulders and knees, the elaborate crucifix on his chest—Enrico's heart started hammering. This man, whoever he was, was part of the Bratva, the Russian *Mafiya*.

The man eyed Enrico and gestured to his own naked crotch. "Like what you see?" he asked in English, his accent confirming his Russian descent. The smirk he gave Enrico insinuated many things, none of them favorable.

Enrico held the man's eyes and started lathering up, as if he weren't in the least bothered. "Just admiring your artwork."

The man flexed his pecs and biceps, then stepped under the spray at the shower head beside Enrico's. "You know what they mean?" the man asked.

Enrico didn't dare take his eyes off the Russian. "I do."

The Russian bent over his things as if to get his supplies, and Enrico's heart leapt into his throat. He tossed the bar of soap and lunged for the toothbrush in his pants pocket just as the Russian came at him with a sharp piece of metal.

The guards stepped back to the entrance to the showers and crossed their arms. No help there—they'd both been paid to arrange this. Would they jump in to finish things if the Russian failed? He'd have to worry about that later.

As the Russian slashed at him, Enrico danced back, sliding in the water, doing his best to avoid tripping over the lip of the shower area. Enrico's feet hit damp concrete, a far less slippery surface, and he waited for the Russian to close in. When the man came at him again, aiming for Enrico's throat, he countered the attack with his forearm, receiving a deep slice from his wrist halfway to his elbow, but the pain didn't even register. The need to stay alive was his sole focus.

The toothbrush was a miserable weapon—useful only on the vulnerable areas around the head and the neck, and the soft belly. And it wouldn't slice a man the way that sharpened piece of metal would. All he could do was stab.

Enrico saw an opening and attacked, jabbing the toothbrush into the base of the man's throat. His hand, slick with soap suds, slid down the handle of the toothbrush, and he dealt the Russian only a skin prick. The cost was a slash to the other arm and a glancing cut along the ribs.

Madonna. He needed to get the soap off his hands. And that meant risking going under the water again.

The Russian laughed and pushed Enrico back. Then his face turned cold. "This is for my cousins and my uncle Ilya." He brought the shiv up in a quick punching stab, aiming for Enrico's right side and the vulnerable liver and spleen.

Enrico blocked again, managing to grab the Russian's forearm. He pivoted, dragging the Russian around. Enrico stepped under the Russian's showerhead, and tried to rinse his right hand while the man struggled in his grasp, slippery now as a fish, both of them grunting from their efforts. Enrico's left foot went out from under him, and he was down, the Russian on top.

He had to flip the man; he needed the upper hand, or he was dead. The sinewy Russian cursed and laughed, his grim smile as he drove his weapon toward Enrico's throat all Enrico could see. Grabbing the man's face, Enrico jabbed his fingers into the Russian's eyes until the man pulled back to save them, and with his opponent off-balance, Enrico rolled him onto his back and slammed the man into the tiles, his head hitting with a hard crack, blood-tinged water splashing as they grappled for purchase.

Fighting to hold the Russian's improvised knife out of the way, Enrico pressed the sharpened point of the toothbrush to the side of the Russian's neck, where the carotid artery pulsed. If only he could get a little more punch behind his thrust, he'd have him. The Russian was putting up a hell of a struggle though. He tangled his legs in Enrico's and fought to flip them over. That couldn't happen.

Gulping in a lungful of air, Enrico roared as he bore down, yelling in the Russian's face to startle the man, who flinched and gave the barest millimeter, but that was all he needed.

The sharpened point of the toothbrush sank home, and blood gushed over Enrico's hand in a dark crimson gout. The Russian's eyes widened and for a few seconds more, the man fought with everything he had left, but it wasn't enough. His jagged blade nicked Enrico's left ear, but inflicted no further damage.

The man shuddered hard, then lay still. Enrico wheeled on the guards still standing at the doorway, but they made no move against him. "I want the warden here, right now," Enrico said.

Sleepy Eyes nodded and smirked. "Don't trust us?"

"You're either very brave or very stupid. And if you don't get me the warden right now, you'll prove how stupid you are. I hope you got the money upfront."

Sleepy Eyes conferred with the other guard, who left to get the warden. Enrico staggered up and over to the shower head he'd been using. He kept his eyes on the guard as he rinsed himself under the spray, his heart still thrashing in his chest. Blood ran down both his arms, thick and warm, and he fought a wave of dizziness. He took one breath, then another, the water making his cuts burn.

The Vilanoviches were back. And that meant no one in his family was safe. He had to alert Trapani. And then all he could do was pray.

———— ♦ ————

Ruggero paced back and forth across the street from Loredana's apartment. An hour ago, he'd gotten a call from Trapani about an attack on Enrico, so Ruggero had immediately driven to Milan to watch over the judge personally. He'd just joined the man on duty and sent him around the block to watch the apartment from the other side. There wasn't a back entrance to the building, but walls could be scaled, and now wasn't the time to take chances.

He lit up another cigarette, then realized his pack was nearly empty—he'd been smoking too much, too quickly, as if this were his last chance to ever do so.

He forced himself to stand still, to take a long drag and then let it out slowly, to feel the wave of calm flow over him. There was something almost magical about the process, though it was nothing more than a stew of brain chemicals called forth by the nicotine.

He ought to quit smoking, to put this dependency, this weakness, behind him. Then again, why? It wasn't like he had a family and a long life to look forward to.

With a shake of his head, he pushed those thoughts aside. He needed to focus. His mission right now was to keep Loredana Montisi safe. Trapani was requesting an emergency hearing to ask that Enrico's custody be changed to house arrest. If anything happened to Loredana, that request would take longer to fulfill. And the entire trial would be put in jeopardy; in fact, the ruling she'd made regarding the gun could possibly be vacated and the whole ordeal could start over again.

And that couldn't happen. Every day Enrico spent in jail was an opportunity for Lorenzo Andretti to try to kill him. And this time Lorenzo had sent a Russian, which meant the Vilanoviches were involved, and they certainly had their own agenda and their own reasons for wanting to destroy the Lucchesi *cosca* and everyone associated with it.

Lorenzo would go after Enrico again, as soon as possible; Ruggero was certain of it. Right now, Enrico was holed up in the warden's office with two guards from another prison to watch over him, but that was obviously only a temporary measure until the hearing. Should Judge Montisi rule against house arrest, Enrico would be dead within hours or days of being remanded to the system, even if a transfer were arranged. Lorenzo's reach stretched far and wide, and there was nowhere in the prison system where Enrico wouldn't be in danger.

They had to get him home. And they had to keep Loredana safe. Ruggero could do nothing about the former, but he'd be damned if he'd fail in the latter.

He had to talk to her again. He'd already gotten her number the same way he'd obtained her address—through his contact at the phone company. Thumbing through the address book of his burner phone, he selected the entry he'd programmed. It was best not to leave an obvious tie between them, in case anyone ever dug into her records.

The phone rang four times. Was there a tap on her line? Possibly. He had to be very careful what he said.

Finally she answered. When he heard her voice and the caution that underlay its velvety richness, he smiled. *Good girl.* She was wary.

He didn't bother to give his name. "Are you aware that Enrico Lucchesi has been attacked?"

"Who is this?" she asked.

"We've spoken before."

He heard her intake of breath. "I remember."

"*Bene.* I'd hate to be unmemorable."

"It's not every day I get a threat in person."

"I wasn't the one delivering it."

"I'd be a fool to believe he wasn't working for you."

"He has nothing to do with me. And you know it."

"No, I don't. And I should hang up right now."

That was the last thing he wanted. "*Per favore,* do not."

A lilt came into her voice. "So now I get a 'please'?"

"You must be very careful."

"Just stop there. I see through your act—"

"It's no act. It's the fucking truth." The words hung between them, his profanity making him wince. He shouldn't be swearing in front of her. But who was he kidding? She already thought he was scum. He could hardly lower her opinion of him.

"I can't trust a man like you."

"You think I'm a thug."

The silence drew out, and he was shocked by the sudden drumming of his pulse. He actually cared what she thought of him.

Finally her reply came. "Can you swear to me that you are anything but?"

The question, so soft, so devastating, stung more than he'd ever admit. "You know I'm not behind the attack on Lucchesi. So ask yourself—who is? And who else have they threatened?"

"I'm hanging up now."

"Just promise me you'll carry your own gun."

"I don't own a gun, and I don't know how to use one."

"You'd better get one, and you'd better learn."

"That sounds like another threat. Or is that another 'warning'?"

Oh this woman! He could strangle her. Or at least put her over his knee. He reined in his frustration. "Stay alert. Trust no one."

"I've been threatened hundreds of times. My men will protect me."

"Not when they're working for someone else." He stared up at her living room window, saw her pacing in front of it. He walked out from his hiding place into the full daylight and waved until she stopped and looked down at him, her mouth open. She needed to understand just how much danger she was in. If he had to scare her to make that clear, so be it.

———————◆———————

A man—*that* man, Ruggero Vela—stepped out of the shadows of the doorway across the street from Loredana's apartment. He waved at her, once, twice, three times, until she stopped pacing and looked down, their eyes locking despite the distance.

He was watching her. He knew where she lived.

He was *stalking* her.

"I can see you," she said, fighting to keep her voice from quavering. She didn't quite succeed.

"I know." He took a drag on a cigarette and blew smoke in her direction, a challenge and an insult all at once. "I'm keeping an eye on you."

"So you know when to pull the trigger?" Her heart pounded madly, so out of control she pressed a hand to her chest.

He chuckled. "I told you before. That is not my intent. Nor is it my job."

Stefano came into the room. He'd been in the kitchen, getting a fresh cup of espresso. "What's going on?" he asked.

She didn't bother to cover the receiver. "There's a man outside. And he's watching me."

With a curse, Stefano plunked his cup down, splashing dark liquid on the walnut end table by her mother's favorite chair. He was out the door and gone before she could say anything more.

Loredana looked back out to the street, searching for Vela, but the man had disappeared, and the phone started to beep in her ear.

A moment later, Stefano rushed out into the street, gun drawn, his head whipping back and forth as he scanned the road up and down. He turned and gave her a questioning look, as if hoping she could tell him which way Vela had gone. She shrugged, and he headed off to the right. A couple minutes later, he jogged back in the opposite direction, then stopped in front of her apartment and shook his head.

She motioned for him to come back up, her mind racing. If Vela was telling the truth, and Enrico Lucchesi had been attacked, she could be next. The threat she'd disregarded could be all too real.

With trembling fingers, she called San Vittore prison and identified herself, then asked for the warden. When the man came on the line, she blurted out her question: Had Enrico Lucchesi been attacked? He confirmed the attempt on Lucchesi's life, and her stomach flipped. He then assured her that Lucchesi was alive and had just been patched up by the prison doctor.

She thanked him and hung up, her hand shaking as she placed the receiver back in the cradle.

If Vela had told the truth about that, had he been telling the truth about the threat against her?

Stefano was hovering behind her. "Are you all right?" he asked.

"I'm fine."

Her mother came into the room. "Phones ringing, doors slamming, people running around—what the hell is happening?"

"It's not safe for you here," Stefano said. "Either of you."

"I'm not letting them drive me into witness protection," Loredana said, but she was speaking to her mother more than to Stefano.

Nora came forward and put an arm around her. "Come, let's talk." She steered Loredana into the kitchen and shooed Stefano away. "You're not helping," she said lightly.

"*Signora*, it's not safe, and—"

"Go." Nora pointed to the doorway, and she directed Loredana to one of the chairs at the tiny table in the corner. The family had always taken their meals in the dining room, but this cozy little table had provided a place for the girls to do their homework while Nora had cooked, or to joke with their father after they'd washed the dishes.

Loredana's eyes welled unexpectedly. So much they'd lost, all of them. And now Allegra and Gisella had moved on, started new lives, while she and Mamma had stayed behind, surrounded by ghosts.

"Tell me what's going on," Nora demanded, pressing a hot cup of espresso into Loredana's hand before taking a seat across from her.

Loredana quickly recapped her conversations with Vela and the warden. "If someone has attacked Lucchesi, the threat against me could be real."

Her mother held her eyes. "I think you have to assume it is."

"So if it's not Lucchesi who threatened me, who is it?"

"Maybe it's as this man said. An enemy of Lucchesi's is at work."

"But if that's true, if it's someone who can orchestrate all this, then it's someone very powerful."

"Or someone with powerful friends."

She studied her mother. "What are you saying, Mamma?"

"The person who attacked Lucchesi wanted to make sure he'd stay in jail. He wanted a judge who wouldn't give Lucchesi house arrest. He wanted a judge who couldn't be bought by Lucchesi."

"You're saying this case wasn't assigned to me at random."

"I doubt it, *dolcezza*."

"But who could pull those kinds of strings?"

"Someone I think you do not want to tangle with."

"So you're saying I should just do what they want? Keep Lucchesi in jail until they slaughter him?"

"If he's in the Mafia, what does it matter?"

"Mamma!"

Nora shrugged. "You were convinced before that he was a Mafioso. What's changed?"

All Loredana's misgivings about this case—the shoddy police work, the "coincidence" of the FIU investigation occurring at the same time the gun in the Dinelli case surfaced, the threat warning her to convict Lucchesi or else, and now the attack on him—could it be that Enrico Lucchesi was being framed?

And could she be the blunt instrument someone was using to engineer Lucchesi's demise?

"Even if he is a Mafioso, this isn't how I operate. I can't convict a man for something he hasn't done."

"If he hasn't done this, he's done something else."

"I need more than suppositions. I need proof."

Her mother took her hand. "Life isn't always that clear-cut. What's your intuition telling you?"

"So far, there's no evidence Lucchesi has done anything wrong. And someone obviously wants him dead."

"Then why not just shoot him in the street?"

"Because—" Because Lucchesi had cold-eyed men like Vela around him. But it wasn't a crime to have private security. And a wealthy banker would certainly be a target for all sorts of unsavory characters.

Enrico Lucchesi could be exactly what he claimed to be: a businessman, nothing more.

Except—except that Vela spoke fluent Calabrian. That right there, that fact alone, was more damning than anything the prosecution had presented to her.

But she'd never have known that if Vela hadn't tried to protect her.

"*Cara*, you know why they've had to go to such lengths to make Lucchesi vulnerable."

She met her mother's gaze. "Mamma, I know nothing. Not a damn thing. But I can find out one thing—*if* I put Lucchesi on house arrest. I've already tossed out the gun, and nothing happened to me. But if I take Lucchesi out of jail, and someone comes after me, I'll know the conspiracy against him is real."

"You're willing to take that gamble?"

"I have to know what I'm dealing with. And if there is a conspiracy, I'm not going to be someone's puppet."

Her mother's lower lip trembled. "I can't lose you too."

Loredana put a hand over her mother's. "You won't. I have the guards. And I'm going to get a gun."

CHAPTER 8

If Loredana hadn't already been half-convinced there was a conspiracy against Enrico Lucchesi, she would be now. The biggest headline of the day on the front page of the *Corriere della Sera* was "Shady Dealings at the Banca di Falcone: FIU Insider Breaks Silence." The article, which she'd read in the back of a car while Stefano and another *carabinieri* officer drove her to the courthouse, detailed the FIU's concerns regarding a "cover-up" at the bank and possible Mafia ties.

Conspiracy or no, there was something about Lucchesi that made her wonder. The man had been surrounded by violence again and again. He was slick and urbane, well-educated, not in any way the rough sort of man who typically appeared before her. Lucchesi was something new; a new breed of Mafioso, perhaps? Born and raised for the twenty-first century, a man who stole with his mind, not his fists. Corvi had said it; if it smelled like the Mafia…

And yet, she had nothing concrete to go on. Nothing solid, no tangible proof that Lucchesi was anything more than he claimed to be.

That lack spoke volumes. So far, the prosecution's case seemed built on supposition, on smoke and mirrors.

She looked over the courtroom and waited for the crush of reporters to find their seats and settle down, her stomach churning. Was she doing the right thing, taking this gamble? Should she really risk her own life over technicalities?

Except they weren't technicalities. They were principles, the principles that had guided her entire life. "Justice" wasn't some remote, abstract concept—it was a real thing that she could grant, in a system that sometimes seemed bent on anything but.

Like now.

As her mother had said, Lucchesi could very well be guilty of something. But unless she had proof, not mere suspicion, to guide her, she'd be no better than the rabble of reporters crowding the courtroom and packing the hall outside, clamoring for blood.

How far she'd come from the woman who'd been intent on convicting Lucchesi just twelve days ago.

She signaled the clerk to call for order, and everyone quieted. Taking a deep breath, she surveyed the teeming courtroom, the expectant faces, the pens poised above notebooks. What she was about to do wasn't going to be popular. She'd be pilloried by the press. But someone had to do it.

"Avvocato Trapani, I believe you have a motion for the court?"

Trapani stood. "Yes, Giudice. Yesterday morning, my client was viciously attacked by a fellow prisoner and nearly lost his life. My client is not safe in San Vittore prison. We petition the court for house arrest."

Corvi popped up from his chair. "Giudice Montisi, the defendant should be moved to another facility instead."

"We doubt he will be safe anywhere within the prison system," Trapani said.

Running a hand over his thinning hair, Corvi smiled. "Given the headlines this morning, I think we all know why."

"Objection," Trapani thundered. "Baseless slander and innuendoes are not proof of anything. Anyone can say what they like to the press."

Loredana had to agree. "Accusations from an unnamed 'source' do not belong in a court of law, and you do your office no credit by alluding to such, Pubblico Ministero Corvi."

Corvi scowled at her. "There is a preponderance of evidence showing that the defendant has questionable ties. Too many people have died around him."

The prosecutor was right, but given the stakes, could she continue to risk Lucchesi's life on what they had to date? "Avvocato Trapani, is there any reason that a transfer to another prison would not solve the problem?"

"Two guards were present during the attack on my client. They did not intervene, because they'd been paid not to. No prison will be safe for my client."

"They'd been paid?" Loredana asked. "By whom?"

"They knew nothing about the man who'd paid them, not even a name. The *carabinieri* so far have been unable to turn up any leads. However, we believe this person is a business rival of my client."

Corvi jumped in. "And the attacker—what happened to him?" Triumph showed in his eyes.

"He died from his injuries."

"So your client murdered him."

"It was self-defense, not murder. The guards who were present gave statements to that effect."

"Still, this means your client is capable of killing a man with his bare hands."

Trapani pressed a hand to his heart. "Pubblico Ministero Corvi, I do believe we are all, each one of us, capable of such an act when we have no other choice."

Corvi turned to Loredana. "Giudice, what he is not telling you is that Dmitri Vilanovich died from a stab wound to the neck. Lucchesi had a weapon on him, a weapon he'd painstakingly created himself from a sharpened toothbrush. That shows intent and cunning."

Trapani shook his head. "It shows nothing more than our client feared for his life. And with good reason, as it turns out."

Loredana noted the bandage on Lucchesi's left ear, another on his right hand, a bruise on his cheek. And that was just what she could see; the report detailing his injuries made clear the conflict had been brutal. Lucchesi had fought hard. Much harder than she'd have expected from a mere businessman. And he'd made a weapon for himself.

But the fight he'd been in had nearly been fatal; one of his arms had been sliced to the bone, and he'd lost a great deal of blood. This was no carefully engineered scene of playacting.

Still, she studied Lucchesi, looking for signs of coldness, a lack of remorse. The defendant seemed steady, though exhausted, and when he met her eyes, she didn't see anything other than a man who'd barely kept himself alive.

And killing in self-defense wasn't against the law.

Loredana raised a hand. "I am ready to make my ruling," she said, and both men took their seats. She allowed herself another look at the defendant, and then risked meeting eyes with Ruggero Vela, who held hers unflinchingly, his own steady and intense. "Considering the disturbing behavior of the *agenti* at San Vittore prison and the fact that they'd been bribed, I can only conclude that the defendant would be safer outside the prison system."

A roar went up in the courtroom, and Corvi slammed his fist on his table. Loredana raised her voice. "The defendant will surrender his passport and receive a monitoring anklet. The defendant will be subject to twenty-four-hour monitoring and will not be allowed to journey beyond a four-kilometer radius from his home, except in the event of a medical emergency or to travel to and from court. Should the defendant violate the boundaries set or tamper with the anklet in any way, the defendant will be remanded to the custody of Bollate prison, without delay."

"Thank you, Giudice Montisi," Trapani said.

She adjourned the court, and the paparazzi went wild, scrambling out of their chairs to approach the prosecution and defense. Loredana stepped down from the bench, and Stefano met her at the door. A swarm of reporters stormed her way, microphones and cameras at the ready, but Stefano kept them at arm's length. Two more officers joined them outside.

They pushed through the throng as questions flew at her.

"Why did you do it?"

"Have you gone soft on the Mafia?"

"Does this mean you'll dismiss the case?"

She responded with "No comment" over and over, desperate to leave the crush of people surrounding her. Only Stefano's steady presence and warm hand at the small of her back kept her grounded.

Looking for the light coming through the doors that led outside, she suddenly froze. The young Calabrian in the tracksuit, whom she hadn't seen earlier, was standing less than three meters from her, propped against a wall. When their eyes met, he smiled, then made a cutting motion across his throat. "*Madonna,*" she muttered, her body going cold.

"What is it?" Stefano whisper-shouted in her ear.

"That man"—she pointed him out—"the one in the gray tracksuit. He just threatened me." Stefano started toward him, and the other officers closed ranks around her, surrounding her in a wall of black.

The Calabrian bolted outside the front entrance, and Stefano followed. The guards with her halted their progress just inside the doors and radioed their superior. Ten minutes later, Stefano returned. Alone. "The bastard's a damn rabbit," he said.

She couldn't stop seeing the sinister smile on the man's face. Her fingers trembling, she reached out and took Stefano's hand. He put an arm around her. "I've got you," he murmured. "I'm not going anywhere."

Loredana nodded, but didn't let go of his hand until they reached the relative safety of the car. He got in back with her, instead of riding up front with the driver, and called in what he knew and asked for additional assistance.

Vela was right—there *was* a conspiracy against his employer. And now she'd angered the person—or people—behind it twice. There probably wouldn't be a third time.

She turned to Stefano. "I want you to get me a gun and teach me to shoot."

"You're serious?"

Loredana held his eyes. "I am. And I want start learning tomorrow."

———— ◆ ————

Italo Baldassare seemed intent on breaking Lorenzo's *cazzo*. If Lorenzo didn't need him, he'd happily put a bullet in the prime minister and pat his weeping children on the head.

Sitting back in his chair, Lorenzo stared at the fire roaring in the hearth while Baldassare whined in his ear, the phone line making the man's voice tinny. "Are you going to take care of her or not?" Baldassare asked.

With a sigh, Lorenzo thought about snapping Baldassare's neck. When he'd been a young man, strong from working the family farm, such a thing would have been possible. Now, he'd have to send one of his men to do it. The arthritis, that creeping plague, was moving into his hands. "She won't be a problem."

"I can't afford to lose this appeal."

Politicians—what a useless lot of fuckups. This one couldn't keep it in his pants, and he couldn't keep his hands out of a million pockets either. "If you're so fucking worried, why didn't you just arrange for another judge?"

"I didn't think I'd get *her*. What were the odds? And I'd already called in a favor to arrange things for the banker. At your request."

"You owed me."

"I am aware." Baldassare huffed. "Besides, once I found out it was her, I thought I could use my 'tough on the Mafia' campaign to buy her goodwill. But all you've given me is the banker. And apparently, even though the press is gobbling up the story, *she's* not impressed. She just let him out!"

"Don't worry. I'm working on the co-judge in your case. Once she's out of the way, he'll take over and rule in your favor. I'll make sure of it."

"Well, I still need someone else to go after. The election is too close, even with the support of you and your... friends. I need more goodwill with the public. And I need to give that judge a good excuse to acquit me. He can't say I'm in bed with the Mafia if I'm spearheading an effort to put them in jail."

Porco Dio, would this fool never shut up? He'd try the Pope's patience. Probably already had.

It was bad enough that they couldn't meet in person because of who Baldassare was, which meant discussing sensitive matters on the phone, something Lorenzo hated. Almost as much as he hated having to put up with Baldassare.

Lorenzo rolled an unlit cigar between his fingers; he was going to need one after this call. Though he hadn't planned to make such a move until after Lucchesi was gone, Lorenzo supposed now was the time. Fortune favored the bold. "Sic your investigators on Vittorio Battista."

"Battista? He practically owns Capri."

"And a good chunk of the construction business in the Tyrrhenian region."

"Then that's where we'll start," Baldassare said. "I can see the headlines now: 'Jet-Set Mogul's Secret Criminal Life Exposed.'"

Lorenzo chuckled despite himself. Battista would be furious. For decades now, he'd quietly built a life of ease and secrecy. That was about to end.

"You're sure you've got her handled?" Baldassare asked. "Your Russian blew it."

Lorenzo's face flushed hot. How dare Baldassare question him? "When I tell you it's handled, it's handled. Need I remind you of what I can do?"

"I'm just nervous."

"No. You're insulting. And no one insults me." Lorenzo's heart was beating fast, and he forced himself to hide the rapidity of his breathing from Baldassare.

"I meant nothing by it."

"*Davvero?* Because that's not how it sounded."

"*Mi dispiace.*"

Lorenzo's fingers tightened on the phone, and he ignored the twinge of pain that shot through his hand. "You don't sound sorry enough."

Silence. Then: "I meant no disrespect. Remember what we're working toward. The future. A future you can't have without my help."

"Remember your place. Remember who put you where you are now."

"I do."

Lorenzo loosened his grip on the phone and hung up. He ran a hand across his face. Baldassare did have his purpose. And Lorenzo had to tolerate him for a while longer. Quite a while in fact. The plan he was working on would take at least a few more years to unfold. But once it did, he'd have this country in his fist.

He picked up the phone and punched a few buttons, barked an order, then hung up. A few minutes later, his grandson Marcello walked into the room. "You wanted me, Nonno?"

Lorenzo motioned to the other chair beside the fireplace. He cut another cigar for Marcello and they lit up, questions on Marcello's face, in his eyes.

Sometimes it staggered Lorenzo, how closely Marcello resembled Remo, the son he'd had to kill. The first son to betray him. Would Marcello do the same someday?

Puffing on his cigar, Marcello leaned forward, a lock of unruly black hair tumbling over his brow, his dark eyes fixed on Lorenzo. "What is it, Nonno? It must be bad if you're having two cigars in one week."

"I've just spoken to Italo."

A smile flashed across Marcello's face. "What did he whine about now?"

Lorenzo couldn't help laughing. Marcello hated Baldassare too. "The usual. 'Fix my trial.' 'Get rid of that bitch.' He's as irritating as a crying baby." Lorenzo waved his cigar in the air, the fragrant smoke circling around his head.

"Impatient little prick."

"You should talk."

Marcello laughed, the sound rich and confident, and so reminiscent of Remo, though Marcello was now forty-three; Remo had died at twenty-five. Lorenzo had few regrets, but how he'd raised Remo—had he been too hard on the boy? Driven him into the arms of the Russians?

"Speaking of impatient," Marcello said. "Has he ensured the party's endorsement? They'll accept me for mayor of Reggio Calabria?"

Lorenzo nodded. "He tells me it's done. And then we'll have no more trouble from that interim council those do-gooders put in place."

Taking a draw that hollowed his cheeks, Marcello stared into the fire. "How long until I'm president of Calabria?"

Lorenzo chuckled. "You have to be mayor first."

With a nod, Marcello acknowledged him. "But with Baldassare's backing, it shouldn't be long. And once I'm there, we cut his feet out from under him."

"And then *you* run as the 'tough on the Mafia' candidate for prime minister."

It was Marcello's turn to chuckle. "It's too bad so few people will ever know about your genius, Nonno."

"Doesn't matter. Winning matters. Only a fool courts appreciation from his sheep."

Still, he had to admit, it was a brilliant plan. All Marcello had to do was appear tough on crime, to look like he was cleaning up Calabria, that he was fighting back the Mafia scourge. With Lorenzo's position in La Provincia, he could order the families to suppress any violence, could order a certain percentage of forfeiture to the police, and could make Marcello look like a godsend to all those who hated the Mafia. And with what Lorenzo knew, they could use the Italian government to crush the Camorra and Cosa Nostra, and all the families among the 'Ndrangheta who proved troublesome.

Soon, the Andrettis would own the 'Ndrangheta. Soon they'd own Italy.

And Lorenzo would be the king behind the throne.

———— ◆ ————

Enrico settled into the leather seat in the back of the Mercedes limousine, Kate pressed against his side, tears streaming down her cheeks. "You're free," she whispered and stroked his face.

Dio, how he'd missed her touch. He pulled her close and kissed her hair, drinking in her scent. Finally he could relax, if only for a few minutes. "Not quite free," he murmured and jiggled his right ankle, which bore the unfamiliar weight of the monitoring device. As well as the weight of Tommaso's leather coat, temporarily wrapped around it to hopefully thwart any bugs that might have been implanted in the anklet.

"You're with me, and that's all that matters."

It was. And it wasn't. He'd done a lot of thinking in prison; there'd been little else to do. And he'd realized something. He'd been thinking too small, too selfishly, when he'd told Kate a while back that they were going to run, to escape all this. He'd been dreaming. And it was the wrong dream.

But what if Kate didn't agree? He could lose her again, this time forever. His stomach tightened into a ball.

Ruggero turned around in the front passenger seat, Tommaso behind the wheel. "We need to talk."

"We do." Enrico nodded. "But I need to speak with my wife first."

Ruggero held his eyes. "We don't have much time."

"We'll talk at the house. All of us." He pressed the button to raise the privacy glass and turned to Kate.

She wiped her eyes and let out a long exhale. "I missed you so much."

He smiled and cupped her cheeks. "I missed you more." Leaning forward, he pressed his lips to hers, their first kiss alone in two weeks, and the feeling of relief, of homecoming, nearly brought tears to his eyes. "*Ti amo, cara.*"

"*Ti amo.*" Her voice wavered, almost broke, and he wrapped his arms around her. How fragile she looked.

They sat in silence, just breathing, for several long minutes. He loved this woman, loved her more than he'd ever thought possible. Losing her would kill him. But he had to tell her the truth, and he had to tell her now. He waited until the tightness in his throat abated before he spoke again. "Remember what I said to you, the day of Sandro and Matteo's *comparaggio*?"

"About how we were going to leave?"

"Yes."

"Are we?" she whispered, her eyes round. "Now?"

"I wish. But no. We must stay. For good."

Her brow furrowed. "I thought you didn't want our son to grow up in this life."

"I don't. But I have another son to think of now. And so many others I cannot abandon."

"Tonio and Ruggero can manage."

"They could. But I've never been a coward. I've never been an oath breaker. I cannot start now."

"You're sure?"

He touched her belly, grown round with their child. "Can you live with this decision?"

She placed a hand over his. "Dear God, I'd love to run away." She closed her eyes for a moment before opening them and looking directly into his. "But I'm not a coward either. I told you I'd stand by you, and I meant it. When I married you, I knew what I was getting into. We have a family here. People who need us."

Relief flooded through him. He'd needed her agreement more than he'd realized. If she'd said no, it would have killed him to let her go, to let her and their child walk out of his life. But he'd promised her once that he'd let her leave if she wanted. And he meant it. He never wanted to hold her against her will. That wouldn't be loving, or respectful, or honorable.

That wouldn't be who he was.

"There's more," he said, and her hand tightened over his. He lowered his voice even further and spoke directly in her ear. "There will need to be a new *capo di tutti capi*."

"To replace Lorenzo." He nodded. "It'll be you?" she asked.

He shrugged. "Perhaps. I must accept if the opportunity is given to me."

"I didn't think it was 'given' to anyone."

"There will be an election. Not even Lorenzo was able to just take what he wanted."

"You want it? All that responsibility?"

He flipped his hand over beneath hers and interlaced their fingers. "It could be my chance to change everything. To chart a new course for the 'Ndrangheta. One that doesn't involve drugs. Or the exploitation of women."

A smile tugged at the corners of her luscious mouth. "My crusader."

"I've got to try. It's what Papà would have wanted. It's what I believe in. And that kind of 'Ndrangheta is what I want for my son. For all of my sons."

"Vittorio will back you. Who else?"

"Gianluca. At least a dozen families."

"That is not enough."

"No. But I have to try anyway. It might not happen in a year, or even a decade, but I'm nothing if not persistent."

Her smile broadened and her eyes glistened with unshed tears. "Rinaldo would be so proud."

Enrico's throat closed up. If only he'd had the courage to bash against those walls that had risen between him and Papà all those years ago, after Carlo Andretti had destroyed their family. They'd barely reconciled before Papà was killed, and it hadn't been enough to fill the hole that had opened up between them. And now it was too late.

He couldn't change the past. But he could change the future. And if it wasn't for Kate, he'd never have embraced his father again, he'd never have told him how he felt. She was his rock, his anchor. "I owe you so much, *cara*."

"*You* did it, Rico. You reached out to him. I just held your hand."

"And I will need you by my side in all the trouble that is to come."

"Always, *caro*. Always."

"You are too good to me. When I think of what you've given up to be with me, the sacrifices—the lack of stability, security, basic safety—"

She put a finger to his lips. "They're not sacrifices, when I have you." Her mouth curved into a grin. "Besides, when I think of the sacrifices *you've* made—giving up having a wife who's agreeable, doesn't fight with you, and doesn't have a potty mouth—"

He chuckled and pressed a finger to her lips in return. "I wanted a challenge. And I happen to like your potty mouth. Especially in bed."

"Shall I keep that in mind for later?" she said teasingly.

"I did not think I was being subtle." He pinched her ass and pulled her onto his lap, making sure she felt his erection.

She laughed and ground against him, making him groan, and he kissed her until her breathing quickened and he remembered all over again the first time he'd ever held her. He was the luckiest man alive.

But how long would his luck hold?

CHAPTER 9

They were all assembled at the house again, even Don Battista, who'd flown up on his jet as soon as he'd heard that Enrico had been granted house arrest. They had little time before Lorenzo would make his next move.

Strasser had come to the house, looked at the anklet, and conferred with Orlando. In a matter of hours, the two of them had hacked into the system that monitored the anklet, and once they had control, they were able to remove it. They stuck it in a soundproof box on the back terrace so that they were guaranteed privacy. All they had to do was remember to put it back on Enrico when he had to go to court—and restrict their talk to trivialities while he was wearing it.

Of course, if someone was listening, the lack of sound would be suspicious. Then again, listening in on Enrico's conversations while he was wearing it wasn't legal. Not that such a thing would stop someone like Corvi, who'd manage to find some way to claim he had a legal bug on Enrico. If Corvi did try to claim that the anklet had been tampered with, he'd have to expose his deception… and he'd have to prove the tampering, which Strasser and Orlando felt confident would be hard to do.

Once the anklet had been handled, Ruggero paced around the drawing room, waiting for everyone to gather. Half a day had already passed—half a day during which the Russians could be finalizing their plans, during which Lorenzo could have dispatched his hitmen to take out Loredana.

And here Ruggero was, waiting.

The sun had come out, bathing the lawn and gardens and trees outside in a golden glow. Luca was out back with Cocco and Bianca, romping about with the unending energy kids always had. Ruggero mustered a half-smile. At least one person in this household hadn't anything to worry about.

Elena came in, and he turned, unsure what to say. Since she'd arrived, he'd done his best to make sure they were never alone, and all he could hope for now was that the others would stop lingering over the lunchtime feast that Nonna

Drina and Maddalena had prepared to welcome Enrico home.

"He's a beautiful child," Elena said, watching Luca throw a ball for Cocco.

"Yes." Ruggero turned back to the scene outdoors and clasped his hands behind his back, grateful that he had an excuse not to look her in the eye. She came up beside him and rested one of her hands on the window frame.

"You've been avoiding me," she said.

"I've been busy."

"And you've made sure we never have a minute together when you are here. So when you slipped out earlier, I decided to follow. The others are still finishing their espresso."

"We don't have all damn day."

She touched his shoulder, and he flinched at the contact, his throat suddenly constricting. "I'm not going to bite."

He kept his eyes on Luca and the puppy. "It's what I deserve."

"For what?"

"Papà." The word was bitter in his mouth. Heavy.

"That was twenty years ago. You were a boy."

"I was old enough to know better. I never should have left my post."

"He told you to go."

"I never should have complained. If I'd kept my fucking mouth shut and done my fucking job—"

She squeezed his shoulder. "He might still be dead. You can't know that it would have made any difference."

He met her eyes. Damn her, and damn her pity. "You weren't there. *I* distracted him, Elena. *I* abandoned my post. It's on me."

Her face contorted with anger, her eyes aflame. "It's on *Papà*. He shouldn't have let you join. This has been no life for you. I remember the boy who always had his nose stuck in one book or another. I remember the boy who wanted to go to university someday. The boy who wanted to be *more*." Her words were choked, and his hands drew apart, clenched into fists at his sides now.

"What do you want from me? The Lucchesis kept a roof over our heads. Who took care of your family when your husband became too ill to work? Who paid for Orlando's education?"

"You did," she whispered. "But you paid too high a price for it." Her eyes glistened with tears.

He held on to his anger, afraid to let it go, afraid to feel her tears. "I'm shocked you took the money."

"I had to. We had to."

"Even though you hated me." He said this last to the window, unable to bear the look on her face.

"What are you saying?" Surprise filled her tone. "I never hated you."

He snorted. "You couldn't wait to leave after Papà died. You packed up as soon as the funeral was over. And then you moved as far from me as you could get and still be in the same country."

"That had nothing to do with hating you."

"You're lying. Again."

"Look at me," she said, her voice laced with a commanding note he hadn't heard since childhood. He finally turned. A tear rolled down her cheek and she wiped it away. "How was I supposed to feel? Papà was dead, and he'd entrapped you in the same life, with the same risks." Her voice wobbled. "I couldn't watch you die too."

More tears spilled down her cheeks, and he resisted the impulse to pull her close. "You're my brother, but you're more than that. I took care of you from the minute you were born. I raised you. And I didn't want to lose you too. Not after Mamma and Papà. I *had* to leave."

His vision blurred and he rubbed at his eyes. *Cristo.* He wasn't a child, coming to her with a scraped knee.

"*Mi dispiace*, Ruggero. Please forgive me. I should have realized how you'd feel." She touched his cheek, her fingers finding the scar. "I should have stayed. Made you get the surgery for this."

"No." His voice was rough, as if he'd swallowed a mouthful of gravel. "It's the least of what I deserve."

"You're wrong. Papà wouldn't like what you've done to yourself."

"I'm doing what he did."

"He had a family. A life outside the business."

"You think I should drag a wife and children into this? When I could be killed any day?"

Elena motioned to Luca and Bianca outside. "So Antonio doesn't deserve them?"

"He isn't a guard anymore."

"Neither are you."

He snorted again. "That's over. Don Lucchesi is back."

"That may be. But my point still stands. You deserve more than you've been giving yourself."

He looked out the window again and sighed, his breath fogging the glass. "Leave it, Elena."

She touched his hair, the caress soothing, and he closed his eyes. "I won't. I've been a horrible sister to you. And that stops now."

He turned to her. "I said to leave it alone, and I meant it."

"*Ti voglio bene.* I want the best for you. I want you to be happy. And so I will not leave you alone."

Antonio and Don Battista came in, sparing him any further discussion with Elena. His chest felt a little lighter, but a heaviness had settled in his gut. Maybe if they'd had this conversation all those years ago, things could have been different. Now… He didn't know how to be any other way. He didn't know how to be anything other than what he was.

He wasn't fit to be a husband, a father. He was fit to be only one thing: a killer. A taker of lives, not a creator of them.

And now he needed to persuade Don Lucchesi to let him fulfill his destiny, to do the one thing he knew how to do best.

The others filtered in: Enrico and Kate, Nick and Delfina, Orlando. At last they could start. And Ruggero could finally get back to Milan to keep an eye on Loredana.

Everyone dispersed to the various chairs and sofas, arranging them in a loose circle. Maddalena brought in a tray with drinks and sweets. Ruggero kept his post by the window. He didn't have much to say, and it wasn't his place to set policy anymore, just to enforce it.

And that was fine by him.

Elena sat next to Orlando on one of the sofas. She looked at Ruggero and patted the open spot on her other side, but he pretended he hadn't seen.

Tonio picked up on the gesture, however. "We're waiting for you."

"I'd prefer to stand."

Don Lucchesi leaned forward. "Ruggero, you're not on guard duty. Sit."

"I'm not?"

"No. I should have done this some time ago. I'm making you an underboss."

"Of what?" Ruggero couldn't keep the edge out of his voice. There wasn't room for another underboss, and they all knew it.

"We'll figure that out later. For now, you're on special assignment."

Scrubbing a hand over his face, Ruggero let out a little huff. "That sounds like a nice way of dismissing me."

The don held his gaze. "I'm serious. You're more than a guard. We will find you a place. As of now, you work directly for me, and only me."

"*Sì, capo.*" Ruggero took an open chair, ignoring Elena's pointed glance and repeated gesture that he join her.

Enrico looked around before speaking. "We're at war. We have been for some time now, but it's been covert. Now that Lorenzo has called in the Vilanoviches, I'm afraid it's about to become very, very public." He looked directly at Ruggero. "I'm going to need you to help with strategy."

"I thought my job was to keep Lor—the judge—safe."

Elena raised an eyebrow at his slip, but no one else seemed to notice.

"It is. That's still critical. But we have to think past the trial. Assuming you keep her alive and she acquits me, Lorenzo will be furious. But we can't assume he won't have a Plan B. And a Plan C. He's made it plain that he intends to kill me."

"Which is why you have to let me eliminate him now," Ruggero said.

"That's just the problem. Until the trial is over, our hands are tied. No one around me can die. I can't risk it. If we go after Lorenzo, the FIU will never let up."

"I can get rid of Parodi."

Enrico held his eyes. "How would that look?"

"We buy him then."

Orlando shook his head. "He's a weasel. We could never trust him not to turn."

"What about Sal?" Ruggero suggested. "Hitting him would hurt Lorenzo. He's Lorenzo's right hand, no matter what any of them claim."

Delfina spoke. "I don't think that's a good idea."

"Why not?"

"Because Papà has him and Angelica staying in the guesthouse now. Where he held Nick."

"Which is still full of bugs," Nick said.

"Dario is spying on Sal?" That was news.

"And by extension, Lorenzo," Delfina said.

"Can you get access to the recordings?" Enrico asked her.

"I don't know if Papà has changed the locks on the office in Como where the computers are, but I know where it is and I know the password to the system—as long as that hasn't changed either."

Enrico looked at Nick. "Can I ask you two to try?"

"Of course." Nick squeezed Delfina's hand. "We want to help however we can."

It wasn't the most delicate question, but someone had to ask it. "Any progress on the baby?" Ruggero asked.

Delfina looked down and shook her head. "I just took another test."

"*Bella*, it'll happen," Nick said.

"When it'll be too late to matter. We need this baby now."

She looked so miserable, Ruggero felt bad for bringing it up. "If your father is spying on Sal, that means he's not on Lorenzo's side—at least not yet. And that means he could be of use to us."

Delfina raised her brows. "I doubt we'll get a lick of cooperation from him. Even if I do get pregnant."

"Dario has surprised us before," Nick said.

"That was when Cris was around. Now..." Delfina trailed off, her eyes going to her father-in-law.

"I have to hope that Dario will forgive me someday," Enrico said. "He's no idiot. He has to realize this was ultimately Lorenzo's doing."

"You're right. He's not stupid, but if anyone can hold a grudge, it's my father."

They'd wasted enough time worrying about Dario. They needed to get practical. "So if we can't eliminate anyone right now, we have to prepare to fight," Ruggero said. "And that means we need more men. We still haven't recovered from the last time the Russians attacked."

"How many do you need?" Don Battista asked.

"Can you spare three dozen? I need to split them between the lake and Milan."

"You'll have them in forty-eight hours. They'll need training on the territory."

"Beppe and Tommaso can help." The promise of more men was encouraging, but these were still half-measures. He looked at Enrico. "The minute this trial is over, you must allow me to pursue Lorenzo. To end this."

"Attacking him in Calabria, in his home, would be suicide," Antonio said.

Enrico nodded. "Then we'll have to draw him out."

"How do you plan to do that, my son?" Don Battista asked.

"I don't know yet, but we'll think of something. Perhaps the *mandamenti* will have to meet?"

Don Battista stroked his mustache. "I'll work on a pretext for it. Still, it'll be dangerous. You'll have Sal and Lorenzo there. And they won't come alone."

"But Lorenzo won't be in his fortress, either." Ruggero never relished killing, but this time would be an exception.

If only they didn't have to wait. But Don Lucchesi was right. They had to be careful, or all would be lost.

Ruggero rose. "I need to get back to Milan."

Elena followed him out and into the front hall, where he donned his coat and gloves. "This judge. She's not just a job to you."

Minchia. He was careful to meet her eyes. "I don't know why you'd say that."

She put her hands on her hips. "You think of her as Loredana."

"I have to call her something."

"Giudice Montisi won't do?"

He finished buttoning his coat, doing his best to pretend she wasn't there, staring at him, victory stamped on her features. "I'm not sure when I'll be back." He turned to go.

She stopped him with a hand on the arm. "I'm going to speak to Don Lucchesi about finding you a wife. It's time."

"If I plan to marry, I'll find my own wife."

The look she gave him was soft. "The judge is beautiful, yes. But impossible."

"Tell me something I don't know."

She squeezed his arm. "We'll find you a girl from a good family."

Closing his eyes, he sighed and shook his head, but kept his tone light. "I should have left you in Calabria."

She chuckled and rose up on tiptoe to kiss his cheek. "Someone has to look out for you."

"If this is how you look out for me, remind me never to piss you off."

"We'll talk about this when you get back."

"No, we won't." He opened the door and she followed him, holding it open behind him.

"You've forgotten who you're talking to."

He smiled then, but didn't let her see it. He'd never hear the end of it. Just as she'd never give up on the wife issue until he was at the altar.

He descended the stairs, salt crystals crunching under his shoes, then cut across the frosty grass to the Maserati. Maybe Elena was right; maybe a wife was what he needed.

Though he couldn't imagine a woman who could ever shove Loredana Montisi out of his mind.

———◆———

Loredana's heart sped up as Stefano pulled up in front of the gun range. It was just the two of them, once they'd left the insanity of the courthouse behind. Today had been the start of Italo Baldassare's appeal on his election-fraud case, and every news outlet in the country—and many from outside it—seemed to have sent at least one reporter. Though she'd been asked many questions about the Baldassare case—all of which she'd refused to answer—there were also quite a few about the Lucchesi case. She'd thought she and Stefano would never escape.

But now here they were. And she was going to learn how to shoot a gun.

She'd never even touched one before. After her parents' shooting, the mere thought of holding a gun made her queasy. Pulling a trigger, taking a life. Killing someone's father, brother, husband, or son. How could she ever?

She had little choice though; she had to be prepared. The messages from the man in the tracksuit had been unambiguous. And if that man's boss had engineered the attack on Lucchesi, he certainly meant business.

Stefano had changed out of his uniform; it was the first time she'd seen him in casual clothes, and the navy blue cable-knit sweater and jeans with boots suited him well. He'd suggested she change as well, and she'd chosen a dark red sweater with black slacks and low-heeled boots. Even though she didn't think her outfit the least bit sexy—okay, the sweater *did* outline her breasts quite well—the suggestive smiles Stefano had sent her way during the drive made her feel like a queen. She'd almost forgotten why they were together during his time off.

The memory of Ruggero Vela standing outside her apartment, smoking and staring up at her, flashed through her mind and made her stomach flutter. *He* was the reason why she was in this car.

Stefano turned off the engine and helped her out, his strong leather-clad hand closing over hers, and she was only a little surprised when he didn't let go. He drew her close instead, his other arm going around her back.

Another flash of Ruggero Vela, caging her against the wall at the courthouse, that suggestive grin he'd given her, the heat radiating off him. The intensity of his stare as he'd stepped closer, giving her no quarter. She put a hand on Stefano's chest. "I'm quite capable of standing on my own," she said.

Stefano leaned down, his lips brushing over hers. "It's slippery out here. I wouldn't want you to fall."

"And you felt the need to kiss me because...?"

"Because I want to."

His mouth feathered over hers again, and her heartbeat grew erratic. She closed her eyes, but when he deepened the kiss, it wasn't Stefano she pictured. It was *him*. Ruggero. Why?

"We'd better get inside before I get too distracted and you never get your lesson," Stefano said.

"I wouldn't want that." Though it was hard to tell which of them was more distracted. He truly was a handsome devil.

He escorted her inside the low-slung concrete building. At the counter, he presented the steel case he'd retrieved from the trunk, and she got her first glimpse of the gun he'd chosen for her. He purchased a box of ammunition and rented hearing protection for the two of them.

The muffled sound of gunshots penetrated the cinder-block walls and the reinforced glass door that separated them from the range itself. They were really going to do this. Her stomach flipped over. *She* was really going to do this.

He handed her the eye and ear protection that he'd rented, making sure she donned it before they went inside. She followed him into the range and to their assigned station, the scent of gunpowder acrid in her nostrils. Someone fired a gun as they passed, and she jumped. "Easy," Stefano said and patted her shoulder.

"First, let's go over some basic safety rules," he said, speaking loudly enough to be heard. He opened the case and removed the gun. "This is a Beretta 92FS. Similar to the one in your trial. Always, always, always treat a gun as if it's loaded, even when you know it's not. That way you'll never shoot it by accident. I've seen two officers forget that rule. One of them lost a finger." He picked up her left hand. "Wouldn't want that to happen to you." Then he kissed her knuckles and she had to look away. He was utterly shameless.

"Eyes on me, please," he said, amusement tingeing his voice.

"Stop flirting, then."

He raised a brow. "I thought you were enjoying it."

"I thought you didn't want to get distracted."

"Am I distracting you?"

"Stop fishing for compliments. You're as bad as a woman."

He laughed. "Okay, then." He pointed to the various parts of the Beretta, noting them one by one. "When you're holding a gun, make sure the muzzle is pointed down, at the ground, and your index finger is resting on the trigger guard, not the trigger itself. Don't ever point your weapon at anyone, unless you're ready to kill them."

She swallowed hard and took the gun from him, a nervous thrill coursing through her at the feel of the cool, heavy metal. So much power, and she held it in her hands.

He pointed at the various parts again, making her touch them and repeat the names. He showed her how to rack the gun, and the button to press to eject the magazine. "Ready to try it?" he asked.

Not in the least. "Can I watch you first?"

"Certainly, *bella*." He loaded the empty magazine with bullets and slapped it home, then racked the slide and aimed at the target. He pointed out the sight at the end of the gun's muzzle. "This tells you what you're aiming at."

Then he demonstrated the proper grip and stance, his deft movements and ease with the gun impressing her. "Do you shoot a lot?" she asked.

"I was a sharpshooter in the military before transferring to the *carabinieri*." He squeezed off a few rounds, and her heart jumped with each shot. Then he pushed a button on the wall to retrieve the target. His shots were all tightly grouped at the center. Stefano definitely knew what he was doing. He plastered the target against his chest and tapped it. "Aim for here. Center mass. Don't go for the head, and don't try to wound someone. Always shoot to kill. It's hard to hit a moving target, especially when you're afraid for your life."

"What if I only wound them?"

"Pull the trigger and don't stop until the gun is empty. Don't expect one bullet to do it. This isn't the movies."

He handed the gun to her. This time it was warm, and the smell of gunpowder lingered in the air around it. Nestling up behind her, he showed her how to sight the gun, his strong arms surrounding hers, his large body pressed against her back. "Now breath out, and squeeze the trigger without jerking the gun off the target."

Her heart started pounding. "You can do this," he said, his warm breath washing over her cheek. She started to pull the trigger, squinting in anticipation of the shot, and was surprised by how much strength it took. She held her breath, dreading the moment when the gun would bark and jump in her hands.

The loud pop of the bullet detonating surprised her nonetheless, and she jerked. Stefano tightened his hold on her. "Easy," he murmured. "Now again."

She pulled the trigger, and though she still flinched when the gun went off, it wasn't quite such a surprise. "Again," he said. She kept going until the magazine was empty.

He pushed the button to call in the target. She'd actually hit it a few times, though her shots weren't dead center like Stefano's.

"You're flinching when you fire," he said. "It'll pass, once you get more comfortable with it. Do another magazine. This time I'm not going to brace you."

She took aim and pulled the trigger, startled at how strong the recoil was without his help. The shot went wild and completely missed the target. "How am I going to do this on my own?"

"You'll get the idea."

"I'm going to need a lot of practice."

He chuckled. "You didn't think an afternoon would turn you into Clint Eastwood, did you?"

"No, but..." She looked mournfully at her untouched target. "I'm awful."

"Keep practicing, *bella.*"

He corrected her stance and her grip and gave her some more pointers. She might have done better had he not pressed himself against her bottom, revealing that she wasn't piquing just his sense of humor. She closed her eyes for a moment, and again Ruggero Vela came to mind, his eyes locked on hers, his hard body just millimeters away. Heat flashed from her cheeks to her belly. Why him? Why not Stefano?

Dio mio. She really did need to get laid. That had to be it, if she was getting all worked up over a look. Vela hadn't even touched her. She pushed backward against Stefano and focused on the target. In a low voice, she asked, "Do you live at the barracks, or do you have a place to yourself?"

"I have a place outside the barracks. And no nosey *mamma* to spoil things." His hands drifted from her elbows to her hips, and he pulled her tightly against his hard groin. "There's a good restaurant on the corner too."

She turned her head to look at him. "Are you actually asking me on a date?"

He held her eyes. "It's whatever you want it to be."

What did she want? Strings, or no strings? "Can I tell you later?"

"You're not seeing anyone, I'm not seeing anyone. Let's just find out what develops, yes?"

She nodded. "Now back up, or I'll waste another magazine." He gave a throaty chuckle, his eyes twinkling, then kissed her just below the ear, the soft caress in such a sensitive place making her shiver. She turned and pushed him away, trying not to let him see the effect he was having on her.

She blew out and tightened her grip on the gun. Sighting on the target, she squeezed the trigger, again and again, until the magazine was empty and her wrists and forearms were aching. But her mind kept going elsewhere—what would it feel like to have Ruggero Vela kissing her lips, her neck, his big body pressed to hers, those brutal hands and hard eyes focused on her and her pleasure?

This has to stop. She ejected the empty magazine and handed the gun back to Stefano. He called in her target, and she was pleased to see that she'd done a little better. He noticed as well. "Ah, *bella*, it looks like I *was* distracting you before."

She smiled up at him, but she could think of only one thing. *What is it going to take to get me to stop thinking of that man?* A quick romp with Stefano might not do it. But if she were to get involved with him, to turn it personal, perhaps *that* would redirect her wandering thoughts.

She watched Stefano pack up the gun, listened to him explain how to disassemble and clean it, but over and over, her mind drifted to Ruggero Vela. What would the same lesson be like, coming from him? Would he be as patient, or would he laugh at her?

No, she decided, he wouldn't laugh. He didn't seem like that sort of man. Brutal yes, but not cruel. Efficient, serious, deadly. Those were the words that sprang to mind.

She let her eyes rove over Stefano, drinking in his masculine beauty, the way the florescent lights glinted on his dark hair, the way they sharpened his cheekbones and accentuated the hollows beneath them, making him look sterner and more severe than usual.

Making him look more like Ruggero Vela. Was that why the man had taken over her brain?

Stefano snapped the case shut and retrieved their coats from the pegs on the wall. *Dio,* her plan had better work. She couldn't keep thinking about Vela. She couldn't. First off, the whole thing was impossible. Secondly, the whole thing was… impossible.

She shouldn't find Vela the slightest bit attractive. She couldn't.

"You okay?" Stefano asked.

Blinking, she looked up at him and forced a wide smile. "Perfectly." What a liar she was.

He took her elbow and escorted her outside. The late afternoon had given way to twilight, and the sky had grown heavy with clouds. They were nearly to the car when Stefano stopped. "Looks like snow," he said.

She followed his gaze upward, and it took her a second to register that Stefano had stiffened beside her, that the sudden, tight grip on her bicep wasn't his.

Planting her feet, she swung her head to see who had grabbed her. A black balaclava covered the man's face, and that, almost more than the gun he held, was what chilled her.

"Stefano!" she gasped, and the man raised the gun and pointed it in her face.

"Shut it." The man's voice was gruff, his tone final.

Her teeth clapped together, and she turned to see what was happening to Stefano. Another man, his face also covered with a balaclava, had a gun shoved against Stefano's temple. Stefano's lips were pressed together, his whole face rigid. "Do what they say," he said, his voice low and clipped.

The two men urged them toward a white panel van, where a third man waited, his face also covered. That was a good sign, wasn't it? If the men were hiding their faces, maybe this was just a kidnapping, not an execution.

The men hustled them inside, and the third climbed up front. They sped off, a spray of gravel hitting the underside of the van, the tires slipping on the snow-covered drive. The man holding Stefano swore at the driver and told him to slow down or they'd attract attention.

The driver cursed him back. He sounded young, nervous. She studied the two men holding her and Stefano, the four of them huddled on the bare floor of the van. An empty glass bottle of mineral water rolled back and forth, clinking on the metal flooring, until the man nearest her stopped it with his foot. Their captors looked to be of medium build, the width of their shoulders and the lankiness of their frames suggesting that they too might be younger.

Younger meant less experienced, and hopefully, less hardened. Less likely to kill? A sick feeling shuddered through her and her stomach roiled. Was this how it was going to end?

"You think anyone saw us?" one of the men asked.

"No," Stefano said. "We were at the far end, under the trees, out of the lights. That's why I picked it."

What? The nausea sharpened and her vision faded. Had she heard correctly? He reached over and gently tipped her jaw up, closing her mouth. "You're going to catch flies, *bella*."

"You? You're working with them?" Her mouth was so dry the words cracked.

"They pay better. And for you, someone was willing to pay a lot."

The van swayed around a corner, and she barely held back a dry heave. "Am I going to live?"

"For a while. How long depends on you." The smile he gave her was hardly reassuring.

CHAPTER 10

Fat, heavy snowflakes careened into the windshield of the Maserati. Ruggero started the wipers with a curse and tightened his grip on the wheel. "Just what I need," he muttered. The snow fell fast and thick, cutting his field of view to no more than a few meters. It was like driving into a black tunnel with confetti being thrown in his face.

Had they killed her yet? He exhaled slowly, forcing himself to focus. He'd lost the van twenty minutes ago. Her kidnappers had spotted the tail once they'd reached the countryside, and they'd whipped around several curves and taken one of the roads that branched off from the autostrada.

But which one? Apparently not the one he'd chosen.

Cursing again, he slowed and wheeled the Maserati around, heading back to the autostrada. Between the dark and now this damn snow, would he find her in time, or would he find her bullet-ridden body?

His heart pounded and his gut tightened. The continued dump of adrenaline was making him jumpy. He needed to think, to concentrate, to focus. This was not how he operated. This was not who he was.

He was a man who did his job, and his emotions stayed out of it.

Ruggero doubled back, then took the next turnoff, another winding lane that crawled into a dense wood. Just his luck that they hadn't headed into farmland. This area was full of vineyards and olive groves, and the land lining the roadways was heavily treed.

This had to be the way they'd gone. If the damn snow had started earlier, he'd have been able to follow their tracks. Now it merely proved a hindrance.

He rounded a corner a bit too fast, and the tires slipped. He forced himself to slow, to keep his eyes peeled as he scanned for signs of habitation through the thick, swirling snowfall. There were no streetlights out this far, and his headlights illuminated the road, but little else around him. He switched on the fog lights, which provided a bit more visibility along the sides.

He almost drove past a small, rock-walled farmhouse set back from the road, but a flash of light at the base of an imperfectly shaded window caught his eye. He surveyed the area around the house, and there it was—a white Fiat Doblo cargo van parked to the side.

Cutting the headlights and engine, Ruggero coasted off the road, stopping near the end of the driveway that led to the house. He'd declined the built-in navigation system that came with the car; he didn't need to make it easy for anyone to track him. Pulling up the navigation app on a burner phone instead, he hoped it would give him a location he could relay to his men in Milan, but the phone kept losing the GPS signal. "Come on, come on," he muttered, staring at the recalculating message and willing it to stop, to settle on a location. "I'm not even fucking *moving*," he grumbled, but the phone ignored him. "Recalculating" flashed again and again.

"Damn it." Finally it stopped and gave him a location. He called one of his men, relayed the info, then hung up. They were at least twenty minutes away, and he couldn't wait. He was going to have to go in alone.

Three to one. He'd survived worse odds.

Making sure the phone was on silent, he slipped it into his pocket, then grabbed the spare Beretta from the glove box and screwed a silencer onto it. He was already wearing gloves. He pocketed a spare magazine and took a deep breath.

She had to still be alive. And if she wasn't, well… These men would die with her.

He exhaled slowly and closed his eyes, willing his breathing to even out, his nerves to settle. This was a job, like any other. It was a job.

He opened his eyes and focused on the house. There were three men who had to die, and one other that he'd have to decide about. That was the job.

Slipping out of the car, he closed the door soundlessly, then picked his way across the gravel drive, until he could approach the house through the snow-studded grass. He stumbled over a rock, but recovered quickly, the fresh blast of adrenaline enough to make his back cold with sweat.

Snowflakes coated his eyelashes, his hair, his cheeks, and he impatiently wiped them away as he approached the house and sidled up to the window where the shade hadn't been pulled all the way down. A couple centimeters of light spilled out, and he peered inside.

Three young men were gathered in the main sitting area, their chairs scattered around a large hearth that hosted a roaring fire, the rustic furnishings resembling those in the house Ruggero had been born in. A lamp near the door had been switched on, but otherwise the room was dark, and the men were passing around a bottle of wine and chatting. One of them stubbed out a cigarette in an overflowing ashtray.

No sign of Loredana. Or Stefano. Were they already dead?

"Hurry the fuck up," the one nearest the front door yelled, looking toward the darkened hallway at the back of the house.

Who was he yelling at? Did they have another accomplice?

Merda. That meant four to one, and the odds slipped further from his favor. And what, exactly, did "Hurry the fuck up" mean? Was one of them back there with her, killing her, or—

A woman's muffled scream rang out, and Ruggero's heartbeat quickened.

Loredana was alive, but probably not for long.

He couldn't wait. He took one more look at the positions of the men and slipped out his knife, switching the Beretta to his left hand.

One of the men patted his pockets and cursed, then rose. "Left my cigarettes in the van," he said, and started for the front door.

Ruggero pocketed the Beretta and took a deep breath. He almost smiled. A lucky break. He eased around the corner and squatted behind a large, denuded bush by the front door. The man came out and headed to the van.

Silently, Ruggero sprang up behind him and slapped a hand over the man's mouth, arching the bastard's head back for a swift, deep cut that severed the arteries at his neck. Blood sprayed out, black in the faint moonlight, and Ruggero eased the body to the ground, then dragged it off to the far side of the van. He opened the van's door and heaved the man inside, then slammed it shut.

Keeping the knife in his right hand, he took the silenced Beretta in the other. That left two men, who hopefully hadn't moved, and a third somewhere in the back.

He stomped up the front steps in imitation of the man he'd just killed and shook the snow out of his eyes and off his clothes before opening the door. The men were still in their chairs and didn't look up when he came in.

Their mistake.

Raising the Beretta, he shot the man closest to him. The other's mouth dropped open. "*Madonna*," the second man gasped, and dived for his weapon.

Ruggero took aim, but a crash and another scream from the hall behind distracted him. He took his eyes off the man for a second, and that was long enough for him to get his gun. Without thinking, Ruggero hurled his knife, and the blade sank deep into the man's chest. He gaped at Ruggero, his hands reaching up as if he'd pull out the knife, but then his arms fell to his sides and his gun clattered to the floor.

Another scream penetrated the rush of blood in Ruggero's head, the harsh sound of his amped-up breathing. Had they heard him? He retrieved his knife and turned toward the darkened hallway. How many men were there? And most importantly, where were they?

———◆———

The knife ripped through the front of Loredana's sweater, the yarn parting easily as Stefano thrust the blade upwards, the tip searing along her belly. She pressed a hand to the wound, afraid to look at the blood that coated her fingers. "You bastard," she spat.

He smiled. "I was trying to make this easy on you. There's even a bed in here." He gestured to the mattress shoved up against the wall. "But I've run out of patience." He motioned with his thumb over his back. "They have too."

She pulled the sides of her sweater closed over her bra. "I gathered that."

Pocketing the knife, he grabbed her wrists, pulling them apart and hauling her against him. The cut on her belly burned when it touched his sweater. She struggled to get away and kicked at his shins, and his grip tightened on her wrists, the bones grinding together, the pain so intense she cried out. "You don't have to do this," she said. "If it's money, a promotion, whatever, I can match what they're giving you. I can make sure you get a nice posting in Rome. Or wherever you want. I have friends."

"I have better friends. Ones who are more powerful than yours." His eyes roamed her face. "You just couldn't do what you were told, could you?"

"How can you do this? How? You swore an oath."

"My boss hates me. I fucked his niece and didn't marry her. He was planning to send me to some wretched little backwater in Calabria as soon as he could get the paperwork approved. And you know how long *carabinieri* officers last down there. Not long, unless they make friends. That fellow in the tracksuit—he was more than happy to work with me and arrange this little party for you."

The coldness in his tone, in his eyes, made her shiver. How could he have flirted with her all afternoon when he knew what was coming?

And how the hell was she going to get out of here?

She closed her eyes and swallowed. There was, perhaps, one way. Steeling herself for what was to come, she looked up at him. "What can I do to survive this? If they want Lucchesi in jail that badly, I can make it happen."

He smiled. "Now you're on the right track." He let up on her wrists a bit. "You think you can stop my transfer?"

"I know I can. And I can get you a promotion too."

His eyes slid over her face again. "You're a talented talker, Giudice Montisi. I wonder what other talents your tongue has."

She pasted a seductive smile on her lips and descended slowly to her knees, his hands on her wrists steadying her. Sitting back on her heels, she gazed up at him, and his grip tightened, his eyes flaring with hunger when she tried to reach for his belt buckle.

If she bit him when he was in her mouth, would he be too distracted by the pain to kill her, or would he snap her neck? Or could she get the knife out of his pocket without him noticing?

The door opened behind him, and her heart jumped into her throat. *Madonna*, this was going to turn into a gang rape. She had no hope of overpowering two of them. But maybe if she kept her head, maybe she could figure out something. Dio, per favore, *keep the others outside...*

"Get the fuck out," Stefano said without turning. "I'll be done in thirty minutes. *Then* she's yours."

"Is that right?" came a low, gravel-strewn voice, a voice that slid over her nerve endings and sparked a fire in her chest. Ruggero was here—but was he a friend or a foe? She tried to peer around Stefano's hip, but he jerked back suddenly, his hands releasing her and clawing at the arm clamped around his throat.

Her heart pumping wildly, she scrambled away, trembling at Ruggero's bloody knife glinting in the dim overhead light. Raising the blade, he brought it to Stefano's left eye, and the bastard went still.

Ruggero chuckled, then relaxed his hold on Stefano's neck, replacing his arm with the blade, and putting an arm around Stefano's chest to restrain him. "So Giudice Montisi," Ruggero said, "what shall I do with him?"

"The others are dead?" she asked. He nodded, and she let out a long shuddering breath. "He needs to be charged."

"I have an idea," Stefano said, his voice thin but steady.

"What?" she asked, surprised he'd said a word.

Ruggero's eyes met hers, then his gaze dropped lower, to her exposed bra, before dipping to her blood-streaked belly. He grimaced then and nicked Stefano's throat. A drop of blood rolled down Stefano's skin. "I ought to gut you like a pig," Ruggero snarled.

Was Ruggero actually upset that Stefano had cut her? She pulled the edges of her sweater together, suddenly feeling the cold.

"Listen," Stefano said. "No one has to get hurt. I'll say I overpowered them and saved us both." He looked at Loredana. "You arrange a promotion and transfer to Rome for me, and I won't say a thing about how you've been working with Lucchesi all along."

Shock speared through her. "You wouldn't dare."

He smirked at her. "I know what happens to officers who end up in prison. I'd be passed around like a party favor. I'm *not* going."

"No, you're not," Ruggero said, and with a quick jerk, he sliced across Stefano's throat.

Loredana gasped and jumped away from the arc of blood spraying from Stefano's neck. "What are you *doing*?" she screamed.

Ruggero wiped the knife on Stefano's sweater, then pocketed it before lowering the body to the floor. He straightened and looked her in the eye. "Saving you from a heap of trouble." He eyed her torn clothes, her bloody hands. "Or did I get this all wrong? You *were* on your knees for him."

Fury ripped through her. She lunged forward and slapped him across the face, smearing his cheek with blood. When she raised her hand to do it again, he grabbed her wrists. His grip was like iron, and she cried out at the pressure on her already bruised flesh. He immediately let go.

She stood there, staring at him, her chest heaving. A shudder racked her body, then another. He stepped closer, set his hands on her shoulders, his eyes holding hers the entire time.

"He was trying to rape me," she said, the words shaking as much as she was.

"I know." One of his thumbs smoothed over the top of her collarbone, and her eyes filled with tears. "Don't cry," he said. "Don't cry for him, or any of those bastards."

"I'm not." Her voice broke, the shuddering so deep inside she thought she'd rattle apart. She was cold, so cold, and he radiated heat. She wanted to step closer, to warm herself against him, but how could she?

He slid his hands up and down her arms, chafing them, but it didn't warm her. Tears poured down her cheeks and she pulled tighter at her sweater, the shaking so bad she thought she'd collapse. Her knees wobbled, and he decided the matter, pulling her close, pressing her against his chest, opening his leather jacket and tugging it around her.

He cradled her gently against him, as if she were an injured bird, and the tears poured ever faster, sobs racking her. He cupped the back of her head with one of his hands, his fingers rubbing softly over her hair. "Shh, *bambina*. It's all right," he murmured. "I've got you."

His body was stiff against hers, rigid, though his tone was soothing. Her arms were mashed up against her chest, creating a wall between them, a wall she was afraid to drop. Clearly, he was as uncomfortable as she was.

Another shiver racked her. She was going into shock, wasn't she? She needed to keep warm, to calm herself. She needed… to get closer to him. She eased her arms down, then brought them up around his back. He shifted uneasily, but allowed the contact until she was pressed full length against him. Hard as granite, the muscles clearly defined, his body reminded her that he was lethal, a killer, and yet he was warm, and that was what she needed.

She couldn't stop the tears, and she nestled her damp face into his black turtleneck, inhaling the scent of him—a hint of cigarettes and that lemony cologne he wore. The familiar fragrance seemed to calm her, though why she didn't want to guess.

A light humming in her ear made her start, and Ruggero tightened his hold a fraction until she relaxed. After a moment she realized it was a lullaby, one she hadn't heard in a long time. Her mother used to sing it to her when she couldn't sleep.

Loredana exhaled against his chest and tried to gather herself. *It's over; I'm safe. He's not going to hurt me.* She repeated those thoughts several times, but something niggled at her. Then she realized what it was, and her tears abruptly dried up. "I can't let you and your boss get your claws in me."

"My boss?"

"Enrico Lucchesi."

He laughed. "I'm an independent contractor."

"Then what are you doing here?"

"My job."

"I haven't hired you."

"But you will." He smirked at her, so damn sure of himself.

"Independent contractor, my ass."

He shrugged. "That's what I am. I protect people, and I solve problems."

"I'm trying to be serious."

"So am I." He searched her face. "Would you rather be dead?"

"Of course not. But there's a catch. There always is. Some price I'll have to pay. And it won't be money."

"You don't owe anyone anything. Just do your job."

"You mean, do what *you* want."

His brows lowered. "You can see what's going on here. Someone has a strong interest in this case and in making sure my current employer ends up dead. You're the only judge who can be trusted not to follow that person's agenda."

"I have to recuse myself from the case."

His face turned stony, and she shivered. Would he kill her too? He pulled her closer, stroked a hand over her back. "Listen to me. If you recuse yourself, who will get the case?"

"My co-judge. Paolo Zambrotta."

"You're certain?"

"That will be my recommendation so that the trial can continue."

"I need to show you something." He stepped away from her and looked around, then retrieved her coat from the bed where Stefano had tossed it. He handed it to her, then crouched down to inspect her belly wound. She trembled when he touched her, and he quickly removed his hand. "Sorry. I needed to see how bad it was."

She buttoned the coat. "Think I'll need stitches?"

He shook his head. "It's clotting already, so it's not deep."

A car crunched up the gravel driveway, and they both stiffened. Ruggero pulled out a phone and dialed a number. "You're here?" he asked someone.

She faintly heard a reply, then he said, "We're coming out. They're all down."

He took her elbow and walked her through the house. She caught a glimpse of the two blood-soaked men sprawled on the floor of the sitting room, then they were headed out the front door and down the steps.

They met three men at the base of the stairs. Ruggero motioned to the van. "There's one in there, three inside. The one in the back is going to need new clothes. Her blood is on them and on his knife. She was never here."

The men nodded, and Ruggero crouched down and grabbed a handful of snow and wiped it over the cheek she'd slapped, erasing the smear of blood. He rubbed the snow all over his gloves, then dipped his knife in the snow as well, scrubbing it before pocketing it again. Then he led her down the drive to a Maserati parked at the very end.

"Was that your clean-up crew?" she asked.

He didn't answer, just opened the passenger door for her and waited for her to get inside. Crossing in front of the car, he whipped the door open and slid behind the wheel, not looking at her. So maybe she'd pissed him off with that smart-ass comment, and maybe she shouldn't have. She'd most likely be dead if it wasn't for him.

The engine purred to life and he had them on the autostrada to Milan within minutes. "Where are you taking me?" she asked, making her voice soft this time.

"You'll see."

She studied him in the dim light from the car's dash. She should be terrified right now, she should be trying to plan her escape. But if he intended to harm her, he sure had a funny way of going about it.

They stopped at a service station outside Milan. He made a call while he filled the car, then he went inside and came back with two steaming cups of espresso. He handed one to her, then dug a couple things out of his pocket. One was a package of wipes for her bloody hands. The other was a package of Baci, the dark chocolate and hazelnut "kisses" from Perugia.

"I thought you could use a little sugar," he said as he put the car in gear again.

"*Grazie*," she murmured. She cleaned her hands, then put one of the chocolates in her mouth and let it melt on her tongue before she bit down into the crunchy hazelnuts at the center. Chocolate had never tasted so good.

When they reached Milan, instead of going to her neighborhood, he pulled onto a tree-lined avenue, one of the surviving sections of grand old homes in the city, and stopped in front of an imposing palazzo. "Guess who lives here?" he asked.

"I can't imagine."

"Paolo Zambrotta. Your co-judge."

She laughed. "You must be joking."

"Well, officially, his mistress lives here."

"And you would know that because…?"

"Because he's in the pocket of the man who wants my current employer dead."

She stared at the house. "Anyone could be living there."

He put the car in park, but kept the engine idling while he got out. He stepped up to a planter near the entrance and scooped a handful of gravel out of it, then pelted it at the front windows—not hard enough to break the glass, but enough to make a racket.

The light out front turned on, then the door opened and a man stepped out. His hair was mussed and his shirt untucked, but she'd know him anywhere. Paolo Zambrotta. "What the hell are you doing?" he shouted at Ruggero.

Ignoring the question, Ruggero strolled back to the car and got behind the wheel.

Zambrotta yelled at Ruggero to get the fuck out of there and gave him the horns, then went back inside.

Ruggero eased the car away from the curb. "Now do you believe me?"

She unwrapped another Baci. She could hardly believe it, but she wasn't going to argue. No judge could afford to live here honestly, and she knew the man didn't come from money. "You've made your point."

He exhaled softly. "So now the question is: What do I do with you?"

A shiver ran over her skin. "What do you mean?"

"I can't take you home, and you can't stay with me."

"Of course I can go home—"

"And who will guard you?"

She could have smacked herself. She really must be in shock. "I don't know what to do."

"We can go to a hotel for the night."

"What about my mother?"

"I have men watching her."

All of a sudden she remembered and bolted up straight in her seat. "My purse!"

"The men will find it. They won't leave a trace of you in that house. You'll have it back by morning."

"I'll pay you back for the hotel."

"Don't worry about it."

"I can't be beholden to you."

He laughed, a warm rumble that went on and on until she started to smile. "Okay, I'm being absurd, aren't I?"

He turned to her and his lips curved up slightly. "Just a bit."

She settled back in the seat and unwrapped another chocolate. "Want one?"

"I bought them for you."

"You must like them too, or else you wouldn't have chosen them."

A corner of his mouth turned up and he nodded, then accepted the chocolate she held out to him. Taking one for herself, she said, "If anyone had ever told me I'd end up in a car eating chocolates with a Mafioso who'd just saved my life, I'd have died from laughter."

He said nothing, but his hands tightened on the wheel, and she swore the temperature in the car dropped several degrees. He didn't look her way again, just took them into downtown and didn't stop until they were at one of the most lavish hotels in the city. He grabbed an overnight bag from his trunk, then escorted her inside, his hand at the small of her back, his eyes sweeping the lobby as they approached the front desk.

When Ruggero spoke, the male clerk straightened his posture. In contrast to how he addressed her, Ruggero's voice was the low, commanding rumble of a man other men didn't argue with. The clerk looked uneasy as he studied the scar on Ruggero's face, but the sudden appearance of a thick wad of euros got them a suite on the top floor.

When they reached the suite, Ruggero made two calls—first to room service, where he ordered for both of them without asking what she wanted, then he called the concierge and asked for someone to bring up a first-aid kit.

They sat at opposite ends of the sofa that dominated the sitting area of their suite, neither of them saying a word. He hadn't spoken to her since her crack in the car. "Look, I'm sorry about what I said—"

He raised a hand. "If I were a Mafioso—which I'm not—well, that would just be the worst thing in the world, wouldn't it? Never mind that it was a *carabinieri* officer who sold you out. A Mafioso couldn't possibly be any better than dog shit you'd scrape off your shoe."

She started to interrupt, but he gave her a stare that made her close her mouth. "I grew up in Calabria; I understand those people. You don't have a fucking clue what desperation drives them into that life. You and your privilege and your money. Not a fucking clue."

She bristled at his tone. "How could I *not* think you were in the Mafia?"

"Seventy percent of the *carabinieri* are from the South. Just because I'm from Calabria, that doesn't mean anything."

Was he serious? His expression said he was, that he meant what he said. If he was lying, he was damn good at it. *Psychopaths always are.*

"What am I supposed to think? You just killed four men."

"And those men planned to kill you. Or did that escape your notice?"

"I'm a *judge*. I've broken the law twice now since we've met," she said. "You can't expect me to shrug and say 'oh well' and not question a damn thing."

"Your circumstances have changed. You can't afford to stand on principles and niceties right now, because the man who's after you certainly won't."

A knock came at the door and he rose, slipping out a Beretta as he approached the door. "Who is it?" he asked.

"I've got the first-aid kit you requested, *signore*."

He opened the door and gave the bellman a few euros, then brought the kit over to her. "We need to patch you up."

She reached for the kit. "I can manage on my own."

He started to say something, but stopped himself. "You know where I am if you need help."

She stood, eager to escape to her room and its adjoining bath. "I'm going to take a shower."

He sat down on the sofa, barely looking at her. An apology rose to her tongue again, but she bit it back. She was who she was; she didn't need to apologize for it. "*Grazie*," she said instead.

He looked up at her then and nodded, his face impassive. But she could swear his eyes bored holes in her back all the way to the door to her room.

CHAPTER 11

You can't afford to stand on principles and niceties right now. Those words rang in Loredana's ears. Was Ruggero right? After everything that had happened—the abduction, her near-rape, Stefano's death—maybe he was. She'd certainly let her principles slide when she watched Ruggero kill Stefano, hadn't she?

Loredana took the first-aid kit into the gorgeous marble bath and started the shower. Then she stripped down, wincing at the bruises revealed in the mirror, at the dried and crusted blood on her abdomen.

Taking a shaky breath, she got into the shower, letting the hot spray beat on her chilled skin. She washed slowly, turning the water hotter when she started to shiver again. She closed her eyes, but all she could picture was Stefano slashing her sweater apart, the dark greed on his face when she'd finally dropped to her knees before him.

What would have happened if Ruggero hadn't found her? How could she possibly have escaped? She might have killed Stefano, but what about the others?

Tears leaked from her eyes, mixing with the spray from the shower. She'd watched Ruggero kill a man. She should be on the phone right now, calling the *carabinieri*, reporting what she'd seen, but how could she repay him with jail after he'd saved her life?

And if she were honest with herself, truly honest, wasn't part of her glad Stefano was dead, that those other men were too? If she could have, she would have killed them to escape. They'd planned to rape her, then murder her. And Stefano—the man she'd thought might possibly be more than just a guard to her someday—he'd betrayed her trust in the cruelest way. He'd used her. He'd tried to—

Balling up a washcloth and turning the water to scalding, she scrubbed at her skin, scraping off Stefano's touch. The sobbing came hard again, and she sank to the bottom of the shower, her cries echoing off the tiles. She curled up in the corner, huddled under the hot water, but somehow unable to get warm.

A gust of cool air alerted her to the door opening. A hand reached in and shut off the water, then a large towel descended over her and Ruggero stepped inside and scooped her up into his arms.

"I'm getting you... all... wet," she said between sobs. He'd taken off the leather coat and his suit jacket, but he still wore the shoulder holster and gun over his sweater.

"Doesn't matter." He set her on her feet, careful to preserve her modesty with the towel. Turning away, he grabbed a plush terry robe from the back of the door. He held it out to her without looking, and she swiped at her tears and took a deep breath before slipping it on.

He turned then, and she stood there, staring at him, feeling numb and vacant, her throat tight. "I'm so stupid," she finally said.

His brow creased and he shook his head. "You're one of the most intelligent people I know."

"But I trusted him. I let him kiss me."

His face darkened. "He was a liar and a traitor. You did nothing wrong."

"I should have known. You warned me."

"But not about him. I didn't know who it was. I didn't even know for sure."

"I should have been more alert, on guard, I should have—"

He pressed a finger to her lips. "Stop blaming yourself."

After a moment, she nodded.

"Dry off, then come out and eat. That will help."

She toweled herself off and bandaged the cut on her belly, then put on the robe. She could hardly bear to look at the clothes she'd been wearing, not that they were wearable anyway. They'd have to get her something new tomorrow.

Tightening the tie on her robe, she headed out to the sitting area, where a table had been set up with two chairs. Their meals were under covers at their seats, while Ruggero sat on the sofa idly flipping through a book detailing local attractions. He rose when she entered and pulled out a chair for her.

For some reason, the gesture made her blush, but he didn't seem to notice. He pulled the cork out of a bottle of pinot grigio and poured them each a glass. Then he lifted the cover off her dinner and took his seat.

"*Grazie*," she said, staring at the risotto with chicken, artichokes, and truffles that he'd ordered for her.

"I thought it would be easy on your stomach." He cut into a thick veal chop.

"You're very considerate."

"For a Mafioso."

She reddened. "That's not what I said."

"It's what you meant."

"No, it's not."

He lifted his glass of wine. "Ah, then. I'm very considerate for an uneducated sheepherder from Calabria." He took a sip, his eyes holding hers, as if daring her to contradict him.

She opened her mouth to speak, then closed it. Then she tried again. "I meant no disrespect. You are not what I expected."

He took another bite of the chop. "I'm happy I can dispel some stereotypes about Calabrians." But he sounded just the opposite.

Loredana searched for another topic, something utterly neutral. She took a forkful of the risotto, the earthy taste of the shaved truffles heaven to her tongue. "This is delicious."

"I'm glad you're enjoying it." He spoke to the plate, not to her.

Dio mio, he wasn't going to make this easy. Maybe he wasn't lying about not being in the Mafia. "Why did you choose your line of work?"

He set down his utensils and wiped his mouth with his napkin. He said nothing for a moment, then he turned to her. "I didn't have much choice in the matter."

"Did someone hold a gun to your head?"

"My father did this work. He trained me, and he made the decision not to join a *cosca*. He moved us north, found us jobs working for rich businessmen who needed private security. After that, my path was set."

"You couldn't make your own choice? You couldn't have stayed, you couldn't have joined the Mafia? If you'd wanted to?"

He shook his head. "I'd be turning my back on my family. My blood. Besides, it's not like I had much choice anyway."

"Of course there were other options."

He huffed out a laugh. "Oh yes, the South is just bursting with jobs and opportunity."

"Many Southerners aren't in the Mafia."

He smirked. "You don't say."

She had to chuckle. "I guess I made that point for you."

"Well, it's true. And the South is always on the edge of starving. Until the North stops ignoring the South and starts investing in it, nothing will ever change."

"But there have been construction projects, investments—"

"Half-hearted at best, utterly mercenary at worst. The North supplies materials for those projects at obscene prices and then hires illegal immigrants over native Southerners because they'll work for nothing. And then who do they put in charge of the final results? Their own cronies."

"What should be done, then?"

He leaned forward. "Investments in higher education, pledges to hire the graduates for good jobs located in the South, not just good jobs in the North. Otherwise nothing will ever change."

"Do you want it to?"

A corner of his mouth turned up. "What a question."

"Do you?"

"Of course. I want better things for the South."

"What about better things for yourself?"

"I put my life on the line for rich men. It's what I've been trained for." He tapped his chest. "All I have to offer is a strong body, and a particular set of skills."

"And your children? Will you train them to do the same work?"

"I don't plan to have any."

"But if you did."

He stared down at his plate. "No. It's not what I would want for them." He didn't say anything else for a long moment, then he looked up at her. "What about you? Why did you choose to be a judge, out of everything you could have done?"

She opened her mouth and realized her answer was much the same as his. And then she realized he'd already guessed that. Anyone who'd read the news stories about her could put two and two together. "I didn't have much choice."

He scoffed, mocking her. "You don't say."

She ignored the jibe. "Both my parents were judges, and after my father was killed and my mother retired, she talked of nothing else but the day when I'd take the bench and continue his work."

"What would you have done if you hadn't become a judge?"

She took another forkful of risotto. "I don't really know. I never thought much about it."

"*Davvero?*"

She looked away, her throat tightening. She *had* thought about it. Many times. "The things I wanted to do were frivolous."

"Such as?"

"When I was in school, I enjoyed being on stage. Acting, singing. Performing."

"What was your favorite role?"

"Lady Macbeth."

"Why?"

"She drives the action, and she's not afraid to go after what she wants." She paused. "Unlike me."

He took a sip of his wine. "No one wants to disappoint their parents."

"And what did *you* want to be?"

"Like you, I loved Shakespeare. I would have been happy studying literature for a living, maybe being a professor."

She bit back a laugh. "I have a hard time picturing it."

"I do too, now." He gestured to the scar.

"You could have surgery to minimize it, as I keep reminding my mother."

"Some things shouldn't be forgotten." His face darkened.

There was a story there. "How did you get it?"

Pointedly not looking at her, he took another drink from his glass, then started in on his chop again. "We need to discuss what you're going to say about tonight."

She tried again. "I would like to know the story someday. If you're willing to tell me."

He continued to not look at her. "The men will make it look like a drug deal gone bad. They'll remove all trace of you being in the house and the van."

Okay, so they weren't going to talk about it. Yet. "But they'll leave Stefano. Who was last seen with me at the gun range."

"Yes. So you're going to need to explain why he wasn't with you. It's best if the story is as close to the truth as possible, so here's what I think. You say that six days ago, a man—that *stronzo* in the tracksuit—threatened you at the courthouse. I intervened and gave you my card."

He reached inside his suit jacket and pulled out a silver case. He took a card from it that gave his name and said "Vela Private Security" below it and listed a number. "I recommended that you hire me if you were unhappy with the protection provided by the *carabinieri*. Stefano showed up—late—that day at the courthouse and we had words, but you elected to stick with the *carabinieri* because I also provide protection to the defendant in the Lucchesi case and you weren't sure how it would look. Okay so far?"

She nodded. It was close enough to the truth that she could easily remember it, and had there been any witnesses to what had happened at the courthouse, their story wouldn't contradict hers. However… "You do work for Enrico Lucchesi." She waved the card at him. "Does this company really exist? If the prosecution does prove that he is a Mafioso, can I plausibly claim that I didn't know you were?"

He sighed. "I'm not in the Mafia, and I'm not going to repeat it again. The company exists, and I'm the head of it. The Banca di Falcone pays me and the men on my payroll to provide protection for their employees, chiefly Signor Lucchesi. But several other companies also pay us for security."

"Are any of them *not* owned by Signor Lucchesi?"

"Quite a few, yes."

"Business associates of his?"

He shrugged. "Perhaps, perhaps not. I couldn't say. But even if they were, it would take a long time to prove anything, if anyone were inclined to dig. And in any case, you would be blameless."

"Okay, then. So, what's the rest of my story?"

He continued. "After that initial incident, the same man continued to shadow you and make threats, and today you saw him outside the gun range when you finished target shooting. You and Stefano then had an argument about your safety, and he got very upset. He'd been acting a bit strangely for a while, erratic and high-strung. He'd also come on to you several times, especially today, and you weren't sure it was a good idea to get involved, but you also weren't sure what would happen if you turned him down, so you were stringing him along." He paused. "Will that work with what happened today at the range?"

She thought for a moment. "Yes. We kissed a little and flirted, but I also pushed him away at least once, so if anyone was paying attention, I think they could say I wasn't completely sold. And he was the one initiating everything."

Ruggero held her eyes, saying nothing. He seemed to be studying her, then he nodded. "*Bene.* So after the two of you came out and saw the man and fought about your safety, you demanded that Stefano take you to see me, and he did. Once I heard about how this man had been following you and that he knew where you lived, I suggested you become my client, and I took you to a hotel for your safety."

"*Is* it safe here?" she asked.

"We weren't followed, and I've never stayed here before."

"And you gave the desk clerk a false name." The man hadn't even asked for hers; he must have realized he wouldn't get an answer.

"We'll have to be more careful once you start going to court, but I'll have assistance then to make sure our location stays secret."

"I should call my mother and tell her what happened. She's going to start worrying soon. And I need to leave a message for my assistant that there will be no court tomorrow."

He nodded. "*Bene.*" He took a phone from his overnight bag and handed it to her. "This phone is clean; if someone gets the number, it'll do them no good, because I'll destroy the chip right after you use it, so the phone can't be tracked."

Dio mio, it's like living in a spy movie. She placed the call to her clerk, claiming illness, then she called her mother, surprised by how easily the lies flowed from her lips. It was just like acting; she had a part to play, and she played it.

"Are you sure you're safe?" her mother asked when Loredana finished her story.

"I'm sure, Mamma." That was the first entirely truthful thing she'd said.

"When are you coming home?"

"I don't know yet. I'll have to discuss it with Signor Vela."

"Be careful, *dolcezza*."

"I will." They said their goodbyes and hung up. She turned to Ruggero. "Good enough?"

"*Perfetto*." He removed the chip from the phone, then snapped it in half. "Maybe you should have been an actress."

"Perhaps." She picked up her glass of wine and raised it for a toast. "To what may be."

He tapped his glass against hers and took a swallow. When he set the glass down, he seemed lost in thought. Was he thinking about his own alternative future?

"Ruggero—"

His eyes snapped to hers. "That's the first time you've said my name. I wasn't sure you knew it."

She pointed to the card. "If I didn't already know it, I certainly would now."

"So you did remember."

"How could I ever forget?"

A smile played along his lips. "Our introduction *was* memorable."

It was her turn to look away, her cheeks growing hot. Should she be honest? Her belly fluttered, but she said the words anyway. "I've thought of it more than once."

"So have I." No hesitation.

The fluttering intensified, threatened to make her shiver. Slowly she lifted her gaze, met those silver eyes, that wolf's stare, head on. *I can't stop thinking about you*, she wanted to say, but her mouth had gone dry. The silence lay heavy between them, pulsing with meaning. What was he thinking?

His eyes roamed over her face, studying her. "Are you all right?"

"I suppose so."

"I mean, are you still in shock?"

She took a quick inventory—no shivers; her breathing was normal, well, slightly fast, but normal; and she didn't feel lethargic or cold. "No. I'm fine. Why do you ask?"

"You said you'd been thinking about me."

"So did you."

He chuckled. "Of course I would." He picked up the fork and knife and gestured up and down at her. "You're very attractive, and I'm... not. I wanted to be sure you're okay."

"What are you talking about?"

He cut another piece off the chop. "Every man you meet must think about you."

"I doubt it. But what I'm wondering is why you think I wouldn't find you attractive."

He snorted. "Many reasons."

"Well, I do."

He stopped chewing for a moment. Finally he swallowed and took a sip of his wine, holding her eyes all the while. He set down the glass, that stare making her stomach flip. "So, now you're going to tell me that while you were flirting with Stefano today, you were actually thinking about me." His voice was low, his words carefully chosen, an edge behind them.

She blushed again, an excruciating flush that rose from her chest to her cheeks. "In fact I was. And I'd hoped that if I slept with him, I'd *stop* thinking about you."

He turned that stare on her again, but this time there was something darker in it. "Is that what you thought?" She couldn't read his tone.

She nodded, unable to speak.

He pushed back from the table and rose. "Stop fucking with me." The ice was back in his eyes. He tossed the napkin next to his plate and stalked off to his bedroom.

Should she go after him? She pushed the risotto around on her plate. Nothing had changed since earlier in the day, when she'd concluded that anything between them was impossible.

And yet, everything was different.

She went to his door, hesitating outside it. She heard water running, and she knocked. No answer. Her stomach cartwheeling, she knocked louder. Again, no response.

She tried the knob; it wasn't locked. Opening the door, she called his name, her voice faltering, and she doubted he heard her over the shower. No way was she going to just walk in on him. He may have done it to her, but he'd had a good reason. She didn't.

She sat down on his bed, her back to the open bathroom door, her heart pounding as she untied her robe, but didn't remove it. What was she doing? He was right to question her; *had* she lost her mind?

The water shut off after several minutes, then she heard him padding around. She knew when Ruggero saw her because he inhaled sharply.

Turning her head, she looked at him in the doorway. He was wrapping a towel around his hips, the broad, flat planes of his chest and the rippling muscles of his abdomen and arms gleaming in the light.

There was a tattoo on his right bicep, a bloody stiletto with a serpent wrapped around it, and he bore scars on his chest, belly, and arms, old wounds caused by a mix of knives and guns, from what she could see. He didn't move toward her, didn't say a word. Just stared, as if he didn't believe his eyes.

She said the only thing she could think of. "I'm not toying with you." Still he said nothing, still he didn't move. She rose and approached him slowly, his face giving away so little she wasn't sure she was welcome.

By the time she reached him, her heart was beating so fast she felt faint. Reaching up, she traced the scar that ran beside his left eye, then cut across his cheekbone.

Suddenly he grabbed her wrist, making her wince. "If this is some kind of game—"

"It's not."

"I don't believe you." His chest rose and fell rapidly and a muscle worked in his jaw. She opened her robe, to show him she was serious, and after a glance she almost didn't catch, he looked away. When she touched his chest, he flinched and stepped back.

"I don't understand," she said. "What's wrong?"

Still not looking at her, he said, "Everything about this is wrong. You're not ready for this."

"I am. I'm fine, Ruggero."

His eyes locked on her face, he pulled the sides of her robe together. "You aren't."

The softness of his tone, the compassion in his gaze, brought a lump to her throat. "I *am* fine," she tried to insist, but her voice shook.

"You don't have to be strong all the time, *bambina*." He stroked a hand lightly over her hair, the gravel in his voice softening, reduced to the whisper of water over stones.

Whether it was his words or his tenderness, she didn't know, but Loredana burst into tears. He pulled her into his chest, once again enclosing her in his strong arms.

She sobbed against him, barely aware when he picked her up and carried her to her room. He laid her on the bed, but when he tried to go, she clung to him, unable to ask him to stay, but unable to let him go. He eased down onto the bed beside her and pulled the coverlet across them both. For some reason the gesture only made her cry harder. He was being so kind to her, and why? She'd been nasty to him. He'd saved her life, and all she could do was spew venom. And then she'd tried to seduce him. Why?

What must he think of her?

She blushed fiercely and started to pull away, but he held her close. "What do you need?" he asked, his chest rumbling under her ear.

Loredana took a deep, steadying breath. "I'm fine. Really I am. You can go now."

"That's what you want?"

Not at all. She shook her head and wiped at her eyes.

"Then why send me away?"

She had to admit it. "I'm sorry. I don't know what's happening to me. I've been awful to you. And then I—" She couldn't say it, couldn't form the words.

He didn't say anything for a long time. "And then you what?" he finally asked.

She pressed her face against his chest. "I'm so embarrassed."

He chuckled, the sound making her smile despite herself. "I've already forgotten about it."

"I don't think I *ever* will."

Stroking her hair, he said, "Today has been one of the worst days of your life, yes?" He waited for her to nod. "Everyone reacts differently to stress."

"Apparently, it turns me into a slut."

His hand tightened on her head. "I am sorry."

"For what?"

He sighed. "That comment I made. About you being on your knees for him. I was angry, and I took it out on you."

"Why were you so upset?" She looked up at him.

A muscle ticked in his jaw. "He hurt you."

"And that matters to you?"

He didn't reply, just resumed stroking her hair. She wanted to press him for an answer, but the tension in his body told her not to. Could it be that this brutal man, this merciless killer, had a heart somewhere beneath that cold exterior?

After a time, he started to hum, the same lullaby he'd crooned to her at the farmhouse, and she closed her eyes. She was safe, for now. But how long would it last?

CHAPTER 12

Ruggero didn't know how long he lay in Loredana's bed, cradling her in his arms, but she eventually relaxed against him, her breathing evening out and finally passing into the regular rhythm of sleep.

She'd asked him such a simple question. *Why were you so upset?* And he'd given her half an answer. And then no answer when she'd pressed for more.

Because there was more. And it scared the hell out of him.

He should have known, the minute she'd started to haunt his thoughts, to occupy his dreams. He should have known, and he should have done something about it. He should have tried harder with Chiara, should have tried harder to fuck Loredana Montisi out of his mind. Because that was never going to happen in real life, despite her offer. She was mixed up, messed up, and tomorrow, after a good night's sleep, she'd take a hard look at him and run the other way. Any sane woman would.

Damn him for thinking otherwise, even for a second. Hell was the only thing he deserved, what he brought with him. A woman like Loredana deserved more. She deserved a man who could love her. A man who could keep her safe. A man who could give her children.

He could do none of those things. He could only bring her destruction, disappointment, and death. And that he was determined never to do. Loredana deserved better. She deserved a man who could live with her in the light, not one who clung to the shadows.

By careful degrees, he slid out from under her and placed a pillow beneath her head. She must have been exhausted; she slept the way a child did, the way Luca did after an afternoon of playing with Cocco.

He left a lamp on in the corner of the room so she wouldn't be disoriented when she woke. He should stay with her, but he couldn't. He needed to be away from her. He needed to stop this feeling that had invaded his chest, his gut, this overwhelming need to pull her close and not let go.

He especially needed to get his *cazzo* away from her, because it had even worse ideas.

She wasn't his, and she'd never be his. And he had to get that through his thick skull.

He padded down the hall to his room and closed the door behind him. Letting out a long sigh, he looked down at the erection that hadn't gotten the memo. *Cristo.* She made him feel like a horny teenager, and the memory of her in his arms, the soft lushness of her, the mounds of her breasts, the scent of her hair, that perfect, heart-shaped ass he wanted to squeeze…

Blood thumped through his cock, reminding him that it had been over a month. Reminding him that she was in the next room. Reminding him of that glimpse he'd gotten of her breasts when she'd opened her robe, of the dark triangle of her *figa*, that glimpse he'd stolen, no matter how strong his resolve not to look. It wasn't right of him to take advantage of her like that.

But fuck… he didn't want to be a gentleman. He didn't want to be anything other than a beast.

Stripping off the towel and scrubbing it over his damp hair, he approached the bed and saw the dent in the coverlet that she'd made. He let out a little groan, remembering all over again the sight of her sitting on his bed, waiting for him. The way he'd felt then, wanting to go to her, to push that robe off her shoulders, to fuck her without mercy, to make her cry out his name.

Fuck it. He took his *cazzo* in hand. It was that, or do something he'd later regret.

His mind went to that image of her on her knees. Except he was the one standing before her, and she was more than willing.

Was he sick to think of her that way, so soon after what had almost happened to her?

Yes, he was a sick bastard. *Sick and wrong.*

Instead, he pulled up the memory of her opening the robe. And this time, it fell to the floor, and he didn't hesitate to go to her.

It didn't take him long to come, but as soon as he did, he realized how hollow he felt. He wanted her still, wanted to feel her in his arms, wanted to hear her moaning in his ear. He wanted *her*, not some poor substitute. And every image he conjured up in his mind was nowhere near what it had felt like to actually hold her, touch her…

"Fuck." He lay back on the bed, exhausted and wired at the same time. His *cazzo* begged him to walk down the hall, to open her door, to get in her bed. She wouldn't refuse.

But *he* had to. He had to stop this. She was eroding his self-control; the brutal way he'd killed Stefano right in front of her proved it. She could send him to jail in an instant, no matter what he said or how hard he tried to implicate her. She held his life, his freedom, in her hands.

And for *what*? Because he couldn't control himself and send for someone else to take care of Stefano after he'd taken her away? He hadn't given it a second thought. The minute he'd seen what Stefano was trying to force her to do, every cell in his body had exploded into white-hot rage. He'd played it cool for her, but he'd barely resisted the impulse to stomp on Stefano's face until only a bloody pulp remained. He grabbed a cigarette from the pack in his jacket and lit up, walking over to the window that looked out on the darkened streets of Milan. The Duomo gleamed in the distance, brilliantly illuminated at night, a dusting of snow still falling. God's house, somewhere he no longer felt welcome.

He tried to tell himself that Stefano's death was justified—an eye for an eye. Stefano had taken something from Loredana, and he'd needed to pay for it. But that wasn't the whole truth. Ruggero had hated Stefano the minute he'd realized that Loredana had wanted the man, the minute she'd allowed Stefano to kiss her in the parking lot of the gun range. *That* was the truth.

Resting his forehead against the cool glass, Ruggero studied his reflection laid over the scene outside. The eyes that stared back at him were cold, hard, and the face surrounding them was harsh and unforgiving. He was what he was, inside and out: a killer.

Finding an ashtray, he stubbed out the cigarette and took a deep breath. He had to shut off these emotions somehow, had to crush this longing for her before it crushed him.

———◆———

The phone on the nightstand buzzed harshly, and Ruggero experienced a moment's disorientation as he reached for it. Then the events of the night before came roaring back, tangling up in his dreams of sex and violence.

He glanced at the display. Tommaso. "Yeah?"

"We've got her purse. Want me to bring it up?"

"*Sì.* 1415." He ended the call, then pulled on the change of clothes he had with him. He stopped outside Loredana's door, listening for the sound of her breathing. He finally heard it, the light sighs of someone deeply asleep, and a wave of relief washed over him. She could've bolted in the night, but she hadn't. Maybe because she'd been too exhausted to move.

There was a tap at the outer door, and Ruggero let Tommaso in.

"We cleaned it all up, very carefully. Left that pig naked."

Ruggero couldn't help a half-smile at the image of Stefano naked for his colleagues to find. "*Bene.* Did you replace the chip in her phone?"

"*Sì.* You need anything else?"

"No. But stay close." Tommaso's brows lowered, and something like disappointment crossed his face. "What's wrong?" Ruggero asked.

"Nothing."

The old guard waved him off, but Ruggero wasn't fooled. "Tell me."

Now Tommaso wouldn't meet his eyes. "Truly, it's nothing."

"It's something."

Tommaso's eyes flicked to his, then his face reddened. Oh fuck, was this about Loredana? "I have something I need to ask you, man to man."

Damn it, it was. Ruggero crossed his arms. "Just say it."

Fiddling with the buttons of his coat, Tommaso spoke to the floor. "What would you think about your sister and me?"

Had he heard correctly? Tommaso was interested in Elena?

Tommaso met his eyes, his flush deepening. "Look. Never mind. I can see you think it's a bad idea."

"No. That's not it. Give me a second." He stared at Tommaso, wondering when this had happened. "You two... haven't, have you?"

With a quick shake of his head, Tommaso said, "Absolutely not. I wouldn't even touch her hand without asking you."

"But you've talked to her? You know how she feels?"

Tommaso shrugged, then he smiled to himself. "We flirted a little on the trip up to Milan. I don't think she took me seriously, but she didn't shut me down, either. And I just... Every time I see her, I want to tell her how beautiful she is. But not just to flirt, you know? To really tell her."

Letting out a sigh, Ruggero nodded. He knew. He knew exactly how Tommaso felt.

"So that's a no?"

"You have my permission"—Ruggero put a hand on Tommaso's shoulder and squeezed—"but make sure you have hers. You hurt her, and I'll hurt you."

His broad face splitting into a grin, Tommaso beamed at him. "I'll treat her like a princess."

This time, Ruggero squeezed the back of Tommaso's neck with affection. He'd known the man for over a decade; he was true and loyal, a dedicated soldier, one of the men he trusted most. "You're a good man, Tommaso. I would be honored to have you in my family, if that's what Elena wants."

Ducking his head, Tommaso smiled. "*Mille grazie.*"

Ruggero thought for a second; he could send Tommaso on this errand, but he didn't want to. "I need you to stay here and watch over the judge while I pick up something."

"Of course." Tommaso ambled over to the sofa while Ruggero headed to Loredana's room. He listened again. She was still asleep. He eased the door open and stepped inside. He could just ask her what he needed to know, but he didn't want to disturb her. He crept into the bathroom and found what he was looking for wadded up in the dustbin: the ruined, bloody sweater and her slacks from the night before. Those were going to have to be burned. But not before he looked at their tags. He slipped out with the clothing still in hand and gave it to Tommaso. Motioning to the balcony, he said, "Burn this."

"Will do."

"I'll be back in an hour or so." They were in a fashionable part of Milan; it wouldn't take long to find what he needed.

—————◆—————

Loredana's eyes snapped open. For a moment she forgot where she was, then she remembered. Rolling over, she was disappointed to find the bed empty. Ruggero had left. But what had she expected?

And really, it was for the best. She'd been a mess last night. Shaky, exhausted, confused. He'd been right to refuse her. What on earth had she been thinking? A gun for hire and a judge? It was like something out of a bad movie.

After showering again to tame her hair—she desperately needed a brush—she wrapped herself up in the robe and braced herself for seeing him. What did he think of her after last night?

Heart beating fast, she turned the knob and stepped into the hall. A few more steps brought her into the main room of the suite. It was empty. A series of thuds coming from the balcony drew her attention.

A man she didn't know was out there, stomping on something that smoldered on the concrete. It was far too big to be a cigarette. She walked over to the glazed double doors and opened one, cold air gliding in and snaking up her legs. Up close, she saw gray in the stranger's brown hair. He looked to be in his early fifties, a big barrel-chested man with twinkling eyes. "Who are you?" she asked.

"Tommaso. Ruggero's... friend."

"And what are you doing?"

He grinned at her. "Just some cleanup."

"What cleanup?"

"Your clothes, *signorina*."

"Ah." Yes, the sweater covered in her blood. Maybe a few spots of Stefano's too. She touched her belly, and the soreness of her wound grounded her. She was not sorry he was dead, for if Ruggero hadn't intervened, Stefano would certainly not have been sorry for anything that happened to her. He'd been a charming bastard. She'd thought him different from Daniele, made of sterner stuff, but she'd mistaken Stefano's hardness for something other than what it was: selfishness, pure and simple.

"I have your purse," Tommaso said, motioning her inside and gesturing to where it lay on the coffee table. "I had to change the chip in your phone, but I transferred all your contacts over."

"*Mille grazie,*" she said. Grabbing her phone, she called her office number to check messages. There was only one, from a *carabiniere* who wanted to ask her about Stefano; he was missing. Her stomach started to quiver. "Fuck," she muttered under her breath, and Tommaso chuckled from his seat on the sofa.

"Where is Ruggero?" she asked.

He shrugged. "Out. Said he'd be back"—he checked his watch—"any minute now." He rubbed his belly. "You hungry? I didn't get breakfast." She was, but could she eat, knowing she'd have to lie to the *carabinieri* later in the day? Well, she'd managed a dinner after what had happened last night, so she could manage breakfast, yes? And she could manage the *carabinieri* too. She'd already lied to her mother; they weren't going to be much more difficult.

"Order us something," she said. "Not a lot for me though."

He grabbed the hotel phone. "You could stand to eat a bit more, you know. A man likes hips."

She stared at him for a second, then laughed at the wink he gave her. He was so much more relaxed than Ruggero. He could've been one of her uncles over for a visit, if it weren't for the bulge of a firearm under his left armpit. When he hung up, she sat down across from him. "I want to ask you something."

"Shoot."

"Is Ruggero always so..." She cast about for the right word.

"Intense?" Tommaso asked.

She nodded. That was the perfect word for him.

Again, Tommaso shrugged. "He is what he is."

"That wasn't much of an answer."

Tommaso leaned forward. "He's exactly who he needs to be. Though"—he ran a hand across the top of his graying head—"he could lighten up every once in a while."

"Could I now." They both started at Ruggero's voice. How had he entered without either of them hearing? A flush heated her cheeks. How much of that had he heard?

He held up a carrier bag with the name of a famous designer on it. "Try these on."

Apparently he'd solved her clothing problem. "Whatever you spent, I'll pay you back," she said, taking the bag.

His thick fingers closed over hers. "It's a gift." When she opened her mouth to protest, he cut her off. "I insist."

A strange pleasure filled her at his tone and the rumble in his voice, the heat in his gaze. She nodded and accepted the bag.

She took it into the bedroom, dying to see what he'd purchased. Was it something trashy, or something she'd actually like?

Opening the bag, she saw several boxes, including a small one that had been gift-wrapped. She saved that one for last, and opened the others instead. The first held a cashmere sweater, similar to the one she'd been wearing. The next box held a pair of black pants that were cut to slip over a pair of boots. The last box contained a lacy bra and panty set, both items black.

Everything was exactly to her taste, and it all fit surprisingly well, even the bra. She admired herself in the mirror. The sweater was the same shade of green as her eyes, and she'd bet that was no coincidence.

She eyed the gift-wrapped box. What was in it? And should she accept?

Unable to resist, she loosened the bow, then removed the fancy foil paper to reveal a box of Caffarel Gianduia. She smiled. He must have guessed from her enjoyment of the Baci the night before that she loved chocolate with hazelnuts, and Caffarel was among the very best. How sweet of him.

Someone tapped on the door. "Food's here," Ruggero said.

She took another look in the mirror. Of course, he'd based the choices on what she'd been wearing, but that color—well, he'd certainly been paying attention. She doubted Daniele could have pulled that off after spending a year with her. And she'd spent what? Less than a day with Ruggero?

When she came out to the living room, Ruggero and Tommaso were talking and drinking their espresso at a table that room service had brought in. They both paused at her appearance. Tommaso whistled, and Ruggero elbowed him. But Ruggero didn't take his eyes off her. "Everything okay?" he asked.

"It's perfect," she said. "*Mille grazie.* I couldn't have done a better job myself. And thank you for the Caffarel. They're my favorites."

He looked down, but not before she saw the hint of a smile.

She took a pastry from the tray of sweets and cold cuts that Tommaso had ordered. Sitting across from the men, she poured herself a cup of espresso. Might as well get it over with. "I have to see the *carabinieri* today about Stefano. They said he didn't come in for work."

"You remember what we discussed?" Ruggero said.

She nodded, but she couldn't swallow the bite she'd taken of the pastry.

He leaned forward and reached out, almost as if he were going to take her hand, then he cut the motion short and brought his arm to rest on the linen tablecloth. She glanced at Tommaso, but he seemed not to have noticed. Would Ruggero have touched her if they'd been alone? Her fingers twitched, as if to move closer to his, and she drew her hand back to her lap. She had to stop this. Where could it possibly go?

Nowhere good, that's where.

Ruggero turned to Tommaso. "I want you and the others to relieve the men outside Giudice Montisi's apartment."

Tommaso raised his eyebrows. "You don't want us to go with you to the station?"

"We'll be fine." Ruggero's eyes flicked back to hers. "Besides, I think the judge won't want to have an entourage with her when we go to *carabinieri* headquarters."

With a shrug, Tommaso looked away and scratched his cheek. "You're the boss." He finished his cup, then rose and made a little bow in her direction. "*Signorina*," he said, that smile and wink coming out again.

She couldn't help returning the grin, but hers died when she saw the scowl on Ruggero's face. She waited until Tommaso left before saying anything. "What's wrong?"

"Nothing." He took another sip from his cup, his eyes pinning her to her seat. Clearly she'd done something to piss him off.

"It's not nothing." She crossed her arms. "Tell me."

He looked away, toward the window. "Do you flirt with every man you meet?"

"What?" She realized her mouth was hanging open. "I wasn't flirting with him."

"He was flirting with you."

"It was nothing."

"Was it 'nothing' with Stefano?"

Where was this coming from? "I thought we talked about that last night."

He shook his head. "Actually, we need to stop talking about it." He set down his cup and stood. "Forget I said anything. You can do what you want."

"Of *course* I can." She could barely keep her voice even.

He tapped out a cigarette and gestured to the balcony. "I'll be a minute. We'll leave as soon as you're ready."

Oh! She watched him go, wanting to slap him for his attitude. For the way he just took charge, the way he just assumed she'd follow his lead without question.

Loredana got her coat and purse, stewing all the while, and came back just as Ruggero was stepping inside.

"Ready?" he asked.

"I'll go by myself. You don't need to hover over me."

"You aren't going alone."

"Obviously you aren't that worried, or you wouldn't have sent Tommaso away."

"I didn't want to attract attention. That doesn't mean I think you're safe."

"If I'm not safe surrounded by a building full of *carabinieri*, when *am* I safe?"

Ruggero closed the distance between them, and it took everything Loredana had not to retreat a step when he stopped just inside her comfort zone. "Listen. You are *not* safe. You will never *be* safe until certain people are dealt with. And until they are, you're safest with me. *Capisci?*"

He'd let his Calabrian accent filter into his speech, and a shiver flitted across her back. How quickly, how casually he'd killed Stefano. How quickly he could kill her—or whomever he chose.

"*Capisco.*" She held his eyes, hoping he couldn't see how he'd unnerved her with his presence, with that oh-so-subtle reminder of who he claimed *not* to be, of who she was truly dealing with. Of how the odds were not stacked in her favor.

Finally breaking eye contact, Loredana set down the purse and started to put on her coat. "Allow me," Ruggero said, reaching for it.

She hesitated, then gave the coat up to him. It had been a long time since a man had done this simple thing for her. Her hair got trapped inside the collar, but before she could deal with it herself, he reached in and smoothed it up and over the fabric, his hands grazing her neck, his breath warm on her temple. She put her hands on his wrists before he withdrew them.

"I have never been so confused," she said.

He froze as he looked at her, then he closed his eyes for a moment. "You're not the only one," he murmured.

She released her hold on him and he stepped back, not looking at her.

Her throat clogged with words, feelings, things that she wanted to say but didn't know how, things she didn't even understand.

How did he manage to send her in a million directions at once? She'd been ready to take his head off a few moments ago, and now she wanted him to… what? Hold her? Kiss her?

Loredana took a breath and held it for a moment before slowly letting it out. Yeah, those weren't good ideas. And they weren't going to happen.

Following him out into the hall, she noted how he scanned the corridor left and right before heading to the elevator, but not without making sure she was right behind him.

When the elevator arrived, Ruggero kept himself in front of her until he ascertained that the car was empty, then he motioned her inside. He *was* worried. And he was also protecting her. She should be terrified, but somehow an ember of warmth glowed in her chest.

Yes, Ruggero was doing his job, but she wasn't the only one rattled by this chemistry between them. She wasn't "just" a job to him.

But what exactly she was, and where exactly this could go, was a mystery.

CHAPTER 13

When they got to the Maserati, Ruggero pulled out his phone and called Fuente to make sure he'd be the one conducting the interview. Fuente was compromised, but Ruggero could use that. If he led Fuente to believe that Dario and Enrico were getting along, that news would filter back to Lorenzo. But most importantly, Fuente would report that Loredana was in the Lucchesis' pocket. That would force Lorenzo's hand, and the more impulsively he reacted, the better. Enrico was safely outside the prison system; they could afford to poke Lorenzo and see what happened.

They parked near the *carabinieri* command station in the Vigentino district of Milan. The low-slung concrete building had clearly been designed for function, not elegance. Ruggero scanned the area as he escorted Loredana to the main entrance. Perhaps he should've listened to Tommaso. But what was done was done.

A young clerk took them to Fuente's office, not to an interrogation room. Good. That meant the *carabinieri* had not yet discovered Stefano's body. Fuente rose when they stepped inside. He gestured to the two chairs in front of his desk. "*Prego*," he said. "Would you care for anything to drink?"

"Water, please," Loredana said. Ruggero refused anything. The *carabinieri* didn't have his DNA on file, and he wasn't going to help them get it.

"Do you want me to step out?" Ruggero asked her.

"No." She twisted her fingers together once, then separated them and rested her hands on the armrests, apparently trying to look calm. She almost fooled him. Would she fool Fuente though?

Fuente handed her a bottle of water from a small refrigerator in the corner of his cramped but tidy office. Every item on his desk was lined up carefully, the pictures and commendations on the wall perfectly level and evenly spaced. And as usual, the man was impeccably groomed. Even though he couldn't see them, Ruggero would bet good money that Fuente could admire his own reflection in the shine of his boots.

Picking up a pad and pen, Fuente turned to Loredana. "Giudice Montisi, it's so good of you to come right away. From what we've been able to ascertain, you were the last person to see Brigadiere Gaspare yesterday. I believe he took you to the gun range after his shift ended?"

"Yes. There's been a man hanging around the courthouse. Twice he's made threats to me. I thought it time I learned to shoot. Just in case."

Fuente gave her an understanding smile. "Can you describe this man?"

"Twenties, black hair, very tan skin, usually in a gray tracksuit jacket. Thin, not too tall."

"Any distinguishing marks?"

"No, but from his accent, I'd say he was Calabrian."

"Ah." Fuente glanced at Ruggero. "And how is it that you are in the company of Signor Vela?"

She shifted in her seat and turned it into a flick of her hair over her shoulder. "Signor Vela intervened the first time this man threatened me. He gave me his card, told me he ran a private security firm, and said to call him if I was unhappy with the protection provided by the *carabinieri*."

Fuente smiled again, this time thinly, and tapped his pen against his lips as he turned to Ruggero. "Signor Vela, I wasn't aware you had time to lurk about the courthouse besmirching the reputation of my colleagues."

Ruggero let a shrug speak for him, and Fuente shifted his focus back to Loredana. "Which gun range did Brigadiere Gaspare take you to?" She gave him the name, then he asked, "What happened after you arrived at the range?"

Loredana sighed and leaned forward. "I don't want to say anything out of turn about the sergeant major, but we had a disagreement."

"What about?"

"I'd rather not say. I wouldn't want to get him in trouble."

"We can keep this between us."

She looked down, fidgeting with the hem of her sweater, then took a deep breath. "Brigadiere Gaspare was inappropriate with me."

Fuente raised an eyebrow. "How so?"

"He had been flirting with me for some time, and I had allowed it. But he propositioned me at the range, and I felt that it was inappropriate for us to get involved."

"How did the sergeant major respond?"

"He grew agitated. He said that I had been leading him on."

Fuente stroked his mustache, then he leaned forward. "How did you respond to that?"

She looked down at her lap. "I asked him to take me home. He refused. He said I needed a good hard…" She paused, then continued. "Fucking, was the word he used."

"And then?"

"I got my phone out and called Signor Vela."

Damn. She'd changed the story. They could check her records.

"Why didn't you call Brigadiere Gaspare's superior?"

She said nothing for a moment, then smoothed her hands over her thighs. "There was some truth to what Brigadiere Gaspare said. About me leading him on," she hastened to add. "I admit I enjoyed the attention. He's a handsome man."

Ruggero stifled the impulse to grind his teeth and waited for her to continue.

"I felt it wouldn't be wise to get into a he said/she said disagreement. I told him I'd find my own way home, and that I'd appreciate it if he asked for a reassignment. He said he'd gladly do so. And then he left."

"About what time was this?"

"Late afternoon. I'm not sure of the time, but it was getting dark."

"He was driving his own car? The red Fiat Bravo?"

She nodded. "Has something happened to him?"

"We're not sure. He hasn't reported for duty. He was supposed to be part of your security detail today."

One of Ruggero's men had dumped Stefano's Fiat on the outskirts of Milan. If the *carabinieri* had found it, Fuente wasn't saying.

"Well, perhaps in light of our disagreement yesterday..." She motioned in the air with her hand.

"Yes, he may have taken the day off. As did you. But unlike you, he didn't call in to claim an illness or some such." After a beat, he asked, "Why did you cancel court today?"

She was still for almost too long, then she shrugged. "I didn't want to see him so soon. I was still upset."

"I did not think you were so easily rattled, Giudice Montisi." Fuente held her eyes, but she didn't look away. "Is there anything else you think pertinent?"

"I don't know what else I can tell you. Except..."

Ruggero almost smiled. She was good at this. He could see Fuente taking the bait.

"*Anything* you can tell me might help. He seems to be missing."

"Well, he's been rather erratic lately. On edge, a bit tense. The whole argument between us felt like an extension of that. Like he was upset about something else and he'd finally snapped."

"And you have no idea what was bothering him? Other than you."

She shook her head. "We weren't close."

"And yet you asked him to take you to the gun range during his time off. And you went alone."

"He told me he was a sharpshooter in the military. I figured I ought to learn from the best."

"And this had nothing to do with his feelings—or yours?"

She stiffened, then sighed. "Sottotenente, like I said, I enjoyed the attention. Maybe too much. I didn't realize he took it for more than it was." Then she leaned forward and put a hand on his desk. "I would appreciate your discretion in this matter."

Fuente smiled, his eyes glinting in a way Ruggero didn't like. "I assume, Giudice Montisi, that you are aware of the relationship between Signor Vela and Signor Lucchesi?"

She shook her head, and Fuente chuckled. It was his turn to lean forward. "Come now. Let us speak frankly. You and I, we're backing the same horse." His eyes flicked to Ruggero. "Well, all three of us are."

Loredana straightened in her chair. "I don't know what you're insinuating."

"Either you are hopelessly naïve, or you're a superb actress, Giudice Montisi." He set down the pen and pad. "Is that how you've maintained such a stellar reputation all these years?"

"Whatever reputation I have is one I've earned," she said, the words clipped and even.

"There are whispers that your father was killed because he wasn't as pure as he appeared."

Loredana's face turned crimson and she rose from her chair. "You shouldn't listen to trash."

Ruggero rose with her. Though he'd heard similar rumors, he wanted to punch Fuente for hurting her. However, he'd have to settle for a different sort of score. "You tell your boss—your *true* one—that we've mended fences with his grandson. He'd better tend to his own yard, instead of trying to encroach on his neighbors'." Ruggero didn't wait for Fuente to respond; instead he took Loredana's arm and motioned her out.

She gave him a strange look, but said nothing until they reached the vestibule of the main entrance. She stopped him there and spoke in a furious undertone. "You think you own me, just like you own that slug Fuente. Well, you can tell your boss to fuck off. I belong to no one."

Damn. He should've sent her outside and spoken to Fuente alone. "It's not like that."

"Ah. So if I throw your boss back in jail, he won't ask you to kill me?"

"He's my client, not my boss."

She put her hands on her hips. "Fuente seems to think he is."

"Fuente likes to make mischief."

"You actually think I'm stupid." Her eyes blazed at him.

"Not at all."

After a long pause, she crossed her arms. "So let's say, for the sake of argument, that he *is* your boss. If I send him back to jail, what happens to me?"

"Nothing."

She laughed. "What makes me so special?"

"You're just doing your job. You aren't... part of this."

"But you have killed for him before."

He couldn't help a huff of laughter. "Now who thinks who is stupid?"

"Don't forget I've seen you in action."

He looked around, but no one seemed to be paying them any attention. "You're not so different."

"What the hell are you talking about?"

"You condemn men to life in prison all the time, knowing full well how high the suicide rate is among Italian prisoners. When you're packed in a cell so crowded only one man can stand at a time, how is that not a death sentence?" He waited for her to say something, disturbed to realize how hard he was breathing. When she just stared at him, he pressed the point. "So I ask you, Giudice Montisi, which is crueler: a swift death or a living one?"

Her lips flattened into a thin line. "Take me home. The *carabinieri* can resume my protection."

"You'll be dead in a matter of days, if not hours."

"So be it."

He opened the door and stepped out in front of her. All he could hear was the pump of blood in his ears. He had to calm down, had to salvage this somehow. If she died before the trial ended, if she ruled against Don Lucchesi—

A sudden movement to his left alerted him to something out of place. He pushed her to the ground without thinking, then he saw the flash and heard the crack of a gunshot.

———◆———

Loredana fell to her knees. Why had Ruggero pushed her? Was he *that* kind of man? A gun blast sent a cascade of ice over her body. Ruggero!

Crouching over her, he whipped around, gun out, and fired, pressing her flat at the same time. Every cell in her body screamed at her to run, but she forced herself to stay still, to look to Ruggero for guidance.

He fired several times at a gunman squatting behind a car. The shooter suddenly bolted away, and then a younger man to their right took off at the same time. The kid had a gun in his hand, but he hadn't fired it, and Ruggero wisely didn't shoot him, even though he easily could have. Instead, he grabbed her by the arm and hustled her up and inside, barking at the officers rushing toward them. "Get me Fuente. *Now.*"

She stood trembling beside Ruggero as he spoke to Fuente in the corridor, issuing orders as if he were the man's superior. "You will send a message for me. This trial *will* proceed. There's no stopping it. But I will stop anyone who gets in the way." He punched a finger into Fuente's chest. "And that includes you." He leaned forward and lowered his voice. "I don't care if he cut off your boy's ear. I'll take the other, and more besides, if you *ever* cross me again."

Staring at Ruggero, Fuente said, "You need to make a statement about the shooting."

Ruggero's eyes narrowed, but he kept his voice down. "You can make it for me. Hell, you probably even know the names of the idiots he sent."

A couple officers started toward Ruggero as if to restrain him, but Fuente broke the eye contact and waved them off. "It's all right. I know this man. He's providing private security for the judge."

When the officers dispersed, Ruggero issued more orders to Fuente. "I want my car checked for explosives." He pulled out his key fob. "And I want you, personally, to get in the car and start it."

Blanching, Fuente took the keys, then called for a couple men to assist him. As Loredana and Ruggero watched from the shelter of the entrance doorway, one man used a mirror on a pole to look underneath the car, and the other brought out a dog, who busily sniffed all around the car, before sitting down beside its handler. The handler shook his head, indicating that the car was clean.

Ruggero gestured to Fuente to get in the car. "That hardly seems necessary," Fuente said.

Crossing his arms, Ruggero stared the man down. "I believe it is."

Fuente shrugged, but his nonchalance was gone.

"What if it's rigged?" Loredana whispered.

"It's not," Ruggero said in an undertone. "I've had a motion-activated camera installed on the car to make sure I know if someone fucks with it." He held up the phone in his hand, which he'd been looking at while she'd been following the inspection. "They didn't touch the car. But obviously, he's not sure what they did."

His movements rigid, Fuente unlocked the car and got inside. A few seconds later, the motor growled to life and Fuente stepped out with a smile. "Satisfied?"

Ruggero took her elbow and led her to the car. As they reached Fuente, Ruggero jabbed him in the chest again. "Your boy gets to keep his ear."

His voice was low, savage. Meant to be remembered and respected.

Was this what his life was always like? Dodging bullets and making threats?

With shaking hands, Loredana buckled her belt, then settled back against the seat. Twice now, in twenty-four hours. Twice they'd come for her.

He got in and said nothing, but he handled the car like it had offended him, whipping it around corners and careening down streets. Finally she found her voice. "You need to slow down and calm down."

"What I need is—" He cut himself off and pulled over on a side street not far from her apartment. He kept the car idling and turned to her. "Are you hurt?"

She shook her head. "One of my knees might be scraped, but that's it." She met his eyes and asked the question that had been bothering her. "Did you mean what you said to Fuente? About his boy?"

Ruggero's brow creased for a second, then he shook his head. "No. I'd never hurt a kid. But *he* doesn't know that." He stared at her for a second. "You don't believe me."

He'd been enraged at Fuente, but he'd seemed genuinely baffled by her question. "Strangely, I *do* believe you."

He grunted and shook his head. "Strangely." Then he pulled out his phone and called someone. They spoke for a few seconds before he hung up and eased back into traffic. "I assume you still want to take your chances with the *carabinieri*—"

"No." She shook her head. "I can't trust them."

"But you *can* trust me?" He glanced at her, his gaze searing.

"Yes." Maybe it was stupid of her to feel that way, but this was the second time he'd saved her life. Mafioso or not, she needed him. For the duration of the trial, no doubt he'd do everything he could to keep her alive.

Loredana almost had to laugh—earlier she'd thought Ruggero different from Daniele because he'd remembered the color of her eyes. What a meaningless comparison. What mattered, what truly mattered, was that Daniele had run when she'd been in danger, whereas Ruggero had run toward the danger and snatched her from its jaws. And not just the one time.

Ruggero exhaled loudly, as if he were surprised by her faith in him. "Your mother may become a target. I can keep men here to watch her, but it would be better if she were somewhere else. Preferably directly under our guard."

"I'll try to persuade her. But she's extremely stubborn."

He chuckled. "Never would've guessed."

He pulled up near her building, and four men materialized out of cars and shadows, all of them converging on the Maserati. Panic rose up in her for a second, until she saw Tommaso's face.

She started to open her door, but Ruggero put a hand on her arm. "Wait." Tommaso reached the door and opened it, with a second man flanking the other side. The remaining two did the same for Ruggero. Ruggero came around the car and took her elbow, then the group of them entered the building. Two of the men stayed in the lobby, while Tommaso and one of the men followed them into the wire-cage elevator.

They approached her door, and she saw the surprise on the face of the *carabinieri* officer standing outside it. He touched his cap and addressed her. "Giudice Montisi, who are these men?"

"My new security detail. You and your colleagues are dismissed."

"*Signora—*"

"*Giudice*," she corrected him. "There's been an incident. I have chosen to employ my own security."

She motioned the *carabiniere* aside and unlocked the door. Ruggero followed her in, while Tommaso and the other guard remained outside. She found her mother in the kitchen talking to a second officer. Her mother looked from Loredana to Ruggero, then back again. "Mamma, we need to talk," Loredana said.

"Who is this?" Nora asked. "What's going on?"

The officer, who was eyeing Ruggero, put a hand on his gun. "Giudice Montisi, this man is armed," he said.

"I am well aware of that. He's the head of security at the firm I've hired to protect me."

The officer's brow creased. "The *carabinieri* are in charge of your protection."

"Not any longer. You've been dismissed."

"I'll have to speak to my superior."

"You do so." She pointed to the door. "Outside."

The man started speaking into his radio, but he left as she'd ordered. Now it was Ruggero's turn. "I need to speak to my mother. Alone."

He nodded, then went into the other room. Loredana sat down at the table, suddenly exhausted. Her mother reached over and took her hand. "What is going on? You told me you'd hired some security, but these men, I know who they are."

"Mamma, the situation is dire. Someone is trying to kill me, and he's been using the *carabinieri* to do it. Twice now."

"Twice?" Nora's eyebrows rose into her hairline. "You lied to me last night, didn't you?"

"I can't go into details. Trust me when I say that the only reason I'm alive is because of Signor Vela."

"The one with the scar?" When Loredana nodded, her mother continued. "*Dio mio.* Now there's a nasty piece of work if I've ever seen one."

"He's not what you think—"

"He's *exactly* what I think."

Loredana stared at her mother. "I need his help right now, or I'll be dead in the next couple of days."

"They're vipers," Nora hissed. "As soon as you're no longer useful to them, they'll slit your throat. I should know!" She smacked her hand on the table for emphasis, her voice thick with emotion, her eyes welling with tears.

Loredana's own vision blurred, and her throat clogged up. Had Fuente been telling the truth about her father? "Mamma, I need to ask you something."

"What is it, *dolcezza*?"

"Papà was honest, wasn't he? Someone said today that he'd taken bribes."

Nora stiffened, her eyes flashing. "You'd listen to stories told to you by these scum?"

Loredana took her mother's hand. "It was a *carabinieri* officer who said it."

Nora turned red. "Your father was a good man, the most honest man I've ever known. He did no such thing."

Loredana studied her mother's face, relieved to see the utter conviction on it. If Papà had taken money, he'd probably have confided in Mamma. And since she was sure he was clean, that was good enough for Loredana. Fuck Fuente. She'd let that lying, double-crossing bastard get in her head. She squeezed her mother's hand. "I thought the man was needling me. I just had to be sure."

"Your father is the one true thing we've ever had in our lives," her mother whispered, her voice cracking.

Loredana wrapped her arms around her. "I'm sorry, Mamma." She held her until her mother pulled back and wiped her eyes. It was now or never. "Mamma, they could try to get to me through you. I want to take you away from here, to get you proper protection."

"You mean *them*?" Nora said, gesturing to the room Ruggero had disappeared into. "I'd rather lie down in a snake pit."

"Please, Mamma. I don't trust the *carabinieri*. If you won't come with us, at least go to Allegra or Gisella."

"I can't trust these thugs, and neither should you."

"Those 'thugs' are the only thing between me and a grave right now. They've given me their word."

"The only oath that matters to them is the one they've given their *capo*."

"I don't have any choice." Loredana raised the hem of her sweater and showed her mother the bandage on her belly. "Someone I trusted with my life tried to gut me last night. And I was betrayed again today, by someone in law enforcement. Two men shot at me outside a *carabinieri* station only minutes ago, right after I finished giving an official statement. They were waiting for me, and almost no one knew I was going to be there. The person who saved me both times is Signor Vela."

Her mother grasped Loredana's hands. "*Dolcezza*, has it occurred to you that this could all be a setup to gain your trust?"

Loredana's stomach fluttered. Her mother had hit on her greatest fear. And Ruggero had specifically asked for Fuente. Yet... "It has. But my gut tells me I can trust this man."

"It's his boss you should fear. Vela's just a puppet taking orders. What does his *capo* want from you?"

"Alleged *capo*. All he wants is a fair trial."

"An acquittal is what he wants. And he doesn't even have to pay you to get it."

"Mamma, I've told you from the start that something seemed fishy about this case."

"So you believe murderers over your colleagues, over law-enforcement officers?"

"You haven't seen what I've seen."

Nora's eyes hardened. "I've seen plenty, and you'd do well to remember it." She sat back in the chair and crossed her arms. "Go then. 'Trust' your new friends. I won't weep when they bring me your body."

"Mamma—"

"I won't!" But there were tears in her eyes already.

"Promise me you'll go to Allegra or Gisella."

"I'll do better than that."

"What do you mean?"

"If someone does come after me, I don't want to be anywhere near my grandchildren. I'll stay with a friend."

"Which one?"

Nora huffed with laughter. "As if I'd say while your enforcers are here?"

"Fine, Mamma. I just want you safe."

"And that's what I want for you too."

"I will be," Loredana said, but she wasn't sure for how long. Yes, Ruggero would protect her—during the trial. But once it was over, what then?

She took a deep breath. She couldn't worry about that now; she had to focus on the day to day. She wrote her new number on the back of a receipt sitting on the table. "You can call me at this number. Share it only with Gisella and Allegra. No one else."

Nora took the paper. "What about the *carabinieri*?"

Loredana shook her head. "Just you three." Rising, she said, "I need to get some things."

Nora wiped her eyes, but didn't look at Loredana. "Go then."

"Mamma."

Nora looked up. "I can't lose you too."

"You won't."

Nora's lips trembled, then she opened her arms, and Loredana stepped into her embrace. "I love you, *dolcezza*."

"I love you too, Mamma." She kissed her mother's cheeks, then stepped away, wiping her eyes.

She hurried to her room and filled a bag with clothes, then grabbed her briefcase packed with work files and her laptop. When she was ready to go, she found Ruggero standing in the doorway to her bedroom, watching her, his face grave. "She won't leave with us," he said.

Loredana shook her head. "No." He stepped forward until he was just centimeters from her. "We'll still watch over her," he said in a low voice. "She'll never know we're there."

"You could save her life and she wouldn't trust you. Not after Papà."

He shrugged. "She matters to you, so she matters to me."

He looked so sincere, so serious. "You swear to me, on your parents' graves?"

Loredana asked.

"I swear to you on my own." He reached for her suitcase. "Ready?"

She looked around, trying to see the room through his eyes. How small it was, how bare. She'd never cared what it looked like—she'd been waiting for that day when she had a home of her own. When she married. And now—now she'd be lucky if she ever saw this room again.

She turned to Ruggero and nodded, swallowing hard. She was as ready as she'd ever be. Who knew if they'd even make it across the street?

CHAPTER 14

Somehow they reached the hotel without incident, but Loredana couldn't shake her mother's words, or the fact that once the trial was over, she was on her own. She couldn't stop pacing around her room in the suite.

She'd already unpacked her things and arranged them in the closet and dresser. Then she'd tried looking over the files on the Lucchesi and Baldassare cases, but it was all gibberish; she just couldn't concentrate.

Loredana glanced at her watch. It had been many hours since her half-eaten breakfast, and her stomach was complaining. But she didn't think she could be in the same room with Ruggero right now without asking questions he probably wouldn't answer.

Someone tapped at the door. Ruggero, or Tommaso? "Come in," she called.

Ruggero stepped inside. "Tommaso reminded me that we missed lunch. Want anything?"

She patted her belly. "I'm starving." She followed him out to the living room, surprised not to see the other guard. "Where's Tommaso?"

"I sent him and the others out to eat. We're safe here." He handed her the room-service menu, and after flicking through it, she told him what she wanted. When he finished placing the order, he sat on the sofa across from her. "This isn't an ideal situation, but what specifically is upsetting you?"

"Why do you ask?"

"You've had your arms crossed the entire time, and you're jumpy as a cat."

So he wanted to talk. Surprising. "The better question might be: What's *not* upsetting me?"

He cracked his knuckles. "Tell me what's on your mind."

She tried to hold his eyes, but at the last minute she looked down at the tiles. *Coward.* "I have no value to you once this trial is over."

When she forced herself to look up again, he was studying her. "I don't know what you mean."

"I serve a purpose for your boss—"

"My client."

"Your client, then. And when that purpose is over…"

He crossed his arms and said nothing.

She tried again. "I'll be on my own, yes? And someone will still want to kill me."

He sighed and said nothing for a long time. Then he nodded. "Yes… and yes."

"At least tell me who this person is."

He rubbed a hand across his face. "Lorenzo Andretti."

The name sounded familiar. Then she remembered. "He was mixed up in the bank case."

"Yes."

"I don't know much about him—besides his suspected Mafia ties."

"All you need to know is that he's vicious, greedy, and will not stop until he's got what he wants."

"And what is that?"

"Let's just say you're standing in the way of his plan."

A thought suddenly occurred to her. And it wasn't a nice one. "You used me today. You used me to send a message to Lorenzo Andretti."

A nod. Then he said, his voice soft, "He'd already targeted you before this."

True. Completely, depressingly true. "How can I protect myself once this trial is over?"

His lips pressed together. "I don't know. Yet."

Why couldn't he just be frank with her? She almost blurted it out. But she knew very well why. He was helping her now, but she was the enemy. And he'd taken a vow that demanded his silence about who he truly was.

"Ruggero, let's be honest. I've broken the law twice now because of you. I should have recused myself from this case after the first time you spoke to me. But I didn't. I wanted to put Enrico Lucchesi in jail, and I was damn well determined to do it. And then when you killed Stefano—" She paused for a second, and gathered her courage. "I could have called the *carabinieri* when you brought me here. I could have and I should have. I could have run away in the night. But I didn't. You know why?"

He glared at her. "Why." Not a question. A demand.

"Because I wanted him dead. And I didn't want to hurt you."

He raised a brow. "And?"

He was going to make her say it. "And I wanted to stay on this case."

"Why."

"Because I'm beginning to believe there's a conspiracy against Enrico Lucchesi."

"At last."

"I want justice to be done here, and what I see happening isn't justice." She swallowed hard. "I need your help. Now, and after this trial is over."

She waited for him to say something, but he didn't. She tried again. "I need to know what would happen if your boss asked you to kill me when I'm no longer of any use."

"Let's not deal in hypotheticals."

She had no trouble staring him down now. "You're evading the question."

He was silent for so long she thought he wasn't going to answer. Finally he said, "You want honesty? I'll give you honesty." He took a deep breath. "I would do anything he asked of me." He paused. "Anything but that."

Was he really admitting who he was? "You'd actually defy your boss for me?"

"Not that he'd ever ask me to. He believes in the old codes. Women and children aren't part of this, and they aren't to be harmed." He ran a hand through his hair. "But even if he asked, I couldn't kill you." He let out a defeated sigh. "I can't."

"Why?"

"Because I'm a fool," he spat. He went out on the balcony. She rose and followed him outside. Ruggero wasn't going to hide from her; she was going to get answers.

"What does that mean?" she asked.

He ignored her and pulled out a pack of cigarettes and lit one. She watched him take a drag, but when the smoke started flowing from his nose and mouth, she lost it. She snatched the cigarette from his lips and tossed it to the floor, crushing it with her shoe.

"What the hell?" he asked.

"My grandfather died of emphysema."

"Why would you care what happens to me?"

"No one deserves that kind of death."

"Even a Mafia thug?"

"Even a *man* like you."

Something in his face changed, darkened, and his eyes lasered in on her. He grabbed hold of her arms. "Is that how you see me? As a man? Or do you see me as a Mafioso?" He pulled her close, his eyes flicking back and forth across her face, before dipping down to stare at her lips.

Both of them were breathing hard. She placed her hands on his chest, his muscles twitching beneath her palms. Her heart was pounding, her stomach flipping. "I see you as a man," she said, the words just barely above a whisper.

Before she could second-guess herself, she leaned in, rising up on her toes, and pressed her lips to his. For just an instant, he kissed her back, then his hands clamped down on her biceps, and he broke the contact. "What the fuck are you doing?"

"I don't know."

Those wolf's eyes drilled into hers. "You'd better know, Loredana. I'm not a man you can play with."

She stared at him for a moment that stretched on and on. What did she want? She knew; she just needed the courage to own up to it. Then she stepped closer and raised her lips to his. "I'm not playing with you," she murmured against them.

With a groan, he hauled her flat against his well-muscled body, his mouth coming down on hers in a searing kiss. She clutched his suit jacket as he took control, his tongue delving into her mouth, his hands fisting in her hair, his rigid cock pressing into her belly.

She shouldn't be doing this, she knew it, and yet she couldn't stop. And why should she? She might not have much time left, and if she was going to die, she was going to die happy—or something like it.

This man—this hard, brutal man—he'd protected her, he'd cared for her, he'd dried her tears and held her on the worst night of her life. He'd shown her tenderness, even though it clearly wasn't in his nature. And he'd asked for nothing in return, nothing for himself.

And she knew he never would. He'd deny himself everything. So she had to be the one to bridge the gap. To take them both where they wanted to go.

Loredana pulled back, and he instantly released her. "Shit." He ran a hand over his coal-black hair. "We can't—"

She touched his lips. "We can, and we will. We're adults, aren't we? We both know the score."

He twisted the gold signet ring on his right little finger, anguish on his face. "I can't." He looked up finally and stared at her. "I can't."

"Ruggero—"

"You don't understand. I've taken a vow. A deadly serious one. And I've broken it." His gravelly voice thickened. "And now, I've put everyone I know, everyone I love, at risk." He took her by the arms. "What are you, the renowned Giudice Montisi, going to do with what you know?"

Her throat tightened. The hurt in his eyes was plain. She'd confessed her sins, but they were nothing compared to his. He'd just admitted who he was, that Enrico Lucchesi was his *capo*. No one would kill her for what she'd done. She'd get jail—if the authorities ever learned of her part in Stefano's death. But Ruggero? He'd die for what he'd confessed, and at the hands of those whom he'd betrayed.

"I'm not going to do a damn thing," she whispered, her words strangled. "Not a thing. I've gone too far to turn back, and now I'm in a situation where the rules as I knew them no longer apply."

He closed his eyes. "If you betray me—"

"I won't." She brushed the hair off his forehead. "I can't." He was the only man who'd ever stood up for her, and she wasn't about to repay that kindness with betrayal. She rose up on her toes again and pressed her lips to his. This time the kiss was soft, tender, searching. He wasn't a man who trusted easily. And yet he'd given her a glimpse into his heart, into the emotions he worked so hard to suppress. And that was a rare gift, one she had to treasure.

He held her lightly at first, then drew her close as he deepened the kiss, his hands cradling her head. Their tongues entwined, and her skin tingled all over. *Yes, yes, yes.* She twisted her fingers in his thick hair, wanting him closer, wanting him to know how she felt.

He broke off and took a breath, then pressed his mouth to her neck, just below the ear. She shivered and moaned at the contact. He might as well have kissed her between the legs, because that's where she felt it.

Someone knocked on the door to the suite. Ruggero groaned, then pulled away from her. "Stay here," he said. He drew his gun and answered the door while she watched from the balcony. He kept the weapon down by his leg, out of sight of the room-service waiter, who wheeled in a table.

Of all the rotten timing! She crossed her arms and took a breath. Her lips tingled; she could still feel his hands in her hair, the movement of his mouth against hers, his lips on her neck, the scrape of his stubble. The scent of him— lemony cologne, cigarettes, and espresso—lingered in her nostrils.

Her belly wouldn't stop fluttering. Now that they'd been interrupted, would he put a stop to what she'd started?

Ruggero tipped the waiter and shooed him out of the suite. He closed the door behind the man and stood there, leaning against it, as if he didn't want to come any nearer.

She stepped inside and shut the balcony doors behind her, her fingers trembling as she made sure the doors latched. Her stomach growled at the scent of food, but food could wait.

What she wanted was the man standing before her, the one who was looking at her like she was killing him. She brought her hands up to her blouse and started unbuttoning it. Then she gave him a coy smile and turned to her bedroom, not looking back to see if he'd follow. He was going to have to take this last step on his own.

And dear God, she hoped he would.

She reached the room and left the door open behind her as she started to pull off the blouse, every cell in her body on alert, waiting for him to enter. The seconds stretched out, and all she heard was the rustle of cloth as she shed her shirt, the thud of her boots as she toed them off, the whisper of the zipper as she removed her trousers.

And then she heard it—a muffled curse followed by hard footsteps as he marched into the room. She looked up, clad only in her bra and panties, and he stopped in the doorway. His nostrils flared and he swore again.

"That bad?" she asked, motioning to the bandage on her belly.

"Fuck no." He swore yet again and laughed. "I've lost all control of my mouth."

She laughed with him and waited for him to close the distance. He didn't move more than a few steps though, and his hands clenched into fists. A thrill of alarm coursed through her. Had she horribly miscalculated? "What's wrong?" she asked.

———————— ◆ ————————

Seeing the pulse jumping in her throat, Ruggero followed Loredana's gaze to the fists at his sides. Fuck, fuck, fuck. He needed to get a grip on himself. He'd risked everything, his life, his future, for this woman. And why? Why couldn't he just leave her in the hands of God when the trial was over?

Swallowing hard, he took a deep breath, tried to quell the shaking inside his chest. He'd broken his vow. He'd betrayed his don, his *cosca*.

Why now? Why her?

He didn't have an answer. All he knew, to the marrow of his bones, was that he couldn't walk away from Loredana Montisi. Even if Enrico put a gun to his head, he couldn't abandon her, and he couldn't let her die. And if that meant his own death?

So be it.

He'd put his trust in her, as she'd put hers in him. And he couldn't ruin it all now.

But how to tell her the other reason he was hesitating? The other reason that taking her to bed scared him?

Loosening his hands, he ran one through his hair and finally responded to her question with one of his own. "You're not going to regret this later?"

She shook her head and said nothing. He wished she'd come to him, but he had to close the gap now. She'd been happy, playful, and now she was scared. All because he couldn't be honest about his fucked-up sexual history.

He'd taken the safe path, the easy path, with women all his life. And look where it had left him: without a fucking clue. Yes, he knew how to fuck. That was easy.

But he didn't know how to make love.

Don't just stand here, staring at her; do something. Loredana was beginning to look at him like he'd grown a second head. It couldn't be that hard, could it? He'd seen his share of movies. He knew what women expected. He'd just never bothered to romance one before. He'd never had to.

Well, it was time to try. *Don't screw it up.* His heart was pounding, adrenaline doing a number on his pulse. How fucked up was it that he was calmer planning a hit? He took a deep breath and stepped forward, trying to smile. The look in her eyes said he was failing.

She placed a hand on his chest when he reached her. Trying to restrain him? He took her hand, wrapped his fingers around her cold ones, and blew on them. "Don't worry," he said, as much for his benefit as hers.

Finally she smiled. "I was beginning to think you didn't want me."

This time he was able to give her a genuine grin. "That could never be the case."

Something sparked in her eyes. He raised her hand to his mouth and brushed his lips across her knuckles, gauging her response. *So far, so good.* With his free hand, he took her by the waist and eased her closer. What did she want? That kiss they'd shared earlier, on the balcony, seemed to indicate that she'd be okay if he took the lead. That maybe she wanted him to do so, just as her trembling now seemed to indicate it too.

That, he could do. It was his default mode with Chiara. He tilted Loredana's chin up, then captured her lips with his, pouring all his desire for her into the kiss. She moaned into his mouth, and his half-hard cock was rigid in an instant. He wanted inside her, now. He didn't even want a blow job first; that treat could wait.

He walked her toward the bed, until it met the back of her legs. She let herself fall back and pulled him down on top of her.

Cristo, she was gorgeous. Her long brown hair fanned out around her head, and her green eyes glowed as she looked at him. Reaching up, she traced a finger along the scar that ran across his cheekbone. He grabbed her wrist, and she stopped, hesitating. He searched her eyes for what seemed like minutes: What was she thinking? Did she pity him? "How did you get this?" she asked, her voice soft.

"I don't want to talk about it."

"You'll tell me later?"

Fuck. That was a story he didn't tell anyone. And how likely would she continue to trust him for protection after he revealed his greatest failure? "Maybe." *What a liar.* He'd say anything right now, just to get inside her.

"Okay." She pulled him closer and pressed her lips to that scar, right where it ran past his left eye. His throat tightened, and he had to force himself not to pull away. Instead, he sought her lips again, trying to distract her. Trying to distract himself. She was ruining him, absolutely ruining him. How many times today had she thrown him off-kilter?

Too many to count.

He thrust his tongue in her mouth and she whimpered, her own curling over his, and it was as if her tongue was curving around his *cazzo*. *Cristo*, she was killing him. Loredana Montisi would murder him in this bed, but Ruggero simply could not muster up the energy to care. She was in his arms, nearly naked, and she'd told him she wanted him.

She'd told him she thought of him as a man, not a Mafioso.

This was so fucking wrong; he knew it. Nothing good would come of it.

But…

Fuck. That.

He was having her, if it was the last thing he did before he died. Lowering his head, he kissed her again, this precious jewel, this woman who knew what he was, who he was, who'd seen him kill, and who didn't care.

She trusted him. Him, of all people.

Loredana moaned into his mouth, the sound spiking his lust again. He couldn't wait to get inside her, to fuck her until she begged him to stop. He kissed along her jaw, then down to her throat, enjoying the gasp he wrung from her when he bit down on the soft flesh of her neck. He soothed his tongue over the bite mark, then bit again, sucking on her skin. She tasted of vanilla and cinnamon, of spices he couldn't name.

Clutching his hair, she moaned. "Don't leave a mark."

Just for that… He bit down again and sucked, pleased both by her writhing and the red blotch he left behind. Everyone would know what the oh-so-proper judge had been doing. "Too late," he murmured in her ear.

"Vampire," she hissed.

"I want a lot more from you than blood," he whispered against her neck before moving lower. He nibbled on her collarbone, then reached down to the firm, round breasts she seemed to be offering up to him.

He cupped one in his hand. It filled his palm nicely, the nipple stiff, and sensitive too, to judge by her moan when he brushed across it. He flicked open the front clasp of her bra, then drank in the sight of her dusky nipples peaked and drawn up tight.

He latched onto the one he'd already teased, and she arched beneath him, her fingers on his scalp urging him to suckle her, her moans making his cock so hard he could feel his pulse pounding in it.

Sex with Chiara had been fun, a release, a necessity. Sex with Loredana was something else entirely.

Madness.

He tore her panties down to her knees and thrust a hand between her legs, groaning when he felt her curls against his palm, her wetness bathing his fingertips.

"Wait," she said. "You're still dressed."

"So?" He'd often fucked Chiara that way, just pulling out his cock and going at it. He'd liked that layer between them, that feeling of control, with him clothed and Chiara naked.

"I want to see you. Touch you."

"Later." Maybe. He couldn't afford to lose all control with her. Couldn't get too swept up. This was just going to be a quick fuck, wasn't it? Just the two of them burning off some steam, getting rid of whatever this was between them. That was all.

And he needed to get Loredana back on task. He slipped two fingers inside her, the others curling downward to tap against the rosebud between the cheeks of her luscious ass. She wriggled beneath him when he did it, so he caressed her there again. Hmm... his little judge might be open to what he wanted to do to her, might like more than just his finger there.

He circled a finger around that hole, then pressed against the opening. She inhaled sharply, then placed a hand against his chest. "What are you doing?"

He looked up at her. "What I want."

She smiled. "I haven't done that before."

"Willing to try?" He held his breath, waiting for her answer.

She gave him a coy little smile, similar to the one that had driven him crazy earlier. "Not right now. But maybe."

He pressed the pad of his little finger against that entrance she was denying him, flicking it back and forth with the slightest pressure. She shivered and bucked beneath him. "Later then." He could wait.

She plucked at his black turtleneck. "We should take this off."

He hesitated, then remembered how her eyes had lingered on him the day before when he'd been clad in nothing but a towel. She'd already seen the scars, the tattoos. And well, if she could concede something, so could he. He was glad he'd shed the holster and gun though before stepping into the room.

Sitting back on his heels, straddling her, he pulled the sweater over his head, then tossed it to the floor. She smiled her appreciation as she brushed a hand over his abdomen, and something squeezed in his chest.

She might hate him tomorrow, but for now she was his.

His phone buzzed in his trouser pocket. *Porca vacca!* He grabbed it and answered without looking at the display. "What?" he barked.

"I've been knocking for over a minute now." Tommaso. "I thought you were staying in?"

Fuck, fuck, fuck. He'd known this was a bad idea. "Look, she wanted some air. We're fine."

"They find you?" Tommaso asked, his voice tinged with alarm.

"No, no. Everything's okay. Just... take the day off. Go see my sister."

There was a rustle at the other end of the line, and Tommaso murmured something to the others about giving him some space. After a second, he came back on, his voice lowered. "You know, this hotel is really nice, but I can still hear your voice out here."

Ruggero closed his eyes as his face heated. Fuck!

There was a long silence, then Tommaso laughed. "I'm not stupid. I could see it between you."

Brazen it out, or admit defeat? "You didn't see anything."

Another soft chuckle from Tommaso, then he said, "You're right. Don't know what I was talking about." His voice went up, as he addressed the others. "The judge isn't feeling well. We've got the day off."

Ruggero heard the men talking, the excitement in their voices. "I'll call you when I need you."

"She's in court tomorrow. We'll be back in the morning."

"Not a word about this, Tommaso. I mean it."

The old guard chuckled again. "Not even to your sister?"

"Tommaso," he growled.

"Got it, boss."

They said their goodbyes, then Ruggero set the phone on the nightstand. "We're on our own," he said to Loredana. "No more interruptions."

That teasing little smile crossed her face again. "Do you have any condoms?"

Damn it again. "No." It was going to kill him to say it, but... "There are other things we could do."

She smiled. "There are, but I want everything." Leaning past him, she reached for the hotel phone on the nightstand. "Just one more interruption, and then we're free." She called down to the front desk and requested someone make a trip to the pharmacy.

His cheeks heated again. They were getting those condoms after all.

CHAPTER 15

"I didn't think anything could make you blush," Loredana said to Ruggero after hanging up the phone.

He shrugged, then he shook his head and laughed, his teeth flashing at her, and she swore her heart stopped. She'd never seen him relax, not once since she'd known him, but here he was, unguarded at last. And in front of her.

Because of her.

Dio mio, this man, with his hard face, his scars, his tattoos, his calloused fingers, he did something to her. He made her feel... what? Soft? Safe? Needed?

Something had happened to him, maybe a lot of somethings. Something had put that brutal exterior in place, but now she was seeing *him*. The man he was when no one was looking.

Her throat tightened. She could relate. How many years had she pretended she didn't need anyone? How long had she covered up how badly Daniele's rejection had wounded her?

Ruggero leaned forward and framed her face in his large hands. He kissed her softly, tenderly. "I like how you surprise me," he said. Then he leaned over the edge of the bed and plucked his sweater off the floor. When she protested as he slipped it over his head, he clucked his tongue at her. "One of us has to be dressed when our delivery comes." He cupped her cheek, then kissed her again. "I'm going to wait out there before I start something I won't be able to interrupt."

He rose and let his eyes travel over her body, making her feel just how naked she was, with her bra undone and her panties around her knees.

"Don't move," he ordered, his voice rough. "I want to pick up right where we left off."

He walked out of the room, and a wicked thought occurred to her. He'd enjoyed teasing her, and turnabout *was* fair play.

She shed her panties and bra, and then closing her eyes, she slid her hands down to her breasts, cupping them the way he had. Her hands felt so much smaller than his, but they'd have to do. Wetting her fingertips in her mouth, she teased the nipple he'd suckled on, picturing how absorbed he'd been in his exploration of her body.

With her other hand, she caressed the mound between her legs, her fingers brushing through the hair, seeking that little bundle of nerves he hadn't touched yet. When her fingertip reached it, she shivered, letting a loud moan leave her lips.

Take that, *Ruggero Vela. Don't move, my ass.*

Letting her legs fall open, she pictured him standing above her, watching as she stroked herself. Plunging two fingers inside, she rubbed her *grilletto* with her thumb, imagining that he was doing it, that he was about to put his mouth on her, right *there*.

She let out another loud, half-theatrical moan, and then she heard the metallic jangle of a belt buckle. Her eyes flew open, and there he was, in the doorway, hard cock in hand.

Loredana froze, one hand on her breast, the other between her legs.

"Keep going," he rasped as he stroked himself. "I'm enjoying the show."

She bit her lip. It was one thing to tease him while he was in the other room. It was another to do it right in front of him.

"You wanted an audience, didn't you?" he asked, his voice a low, amused rumble.

Yes, she supposed she had. Her gaze dropped down to the thick, heavily veined shaft he held in his fist, and she imagined what it would feel like on her tongue, how hard it would be deep inside her.

Her mouth went dry, and she stroked herself quickly, greedily, her eyes eating up the straining in his jaw, the flexing of the muscles in his neck, his arm, the rapid breaths he was taking as he fisted his cock, his eyes glued to the hand moving between her legs.

She was going to come any second, with him watching. A blush flooded over her face, her neck, her chest, but she didn't stop. She wanted him to watch her, to see her. She wanted to give that to him.

With a hoarse cry, she arched up, and he let loose a string of rapid Calabrian that she couldn't make sense of.

He swiftly crossed the room and sat down beside her on the mattress, his hand covering the one between her legs, urging her to keep stroking even though she was so sensitive she could barely stand it. She shuddered and bucked under his hand, and he murmured sweet words to her mingled with affectionate curses.

Finally she had to stop, but still he kept his hand cupped over hers, his rapid breathing matching hers in the silence of the room. When she opened her eyes, she saw him grinning again. She met his gaze shyly and he chuckled. "I really do enjoy these surprises." He pressed a kiss to her lips, then drew back. "Keep them coming."

"You weren't supposed to watch me."

He laughed. "Liar."

Reaching over, she glided her fingertips across the head of the rock-hard *cazzo* poking out of his trousers. "Maybe I am." When he shivered beneath her touch, she smiled. "I've never done that in front of a man."

"Then I'm honored." She curled her fingers around him, his cock pulsing in her fist, and he hissed and stilled her hand. "Not yet." He extricated his *cazzo* from her grip and rose, tucking it away. "I still have a package to wait for."

She sighed. "I shouldn't have called for it."

"A little wait won't kill us."

Another idea occurred to her. "Maybe I should warm up the shower?"

His eyes darkened with interest. "Maybe."

He offered her a hand up, then followed her to the en-suite bathroom door. Aware of his gaze on her, she started the shower, her back turned to him. She swore she heard him mumble something about her ass, so she bent over to straighten the mat outside the shower door.

"I could fuck you right now." His voice was thick, guttural.

"And I'd let you." Her eyes met his briefly before she opened the door and stepped inside.

The hot spray cascaded over her body, making her already sensitive nipples ache and sending a zing of excitement straight between her legs. She picked up the bar of soap and lazily stroked it across her breasts.

He swore, loudly, then said, "Don't get too far ahead of me," before he left.

She laughed and lathered up the soap. Oh, she'd wait this time.

The water soaked into the bandage on her belly. Turning her back to the spray, she peeled it off, pleased to see that a scab had formed over the shallow cut. The sight of it was sobering, however. She traced it with her fingertips.

She could have died, *would* have died, if it hadn't been for Ruggero. If he hadn't come for her, risked his life for her. If he hadn't cared…

Tears welled in her eyes just as he came back in, a bag in his hand. She yanked her hand away from her belly and turned to the wall, trying to hide how upset she was, and wiped at her cheeks in an attempt to make it look like she was washing her face.

Within moments he was in the shower, naked as she was, and the feel of his warm skin, of his big arms enclosing her, undid her. She hadn't fooled him for a second. She let out a long shuddering sob against his chest.

"*Bambina,*" he murmured into her hair. "My brave, brave girl."

She didn't want to ruin things. She wanted this, she wanted him.

Lifting her lips to his mouth, she kissed him hungrily, and without hesitation he matched her mood, his tongue twining with hers, his hands slipping down to grasp her butt, to rub her up against the evidence of how badly he wanted her.

Pressing her back against the marble, he urged her legs up around his waist. Positioning himself at her entrance, he said, "I won't come in you. You trust me?" Water droplets beaded on his thick lashes as he searched her face.

She nodded, unable to speak, desperate to have him take her so she didn't have to think anymore, just feel. Just lose herself…

He entered her on a hard thrust, and they both groaned at the sensation. *Dio mio*, he was big. His body was finely toned all over, the cords of his muscles standing out as he held her up, as he moved her up and down on his rigid cock.

The strokes were quick and shallow, teasing, and she wanted more. She wanted to be fucked. Hard and fast. "On the bed," she said. "Not here. I need you in me deep."

He let out a low groan, then he pulled out and swept her up in his arms. She turned off the shower and grabbed a couple towels off the rack and the sack from the pharmacy off the counter before he carried her into the bedroom. She tossed the towels down on the bed and he deposited her on them, then grabbed the bag from her hands, fumbling with the carton and tearing it open with desperate fingers.

"You're killing me," he muttered as he ripped open a foil packet.

"I know," she said softly, then met his gaze.

He stopped what he was doing and leaned forward, pulling her into a kiss. Then he had a condom in hand. Without a word, she reached for it and he gave it to her. Unrolling the condom over the length of him, she used both her hands to smooth the latex all the way down, and he inhaled when she touched him, watching her every move as if it were the most fascinating thing he'd ever seen.

Then he pounced, pinning her beneath him, spreading her knees. He was inside her in seconds, and he felt so damn good. She clasped her legs around his waist.

This was what she so desperately needed. This feeling of possession, of abandon. And when he bit down on her neck again, she didn't care that he was marking her.

She was his, at least for whatever time Lorenzo Andretti allowed her. Ruggero had protected her so far, but how much longer could she escape her fate?

Porca miseria. She closed her eyes and tried to focus on Ruggero, tried to forget about everything else. Before she succumbed to the cold fingers of the grave, she was going to grasp every bit of pleasure this life afforded. She would die with no regrets.

———— ◆ ————

Loredana's *figa* clenched around his *cazzo* again, and Ruggero swore under his breath. He was about to come, and he hadn't been inside her long. Gritting his teeth, he tried to think about something else, anything other than the feel of her slick walls surrounding him, her panting little breaths in his ear...

With a groan, he shuddered, the orgasm spiraling up his spine and hitting him so hard it was nearly painful. He waited for her keen of pleasure, but she didn't make a noise. Hmm... maybe she was just a lot quieter than Chiara.

Except that she hadn't been quiet earlier when she'd made herself come, had she?

Blowing out hard, he opened his eyes and searched her face. Had she enjoyed it at all? "I know that was a little quick," he said. *Don't ask, don't ask...*

She brushed a curl off his forehead and smiled. "I guess I wasn't the only one who was excited."

His cheeks burned. Fuck. He'd blown it. And he couldn't tell her why. How did he admit that she was only the fourth woman he'd slept with—and the first who wasn't getting paid for it?

"It's okay," she said.

"It's not." It really wasn't. He wanted her to enjoy it the way Chiara always did. "Look, it doesn't take me long to get ready again."

"I'm not worried." She gave him that teasing little grin that meant she had something in mind. "There are other ways you can please me."

Oh yeah. He grinned. He could certainly keep her occupied until he was ready to go again. "Give me a second." He went into the bathroom and disposed of the condom and washed off. Whoever the concierge had sent to the pharmacy had decided to buy a jumbo pack of condoms, and thank God for that. Because he intended to use every last one. Loredana was going to remember him with every step she took tomorrow.

When he returned to the room, she was stretched out on her side, her legs slightly parted, her fingers straying over her *figa*. If she wanted to play that game again, he was certainly happy to watch. He palmed his cock, surprised that he was already getting hard just remembering how her back had arched when she'd cried out. "Touch yourself," he said.

She shook her head. "I want you to do it."

He lay down beside her and ran a hand over her belly, then brushed it along the top of the curls between her legs. She shivered and shifted onto her back, and he slid his hand lower, until his fingers found her entrance. She was wet, though not as much as before. He pushed one finger inside, and at her gasp, he added another. He pumped them in and out, hard and fast, and she moaned, but grabbed his wrist. "Slower," she said. "And touch me."

What? "I *am* touching you."

"Not where I want you to."

"I thought this was what you wanted."

"It is. But I want you to touch me where it counts most."

He tried not to show his confusion, but she was talking in riddles. Maybe... He lowered his mouth to her right breast and latched onto her nipple, swirling his tongue around it. She moaned and clutched his hair. He smiled against her skin. Yes! He'd figured it out.

Slowly moving his fingers in and out, he continued to suckle her breasts, moving from one to the other. Her hips moved in needy little circles. "Oh yes, oh yes. Now touch me. Touch me *there*."

Touch her where? Had she changed her mind about earlier? He wriggled his two free fingers down into the crack of her ass and tapped against that entrance she'd said no to before.

She froze beneath him, and he looked up. "I didn't mean there."

"Well, what did you mean?"

"I meant my *grilletto*."

Dio mio. He was an idiot. "Oh."

She snorted. "You know where it is, yes?"

"Of course." It was... somewhere between her legs. He'd seen it in porn, right? That little nub, close to the top of the lips. He kissed her while he felt for it. There was a hard little pearl about a couple centimeters above her entrance. That had to be the spot. When he brushed his thumb over it, she shuddered. "That's it," she moaned.

Okay, learning something new. How come Chiara had never mentioned it? *Idiot. She was getting paid to please you. Not herself.*

He applied more pressure. "Can you wet your thumb a bit more?" Loredana said. "It kind of hurts." He was sticking his thumb in his mouth when she said, "Or you could use your tongue."

Yep, something else he didn't really know much about. How many times had Chiara gone down on him? He hadn't been inclined to return the favor, had he?

Dio, kill me now. Loredana was about to know just how completely ignorant he was. His stomach knotted. And she'd be appalled to know why.

Hell, he was a little appalled at himself right now.

He blew out hard. It was time to come clean. "I don't..." His voice sounded a little rusty, and he coughed. "I don't know how."

She chuckled. "You *are* kidding me."

His cheeks burned again. She'd made him blush a million times today. It wasn't something he did often.

"No woman has ever asked you?" He shook his head. "Who have you been sleeping with? Virgins?"

Far from it. "No."

"Who then?" She froze again. "Don't tell me you're married to some nice girl who's terrified to say a word to you about anything."

"Of course not. I'd never cheat on my wife."

"Then?" She let the question hang in the air.

He looked away. He couldn't tell her.

"Oh *Cristo*," she murmured. "Is this your first time with a woman?"

He groaned. "I haven't been a virgin since I was sixteen."

She took hold of his jaw and tugged until he looked at her. "Be honest. Have you..." She hesitated, then said, "Have you been with men, then?"

"No!" *Dio*, he'd thought Antonio would be the only one to ever ask him that question. Fuck it. He had to tell her. "I've been with call girls."

"Oh." She paused, then said, "Am I the first woman who wasn't a... professional?" He nodded, and her eyes went round. "You've been careful?"

"Of course. I always use condoms."

"Then how come you didn't have any?"

"Because they always did. This was the last thing I expected to happen today." She looked skeptical. "I swear. I'm clean. I was only with high-class girls."

"You've been tested."

"Yes. As part of my physical every year."

She lay back on the bed and put an arm over her eyes. "This is a lot to take in."

"Well, trust me, it wasn't easy to admit. Especially since it makes me look like a real bastard."

She lifted her arm and opened one eye. "How so?"

"Well, it's pretty damn obvious that I've been concerned only with myself, isn't it?"

She sat up and touched his cheek. "It's pretty obvious that you've been lied to. A lot."

"What do you mean?"

"Well, let me guess. They came every time, right? Just from intercourse?"

He shrugged. "Yeah."

She made a buzzing noise. "Nope. Most women don't come that way. And certainly not every time."

"You're kidding me."

She sighed. "And I hate to break it to you: porn is all lies too."

He stared at her for a second, then he just had to laugh. Here he was, thirty-six years old, and he didn't know a damn thing about women. Except... he liked Loredana. He really did. She was bursting his bubble, but the way she was smiling at him and joining in his laughter, the way she was touching his face and kissing him—he was glad she was the one who'd told him. And when she whispered, "Want me to teach you to be a real Casanova?" he couldn't stop smiling.

And he couldn't stop kissing her until they both had to breathe. "Yes," he said. She giggled, and the shine in her eyes gave him that squeezing sensation in his chest again. "So what do I do?"

"Well, you can think of my *grilletto* as a tiny *cazzo*. A lot of what you like done to you, I'll like too. Lick it, swirl your tongue around it, suck on it. And take it slow, light pressure, until I'm really excited."

He pressed her down against the mattress, then parted the lips of her *figa* and blew gently over that nub. She shivered. "And then what do I do when you're really excited?"

"You find a rhythm, quick strokes, and don't stop until I tell you to."

He tentatively licked her *grilletto*, pleased when she moaned. "Yes, like that." Swirling his tongue around it, he gently sucked it into his mouth. She rose up a bit and clamped her hands on his head. "Oh yes."

Smiling, he continued to work that sensitive flesh, enjoying each sound she made. It was actually fun. Not to mention a turn-on. The spicy scent of her was intoxicating, and he was ready to go all over again. But not until she'd come first. If he couldn't get her there with his cock, he damn well would with his mouth.

Flattening his tongue, he decided to experiment a little. He licked a broad swath from her entrance to her clit, and she definitely enjoyed that. "Fuck me with your tongue," she moaned, and his *cazzo* was so hard, he swore he was going to drill a hole in the mattress.

This time, he speared his tongue inside her, and she worked herself hard against him, as if she were fucking his face. She definitely liked that. And then he had a brilliant idea. Why not add his fingers to the mix?

He sucked her *grilletto* into his mouth again, working his tongue all around it, and slipped two fingers inside her. Again, he used his free fingers to tap against that entrance between her ass cheeks, and this time she didn't go still or try to stop him. He dipped his little finger inside her *figa*, getting it nice and wet, then pressed it against that puckered hole again. She shuddered, and he pressed it a little harder, not quite enough to enter. Not yet.

A high keening noise burst from her lips, and he sucked her with increasing pressure, flicking his tongue rapidly back and forth until her hips bucked and she cried out for him to stop.

After her jerking subsided, he kissed the inside of her left thigh, then looked up at her. Her face was flushed and she was breathing hard. He couldn't remember being happier than he was right now.

When she caught her breath, she said, "You're certainly a quick learner."

"I try."

"And good at improvising."

"I have to be."

She crooked her finger at him. "Come here." He crawled up her body until he could look straight into her eyes. He wanted to say something, but he didn't know what. All he knew was that his chest felt light, like he could fly away. And somehow she'd caused it. She placed her hands on his cheeks and kissed him, her tongue fluttering around his. Then she reached down and palmed him. "Ready for round two?"

He didn't have to be asked twice. He put the condom on himself, and when he thrust inside her, he kept his eyes on her face, trying to read her expression. She was slick, so very slick, and the only sounds in the room were their rapid breathing and the slap of their bodies coming together.

This time, when she clenched around him, he still enjoyed it, but he also enjoyed watching her, studying her. He swirled his hips around, and she ground her heels into his buttocks, then asked him to do it again. He was more than happy to oblige. He could do this forever, if she asked.

He slowed his strokes, not speeding them up until she urged him on, waiting until she was moaning, until her face was flushed and she was mumbling expletives and clawing his back. Then he pistoned into her, as fast and hard as he wanted, and when he came, she cried out again shortly after.

Oh yes, this Casanova business was fun. More fun than he could ever remember having. And Loredana, she was the reason. She'd done something to him, made him feel something he'd never felt before.

And even though he was happy, he was also the slightest bit afraid.

This happiness couldn't possibly last.

CHAPTER 16

Ruggero woke up in Loredana's room the next morning. She was running a finger over his scar, tracing its length from just beside his left eye down across his cheekbone. "Tell me about this," she said.

He started to open his mouth, then slammed it shut. What was he doing with her? Telling her who he really was, sleeping with her, showing her a side of himself no one else had ever seen—he'd gone too far, too fast. And all without thinking it through.

"We need to get dressed," he said and rolled over.

"Ruggero, what's wrong?"

He blew out with his back to her as he looked for his clothes. "Look, this can't go anywhere. Let's not pretend any differently."

"I'm not asking you to marry me. I just want to know you."

He pulled on his pants and glanced at her over his shoulder. She'd drawn the sheet up over her chest, hiding all temptation from him. Except her mouth. That gorgeous mouth, those flashing eyes...

"What's the point?" The words came out a little sharper than he'd intended, but perhaps that was for the best.

"I thought..." She paused and frowned. "I don't know what I thought."

His stomach tightened at the hurt in her tone. He wanted to say something comforting, but why? They had no future.

He knew it. She needed to know it too.

He took the rest of his clothes to his room, closing the door behind him. He showered rapidly, his movements rough, almost brutal. He shouldn't have told her who he was. He shouldn't have told her a goddamn thing.

If she ever breathed a word, if anyone ever found out, they'd both be dead.

And it would all be his fault. Because he was weak.

His phone buzzed and he picked it up. Tommaso. "We'll be ready in a few," Ruggero said.

"It's not that." There was a tension in Tommaso's voice that Ruggero didn't like.

"What's happened?"

"Battista's been arrested."

Fuck. And of course, just when they needed his support most. True to form, Lorenzo Andretti had an attack plan for every move they made. Battista had sent them some money and a few men, but it wasn't nearly enough. And now, there'd be no more.

"Where's he being held?"

"San Vittore."

"Here?" He'd expected Naples.

"Trapani says Corvi wants to tie the cases."

"You're fucking with me."

"I wish I had better news."

He ended the call. Now he wished he hadn't turned the damn phone on. He crossed the hall and tapped on Loredana's door. No response.

Shit. Had she bolted? He tried the door and found it unlocked. He stepped inside and heard the water shut off in the bathroom.

He could picture her in there, naked, glistening with water, her hair long heavy ropes lying over her shoulders. *Dio*, he wanted to go in there, to apologize for being such an ass, but he couldn't. Distance was best. He'd said too much already.

The door opened and she stepped out, her hair wrapped in a towel, the rest of her bare. She paused in the doorway, her eyes holding his. "I'm surprised to see you back in here." She crossed her arms. "Especially considering your quick exit."

"Something's happened. Something bad."

She raised a brow, then walked over to the closet. "What?"

"Enrico Lucchesi's godfather was arrested. And Corvi wants to tie the cases together."

"Interesting," she said to the rack of clothing as she searched.

"This is Lorenzo Andretti's doing. You can't allow this."

"I'll need to hear Corvi's rationale."

"Don't you get it? Andretti is trying to take down everyone who opposes him. Everyone who's a threat."

The glance she spared him was withering, her voice cold. "We shouldn't be talking about the case."

"We shouldn't be fucking either." The words came out before he could stop them. She paused in her movements, her back stiffening, then she continued as if she hadn't heard.

If she could pretend, so could he. "We *need* to talk about the case."

She pulled a white fitted blouse and a black skirt out of the closet and laid them on the bed, then went to the dresser and picked out a bra and panties. Then she paused to rub the towel over her hair, and Ruggero couldn't stop himself from staring at the jiggling of her breasts.

Tossing the towel on the bed, she donned her panties and bra before she looked at him again. She put her hands on her hips. "So *this* you want to talk about?"

"It's important."

"All that matters is this case, yes? That's *all* that matters to you?"

"It's not like that."

"Oh, it is. You've made that clear."

"You have to listen to me."

With a slash of her hand, she said, "No. I do not. I will hear the evidence, and *I* will decide what to do. Not you. And not your boss."

"Look—"

She pointed to the door. "Out. I'll be ready in a few minutes."

He could see she wasn't going to back down. And maybe giving her some time to cool off would be the best move.

Because everything else?

Total failure.

———— ◆ ————

Loredana took a last look at herself in the mirror. Hair blown out, makeup perfect, the mark on her neck covered. But her eyes were puffy, her nose a little red. Every time she told herself to buck up, to stop thinking about him, it had the opposite effect.

She was damned if she'd let Ruggero see her cry. Not over this. Not over him. She'd thought he'd started to open up last night.

But whatever tiny crack she'd made, he'd slammed it shut. Right in her face.

If that's how he wanted it, then that's how it would be.

She left the room and pulled on her coat. He was waiting for her on the sofa in the main room, and he rose in one fluid movement.

She met his eyes and saw something there—remorse, perhaps?—before his typical hard mask shifted into place.

He opened the door and signaled to a guard waiting outside. The man preceded them down the hall. This time, Ruggero didn't put his hand on the small of her back when they entered the elevator. He stood apart from her, his hands clasped loosely behind him.

Probably so he wouldn't accidentally touch her.

Because that would be bad. But for which one of them?

They reached the waiting car, a black Mercedes limousine. She and Ruggero got in back, Tommaso and the driver up front, the other two guards following in another car.

She fiddled with the papers in her briefcase, trying to look busy, but aware of every breath Ruggero took, every movement he made. Just before they pulled up to the courthouse, he put up the privacy glass and turned to her.

Her pulse quickened. What now?

He took her right hand in his. "I don't know how to do this." He swallowed, speaking to her hand. "I don't. When you snapped at me about the case, I wanted to hurt you back. What we did last night... it meant more than I made it sound."

"Was that an apology?"

He looked at her then. "I guess I don't know how to do that either." A corner of his mouth quirked up with a hint of a smile.

She allowed him the barest hint of one herself. "I don't know what I'm doing either."

He touched her cheek. "It's my fault. This morning..." His voice trailed off.

"Buyer's remorse?" she said.

He shook his head. "Just too much, too fast."

Ah. And she'd pushed when she should have nudged. "We'll talk more later?"

He nodded, then pressed a kiss to her cheek. She turned so their mouths met. Oh this man. He could be so infuriating one moment, and so endearingly vulnerable the next. He was like a wounded animal—needing help, but lashing out, growling in mistrust.

She couldn't push; she'd have to trust that he'd come to her. Eventually.

And if he didn't?

Her stomach tightened. Well, she'd lived through Daniele, hadn't she?

She'd live through Ruggero too if it came to that. But how long she lived without his protection was another matter altogether.

———————◆———————

The courtroom was packed again, seemingly with every reporter in the country. Apparently the news that Corvi was increasing the scope of the Lucchesi trial had fired them up.

Loredana had seen the front page headline of the *Corriere della Sera* on her way in: "Montisi vs. Corvi: Will the Real Winner Be the Mafia?"

If only they knew what was actually going on. Though whoever had written that headline had unconsciously hit on the underlying truth. Whatever happened here, the Mafia had a hand in it. But she was going to do her best to see justice done.

Corvi was on time today. No excuses about running late. He'd probably been up all night preparing his arguments, to judge by his frazzled appearance.

At the defendant's bench, she saw the new addition to this charade: Vittorio Battista, a balding, heavyset, genial-looking man in his sixties, with a bushy mustache. Though he shared a table with Lucchesi and his lawyers, Battista had brought his own counsel.

This trial was turning into a circus, and she was the ringmaster.

Once the court was brought to order, she called Corvi forward. "Pubblico Ministero Corvi, please explain your rationale for expanding the scope of this case."

Corvi rose. "Vittorio Battista, who has been charged with bribery and fraud in his construction dealings from Calabria to Capri, is the *padrino* of Enrico Lucchesi. The Battista and Lucchesi families have a long history of doing business together as well, and Vittorio Battista is a client of the Banca di Falcone. We believe that Vittorio Battista has laundered his ill-gotten profits through that same bank. Thus, we believe that Battista and Lucchesi have colluded together to commit tax evasion and fraud."

"Have you received any new evidence from the FIU regarding these allegations?"

He shook his head. "Not as yet. We need more time. There's an incredibly complex series of corporations set up around the bank, with accounts all around the world. Unraveling where the money goes once it is withdrawn is a complex and time-consuming process. It may be months before we know the extent of it and where the money is funneled to."

"I see." When Trapani rose to respond to Corvi's allegations, Loredana motioned for him to take his seat. "Not yet, Avvocato Trapani. I have some additional questions."

She turned back to Corvi. "Have you located Sergio Grantini?"

"No."

"Have you any evidence tying Signor Lucchesi to the murder of Giudice Dinelli?"

"Not yet."

"So essentially, you're telling me you have nothing new to report?"

"Giudice, this is a new angle on the case. I need additional time to investigate it."

"You agreed, two weeks ago, to a fast-tracked trial. Will you be unable to meet the expectations of that agreement?"

"Giudice, I hadn't anticipated the complexity of the FIU investigation or the expanded scope of this case."

She held up a copy of the newspaper she'd picked up on the way into the courtroom. "And yet I see you had plenty of time to speak to the press."

Corvi reddened. "I was asked to give a statement."

"I've told you before I will not have this case tried in the media."

"That was not my intent, Giudice."

She smiled. "Intent or not, the effect is the same. I will not stand for it. Nor will I repeat myself again. Am I clear?"

"Yes, Giudice."

She allowed Trapani and Battista's lawyer to make their statements, all while nodding as if she were actually listening. But she'd already decided on a course of action. If Lorenzo Andretti was behind this—and considering that he'd yet to become a target of Corvi's or the FIU's investigations, it looked increasingly certain that he was—then she needed to thwart the man. And there was one way to do it.

Oh, she wouldn't take the final step yet and dismiss the case or give Lucchesi an acquittal. But she'd do the next best thing. And then she'd sit back and see what happened.

When Battista's lawyer quit speaking, she motioned for him to sit. "I agree that it is a hardship for a man of Signor Battista's advanced years and ill-health to be incarcerated in San Vittore for any length of time. Since the charges against him do not include anything approaching murder or physical injury, I am recommending that he be freed, with monitoring, for the next two weeks while the investigation proceeds."

"Two weeks?" Corvi said. "That gives me little time—"

"You're the one who tied these cases together. Therefore, this case falls under the accelerated timeline you agreed to." Corvi looked like he wanted to explode, but he merely nodded and sat down.

Loredana continued. "Regarding Signor Lucchesi, I have decided to remove the monitoring requirement."

Corvi hopped to his feet. "What?"

"You've brought no new evidence regarding the Dinelli case. Frankly, I am on the verge of dismissing it."

A clamor went up in the court and Corvi's face turned purple. "Giudice

Montisi, you cannot do this."

"You seem unable to make a case against Signor Lucchesi. I do not wish to subject him to these onerous monitoring requirements for any longer than is necessary."

Corvi swept a hand across his face. He looked sweaty, almost ill. Probably because he didn't want to face Lorenzo Andretti's wrath. To her surprise, he smiled. "Giudice, I notice that you've dismissed your security detail provided by the *carabinieri* and have provided your own men. Are you aware that these 'gentlemen' providing your security also work for the defendant?"

"Yes. However, they work for a great many people."

"I beg to differ."

She narrowed her eyes at Corvi. He wasn't going *there*, was he? "What are you implying?"

"Collusion. Plain and simple."

Fuck! Corvi wasn't entirely wrong, but what choice did she have? "You have no basis for that accusation. Repeat it, and you won't step foot in this courtroom again." Her hands shook as she dismissed the court, her stomach in knots. Damn Corvi, the sanctimonious little shit. He dared accuse her when he was the puppet of Lorenzo Andretti?

But look who's preaching.

She stepped down from the bench and approached Corvi, wanting to give him a piece of her mind. At the defense table, Ruggero had been watching the bailiff remove the ankle monitor from Lucchesi, but he looked up at her approach, locking gazes with her. Another bailiff was affixing a different monitor to Battista's ankle.

A cadre of reporters charged forward, and she backed away from the crush, stepping closer to the defense table. She was within arm's length of Ruggero when she saw it: a man in the back of the courtroom raised his arm and pointed something white at her. It looked odd—like one of those plastic guns—and she didn't have time to do more than scream before the man pulled the trigger. The person between her and the shooter was Vittorio Battista, and she pulled him forward as she dived for cover behind the defense table, pushing Ruggero down on her way.

A searing pain sliced through the upper part of her left arm, as if she'd been branded with an iron. She looked down, saw a hole in the sleeve of her black judge's robe, and felt something wet and hot spilling down her skin.

People were screaming, scrambling over each other trying to reach the exits, but all she could think about was whether Ruggero was okay. She'd heard two shots. One had hit her, obviously. Where had the other gone?

Ruggero was by her side in an instant, helping her to sit up. "Are you okay?" he asked.

She shook her head and motioned to her arm. "You?"

"I'm fine." He looked over his shoulder, his head moving first to look at Enrico Lucchesi, then to Vittorio Battista. Battista was lying across the desk clutching the side of his head, blood dripping over his fingers. He was conscious though, and that was a good sign, wasn't it?

She tried to move her arm and cried out. "Shh," Ruggero said. "You probably have a torn muscle." He stripped off his tie and wrapped it over her wound, which throbbed with her pulse. He touched her cheek, then dropped his hand away. For a moment she'd forgotten too where they were: in a crowded courtroom, on display for all to see, despite the chaos.

She tried to see if the shooter had been apprehended, but she couldn't tell what was happening in the clot of officers at the back of the courtroom. Not that they were likely to tell her anyway, after her dismissal of their protection.

If only she could tell the truth about what she knew. She no longer had any doubt: Lucchesi, and now Battista, was being framed.

And the man behind it wasn't going to let her ruin his plan.

CHAPTER 17

Ruggero paced back and forth in the hospital corridor, circling between the rooms where Loredana and Don Battista were being treated. In addition to his head wound, the old don was having heart palpitations, and he'd been put on an EKG. Loredana was being stitched up. Both of them would live, but no thanks to Ruggero.

He'd been so entranced by Loredana, he hadn't noticed anything else in the courtroom, and it had been only her own quick thinking that had saved her life and Don Battista's. Maybe even Ruggero's own. It had been a miracle that Enrico hadn't been hit, but given where the bullets went, Ruggero doubted that the shooter had been too far off the mark. Thank goodness those plastic guns weren't all that good yet.

This was all his fault. He shouldn't have played with Lorenzo, shouldn't have flaunted his ties with Loredana in front of Fuente. Oh, it had provoked a response all right. One he should have been better prepared for.

But he'd let his entanglement with her take his head out of the game. And look at how close he'd come to losing everything.

A door opened and closed, and Ruggero turned in time to see the doctor leave Loredana's room. Since the *carabinieri* officer posted outside Don Battista's room wasn't allowing anyone other than medical staff to enter, there was no reason not to visit her. Enrico, Antonio, and Kate were in the hospital cafeteria, making sure Kate ate something and relaxed after the commotion.

As Ruggero reached Loredana's door, a flutter passed through his gut. What the hell? But he knew why it was there. She just might tell him to fuck the hell off and get as far away from her as possible. He turned the handle, bracing himself for a frosty reception.

She was sitting up on the bed, the left sleeve of her blouse hastily cut away, a large bandage covering her deltoid muscle. She smiled when she saw him, and the sweetest relief flooded his system. Maybe she didn't blame him after all.

"Where have you been?" she asked.

"Pacing."

She chuckled. "Honestly?"

He nodded, then drew closer to the bed, gesturing to her arm. "How bad is it?"

She looked at the bandage. "The doctor's writing me a prescription for some pain medication. He said it's a flesh wound. It's going to hurt, and it's going to leave an ugly scar." She pulled a face. "I may never wear anything sleeveless again."

Her tone was arch, but Ruggero could see the concern in her eyes. "You can get surgery for it."

"You think that's what I'm worried about?"

He held her gaze. "No." He pulled a chair up to the bed and took her hand. "This is all my fault. I made a stupid move, putting the focus on you. I could've gotten you killed."

She squeezed his hand. "The focus was already there."

"I didn't even give it a second thought—"

"Shh." She put a finger on his lips. "I survived. So did everyone. Let's be thankful for that."

He nodded, but his stomach was still in a knot. She could have been killed. All because he hadn't been careful. He'd wanted to shake the tree, make something happen. "No thanks to me," he whispered. "I should have protected *you*. Not the other way around."

She caressed his face, her fingers going to his scar. "Give and take," she murmured. "It's okay to let someone help you once a while."

His throat tightened. She touched on something similar to what Elena had said, how she hadn't looked out for him when she should have. But Loredana had. He wanted to say something, but what?

All he could do was stare at her, mute and confused. "Tell me about this," she said, her fingers passing over the scar he knew so well.

The familiar urge to say nothing rose up in him. But he owed her something, so he fought it down. "I got it the day my father was killed. He died because of me." The words thickened in his throat, becoming strangled, but he swallowed hard and pushed on, telling the story of the thwarted assassination attempt on Rinaldo Lucchesi, Enrico's father, the words coming in a rush.

"I was stupid. I let my selfishness take me away from my post. If I'd just been patient, waited, done my damn job..." His voice cracked. "My father died because of me. Because I wasn't doing my job. I wasn't paying attention. And now..." His eyes grew hot with tears, and he looked away. "I did it again. You could have been killed today." He rubbed at the moisture, unable to look at her. He hadn't been a child for many, many years, and here he was, blubbering like a baby. What must she think of him?

She tilted his face back to hers, something warm in her eyes. "Thanks for telling me. I know that was hard."

His stomach was so tight he felt ill. "What are you doing to me?" he whispered. "You ask, and I start talking. I haven't repeated that story to anyone, in over twenty years."

She smiled and brushed his hair. "I did have to ask three times."

He huffed in amusement. "You hardly put the screws to me."

"I want to know you. And I think you want someone to know you too."

His throat tightened again. Hadn't Chiara hinted at that? He'd dismissed what she'd said, but now the impossible was happening: Loredana Montisi knew who he was, knew his deepest shame, and she wasn't running from him. Quite the opposite.

She stroked his cheek, her fingers finding the scar again. "I hope you get some surgery to address this. Not because of how it makes you look—I think you're handsome just as you are—but because of how it makes you feel."

"If you think I'm keeping this scar to punish myself, you're wrong."

"Am I? If not to punish yourself, then why?"

"It's a reminder not to let down my guard."

She stared at him. "I think you've absorbed that lesson well enough. Too well."

He snorted. "Hardly. Look what happened today."

"Everyone makes mistakes."

He almost didn't say the words, but they slipped out anyway. "Mine get people killed."

"And there we go. You *are* keeping it to punish yourself."

Maybe she was right, but shedding the scar felt like cheating. "I can't let it go. Not now. Maybe not ever."

"Promise me you'll think about it."

He nodded. He'd think about it. But some things couldn't be—shouldn't be—erased.

Someone tapped on the door, and a nurse entered with a pill in a cup and some papers. "Here's one to take now. You can fill the prescription at the pharmacy."

Loredana took the pill, downing it with a paper cup of water. "Am I free to go?" she asked.

The nurse nodded. "Here are the discharge instructions. You'll need the stitches out in seven to ten days."

The nurse left the room, and Loredana swung her legs over the side of the bed, careful not to put much weight on her injured arm. Ruggero assisted her to her feet.

"I don't really need help," she said.

"I know. But I want to."

Her face softened and her eyes misted. She touched his cheek. "You do," she whispered, a little hint of wonder in her voice.

Could he blame her for being surprised, after the fiancé who'd run off and the *carabiniere* who'd betrayed her?

"I do," he said, filling his voice with conviction. It was true. And it went beyond the moment, into a realm that scared him. She wasn't someone he could make a commitment to. And yet... hadn't he just done so?

His stomach tightened again. Sooner or later, he was going to have to choose between her and the 'Ndrangheta. But there was no choice, was there?

He'd made his decision long ago, when he'd taken his vows. Vows that he'd never broken, until now. A confrontation was coming, between what he wanted, and what he'd sworn. And if there was anything he hated, it was a man who didn't keep his word.

"What's wrong?" she asked. "You look so unhappy."

"It's nothing. Just worrying about the future."

"Ah, so you *do* worry about things."

"All the time."

"And here I thought nothing got to you."

He grabbed the bag containing her damaged judge's robe, then escorted her out into the hall. He glanced down the corridor toward the guard outside Don Battista's room, and an idea occurred to him. "You think you could get me and the Lucchesis in to see Signor Battista? I think it would be a comfort to him. He's been having some heart palpitations."

She gave him a wry smile that said she saw right through him. "I think I can manage that."

He made a call, and soon Enrico, Antonio, and Kate were there. Loredana donned her torn robe and they followed her over to the guard.

"These people need to see Signor Battista," she said.

The guard looked up from his newspaper. "And you are?"

"Giudice Loredana Montisi. I'm presiding over Signor Battista's case."

"His family is already in there. I'm not supposed to let anyone else in."

She motioned to Enrico. "These people are family as well."

"Any of your last names Battista?" When they shook their heads, he went back to reading the paper.

"What's *your* name?" Loredana asked. "So that I can get it right in my complaint to your superior."

He folded the paper down, the newsprint crunching. "This is highly irregular."

She pointed to the bandage visible through the hole in her bloody robe. "So is getting shot in my own courtroom. Now let these people pass."

He stared at her for a moment, then sighed. "Fine. I don't need the hassle. But if anyone says anything to me about this, *your* name is going in *my* report."

"As I'd expect," Loredana said. She remained out in the hall, telling Ruggero she had some calls to make.

They filed inside. Don Battista's wife and his sons, Fabrizio and Pasquale, were in the room. Before anyone spoke, Ruggero held up a hand for silence. He approached Don Battista and motioned to the sheet covering his legs. "May I?" he asked.

When the don nodded, Ruggero turned back the sheet, checking to see if the monitoring anklet had been successfully placed before the shooting had started. The don's legs were bare. When Ruggero looked at him, Don Battista grinned. "Cautious, as always. Livio taught you well. We can speak, for now. I'm sure they'll send someone to attach the anklet before the day is over. Pasquale scanned the room, and it's free of bugs at the moment."

When Ruggero stepped back, Don Battista motioned Kate forward. "Caterina, I hope you and the child are all right."

She took his hand. "I'm fine." Her voice thickened. "I'm more worried about you."

The old don laughed, but it ended in a cough. "Don't you fret. I will see Lorenzo Andretti in his grave before I ever go to mine."

At the mention of Andretti, the don's wife stepped forward. "Come Caterina, let's leave the men to their business and get you off your feet."

After they left, Ruggero took a deep breath, then said what he had to say. "This is my fault. I let Andretti think that Giudice Montisi is on our side." He explained about his and Loredana's visit to the *carabinieri* headquarters and the threat he'd made to Fuente after the shooting.

Enrico's face darkened. "You should have discussed it with me."

"You wanted me to be strategic. Well, that was strategic." Ruggero turned to Don Battista. "I'm sorry you were caught in the crossfire."

Don Battista waved him off. "Eh, it was good to poke him. Now he's done something reckless. Perhaps something that will get the case dismissed?"

Ruggero scratched at his cheek. "I can't speak for the judge. Though I think she understands the situation quite clearly now."

"That's all for the good." Don Battista turned to Enrico. "Of course, with this attack on me and my businesses, I'm afraid I can't give you everything I promised."

"I will manage."

"Lorenzo has made it clear he wants both of us dead. You must press Gianluca to publicly pick a side. You need men and money. Lorenzo is bound to attack again, and soon. He won't rest."

"I'll speak to Gianluca," Enrico said.

"*Bene.*" Don Battista motioned to Ruggero. "I would like to talk with Ruggero. Alone, *per favore.*"

Everyone's brows went up, including Ruggero's. What did Don Battista want with him? The memory of their talk by the lake rose up.

After the room had emptied, Don Battista motioned to a nearby chair. "This will take a few minutes." He eased himself a bit more upright. "You remember our discussion?" Ruggero nodded. "It is time."

"The trial isn't over."

"Never mind that." He held Ruggero's gaze. "After Livio died, you had to raise yourself. So did Enrico, after what Carlo did to Rinaldo, murdering his wife and sons."

Where was Don Battista going with this?

"You remember what Enrico did next?"

Ruggero had heard the tale from Tommaso. "He killed the four assassins Carlo had sent. He avenged his family."

"Yes. His decision and his plan were clever, audacious. Risky. The brainchild of a desperately unhappy young man who felt he had nothing to lose." Don Battista wheezed in a breath. "But now Enrico has everything to lose. A wife, an unborn child, two sons. Rico is brilliant, and he's the leader we need in many ways, but he hasn't been tested and battle-hardened the way he normally would have been. Toni was his shield from Carlo for many years."

Like Enrico, there was a time when Ruggero hadn't had anything to lose. But perhaps he did now. "You could say I haven't been tested either, then."

The old don took a long look at him. "For you, it wasn't necessary. The day your father died, you learned the basic truth: kill or be killed. You've known it in your marrow, for much of your life. Rico knows it in his head, not his heart. He understands strategy; he understands vengeance. *You* understand survival."

Ruggero nodded, though he felt disloyal for doing it.

Don Battista smiled. "I can see on your face you don't like me speaking so plainly. But it is the truth. Even Rico knows it—maybe not in the same way, but he knows. Why do you think he chose you to help in this war?"

Ruggero shrugged and stood, jamming his hands in his pockets.

"You love him like a brother. You will never betray him. Acknowledging the truth about him is not a betrayal. It is necessary. For you *must* help him. You must do the things he cannot do."

But I have betrayed him. I have. "I am not sure how I can get close to Andretti."

"Everyone has a weak point. So does Lorenzo."

"Yes. But what?"

"What is the thing Lorenzo hasn't done, the thing you would have expected?"

Ruggero stared at Don Battista, unsure what he was hinting at. Then it came to him. "Dario. I expected him to take out Dario after Cristoforo."

Don Battista smiled. "Yes. And why hasn't he?"

"Dario has something he wants."

"Exactly. Though Lorenzo is strong, very strong, he has no presence in the North. Were he to forge an alliance with Dario, he could gain something he's long desired: a foothold in Milan and Lombardy."

"He's taken a roundabout path to it."

"He thought he could manipulate Enrico. When that didn't work, he tried to undermine and break Dario."

Ruggero nodded. Of course. The question was: Had Lorenzo succeeded? And if he hadn't, could they bring Dario around to their side?

Not as long as Dario hated Enrico. There was no getting them into the same room even.

But perhaps there was a way. And perhaps Dario could prove to be the ally Ruggero needed.

"You see what must be done?" Don Battista asked.

"Yes. It will take some time."

"You don't have much. The shark doesn't hesitate when there's blood in the water. And neither will Lorenzo."

———— ♦ ————

Antonio was waiting for Ruggero when he left Don Battista's room. "What did he want?" Antonio asked.

Ruggero shrugged. What could he say?

"He's given you an assignment." When Ruggero shrugged again, Antonio frowned. "I'm not an idiot, and neither is Enrico."

"I can't discuss it yet."

Antonio crossed his arms. "He tell you that?"

"Not in so many words."

"Fine. Then tell me this: What's going on between you and the judge?"

"Nothing."

Antonio laughed. "Now you're being insulting. There's something between you."

Damn it. He did not want to discuss Loredana. "It's nothing."

Antonio shook his head. "You're a terrible liar. You, my friend, really like her. I've never seen you look at a woman like that."

Fuck. Written all over his face, was it? "She's tough. Nerves of steel. Ballsy."

"You *do* like her."

Ruggero almost smiled. It was so much more than that. "No. It's worse. I *admire* her."

With a sly grin, Antonio said, "Tell me. Have you admired what's under that robe?"

Ruggero shrugged again, but Antonio wasn't fooled. His expression turned serious. "What are you going to do?"

"It's up to her. I can't make her do anything."

"You haven't told her?"

Ruggero gave him a withering look; best to lie about what he'd done. If Tonio knew, and he told Don Lucchesi... Yeah, there'd be hell to pay.

"If she knew, do you think she'd leave her job?" Antonio asked.

Ruggero snorted. "I've never met someone so hell-bent on doing the 'right' thing. She's not going to leave the law. Certainly not for me."

And that's what he needed to keep telling himself. Over and over again. Believing anything else was foolish.

CHAPTER 18

While Ruggero was in his meeting, Loredana looked for a quiet place to make a call. She needed to talk to someone who wasn't involved in the whole business, and the one person she could think of was her older sister, Allegra.

The situation with Ruggero confused the hell out of her. He seemed to care for her, and *Dio* only knew that she was starting to care for him much more than was wise. The things she'd done since she'd met him. The things she was still doing... and the things she was thinking about doing... they all went against everything she'd ever believed—about herself, about how one should live, about the way the world worked best.

How had she ever ended up in bed with a Mafioso?

And how the hell was she going to continue doing her job, knowing what she knew?

She pulled out her phone and saw a dozen voice messages and missed calls from her family on it. *Porca miseria.* She always put her mobile on silent when she was in court, and it hadn't occurred to her that the incident had made the news. But of course it had; it must have been on television for hours now.

She scrolled through her phone's contact list with shaking fingers until she found Allegra's number. If she could rely on anyone to give her good advice, it was her sister. Allegra answered on the first ring. "*Grazie a Dio*! Mamma, Gisella, and I have been frantic. No one would tell us anything, and you haven't answered your phone. We saw the news. How are you?"

"I'm fine. The bullet just grazed my arm."

"Have you spoken to Mamma?"

"Not yet. But I will." She hesitated, then said, "I wanted to talk to you first."

"Why?"

Loredana took a deep breath, but it did little to keep her voice even. "I've royally screwed up. And I'm probably going to lose my job. Actually, I probably *should* lose my job."

"What are you talking about?"

It was best not to say too much. "Let's just say that I'm sleeping with the enemy."

"*What* is going on?"

"I can't really tell you. But I think…" Her voice trembled. "I think I should resign after this case."

"Which one? Baldassare?"

"No. Lucchesi."

"Ah." Allegra was quiet for a moment. "Well, I know what Mamma would tell you."

"What?"

"She'd tell you to stay. That you can't possibly be any more corrupt than they are."

Loredana almost laughed. "She'd never say that."

"Come on, Loredana. You *know*."

She didn't like Allegra's tone. "What are you talking about?"

"You honestly don't know?"

Loredana felt a bit queasy. "You're starting to piss me off. No more riddles."

Allegra's voice was hushed. "She's never told you, after all this time?"

"*What* hasn't she told me?"

Her sister said nothing for a long while. Then she sighed. "You need to ask her why Papà was shot."

"I know why."

"You have no idea. And it's time you did."

"Just tell me."

"You're going to have to hear it from her."

"Allegra—"

"I'm not saying another word. Call me after you talk to her. I'm glad you're okay."

Allegra hung up, and Loredana stared at the phone, feeling a hundred times worse than she had before placing the call. A horrible idea occurred to her, and she had to swallow hard to keep down the espresso she'd bought from the hospital vending machine.

Ruggero came up and touched her shoulder. "What's wrong?"

She couldn't speak. All she could do was press a hand to her stomach.

"Are the painkillers making you ill?"

She shook her head.

"What's going on then?"

"I don't know. I don't know what to think."

"About what?"

"About anything." But standing around the hospital dreading what she had to do was only delaying the inevitable. "I have to see my mother. Right now."

"Is it about the case?" he asked.

"No. It's about the past."

"Does that really matter now?"

She held his eyes. "It means everything." She called her mother. "Where are you?" Loredana asked. "I have to see you."

"Are you all right? I saw the news. They said you were alive, but you haven't returned my calls."

"I'm fine. The doctors were stitching up my arm. It's nothing."

"I told you they wouldn't protect you."

"*They* are not the problem, Mamma."

"Well, if you're coming here, you'd better not bring them. I don't want them knowing where I am."

"I'm not sure you have any right to judge them."

"What does that mean?"

"Allegra said something to me. About Papà."

Nora didn't respond for a long moment. Then she gave Loredana the address and hung up. Loredana stared at the phone. Her stomach was sour, knotted. Ruggero placed a hand on her arm. "You don't look good."

"I'm really not."

"You don't have to do this."

Loredana shook her head. "I do." Her mother had lied to her when she'd said Papà was clean. She'd lied, but now she was going to tell the truth.

————◆————

Despite her mother's wishes, Loredana started to give Ruggero the address where her mother was staying. He cut her off. "I already know. I've had men watching over her the entire time." He paused. "I didn't want to take any chances."

Days ago, she'd have doubted his sincerity. "Thank you," she said, meaning it with all her heart.

He nodded and escorted her out of the hospital, calling Tommaso along the way.

She shouldn't trust Ruggero. He was a man brimming with secrets, with lies, with terrible deeds, and still she felt safe with him. He'd made her a sort of promise back in her hospital room. She'd felt the weight of it in his words, in the way he'd looked at her, so solemn, so full of purpose.

She'd waited her whole life for a man who could make such a promise, who'd even be willing to.

It was just her luck that he was the wrong man. But wasn't he the right one, in so many ways that counted?

They soon arrived at an imposing apartment building in a fashionable section of Milan. Loredana had no idea which of her mother's friends lived here, but whoever it was had done well for him or herself. She glanced around for signs of surveillance and finally spotted two men in a car who gave Ruggero slight nods as they walked by.

They and the guards with them were buzzed in, but just she and Ruggero went upstairs. Her mother would be angered enough by Ruggero's presence; no need to have more witnesses to that than necessary.

When they reached the door, Ruggero unholstered his gun, but held it discreetly down by his side. "I'll go in first. Wait out here. Just in case. And don't stand in front of the door."

Ruggero tapped on the door, and Loredana expected the apartment's owner to answer, but it was her mother herself who came. Nora took one look at Ruggero and then she turned to Loredana. "I asked you for *one* thing. One."

"He already knew where you were."

Nora blanched slightly, then she turned and headed down a wide hall that had rooms branching off it. Ruggero followed her inside. "Anyone else here?" he asked.

"I'm surprised you don't already know that too."

"Signora Albani owns the apartment. Lives alone. But one can never be too careful."

"Especially not in your line of *work*." Nora practically spat the words at him.

Loredana didn't hear him reply, and moments later he came back and nodded to her. "Want me to stay?" he asked.

Her stomach fluttered, but she shook her head. He could protect her from many things. But not the truth. That she needed to face alone.

He motioned her into the apartment and then stepped outside, shutting the outer door softly behind him. She followed the hallway into a beautiful sitting room. The late afternoon sun gave the space a warm glow, but Loredana felt cold inside. All this time, she'd been deceived. Well, no longer.

She took a seat in a plumply upholstered chair across from her mother, who'd obviously been doing a crossword puzzle when she'd called, to judge by the open book of them sitting on the table beside her. All those puzzles, over all those years. Had she been trying to unlock how her husband had gone wrong?

Nora shifted in her chair, clasping and unclasping her hands. "Now I'll have to find somewhere else to stay."

"There's no need. Besides, they'll find you."

"Of course they will," Nora snapped. "Don't you see? They're keeping tabs on me so that they can use me against you. If you stop doing what they want, *I'll* be the one who pays the price."

"It's not like that. They're watching over you."

Nora snorted. "When did you become so blind?"

"I don't know, Mamma. Maybe when I trusted you to tell me the truth about Papà."

"I told you the truth."

Loredana's chest filled with heat. "You told me Papà was clean. You swore it, and I believed you. But you lied."

"I didn't."

"If he was so clean, why do the rumors still circulate? Why did Allegra tell me that I don't know the full story?"

Nora shook her head and looked away. Loredana waited for her mother to say something, but she didn't. And then another possibility occurred to her. Maybe her mother had been protecting someone. "If Papà wasn't the one taking bribes, who was?"

A shudder racked Nora and she sobbed in a breath. Tears spilled down her cheeks, and she looked away. Loredana's stomach twisted into a knot. *No.* A chill raced across her back. "It was you?"

Nora nodded and gulped in another breath. "It was so easy. The money was so good."

"Did Papà know?"

Nora shook her head. "Of course not."

"What happened? If you were taking their money, why did Papà get shot?"

"They asked me to do something I couldn't do. They wanted your father to acquit a man who'd murdered a child. The boy had suffered before he died. I might have tried if the death had been an accident. But what the man had done… it was horrible. I couldn't bring myself to try to persuade your father."

Loredana's eyes burned with tears. "So they shot him." She could barely form the words. "Papà," she whispered, and Nora let out a great sob.

"It's my fault. I'm so sorry." She reached out to Loredana, her hand trembling so hard Loredana took it.

She wanted to hate her mother. She'd lied to Loredana over and over. All that bullshit about the law, about justice. About doing the right thing, when all along, she hadn't really believed any of it. And yet—in a way her mother had always told the truth. Loredana caught sight of the ugly scar bisecting her mother's right cheek. Now she knew why her mother had never gotten surgery for it. "You loved him, really loved him, didn't you?"

Nora nodded. "I couldn't tell him what I'd done. I couldn't put him in that position. If he'd known, he would have tried to save me. But it would have ruined him, broken his spirit." She pressed a hand to her lips. "I never expected they'd go after him. I thought it would be *me*." Her voice broke on the word, and she squeezed Loredana's hand. "Forgive me."

Loredana swallowed hard. Could she? "Why did you do it? Why?"

Nora stiffened. "I wanted a good life for you girls."

"We had one already."

"I wanted more for you."

"What more did we need?"

Nora sat back in her chair, withdrawing her hand from Loredana's. Her eyes were stony. "You, of all people, can't judge me."

"And why is that?"

Her mother let out a little huff of disbelief. "I can see it *all* over you. And him. I may have taken money from them, but I never stooped as low as you have."

"What do you mean?" Loredana asked.

"I never whored for them."

A bomb may as well have detonated in Loredana's gut. "You think so little of me? You think that's how he treats me? He may not be perfect, but he's a better man than Daniele or Stefano. Daniele liked how I looked on his arm, and Stefano—" Her voice broke. "He was using me to get something he wanted. And he didn't care what happened to me as a result." She almost blurted the truth, including Ruggero's part in it, but *Dio* knew what her mother would do with that information.

"He's scum, Loredana. He's a murderer." Her mother snapped her fingers. "They all are."

"So are you."

Nora's face crumpled. "I never intended for this to happen."

"Oh no. Of course not. There's no way taking bribes from the Mafia could *possibly* be a bad idea."

"I never thought—"

"No, you didn't. You didn't think. You didn't *care*."

"I loved him," Nora sobbed.

Loredana rose. "And you have to live with that." Her vision blurred with tears. Papà. All those years stolen from him, from them. He'd never gotten to see his grandchildren. He'd never known that Loredana had followed in his footsteps...

But had she really? *Could* she claim the high road? She'd broken the law. She'd done things her father never would have.

And yet—there was justice in what she'd done. Enrico Lucchesi was being framed. Fuente was a dirty cop, and Stefano had admitted he'd worked for another Mafioso. True, Lucchesi might be guilty of many things, but she wasn't going to be the one who convicted him of a crime he hadn't committed. Because if he had done it, there'd have been no need for any of this. The evidence would have been there.

She looked again at her mother, sobbing pitifully in her chair, and closed her eyes, listening to that keening, the sound tearing at her. A lump rose in her throat, full of all the things she couldn't say. "I need to go," she finally managed.

"Loredana, please."

"I need time, Mamma. I need to think."

Her mother let out another wail, and Loredana almost caved. But she wasn't ready. Anger still burned hot in her chest. Anger for Papà. Anger for all the things that could never be. "I'll call you."

When I'm ready. If I ever am.

She turned and tried to shut out her mother's cries. Tears of her own ran down her cheeks and she wiped at them furiously, trying to blink them away, fighting for composure. She didn't want anyone to see her like this. She didn't want anyone to know how thoroughly shattered she felt.

When she opened the outside door and stepped into the hush of the hallway, Ruggero knew. His harsh look of concentration softened, and he took her in his arms. "*Bambina*," he whispered in her hair. She couldn't hold back the tears any longer. She shook from the effort of trying to suppress them, from trying to cry silently, and burrowed her face into his chest, gulping down air as if she were drowning.

He cradled her gently, murmuring something in her hair. "What?" she asked.

"Nothing," he said, raising his voice slightly. Then he hummed that lullaby he'd crooned to her the night he'd rescued her from Stefano and those men. She closed her eyes, and his arms tightened around her.

Her world may have fallen apart, but here he was, holding her together.

———◆———

The whole trip back to the hotel, Ruggero stayed tight by Loredana's side and did his best to keep some discreet physical contact with her—holding her hand in the car, placing his hand at the small of her back in the elevator. He barely said a word to her the entire time, yet she felt his reassurance, his strength. The comfort he was trying to give her.

As soon as they were alone in their suite, he took her coat, gently removing the garment from her and guiding her to the sofa. He sat beside her and entwined his calloused fingers with hers. "What happened?" he asked, his voice as gentle as she'd ever heard it.

Loredana took a deep breath. She could do this. She could do this without crying. "She lied to me. She told me my father was clean. But what she *didn't* tell me—" Her voice broke. "My whole life has been built on lies. She pushed me into the law. She told me she wanted me to make Papà proud. But that wasn't it. She wanted—" Her throat clamped shut and she had to swallow before she could go on. "She wanted me to make up for what *she'd* done to him."

Ruggero's brow creased. "She was the one taking money?"

Loredana nodded. "And she wants me to forgive her." Her vision blurred. Damn it, she *was* going to cry. "And I *can't.*"

"Do you want to?"

Hot tears poured down her cheeks, stung her eyes. "She got Papà killed. Out of greed. How can I forgive that?"

He pulled her into his lap and wiped her tears with his thumbs. "People make mistakes."

"She called me a whore."

"What?" His voice hardened and his hands balled into fists. He opened them immediately, but the coldness of his gaze, the steel in his tone, spoke volumes.

"She figured out that I was sleeping with you."

A muscle tensed in his jaw. "Do you agree with her?"

It took her a second to realize what he was referring to. "Of course not."

"You are nothing like them," he said.

"I realize that."

"I don't think you do." He touched her cheek. "They never—" He cut himself off.

She waited, but he said nothing more. "They never what?" She kept her voice soft, almost felt that she had to hold her breath.

"They never made me *feel*." His voice rasped on the last word.

Tears filled her eyes again. "Oh Ruggero." She sniffed hard, then started to laugh. "What are we doing here?"

"I don't know." He looked away from her. Then his eyes shyly met hers again. "All I know is that I can't even think of not being with you."

She didn't know what to say. He was struggling; if she was honest with him, would that help or hurt? "Well, you might be stuck with me."

Was that disappointment in his eyes? "You'll sort things out with your mother."

Her throat tightened. "I don't see how." Her eyes burned and blurred. More fucking tears. She covered her eyes with her hands. "I'm sorry." *For crying so much. For not being honest with you.*

"You have nothing to be sorry about," he murmured.

"Yes I do," she sobbed. She needed to tell him. He'd been honest; she needed to be honest too.

But before she could say anything, he gathered her in his arms and carried her into her bathroom. He set her on her feet, then turned on the taps in the oversized tub. He added some bath products, and the water foamed, a light floral scent filling the air.

"Ruggero, I—"

He hushed her with a finger on her lips. "No more talking."

Because she'd hurt him? He held her eyes for a moment, and she nodded. Maybe she needed to gather herself. To be sure of what she was feeling, of what she wanted to say. It had been a hellish day—getting shot at, learning the truth about her mother—maybe he was right. She needed a moment of not talking. They both did.

He undressed them both, then helped her into the bath, making sure she kept her bandaged arm out of the water. He got in behind her, his arms going around her body, his knees surrounding hers. They sat like that for a long time, saying nothing. When the water grew cool, he turned on the hot tap again, and let enough water drain out to compensate.

Her stiff muscles relaxed, but her mind whirled. What he'd said to her, what she *hadn't* said to him. What she needed to say. She shifted in his arms so she could look at his face. "I owe you an apology."

"For what?"

"For not being honest out there. You said something to me, and I tried to make light of it."

He stiffened. "That was... a mistake."

She shook her head, her heart pounding in her chest. "It wasn't. What I said was." She reached up and touched his cheek. "I can't imagine not being with you either."

CHAPTER 19

A wave of relief washed over Ruggero. So he wasn't the world's biggest fool.

Loredana straightened herself a bit and leaned in, and he pulled her close. When their lips met, he felt it—how *she* felt, what those words meant to her. What they meant to him. If only things were different, if only he could promise her everything.

He deepened the kiss instead of asking her what he wanted to know. But he couldn't pressure her; if she was going to leave the law, that had to come from her. It had to be *her* choice. Not something he coerced her into.

She pulled back. "What are we going to do?"

"Let's just take it day by day."

"But—"

He put a finger to her mouth, her gorgeous mouth. "No more talking." For there were no answers. And he didn't want to waste a precious second with her.

She looked like she wanted to say something more, then she nodded. He helped her out of the tub, then dried her with a towel, planting kisses on her shoulders, her neck, her breasts, slowly moving south until he was on his knees before her.

Dio, she was lovely, like Botticelli's Venus, rising from the waves. Her hair tumbled past her shoulders, still wet at the ends, her skin glistening in the places he hadn't yet dried.

He pressed the towel to the soft flesh of her belly, careful around the cut from Stefano's blade. He'd never regret what he'd done to the man. Never. He placed a kiss on the healing skin, then rubbed the towel over her thighs, her calves, the delicate bones of her ankles and feet.

He kissed the inside of her right knee, and she shivered. Setting the towel aside, he slid his hands up her inner thighs, spreading her legs slightly apart. She looked down at him, her green eyes glowing, her cheeks flushed from the bath. He slid his fingers higher until he touched the neatly trimmed hair between her thighs.

Remembering what she'd said to him, he drew one hand back and wet his index finger in his mouth, then slid it into the cleft between her legs. She shuddered when his fingers passed over her *grilletto*, and he worked that bit of flesh until it hardened and swelled.

Placing his thumb over it, he pushed one finger, then another inside her, enjoying her gasps of pleasure, the way she wound her fingers in his hair. He'd gladly spend the rest of his life making her cry out like that, making her come again and again…

He worked his fingers in and out, until she was trembling, then he pressed his mouth to her, finding that little pearl. He swirled his tongue around it, then sucked it into his mouth, and she cried out, bucking against him, her legs shaking so hard he grabbed her hip to hold her.

"God, Ruggero," she gasped.

He smiled against her skin. "We're not one and the same, but I don't mind you saying so."

She laughed and pinched his ear. Then she sobered. "I like seeing this side of you." She brushed his hair back. "I like it a lot."

His throat tightened. *I like being like this.* He almost said the words, but it wasn't the time. If he ever figured out a solution, then he could say everything he wanted to. Until then, he'd just have to show her.

Rising, he picked her up, and she laughed, protesting lightly. He carried her into the bedroom and closed the drapes, then dropped her on the bed, pausing beside her. She reached out and took his stiff *cazzo* in her hand. "I think it's time I returned the favor," she said, her voice low and husky.

His *cazzo* twitched, eager to be inside her mouth, between those lush lips. But that was something he'd taken from Chiara and the others too many times. Loredana wasn't one of those girls.

"No. You don't have to." He started to extricate himself from her grasp.

"I want to." She tightened her fingers around him.

"*I* don't want you to."

"Yes, you do," she said. "I can see it all over your face."

"Not right now."

She peered up at him, her fingers caressing him. "Why?"

"Because…" He searched for a reason that wasn't the truth. "Because I just don't," he said, the words sounding lame even to his own ears.

"Tell me the truth." She glided her fingers over the head of his *cazzo*, spreading the slickness of his pre-ejaculate over the tip. He fought not to react, but she did it again.

A light sweat broke out on his forehead. "Because I want this to be different. I want *us* to be different."

She paused in her movements. "Do you think this is beneath me?"

He nodded, and she rose up on an elbow, her mouth so close to the tip of his *cazzo* that he could think of nothing else.

Her tongue darted out, sliding over his cockhead, and he groaned, then shifted back. Damn her. "No." He barely managed the word.

"Yes," she said, then leaned forward and took him in her mouth. For a few seconds—heavenly, tantalizing seconds—he didn't move. Her tongue swirled over him, making him shudder and curse. Then he pulled back.

"I said no." He made the words firm. When she reached for him again, he took her by the wrists and pushed her onto her back, straddling her, her wrists imprisoned in his hands, and an urge came over him that threatened to swamp his control.

She was breathing heavily, her eyes darting up to his hands on her wrists. "You want to be in charge," she said.

He held her gaze. "Yes," he finally said. "That's what I want." He swallowed hard, his heart tapping on his ribs.

She looked again at her wrists, then back up at him. Then she nodded.

Some kind of switch flipped in him. "Stay here. And do *not* move," he said as he rose. "Not a millimeter."

She gave him another nod, and he crossed the room to the bath. He quickly found what he was looking for: the ties to the two terrycloth robes on the back of the bathroom door.

Her nostrils flared when she saw them in his hands and her hips shifted restlessly. Ah, so she truly did like this idea. He fastened one of the ties around the base of the padded headboard where it attached to the mattress frame, then looped it around her wrist.

"Tie it," she said, her voice tight and breathy. "Make it so I can't escape."

His cock jumped. She *really* liked this idea. He knotted the tie around her wrist, then secured the other and tightened the second tie around the other side. Her arms were drawn out now to her sides. He'd given her a bit of room to shift, but not much.

"Bend your knees," he said.

She drew her legs up, closing off his view of her glistening *figa*. "Keep them open," he said.

She hesitated. "Open your legs for me." His voice was gruff, raw. He couldn't remember ever being this excited.

Loredana's arms stiffened against the restraints, the muscles tightening. Then she opened her legs.

"More." He held her eyes. She swallowed, then she let her legs fall open.

"Good girl." He got the ties from the robes in his room. He secured both her legs, then stepped back to admire his work.

She tried to close her legs, but couldn't. He smiled. "Good." He slipped into the robe he'd brought with him. "I'll be back in a minute."

"Where are you going?" she asked, her voice high with alarm.

"To get something."

"You're coming back?"

He gestured to the robe he was wearing. "Where do you think I'm going?"

She blew out. "I've never done this before."

"Neither have I." He'd always been in control, but never this explicitly. Because Chiara and the others, they'd always been compliant, they'd always followed his lead. Loredana didn't—or hadn't, until now.

The fact that she'd agreed to this—and that she was turned on by it—still surprised him. He went out into the main living room and over to the windows, pulling the drapes shut, then headed straight to the minibar. What he wanted was in there.

He grabbed the champagne flutes from the shelf above, then filled the ice bucket and took the bottle of prosecco with him. No doubt the hotel would charge a fortune for it, but he didn't care. All that mattered was the woman waiting for him.

He entered the bedroom, drinking in the sight of her, bound and helpless. He needed just one more thing. Crossing the room to the dresser, he rifled through it until he found a silk scarf in her things. That would do nicely.

He set everything down on the nightstand beside her. Picking up the scarf, he said, "Lift your head."

"You're going to blindfold me?"

He nodded. And waited. Finally she lifted her head off the pillow. He wrapped the scarf around her eyes, then knotted it, making sure she could see nothing. "*Perfetto*," he murmured.

Her lower lip trembled, and that bit of vulnerability made him lean down and kiss her. "You're safe with me, *bambina*."

"I know," she whispered.

He reached down and tweaked one of her tight nipples. Then he stepped away from the bed. He had an idea. There was a vase of fresh flowers on the dresser, and he took a peach-colored rose from it. He tested the petals with his fingertips. Would she guess what it was?

He crossed back to the bed, trailing the rose along the outside of her right leg, up to her hip, then across her belly, her breasts, circling but not touching the stiff, dusky nipples, then caressed the petals up to her throat, along her jaw.

She shifted against the sheets. "That tickles."

He swooped the rose back to her breasts, this time teasing her nipples, making her writhe. "More," she panted.

He played the rose along the skin of her belly, brushing it over her navel, then skimming it along the hair between her legs. Skipping over her *figa*, he feathered the rose along the insides of her thighs until she squirmed and tried to close her legs.

"Keep them open," he said.

"You're killing me."

He chuckled. "I haven't even started." Setting the rose aside, he reached for the prosecco. Her forehead creased as he peeled off the foil, then popped the cork.

"What is that?"

He didn't answer. He poured a glass, then sat down on the mattress beside her. Placing a hand beneath her head, he brought the rim to her lips. "Drink."

She swallowed the sparkling wine, a bit of it dribbling out of the side of her mouth, and he couldn't resist licking it up. He placed his mouth over hers, and she opened to him eagerly. Then she sucked on his tongue until he groaned. Dear God, how he wanted that mouth on him. But not yet.

He set down the champagne flute and took an ice cube from the bucket. He trailed it along her lips, enjoying the sight of her pink tongue coming out to lap at it, then he ran it around her nipples. She shivered and moaned, twisting against the ties that bound her.

Sliding the melting cube along her belly, he brought it down, down, until it rested just above her mound.

She trembled beneath him, her legs moving as if she couldn't keep them still. A soft cry left her mouth, and his cock strained against the cloth of the robe he still wore.

He circled the ice cube around and around, watching a trickle of water drip between the lips of her *figa*. She shivered and cried out. "Please," she said.

"Please what?"

"Touch me."

"Where?" he teased.

She smiled. "You know where."

"Oh, I don't think I do."

She laughed. "It's hardly a mystery to you now, is it?"

"I might need further education on the subject."

Her hips twisted as another drop of water slid between her folds. "Please," she begged.

And there it was—that raw pleading note he'd been waiting for. He slid the cube between the lips of her sex and she stiffened and twisted. "Yes," she moaned. He massaged it over and around her clit, then plunged the cube inside her. She shivered and bucked. He took another cube, a much larger one, from the bucket and ran it over her *grilletto*. "Oh *Dio*," she moaned.

He shifted so that he was between her legs, then he took the cube and fucked her with it until her thighs trembled. "Please," she moaned.

That's when he put his mouth on her. Her swollen *grilletto* felt cold on his tongue, and he enjoyed the way she cried out at the touch, her legs straining against the restraints. "Oh God, fuck me," she begged.

He slid two fingers inside her, then sucked her clit into his mouth. Within seconds she was crying out, her hips jerking, her juices flooding over his fingers.

His cock was so hard, he could've hammered nails with it. All he wanted was to be inside her.

But not just yet.

———— ✦ ————

Loredana felt Ruggero shift off the bed, heard the rustle of cloth. Was he finally going to do what she'd begged him for?

The mattress dipped beside her, then he was straddling her chest. The tip of him—slick and velvety—played across her lips.

Interesting. He'd resisted her offer before, but now that she was restrained, he was asking for it. Some part of him had switched on when she'd agreed to let him render her helpless.

And she wasn't going to discourage that part by refusing.

She opened to him, more than willing to repay him for all the pleasure he'd given her. If only she could see him. She imagined how she must look—bound, her eyes blindfolded, her mouth open and eagerly taking him in. Swirling her tongue around him, she closed her lips, sucking hard, enjoying his gasp and shudder, his murmured curse. "Fuck yes." His voice was raw, guttural. Excited.

He surged in and out of her mouth, testing her limits. For a second, unable to stop him with her hands, she worried that he'd gag her, but he knew just when to pull back.

She couldn't take all of him this way, but judging by his groans, it didn't matter. She sucked at him enthusiastically, greedily, wanting him to lose control, wanting him to let go.

Suddenly he stopped moving and she felt his hands on her skull. Then he pulled off the blindfold. She looked up into his eyes, saw the way his were glued to her mouth, to how she surrounded him. He met her gaze and slowly pushed forward, before pulling back. His thighs were trembling; how he must be struggling against the urge to fuck her mouth.

She increased the suction and played her tongue along the underside of his *cazzo*. He inhaled sharply, then pulled out.

"No," she said. "Let me finish."

He laughed. "I'm in charge, remember? I decide what happens here."

"But—"

He touched her mouth. "I want to fuck you. Hard. And I can't hold back any longer."

A thrill coursed through her at his words. He opened the nightstand drawer and pulled out a condom. As he put it on, she couldn't help rolling her hips.

He saw the movement and chuckled. "You want it too."

"Yes." She pulled at the ties. "Let me touch you."

He shook his head. "Not yet."

"But—"

He raised an eyebrow, then moved over her on his hands and knees. "I decide when," he said, his deep voice rumbling across her skin.

Dio, he was amazing, every muscle rippling, the hard planes of him shifting over her. He held himself just above her, so that she strained up to make contact, but he shifted farther out of reach.

"I can do this all night."

"I hope so."

He smiled and laughed, the rare one where he actually let go. Then he lowered himself so that he could kiss her. Their tongues met in a tangle, and she moaned into his mouth.

What he was doing to her—the way he'd taken over, the way he held back, then gave himself to her—it was just this side of too much to take. She bucked her hips, straining for him, and he slid inside her this time. She almost cried in relief.

He glided in and out, shallow strokes, when she wanted more. But if she demanded anything, he'd hold back. She rose up to meet him, silently begging with her hips. *Per favore, per favore...*

With a groan, he plunged into her hard, again and again until she was practically whimpering, the ties from the robes cutting into her wrists and ankles, but she didn't care, the sense of being helpless only driving her higher.

Finally she came, shuddering hard beneath him, crying out his name. He thrust into her quickly then, muttering incoherently until he too, shuddered and stiffened. "*Cristo*," he murmured, sagging against her.

She shifted weakly beneath him. She wanted to touch him, to cradle him, but she couldn't. He kissed her lips, her cheek, her jaw, then he pulled out of her and disappeared into the bathroom. Water ran for a few moments before he returned.

Sitting down beside her on the bed, he released her right wrist, then leaned over her and freed the other before untying her legs. While she rubbed her wrists, he chafed the marks on her ankles, his eyes on hers. "Did I hurt you?"

"No." She smiled at him. "You about killed me though."

He planted a kiss on each of her ankles, then crawled up the bed until he was lying beside her. He traced a finger along her brows, then down across her lips. "You seemed to like that."

"I did. Very much."

"*Bene.*" He pulled her atop him and she couldn't resist touching his face, his chest, all the places he'd denied her. Leaning forward, she kissed him softly, this man who so confused and delighted her. "Where did you learn all that?"

He reddened. "I spent some time on the Internet, looked up things I could do to you."

How sweet. "Will you tell me something?"

"Depends."

She ran a finger along his bottom lip. "Why did you restrict yourself to only call girls, before me?"

He said nothing for a moment, then he let out a puff of air. "I'm not going to live long. Why leave a widow behind?" He looked away after answering and pressed his lips together into a frown.

"That's not the real reason," she guessed.

He met her gaze then. "I don't have much to offer anyone." He held her eyes this time, and her chest tightened.

"You really believe that?" When he nodded, she shook her head. "The way you take care of me, there's a tenderness to you. I can't believe you don't want more."

He looked away again. "You think I can just do what I want."

"Can't you?"

His hand circled her left arm, just below the bandage, and he squeezed lightly, reminding her of her injury, making the wound ache. "If I get involved with a woman—really involved—I'll have to marry her. That's the way things are." His eyes held hers. "I can get involved only with women who are already part of my world. What I've done, with you, I could die for."

Her throat tightened. So many things she wanted to say. So many things she couldn't. Finally she whispered, "What are we going to do?"

The silence lasted so long, she thought he wasn't going to answer. Then he sighed. "Our jobs, until we can't do them anymore."

And then what? She almost asked the question, but stopped herself. She didn't want the answer.

———◆———

Loredana woke up repeatedly during the night. Again and again, she dreamt of her father's death, but it got mixed in with everything else that had happened—Stefano, the assassination attempt outside the *carabinieri* station, the shooting at the courthouse.

What would Papà want her to do? Would he want her to forgive Mamma? Would he tell her to step down from the Lucchesi case, if not the law altogether? And what on earth would he think of her and Ruggero?

She was pretty sure she knew the answer to the last question. But the others weren't so clear.

Each time she awoke, it was to the steady sound of Ruggero's breathing. He woke easily if she moved too much, and several times he asked if she was all right. She'd reassured him, but she wasn't. Far from it.

She knew what she *should* do, she knew what the law dictated. And yet, this situation was so far outside anything the law was designed to address.

What would her father do?

The question nagged at her all morning as she dressed for court, as she ate a quick breakfast with Ruggero. He studied her across the table, but said nothing. If patience was a virtue, it was one virtue he had many times over.

Finally she turned to him in the car when they arrived at the courthouse, where a pack of reporters awaited her. She reached across Ruggero for the button to the privacy screen. He regarded her silently, those silver-gray eyes seeming to penetrate into her.

She took a breath, then said what she'd been thinking, the words tumbling out in a rush. "I think I need to step down. At the least, I need to recuse myself from the Lucchesi case."

Aside from a slight narrowing of his eyes, his expression didn't change. "This is what's bothering you?"

"Of course.

"You'd already made your decision, I thought. What's changed?"

"I can't do it. I can't."

He took her hand, his eyes not leaving hers. "This is about your father."

She looked away. "He'd be ashamed of me."

He took her chin and made her look at him. "He'd be ashamed of *me*, never you, Loredana."

She sucked in a breath, trying to tamp down the lump building in her throat. "I feel like I'm letting him down."

"He'd want you to live. He wouldn't want you to throw away your life."

"He'd want me to do the right thing."

A muscle jumped in Ruggero's jaw. "So the right thing in this case is seeing a man go to jail for a crime he didn't commit? The right thing is to let a greedy, murderous monster rampage across the country unchecked? The right thing is to do what Lorenzo Andretti wants?"

"No. But how can I go in there and act like everything is okay? How can I hold my head up? Corvi accused me of collusion yesterday."

"And you brazened your way through it."

"Yes, but I know—"

"You know the truth. And the truth is that you, Loredana Montisi, are one of the finest, most honorable people I've met. And I don't say that lightly. You may think in my world that we have no scruples, but we do. Well, some of us. Not men like Lorenzo Andretti. He is the thing we must defeat. And we cannot do that by so-called legal means."

Put that way, it all made sense. The world she lived in—it wasn't her father's world. She'd crossed a line a while back, and she'd kept crossing it. Everything had seemed so simple all those days ago, when she'd wanted nothing more than to send Enrico Lucchesi to prison.

Now nothing was simple. The din of the reporters outside the car grew. "They're going to ask me about Corvi. They're maybe even going to ask me about you."

"You know what to say." He touched her cheek. "You're not even on that case today. You just have to deal with Baldassare. Keep the focus on that." He kissed her softly. "It's going to be okay, *bambina*."

He pressed his forehead to hers, then kissed her again, and a flashbulb from a camera went off outside the window.

They both started, then she flushed. "What if they caught that?"

"Don't worry. The windows are tinted. If they ask why we've been sitting here, say that you had to finish a call."

She nodded and took a deep breath, bracing herself for the onslaught. Ruggero opened his door and came around the car, then opened her door while Tommaso urged the reporters back. She stepped outside, blinking as more camera flashes went off.

The day was crisp and clear, a strong breeze blowing, and she looked up at the courthouse, the same one her father had worked in. He might not entirely understand her decisions regarding the Lucchesi case, but at least today she could make him proud. It was time to hold Italo Baldassare's feet to the fire.

If the Mafia was the great scourge of Italy, Baldassare was its right hand, rewriting laws to suit himself and his cronies, undoing the work so many had dedicated their lives to. Baldassare, at least, she could make pay for his crimes.

Reporters surged forward, microphones and cameras at the ready. An eager blonde in the front asked her if she was all right after the shooting.

"I'm fine. Other than a sore arm."

"Who do you think shot at you?"

Loredana shook her head. "I'm not going to speculate on that."

"Will the Lucchesi-Battista case proceed?"

"Of course. I will not be scared out of my own courtroom." *Take that, Lorenzo Andretti.*

"What about Pubblico Ministero Corvi's accusations?"

Loredana was careful to stop and smile directly into the camera. "Pubblico Ministero Corvi likes the spotlight."

"Are you going to petition for another prosecutor?"

She waved her hand as she reached the top of the steps. "No more questions."

If only she could quiet her own brain so easily. She glanced at Ruggero as they entered the courtroom. How calm he looked, how at ease. How certain he seemed about what he'd said.

Would she ever feel the same?

They'd already heard testimony from several informants and other witnesses; today Baldassare was taking the stand in his own defense, and at the least it wouldn't be boring.

In his late fifties, Italo Baldassare cut an impressive figure. Though not overly tall, Baldassare's fine suits, easy humor, and photogenic smile had made him a favorite with voters and a popular ladies' man. He claimed to be a man of the people, and his frequent anecdotes about his rise from humble beginnings to his success as the head of a multibillion-euro business empire, ranging from construction to sports to media conglomerates, gave him a modest, congenial air.

For years he'd dodged accusations of Mafia association, steadfastly maintaining that he was working for the people and against the Mafia. And yet, he'd rewritten law after law during his time as prime minister, weakening the anti-Mafia statutes that had been put in place in the seventies and eighties. He claimed—not without some justification—that the laws were flawed.

Loredana had no doubt that the statutes worked, even if at times they trampled on people's rights. Sometimes you had to cut down the wheat to get the weeds. The law was imperfect when it came to the Mafia, but they were their own special case. They couldn't always be fought by ordinary means.

Something she now understood more thoroughly than she ever had before.

As Baldassare was sworn in, she glanced over at Ruggero. Maybe he was right. Maybe the things she was doing, though not in the letter of the law, were in the spirit of it.

Maybe sometimes the ends did justify the means.

The prosecutor, Martino Fantoni, stepped forward and got right to the point. "Prime Minister Baldassare, on 6 June 2006, you attended a party given at an estate in Palermo. Is that correct?"

Baldassare smiled and shrugged. "Perhaps. I don't remember the exact date. I have so many engagements."

"But you were at such a party, where you spoke with these men?" He pointed to an easel with a series of pictures on it, labeled with various names.

Peering at the easel, Baldassare said, "I may have spoken to those men. I can't recall."

"These men you can't recall were under surveillance for Mafia association, and several have since turned state's evidence and confirmed their association. And they certainly remember you."

Another shrug. "These people you say are in the Mafia, I don't know who they are. They are friends of friends. We were all at a party. I'm supposed to know who everyone is?"

"Your security detail is supposed to."

"I can't answer for them. All I know is that no one told me."

"So you're saying that you shook hands with these men, discussed various matters with them, and spent over four hours in their company, and yet you didn't know who they were?"

Baldassare turned to address Loredana and the lay jurors. "I meet hundreds of people every year, especially when I'm campaigning. I can't remember them all, and I can't know them all personally. Who could?"

Loredana had to give him credit; he sounded sincere. And it could even be true.

Fantoni held up a printout. "So you don't remember Giuseppe Lavoro, who acted as a paid consultant to your campaign? He didn't stick in your mind at all?"

Out came that famous smile, the one that had won Baldassare votes again and again. "Him, I remember. But I can't say that I know him."

The prosecutor turned to a portable stereo system that had been brought in. "We have on tape a discussion between you and Lavoro and these other people you supposedly don't know. I'd like to play it for the court."

The tape started, with Fantoni naming the various participants, while a typewritten transcript flashed up on a projector. After several minutes of idle chat that seemed to establish that Baldassare had in fact met at least some of these men before, they came to the meat of the matter, cloaked in a discussion regarding local schools.

Lavoro: "The problem with the school system here in Palermo is this: too many matters are decided in Rome. What we'd like is local control. People here, with children in the schools, they should decide on such things, not people who are hundreds of kilometers away, people who don't understand the needs of our children."

Baldassare: "Of course, of course."

Lavoro: "You take my meaning."

Baldassare: "Your needs will be taken care of. I'll see to it personally."

Lavoro, laughing and apparently addressing the others: "What did I tell you? Baldassare is our man."

Fantoni stopped the tape. "What I find notable about this discussion is this: Giuseppe Lavoro at that time did not have any school-age children. Nor did two of the other men participating in the discussion."

Raising his hands palm up, Baldassare said, "Maybe he thinks ahead to the future? Maybe he has a brother or sister with kids in the schools? How am I to know?"

"So you're saying that Giuseppe Lavoro wanted you to sort out matters in a school district he doesn't even have children in?"

"I thought he was a concerned citizen."

Loredana restrained herself from rolling her eyes. She turned to Baldassare. "Prime Minister, may I remind you that you are in a court of law?"

"I'm aware."

"Then take this seriously."

His lips pursed, and the twinkle left his eye. "As seriously as you take your oath to the state?"

Heat rose to her cheeks. "We're focused on you and your behavior. Not on any slander that's been thrown my way."

Baldassare leaned toward her. "I too have been slandered. I have been tough on crime, the Mafia in particular. In the last few years we've practically vanquished the Cosa Nostra power structure, and just this week anti-Mafia forces arrested a major 'Ndrangheta *capo*, Vittorio Battista. And obviously we've angered some people, given what happened in your courtroom yesterday. And yet, here I sit, accused of being on the same side as those thugs."

Loredana wished she could wave a magic wand and send Baldassare to jail for a very long time. But that decision wouldn't be entirely hers to make. Though she could certainly make sure the lay jurors heard as much damning testimony as possible.

Fantoni addressed the lay jurors. "As you may recall, our prime minister spearheaded a law that allowed our countrymen overseas to vote in elections without having to come home. This law affected nearly three million Italians around the globe." When the prosecutor received several nods, he restarted the tape.

Baldassare: "You've made the arrangements in Argentina?"

Lavoro: "*Sì, sì.* It was no problem. Everything is in place." Lavoro chuckled. "Just say the word, and we'll make you a dictator for life!"

Baldassare, laughing: "We'll worry about that later. All I care about right now is winning this election."

Fantoni turned off the tape, again addressing the lay jurors. "What you may not know is that Italians voting in Argentina chose Prime Minister Baldassare's party by a seven-to-one margin—a proportion much greater than he enjoyed anywhere else." He turned to Baldassare. "How do you explain that?"

"Argentina loves me!"

When the jurors laughed, Loredana's stomach sank. Apparently someone needed to lay out the facts a bit more plainly. She addressed Fantoni. "Do you have an explanation for the difference?"

The prosecutor nodded. "I do. The procedures governing the safeguarding of the overseas ballots were not yet fully implemented in several countries, Argentina being one of them. Rigging the vote would be far easier to do there, with fewer watchful eyes."

Fantoni played several more tapes, building the case for collusion, and Baldassare continued to give a series of shrugs, thrown up hands, and the occasional quip in response to his questioning. He seemed to be having, if not a great time, at least a bit of fun at Fantoni's expense, as if the entire trial were some sort of elaborate prank being played in his honor, perhaps one of those celebrity roasts.

The prosecutor was doing his best to remain cool and professional, and Loredana sympathized with his struggle. Baldassare was simply unflappable. No wonder he'd been elected again and again.

When Fantoni finally rested his case, the day was nearly dark. The defense still had its final arguments to make, but that would have to wait.

Just after she adjourned the court, Baldassare coughed to get her attention. She turned to him and was greeted with a smirk and a wink as he stepped down from the witness box. That comment about Battista—was it really as off the cuff as it had appeared? Or had Baldassare been trying to tell her something? If he'd targeted Battista, did that mean he was in league with Andretti?

She looked at Ruggero. There was, perhaps, a way to find out.

CHAPTER 20

Loredana hadn't said much during dinner. Ruggero supposed she was still fretting about her father.

He'd been almost relieved when she'd told him what was bothering her. He'd been afraid it was the sex they'd had.

He could think of little else. He wanted her at his mercy again, wanted to hear her cry out, wanted her to beg for more the way she had last night. He was hard just thinking about it.

When she went to the bathroom to wash up after eating, he headed out to the balcony and lit up a cigarette. He was halfway through when she joined him.

"I wish you'd quit," she said, motioning to his hand.

"I've thought about it."

"Well?"

He shrugged. "Haven't had a good reason."

"What if I asked you to?"

He took another drag. "That might do it."

"Then I'm asking." She stepped forward and took the cigarette from him, then dropped it to the cement and ground it out with her shoe. She looked up at him and touched his cheek. "You'll do it?"

He nodded. "That was my last one."

She smiled, and the joy in her eyes made him glad he'd agreed. Putting her hands around his neck, she rose up on her toes and kissed him. "We'll get you those patches or the gum tomorrow."

"I'll probably need it." Or a vat of espresso. Or both.

This was probably the worst possible time to quit—he still hadn't figured out how to tackle the Andretti problem—but for Loredana, he'd try. He'd try his damnedest.

That pensive look slid over her face again. "Something bothering you?" he asked.

She frowned, then let go of him. "It's something Baldassare mentioned."

"About what Corvi said to you?"

"Sort of. He brought up Vittorio Battista today. I thought at first it was just an idle comment. When he stepped down today, he gave me this look, like he was in on some big secret, and I realized—if Andretti wanted Battista out of the way, maybe he got Baldassare to send the DIA and Corvi after him."

Should he tell her? "There might be a tie between Baldassare and Andretti."

"Might be?"

"And there might be a paper trail that proves it."

"What are you saying?"

He shrugged. "I shouldn't have said even that."

"But you did."

Dio mio. Enrico was going to kill him. "Such a thing might exist."

She clutched the lapels of his suit jacket. "Don't you see? This would put Baldassare away. It would be the smoking gun."

"There's a problem."

"What problem?"

"An 'I have to find out if I can tell you more' kind of problem."

"I can delay things for a while, but not long."

He didn't want to say it, but it was true. Damn it, was there no other way? He hesitated so long, she said, "What is it?"

"It would greatly help if a certain trial ended first."

She looked up at him. "I see." Then she looked away.

He tilted her chin back toward him. "I didn't want to mention it, and I'm not telling you what to do. I'm just giving you the facts."

"I know." Her voice was thick. He tipped his head down, and pressed his lips to hers. Something flashed in his peripheral vision, and he turned and ducked at the same time, pulling Loredana down with him. There was movement at a window in the building across the street, then another flash. Was that a camera?

His pulse quickened. "Go inside. Now."

"What?"

"We've been followed. Pack your things."

"What did you see?"

He ushered her inside, explaining quickly. She paled. "Thank God it wasn't a gun."

"A camera can be almost as bad."

Fuck, he'd been stupid, kissing her out there. That first time she'd ever kissed him out there had been borderline risky, and *Dio* knew he hadn't been capable then of thinking about anything but her, but now that they'd been traveling back and forth to court together... He'd gotten cocky, sloppy, trusting that he and the men would spot any tails from the courthouse.

He couldn't have been stupider. And that needed to stop.

They packed quickly, and he summoned Tommaso and the guards. He could move her to another hotel, but right now, he wasn't going to take any more chances.

They were going to a safe house—one he had here in Milan.

Ruggero's "safe house" turned out to be a pretty bare-bones affair—a clean, spartan apartment in a somewhat rundown neighborhood. Loredana shouldn't have been surprised.

He sent a couple of the guards out for supplies. Tommaso would be staying in one of the rooms, while she and Ruggero shared the other. Officially, Ruggero would be sleeping in the chair, but that was only for appearances.

She was surprised to find a selection of Shakespeare on the shelves in the bedroom. While Ruggero and Tommaso talked in the living room, she picked up a copy of *Macbeth* and paged through it, looking for her favorite speeches. She was near the end when Ruggero came in. She held up the book. "Where did this come from?"

"Me. I stay here sometimes."

"You do?"

He gave her that little half-smile. "Can't always stay in hotels."

Ah. So he was referring to... work. "Which is your favorite?"

Without thinking about it, he said, "'Cowards die many times before their deaths. The valiant never taste of death but once.'"

She smiled. "*Julius Caesar.* I should've guessed." She placed the copy of *Macbeth* back on the shelf, then asked the question that was plaguing her. "Will they try to kill us again tomorrow?"

"Maybe."

She hadn't really expected any other answer. So she said what she had to say, forced it out around the lump that had risen in her throat. "Then the trial has to end."

He stared at her for a long time, saying nothing. He shoved his hands in his pockets and paced away from her to stare out the window at the snow-flecked ground. "You know what that means," he finally said, his voice low and flat.

"I know." She was trembling inside. After tomorrow, she was on her own. And this—whatever it was—between them, would end.

"Is that what you want?"

"No." She couldn't keep the quaver out of her voice. "But it has to end sometime. And every time all of us are in the courtroom, or coming and going from it, that gives Andretti another chance."

Ruggero crossed the room to her. "'It has to end sometime,' you said. The trial, or us?"

She couldn't look at him. "It's both, isn't it?"

"It doesn't have to be."

She snorted. "How would that work? How could it?"

"There's a way."

"What way?"

"There *is* a solution to this." His intense stare was unnerving.

"Are you asking me to quit?"

He took in a breath and she waited, the seconds stretching out. Waited for him to say what he wanted. Finally he spoke. "I can't ask you to."

"Do you *want* me to?"

He pulled her close. "Of course. But I can't ask you to do that."

Could she? Could she do it?

And then… what? Spend her life as the wife of a hitman, or whatever Ruggero was? Could she sit idly by and let him do whatever it was he did?

It was idiotic, but she was going to ask. "Can you quit your job?"

He stepped back from her. "No, *bambina*. That is not possible."

And here it was, the horrible truth. She might as well say it. "It's one thing to be with *you*. It's another to be part of your life."

That hopeful look he'd given her bled away, and the hard mask that he'd shown her so many times before took its place. "I understand."

Her stomach plummeted to the floor. She wanted to take it all back, to undo what she'd said.

But it was all true. And she'd known it all along. Someday they'd have to return to the real world. "It was never going to be forever, was it?" Her eyes filled with tears.

He shook his head, then looked away. He rubbed at his eyes. Was he crying?

She stepped around to see him, and he averted his face. "Ruggero, look at me," she said, her voice breaking. "Look at me."

He took a deep breath, then turned to her. His eyes glistened. "Happy?"

"No." She shook her head and put her arms around him. What had she done to him?

He enclosed her in his arms and murmured in her hair, something she couldn't hear. Something he'd said before, when she'd left her mother, when he'd held her close then.

She pulled back to look at him. "What did you say?"

He wiped her tears with his thumbs. His voice was thick. "I would protect you forever, from everything."

"Oh Ruggero, I—"

He touched her lips. "Don't."

He was right; saying it would only make things worse. But if she couldn't say it, she could show it. "Can you send Tommaso somewhere?"

"I could."

"Then do it."

He left the room, closing the door behind him. She stripped out of her clothes, then sat on the bed.

He came back in, his brows popping up when he saw her. Surely he'd expected this. "You seem surprised."

"I thought you'd wait for me."

"I am. But tonight I want to take care of you." She rose from the bed. "Tonight, I call the shots."

Ruggero seemed to freeze up. "I thought we could do… what we did."

"We could," she said. "But we could try something else too."

"What?"

"Let me take care of you."

"No."

"Why not?" She closed the distance between them and ran a hand over the bulge of his trousers. He was hard already.

"Because… you're not them. They always took care of me. That's not what I want anymore."

"Let me," she whispered in his ear. "Let me because *I* want to."

"You truly want this?" he asked, a sort of wonder in his voice.

"I do." She removed his suit jacket, revealing the well-muscled body beneath it. He wore a shoulder holster over his button-down shirt. She started to remove the holster, but he stopped her. "I take off the weapons."

Weapons, plural? She watched in amazement as he removed not only the holster and set it on the nightstand, but also knives strapped to both arms. He added a switchblade and a set of brass knuckles from his pocket, then another knife and a gun, each strapped to an ankle.

"You're a veritable army."

"I have to be."

"You weren't this armed at the hotel."

"After the first night, no. I had them with me, but not on me. At least, not all the time."

He'd always dressed in his own room. Now she knew why. She started loosening his tie, and he watched passively, his eyes roving over her as she moved.

Would this be the last time she touched him like this?

There had to be another way. There had to be. She swallowed down the tightness in her throat and removed his tie, his shirt, his cufflinks, then watched him shed his shoes and socks. She reached for his trousers, and he grabbed her wrist. "I still don't want this."

"Let me. Please. I promise it will be different."

Something flashed in his eyes, something she couldn't name. Then he released her hand. She unzipped him and pushed his boxer trunks to the floor, along with his slacks.

He stood bare before her, a man very much in his prime. The hard angles of his face gave way to a sturdy neck and torso, the sort of body a middleweight boxer might have, all slabs of muscle. That well-developed torso angled into a V that seemed to point to the thick erection springing up between his legs. She could've spent hours looking at him, but this was for him, not her.

She traced her hands over his face, closing his eyelids, running her fingers across his cheekbones, along his jaw, over his lips. He opened his eyes to look at her, and she closed his lids again. "Just feel," she whispered.

She pulled his head down and pressed her mouth over his. His arms came up and he pulled her close, until they stood pressed together, her softness molding against his hardness. The hair of his chest tickled her nipples, and she moaned into his mouth as he invaded hers with his tongue. She sucked gently at it, then more greedily. He nudged her toward the bed, but she circled back so that he was the one on the bottom when they hit it.

He tried to roll her under him, but she stopped him. "Please, Ruggero. Let me do this. Stop resisting."

"It's not what I want."

She pressed him flat against the bed and straddled him. "It's what you need. Aren't you tired of being in control every minute?"

———— ♦ ————

Ruggero stared up at Loredana. The question caught him off guard.

Staying in control was what kept him alive. It was what kept her alive.

And here she was, asking him to give that up. At least for this night. "I can't."

"You can."

She didn't understand. How could she? "Every time I relax, something happens."

"You mean your father."

"It's more than that. A few months ago, my sister's husband was dying, and there was nothing I could do. I couldn't even go to her. My *capo* needed me. But I failed him twice, nearly got him and his wife killed. Because of my distraction. And the day before yesterday, in the courtroom—my eyes were on *you*."

She looked down at him, then she touched his cheek, tracing the scar. "You can't be responsible for everything. You can't take on that burden. No one can. You're wound so tight, it's a wonder you haven't cracked."

But hadn't he? He'd broken his vow. He closed his eyes. "Maybe I have."

"You mean me?"

He nodded, still not looking at her. She'd be out of his life tomorrow, and maybe that was for the best.

And maybe it would kill him.

"Look at me," she said, her voice hoarse with tears. He opened his eyes and gazed up at her in the dim light. She was glorious, wonderful, everything he thought he'd never have. Everything he couldn't.

"No matter what happens with the trial, I will keep you safe," he promised.

"And what will your boss think of that?"

"Don't worry about it. I can find someone to watch you."

She touched his cheek. "I don't want you to get in trouble because of me."

"And I don't want you killed."

They stared at each other for a long time, then she leaned over him, her hair forming a curtain around them as their lips met. "No more talking," she murmured against his mouth.

Did she believe him? He'd find a way, even if he had to beg Enrico. They could ill-afford to guard her indefinitely, but perhaps, at least through the Baldassare trial…

But in any case, he wouldn't be the one with her. And he'd have no opportunities to be with her alone.

No chances to touch her, to kiss her. No chances to show how much he cared.

She cupped his jaw in her hands, held him still while she kissed him, her tongue wrapping around his, her hips rocking on his belly, her sweet, delectable breasts pressing into his chest. *Dio*, this woman, what she did to him…

Loredana pulled back. "Close your eyes," she said. They were alone in the house; he was unarmed, though his weapons were within reach. And no doubt Tommaso hadn't gone far—he was probably sitting outside in one of the cars, watching over them. But still…

"Let go. For me," she said. "Please."

"Okay." He closed his eyes, glad she wasn't trying to blindfold him. Or cuff him. He cracked an eyelid to see what she was doing. She was watching him.

"You're impossible," she said.

"Wasn't sure what you were up to. I thought maybe you'd try to turn things around on me. Tie me up or something."

"I should." At the look on his face, she laughed. "I figured that wasn't going to fly." She studied him for a moment. "Since you can't keep your eyes closed, I'll give you a choice. Either close your eyes, or link your hands together behind the rails on the headboard. And keep them there."

He smiled. So she did want some payback. But she was taking it easy on him. He laced his hands through the rails behind his head and clasped them together. "This what you had in mind?"

"Exactly. You aren't allowed to touch me until I say so. Promise me."

He nodded. It wouldn't be easy with this much temptation right in front of him, but he'd play her game.

She scooted down his body until her luscious ass bumped up against his straining cock. Another centimeter or two and he could be inside her. But she didn't raise herself up to take him in. Instead, she pressed her lips to his ear, then his neck, kissing her way to his chest. She circled her tongue around one of his nipples, then took it in her mouth. When she gently bit it, he twitched, surprised to find that it was so sensitive. Did she feel the same, or even more, when he did that to her?

With agonizing slowness, she moved farther down his torso, and finally, finally, she was straddling him, her slick *figa* gliding back and forth across his aching *cazzo*. "Put it in you," he said.

She looked up at him and smiled. "No." Then she continued her descent, kissing a path across his ribs, his belly, his navel.

Shit. She was going to go down on him, wasn't she?

As much as he wanted it, he was torn. He'd taken advantage of her last night, had reveled in her helplessness as he'd used her mouth. Shame flickered through him. He shouldn't have done that. Shouldn't have done any of it. And yet… she'd really seemed to like it.

But if she'd liked it so much, why had she turned the tables on him? Had she lied? The way she'd flushed, the way she'd cried out, the gush of her fluids when she'd come—she couldn't have faked all that.

She *had* liked it. But maybe like him, she was a little frightened of it too.

Her lips trailed along the muscles that crested his hips, first one side, and then the other, then she nuzzled the skin of his inner thighs. His cock ached for her touch, her attention, but she deliberately ignored it.

She sat up, her hands kneading the muscles of his thighs, and he couldn't take it anymore.

"Fuck me or suck me," he rasped.

She laughed. "You don't get to make demands tonight."

"I thought I was supposed to let go."

A coy little smile played across her lips. "That is what I said."

"So?" He held her gaze and his breath, not sure which option she'd go for. Not sure himself which one he wanted.

Bending forward, she took his *cazzo* in hand and let her breath wash over it. She blew on that sensitive skin and he jumped, almost letting go of the headboard railing. Then she sat back.

"You're killing me," he growled.

She chuckled. "I know. You teased me a lot more last night."

"And I will again if you don't do something, and quick. It's not like I'm tied up or anything."

"You promised."

He had. *Not so easy when you're not in charge, is it?* "Don't make me break it."

"I was thinking this morning that you had infinite patience, but I was wrong. You do have your limits." She lowered her mouth to his cock and blew on it again. "And I'm going to test them." Then she swiped her tongue across the head and he shivered. It felt so damn good. Like heaven.

To his surprise, she rose up, then turned and straddled him so that her luscious ass and glistening *figa* were facing him. She looked at him over her shoulder, a challenge clear in her eyes. "I want to ride you. But you have to get me ready."

She backed up so that her *figa* hovered over his mouth. He breathed her in, her spicy scent hardening his cock like nothing else could. He strained up to reach her and started to unclasp his hands to pull her thighs apart, to hold her in place...

"Uh-uh. No touching. I'm in charge. Remember?"

"Tease."

"If that's your nice way of saying 'bitch'—"

He nipped at her inner thigh. "I'm not nice, but that's not a word I'd use for you."

She spread her thighs and lowered herself. "Let's see what else you've learned from the Internet."

He'd never been in this position before, never been the one being commanded, controlled. And yet his cock pulsed like a second heart, and he wanted nothing more than to please her, to make her cry out his name. She hovered just above his reach, and he licked the soft flesh of her inner thigh, silently begging her to descend just a few centimeters more...

She sighed and spread her legs further, bending her arms and placing her hands on his hips, her mouth once again dangerously close to his cock. Her breath washed over it, but he tried to ignore the sensation. He was going to do right by her.

At last her little pink *figa* was within reach. He ran his tongue the length of it, inserting his tongue between the lips, seeking out her entrance. She opened wider, and he speared his tongue inside her, fucking her with it. She moaned and rocked down onto him. If only he could use his fingers...

Fuck it. He freed his hands from the railing and grabbed her inner thighs before she could protest, penetrating her with both thumbs as he sucked on her *grilletto*.

Loredana moaned and pushed herself closer. "You're a bad boy," she gasped.

He chuckled against her flesh. "You don't seem to mind."

"But I do," she panted, still grinding against him. "You disobeyed me."

"You like it," he managed to say between licks and probes. "You wanted me to do this."

He plunged his right thumb deep inside her, then pulled it out and brushed it over her other hole, the one she'd denied him so far. She laughed. "No."

"Yes."

She rose up and looked at him over her shoulder. "Not today." She held his eyes. "Now put your hands back behind that railing and clasp them together."

He smiled at the flush on her cheeks, the mock disapproval in her eyes. But he did as she asked, and she repositioned herself so that she was facing him full-on again, her *figa* now temptingly close to his cock. "I need a condom," she said.

"Right inside coat pocket."

She left him for a moment, then returned with a foil packet. Tearing it with her teeth, she held his eyes all the while as she rolled it down his length. *Dio mio.* How had he ever lived without her?

Straddling him, she reached between her legs and guided his cock to her entrance, taking in just the tip of him. His *cazzo* pulsed and twitched, and it took all his restraint to keep his hips still. Centimeter by centimeter, she descended over him, swirling her hips and making him shudder.

Had it ever felt this good before?

She leaned forward, rising up to his tip, then slowly descending again until their hips met. She repeated the motion, adding a hip swivel on the way down that made him groan. He wanted her to go faster, but she seemed to delight in making him sweat, in drawing out his pleasure… And that's when he realized what she was doing.

And why.

She was giving him a gift.

Something to remember her by.

"Stop," he rasped.

She stilled and met his eyes. "I know why you're doing this," he said. "You don't have to."

Loredana held his gaze, then she shook her head, her eyes glistening. "I do have to. I want to."

"But—"

"Be quiet. Before I gag you." Then she resumed her slow, sweet torture of him.

He wanted to touch her, wanted to hold her, kiss her. Didn't want to just lie there and accept this gift. But she was making the rules tonight, and he'd given his word.

She kept to her torturous pace until he was sweating with the effort of keeping still, of not giving in to his instincts, of not giving in to his need to pound into her. "Tease," he said again between gritted teeth.

Loredana laughed and sped up her movements. Up and down, her hips swiveling, her inner muscles clenching tighter until he was groaning, his arms straining, his hands wanting to come unclasped.

"I can't hold back," he said.

In answer, she took him in deeper, and when she tightened around him again, he came with a roar.

She rode him mercilessly, her breath shuddering, her *figa* pulsing around him, until he had to beg her to stop. He was panting, his heart racing, his breathing harsh, as if he'd been running.

As soon as he caught his breath, she'd be getting no mercy.

She sat back on her heels and looked at him. "You can touch me now. If you want."

He freed his arms from the railing and sat up, pulling her into a punishing kiss. He'd never been with a woman so sexy. So giving. So precious.

How was he going to let her go?

He wasn't a man who believed in prayer, but he said one in his head anyway. *Dio*, *help me. Help me keep her.*

He flipped her on her back and spread her legs. Still kissing her, he found her *figa*, slick and warm, so ready for his fingers, his tongue, his cock. She was getting it all the minute he recovered.

She moaned into his mouth and he dropped down to her *figa*, flicking his tongue over her *grilletto* until her thighs trembled. "Ruggero, please," she begged. He slid two fingers inside her, searching for that spot he'd read about. Thank God for the Internet. So much useful information. Her back arched and she moaned when he found it.

"Yes, yes," she said. "Don't stop."

There was no way in hell that he was going to. He worked her harder, faster, her breath coming in great gasps, her hips bucking into his mouth, into his hand, her fingers twining in his hair. "Yes!" she finally cried and shuddered, her limbs convulsing.

And damn, just like that, his *cazzo* was ready for more. He couldn't remember the last time he'd recovered so quickly. She'd bewitched him, and he didn't care.

Grinning, he kissed her belly, then left her for a moment to get another condom. She lay sprawled out, panting and flushed on the bed. So lovely.

He rolled on the condom and positioned himself atop her, sliding inside her even though she weakly protested. "You really want to stop?" he teased.

She laughed and punched him lightly on the shoulder. "No."

He thrust into her hard and she moaned. "Please."

"Please what?"

"Just more, please. More."

She wrapped her legs around his hips and pulled him tightly to her, her hands clutching his shoulders. He bit into the soft flesh of her neck, where it met the shoulder. She cried out, jerking beneath him, and that raw response unleashed something in him. Something animalistic, primitive. She was his, and he was keeping her. Somehow. Some way.

"You're mine," he whispered against her neck. "You hear me?"

"I do," she panted.

"Mine," he said, punctuating it with a thrust.

"Yours."

He pounded into her relentlessly, her little cries and moans the fuel that fed his desire, his need for more.

He wasn't giving her up.

He wasn't.

He'd find a way to keep her. Or die trying.

CHAPTER 21

Ruggero woke with a start. Someone was leaning over him—Loredana. She was dressed, her hair still damp from the shower. "Wake up, sleepyhead."

He smiled up at her, then he remembered. She was going to dismiss the case today. And he was going to have to give her up—for a while anyway.

He'd find a solution. Somehow. She turned away from him, and he caught her wrist. "*Bambina*, listen. I meant what I said last night."

"'Mine'?" she asked.

He nodded. "I'll figure something out."

She gave him a tentative smile. "You're going to need a miracle."

"Then I'll get one." He rose and kissed her, conscious of the fact that he was naked, while she was clothed. She'd turned his world upside down entirely. Upside down and inside out, and he couldn't imagine going back to what he'd been.

Who he'd been.

A heart beat in his chest after all, and he wasn't going to silence it again. And unless *Dio* was cruel beyond measure, He wouldn't have put Loredana Montisi in Ruggero's path, only to tear her away.

When she pulled back from him, she said, "Tommaso picked up something for breakfast."

He smiled. He knew what she was doing, how nervous she was. "Have faith," he said, and kissed her knuckles.

"Okay." She said it almost shyly. But it was a start.

He was just stepping out of the shower when his phone rang. He looked at the display. Fuente. What the hell could he want? "Yeah?" Ruggero said.

Fuente chuckled. "Manners, Signor Vela."

"Fuck manners. Why are you calling?"

"I have something very interesting that I'd like to show you and Giudice Montisi."

The back of Ruggero's neck prickled. Why the both of them? "What does this have to do with the judge?"

"You'll see. We need to meet, as soon as possible."

"She's in court today."

"I know. Can we meet in her chambers, before she starts? It won't take long."

Was this some kind of trap? "If you're thinking of pulling something—"

"I have no such intentions. I'm merely giving you both some information. Critical information."

"About the case?"

"In a way. Yes."

They fixed the time, and Ruggero hung up. He didn't like the sound of it. But he wanted to know what Fuente had to say, all the same.

He quickly explained to Loredana and Tommaso, and they ended up eating pastries in the car and taking their espresso to go. Not that either of them were that hungry, but they had a long, difficult day ahead.

Fuente was waiting outside Loredana's office at the courthouse when they arrived. He held a large manila envelope in his hand, and Ruggero barely resisted the impulse to grab it and rip it open.

They followed Loredana inside her chambers. She stowed her belongings in her desk, her movements stiff. Fuente was far from her favorite person, and no doubt his presence called to mind the shooting outside the *carabinieri* station—a shooting Fuente had certainly had some hand in.

Loredana composed herself at her desk, then she motioned for Fuente and Ruggero to take the seats in front of her. Fuente did, but Ruggero moved off to the side, between Fuente and the door, and remained standing.

Fuente gave him the eye. "Signor Vela, you insult me. I gave my word."

"As if that matters."

Fuente shrugged and placed the envelope on the desk, pushing it toward Loredana, then he removed his cap and crossed his legs, settling back against his chair.

"What is this?" she asked, not touching it.

"Open it and you'll see."

She picked up the envelope as if it might bite her, then she pulled out the contents and set them on the desk, pressing a hand to her mouth. The pictures weren't the best quality, but they were clear enough: Ruggero kissing her on the hotel balcony, another of him kissing her in the back of the limousine, though the photo was heavily marred by the tinting of the windows and the high flash used to penetrate them.

"Where did you get these?" Ruggero asked.

Fuente smiled. "A certain man with a certain case."

"Baldassare," Loredana said.

Fuente stroked his mustache. "You *are* smarter than you appear."

Ruggero clamped a hand on the man's shoulder, and Fuente turned to him, wagging a finger. "Before you get all indignant, let me remind you both that the judge has not been willing to take the hints thrown her way. On *either* case. And that, all by itself, is at best naïveté; at worst, it's downright foolish."

"What does he want?" Loredana asked, her voice hoarse.

"Must I spell it out?"

She said nothing for a while, lost in thought, then she sat back in her chair and met Fuente's eye. "Well, I want something in return."

Ruggero barely hid his surprise. *Where the fuck is she going with this?*

Fuente leaned forward, his hat in his lap, his hands laced together on his knee. "So you're starting to understand."

Loredana mimicked his gesture, clasping her hands together on the desk. "If I'm going to lose my job over this, I need to make it worthwhile."

"Who said anything about losing your job? Unless, of course, you choose not to cooperate."

"I'll lose my job because I won't be a puppet."

"What do you want?" Fuente asked.

"I'm not going through an underling." The bite in her voice made Ruggero smile. "I want to speak to him myself. I want assurances about my future."

"You want to meet with Baldassare?" Fuente asked, as if there couldn't be a more absurd idea.

"I want to meet with him... and Andretti."

Fuente said nothing for a second. "That's never going to happen."

"It has to, or I'm not budging."

"You'll face the consequences of these," Fuente said, tapping the photos.

"And they won't get what they want. Because I won't resign. There will have to be an investigation, and that could take months. Meanwhile, the cases in question will conclude... under my watch."

Fuente stared at her for a while. "Don't expect miracles."

"If I go down"—Loredana pointed at herself, then pointed at Fuente—"*you* go down with me."

Fuente waved his hands in surrender. "No need to shoot the messenger." He placed his cap on his head and rose. "I'll see what I can do."

Shooting the messenger seemed like a fine idea to Ruggero, and for just a moment, he refused to get out of Fuente's way. Fuente smiled at him. "Signor Vela, it has been a pleasure. As always."

"The pleasure is all yours," Ruggero growled. He waited until Fuente closed the door and his footsteps receded down the hall, then he turned to Loredana. "What the fuck do you think you're doing?"

"My job."

"You're going to get yourself killed."

"I'm going to get the two of them on tape trying to bribe and threaten a judge."

"You'll never get near them with a recording device."

"I won't have to."

"What do you mean?"

"Fuente will be wearing it."

"You can't be serious. He'll never do it. Not that he can be trusted in the first place."

"I'll get him to help. Trust me."

Ruggero swallowed hard, trying to tamp down the alarm her words and demeanor were causing him. "I can't let you do this."

"It's not a matter of 'letting' me do anything. I'm doing it."

"You will *not* do this."

"If you don't like it, you know where the door is." She pointed to it, as if he needed help finding the way.

Cristo. What the hell was he going to do? He glanced at his watch. She was due in court in ten minutes.

If she meant what she'd said to Fuente, she wouldn't be ending the Lucchesi-Battista case today. In a way it was a relief, but it was only a temporary reprieve. The meeting with Baldassare and Andretti would only get her killed.

Unless he helped her. And that meant a radical change of plan. "If you're doing this, I'm helping you."

"I was hoping you'd say that." Her shoulders relaxed slightly.

"But we do it my way."

She pursed her lips. "I figured you'd say that too."

"Cancel court today, however you have to. We need to make a trip."

"Where?"

"You trust me?"

"Of course."

"Then you're going to have to trust him too."

Her eyebrows raised. "Him? You mean your boss."

He nodded, and after staring at him for a moment, she phoned her clerk.

There'd be no court until Monday. They had three days to make her plan work, assuming Baldassare and Andretti agreed to the meeting. They could delay the inevitable for only so long. And Ruggero was sick of delays.

It was time.

———◆———

Loredana couldn't believe she'd agreed to a meeting with Enrico Lucchesi, but she had, and there was no turning back. Ruggero drove like a demon despite the wet, icy conditions, and they eventually left behind the two cars escorting them. They made the trip from Milan to Como in less than an hour, the Maserati easily chewing up the snow-covered mountainsides as they crossed in and out of Switzerland, the Alps whizzing by on their way to Lake Como.

Lucchesi's estate was outside Como itself in the quaint little town of Cernobbio. The closer they drew to the lake, the harder the rain fell, pounding on the roof of the car and making everything outside the windows a watery blur.

Eventually, they stopped at an imposing wrought-iron gate. After they were buzzed through, they headed up the long gravel drive to a cream-colored villa looming in the distance.

The rain ceased as they headed up the drive, and the sun weakly poked through the clouds.

Loredana took a deep, shaky breath. What if Lucchesi opposed her plan? What if he refused to trust her?

He had no good reason to. No reason at all, other than whatever credibility Ruggero could lend her.

For an instant, she questioned her sanity. She was allowing Ruggero to take her into the lion's den. She was about to ask a Mafia don for help. She was about to break every rule in the book.

And why?

Because she wanted justice. Baldassare and Andretti couldn't be allowed to continue unchecked. If there was to be any hope for a stronger Italy, she needed to do her part.

But what reason did she have to believe that Enrico Lucchesi would be any better? Sure, he had an impressive history as a philanthropist, and other than the specious accusations regarding Judge Dinelli's death, he'd never been accused of anything worse than tax evasion.

Except... there were all those troubling deaths around him.

Ruggero stopped the car near the front door of the villa, the cessation of the engine leaving a sudden silence. "You're sure he won't decide to put a bullet in my head?" she asked.

"I'm sure." Ruggero took her hand and kissed it. The engine ticked as it cooled, and she stared out at the villa, her stomach flipping. The crunch of gravel behind them signaled the arrival of Tommaso and the rest of their escort.

She couldn't put it off any longer, and she reached for the door handle. Ruggero put a hand on her wrist. "I'm going to have to talk to him first. I'm not going to lie to you. He isn't going to like it. But I think he'll see reason."

"You *think*?"

"I can't promise it."

"A moment ago you were sure."

"That he won't kill you. Doesn't mean he'll agree to your plan."

How completely disheartening. "You really aren't good at reassuring me." She thought back to when they'd first met at the courthouse, the way he'd backed her against the wall.

"Pretty lies won't help."

She sighed and slumped against the seat. "It's only hard truths with you, yes?"

He gave her that half-smile of his. "Would you want it any other way?"

"Was that a double entendre?" She almost laughed.

He did laugh. "And I thought I was the only one with sex on the brain."

She smiled and kissed him on the cheek as the guards filed into the house. Tommaso stood on the step, waiting, and she felt his gaze as she and Ruggero exited the car and approached the house. He stopped them before they entered, his gaze on Ruggero, his expression a mix of compassion and defiance. "I had to tell him. He's not happy."

Ruggero nodded. "I figured you would."

"You might have made that call yourself."

"And have him tell me no?" He put a hand on Tommaso's shoulder. "Sometimes it's better to ask for forgiveness than for permission."

"You'd better hope this is one of those times." Tommaso looked at Loredana and bobbed his head, stepping out of their way.

They entered a grand foyer that extended up two stories. Loredana had expected some overblown, gewgaw-strewn monstrosity, but she should've known better. Like the man himself, Lucchesi's home was elegant, tasteful, and subtle. There was wealth here, plenty of it, but nothing ostentatious. Nothing that said Enrico Lucchesi had a fragile ego or anything else to compensate for.

Her heels echoing on the marble, Ruggero escorted her to a drawing room, from which emanated the excited shouts of a little boy and laughter from several adults, punctuated by the sharp yips of a small dog. They paused in the doorway, and she took in the cozy domestic scene: Lucchesi and his wife sitting side by side on a loveseat, a blond-haired boy of five or six rolling on the carpet with a fluffy white puppy, assorted other adults watching.

From the files she'd read, she recognized Antonio Lucchesi, Enrico's adopted son, and Nick Clarkston, an Interpol agent who'd been involved in a massive shootout at the lake several months ago. What was *he* doing here? And why was he so comfortable in Lucchesi's home?

Clarkston had his arm around a heartbreakingly beautiful young woman, with long dark hair and exquisite model-worthy looks. Antonio Lucchesi held hands with an attractive, rather voluptuous young woman with caramel-colored hair. Two older women sat at a table nearby, chatting and playing a game of cards with a young dark-haired man.

It didn't take long before the room grew silent, save the boy's laughter and the pup's mock growls as they tussled over a ball.

Ruggero placed a hand on the small of her back, his touch steadying and reassuring her. Surely it was a good sign that all the women were here, that she hadn't been bundled off into some dank cellar?

It wasn't that she didn't trust Ruggero; it was the frost in Enrico Lucchesi's gaze that gave her pause.

Why should he trust her? Why should he have a damn thing to do with her at all?

After a moment, Lucchesi rose, and Ruggero nudged her into the room. "Welcome to my home, *signora*," Lucchesi said as they approached. She didn't correct his dropping of her title. They all knew who she was, and no doubt he was giving her a message regarding who was king here.

"Thank you," she said, forcing her voice to sound more confident than she felt.

Lucchesi's gaze left hers and turned positively arctic when he looked at Ruggero. "We need to talk. Now."

Ruggero pressed his hand against her back, then he was gone. Antonio Lucchesi followed, no surprise, but then so did Clarkston and the young dark-haired mystery man. What was going on here? Was Clarkston a dirty agent? Had his "undercover" work for Interpol last year been a mask for something else entirely?

Her pulse raced as the men's footsteps receded. A door was opened and shut somewhere in the recesses of the house. She looked at the women awkwardly, her eyes lighting on Lucchesi's wife, who met her eyes with a hint of her husband's frost. Then she sighed and shook her head. "I want to be angry with you for keeping him in jail, but… you were only doing your job."

"I'm glad you understand. It wasn't personal."

Signora Lucchesi rose gracefully from the sofa, despite the size of her belly. "Please, come make yourself comfortable. Are you hungry?"

Loredana shook her head. "No, thank you."

"Then let me introduce you." She stepped forward with her hand extended. "I'm

Kate." She motioned to the woman with caramel-colored hair. "That's my daughter-in-law, Bianca, and this"—she motioned to the gorgeous dark-haired woman—"is my other daughter-in-law, Delfina."

Other daughter-in-law? Lucchesi had no natural children, aside from the one his wife carried, unless… unless Delfina or Clarkston was his child. The resemblance between Lucchesi and Clarkston was striking. But how could an Interpol agent be the son of a Mafia don?

The older women came forward. The younger was in her mid-forties, the other in her early fifties. "This is Francesca, Bianca's mother," Kate said, referring to the younger woman, "and this is Elena, Ruggero's sister."

Sister? She must be the one he'd mentioned, the one whose husband had died.

The women exchanged greetings, and Francesca and Elena joined their group on the sofas and chairs arranged near the crackling fireplace. They took their seats, and the blond boy finally seemed to take notice of the awkwardness among the adults. Silently, he regarded her, then he went over to Bianca and nestled himself into the space at her side. She put an arm around him.

Loredana took the open spot beside Kate and leaned toward the boy. "My name is Loredana. Who are you?"

He looked up at Bianca, who nodded, then he turned his gaze back to Loredana. "I'm Luca." The puppy bounded over to the couch, and he picked it up. It licked his face, making him giggle. "This is Cocco. You can pet him if you want." His blue eyes studied her as if he wasn't quite sure what to make of her.

"I'd like that." Luca hopped off the couch and brought the squirming pup over to her. She scratched the dog's ears, and Luca smiled. "He likes you."

"And I like him."

"Want to play with us?" Luca asked.

She looked at Kate. "A little later."

"Okay." He set the puppy down and it promptly raced over to the ball in front of the hearth, Luca right behind it.

"He's adorable," Loredana said to Bianca. Luca's mother smiled, but there was something tentative about it.

"He's having a good day today," Kate said. "Normally he won't go near strangers."

"Why?"

Bianca spoke up. "A few months ago, there was… an incident. His adoptive parents were killed in front of him."

"Adoptive parents?"

Bianca nodded. "Tonio and I, we're his biological parents. But I had him when I was very young, and my father forced me to give him up." Her eyes grew moist and her voice thickened. "It's only by the grace of God that we got him back."

Her mother reached out and squeezed Bianca's hand. "*Dolcezza*, that's all over now."

"I know, but…" She looked over at her son wrestling with the puppy. "I just hope it will be over for him someday."

"Is he having nightmares?" Loredana asked.

Bianca nodded. "And sometimes he refuses to leave the grounds. He'll almost have a panic attack."

Loredana understood that all too well. Her own eyes pricked with tears. "My father was shot to death in front of me when I was twelve. It's not something you forget—or let go of easily."

Bianca wiped her eyes. "I'd forgotten. How long did it take you?"

"Months before my heart stopped racing every time I left or returned from the apartment. It happened right outside our building."

"At least he doesn't have to go through that every day," Bianca said.

"It might help him to go back, to see where it happened, and that everything's okay there now."

Bianca looked over at Luca. "That's what the psychologist says. I'm just not so sure."

"It did desensitize me. Eventually."

"Maybe we'll try it. He's been getting stronger every day. Cocco helps."

Loredana dabbed her eyes and smiled. "I noticed he brought the dog with him." She paused. "I'm impressed that he came over to me without you."

Bianca returned her smile. "So am I."

Luca appeared at Loredana's side. He was dragging a long blue knitted scarf with him, handmade, and not very well, from the looks of it. He offered her the end of it. "You can pet it if you feel sad."

Loredana stroked the scarf, tears threatening to spill. "It's very soft."

"It's warm too." Luca pressed the material against his cheek.

"Thank you." Loredana handed the end of it back to him. Cocco came up and tugged the other end of the scarf and Luca followed the pup back to the fireplace.

Loredana wiped her eyes. "I'm not sure I'm doing the right thing. Being here."

This time Elena spoke. "Do you love my brother?"

Loredana blushed; had Ruggero said something to her? "I don't know why you're asking."

Elena raised an eyebrow. "He wouldn't have brought you here if he didn't trust you. And he wouldn't trust you lightly." She paused. "I also picked up on something when he mentioned you before."

"I'm not sure what to say."

"It's a simple question. Do you love him?"

Loredana nodded. "I don't think he's there yet. If he'll ever be."

Elena held her eyes. "He may not know it yet, but he is. I can see it all over him."

Loredana's stomach flipped. Could Elena be right? He hadn't said the words, but what he had said to her—*mine*—echoed in her head. She met Elena's gaze. "I hope so."

Elena smiled. "Ruggero doesn't think himself capable of such a thing, but he has a heart." She paused. "Just don't break it."

"I don't want to. But this situation—"

Kate touched her hand. "Yes, it's all kinds of fucked up."

The profanity left her mouth so casually that Bianca and Delfina laughed, and Loredana did too, a bit shocked.

Kate smiled. "*Mi dispiace.* I'm not one to mince words."

"Neither is Ruggero," Loredana said.

Elena sighed. "The mouth on my brother. I never could get him to stop. Papà was a horrible influence."

"Actually," Loredana said, "I think he was a good influence. Ruggero may be difficult, but he's... genuine. True."

Elena nodded, her smile open. "Yes, he is that, for all his faults."

Loredana just hoped that Ruggero's trust in his *capo* was as well-placed as hers in him. Or else she'd just made the biggest mistake of her life.

She looked at the doorway he'd disappeared through. How soon would she know her fate?

CHAPTER 22

Ruggero hoped the women would take pity on Loredana; it was clear from Don Lucchesi's expression that Ruggero couldn't expect an easy time of it himself.

Nor should he.

When they entered Enrico's study, the don settled into the chair closest to the fire. Antonio, Nick, and Orlando took seats on the sofas to either side of the don. There was a spot on the sofa next to Orlando, and an open chair at the other end of the coffee table from the don.

But Ruggero didn't deserve to sit. Not unless the don told him to. Instead, he went over to the window that ran the length of the room and put his back to it so he faced them all.

No one said a word. Ruggero knew what Enrico was doing. He'd seen him do it before, to other men. He was letting him sweat, letting the silence do its work, letting it fill Ruggero's head with doubt and worry.

It was no less effective for all that Ruggero knew it was a ploy. After all, when Enrico had doubted Tonio, he'd been prepared to take the necessary steps, that day they'd taken Tonio out onto the lake and the don had questioned him.

For all of Enrico's love for Tonio, he'd been prepared to protect the family. His wife, his unborn child, his son Nick. And everyone in the *cosca*.

Though the don had called Ruggero "friend," he had no reason to be any more merciful to Ruggero than he'd been to Tonio.

Or to his cousin Domenico. The cousin who'd betrayed him. The cousin Enrico had executed himself.

Finally Enrico broke the silence. "What does she know?"

"Enough. I haven't said it directly, but I stopped denying it."

"Why is she here?"

"She's in danger."

"She's *been* in danger."

"Well, it's changed. Because of me. Because she trusted me."

"Trusted you how?"

"She believes there's a conspiracy against you and Don Battista."

"And?" Enrico raised a brow.

"And I—" He hesitated, then swallowed. "I was intimate with her."

Enrico slammed his fist on the arm of his chair. "I asked you to be strategic. I didn't think seducing her would be part of the plan. Or is that the mysterious mission Don Battista gave you?"

"He had nothing to do with this."

"Then what did he ask you to do?"

Ruggero frowned. "He told me I'd have to make sure Lorenzo was dealt with. And I'd have to work on fixing things with Dario."

"Does he think me incapable?"

"No. He just felt you'd need help. And you wouldn't ask for it."

A muscle twitched in Enrico's jaw. "Fair enough." He took a breath, then said, "So what happened with the judge?"

What the hell could he say but the truth? "I wanted her."

"You wanted her? *That's* your excuse for exposing us?"

"If you wish to put a bullet in me, that is your right."

"It damn well is." A muscle ticked in Enrico's jaw. His voice had a raw, rough edge.

Antonio held up his hands, looking from Ruggero to Enrico. "If I may speak for Ruggero, who I'm sure doesn't feel he can say this—what about Kate? You risked everything for her."

"I am the *capo* of this *cosca*."

"You made Ruggero *capo di società*." Antonio's words hung in the silence.

Ruggero's heart pounded in his chest; he couldn't let Tonio do all the talking. He needed to say something. He was fucking this up. Ruining it. Ruining Loredana's chances of surviving this mess. Fuck his own chances; *she* was the one who mattered. He inclined his head, breaking eye contact with Enrico. If he had to beg, he'd beg. "Forgive me, Don Lucchesi."

Enrico studied him for several moments. "What happened?"

Ruggero couldn't answer. How could he possibly explain? "*She* happened," he finally said.

"I admit she's stunning, but I thought you, of all people, could keep it in your trousers."

Ruggero dropped his eyes to the carpet. "I can't explain it."

"I can," Antonio said. "*Colpo di fulmine.* The thunderbolt has struck. You're in love with her."

Was he? He wanted her, he adored her, but was this love? "I wouldn't go that far—"

Enrico cut in. "You already have. Too far. You slept with her. You brought her here, under this roof. You're asking me to protect her, to help her. You've claimed her."

Mine. The word flashed into Ruggero's head. *Yours,* she'd said. He raised his eyes and looked at Enrico. "Yes."

Enrico held his gaze. "You expect me to trust her?"

Heat flashed through Ruggero's chest. "After all she's done? After what she's gone through for us?"

"She may just be trying to save her skin."

"That's not how she is."

"So you say."

"So I *know*."

Enrico scrubbed a hand over his face. Then he sighed. "Were she part of the family, then it would be different."

Ruggero's stomach knotted. "You don't mean—"

"That's *exactly* what I mean." His eyes drilled into Ruggero. "Marry her, and then she can't turn against us."

Ruggero's mouth went dry. "Marry her?" he croaked.

"You want me to protect her?"

"I need to think."

Enrico looked at his watch. "You have twenty-four hours. And you stay with her, in Dom's house, away from the others. I can't have her overhearing something she shouldn't."

"She has a plan to take down Baldassare, and Lorenzo with him."

Both of Enrico's brows rose to his hairline. "She does?"

Ruggero quickly explained their discussion with Fuente. Then he said, "She's willing to dismiss the charges against you. What if we help her build a case against Baldassare? What if we give her access to the information we have?"

Enrico blew out. "There's only one way she's going to get access to that information. *Capisci?*"

"And if she says no?"

"Then she's on her own."

"And me?"

Enrico shook his head. "You've already told me what I *should* do."

Yes, he had. But would Enrico do it? Months ago, Ruggero wouldn't have protested. He'd have accepted his sentence. But now—now he had something to live for. Something to fight for.

Enrico held his gaze. "Don't make me regret the faith I've shown in you. The faith I'm showing now, by tolerating her presence."

Message received. No more fuckups. Or this would be his last.

———◆———

Ruggero left Enrico's study. *Marry her.* How could he?

And yet, how could he not?

He was only a step or two out the door when Antonio called to him. "Ruggero."

Stopping, he waited for Antonio to reach him. "What?"

Antonio gave him a somber look. "You should see your face." He motioned to the open door to the library. "I think you could use a drink."

There were certainly worse ideas. *Like asking a judge to marry a Mafioso.* He followed Antonio inside, a hush falling over the room when Antonio shut the door behind them.

The study desk that Orlando had taken over was piled high with papers, but the stacks were orderly, precise. Like his nephew, the man he was only now starting to know.

They were rather alike in their way; Ruggero too, liked everything in its place, the various aspects of his life safely walled off into compartments, with no place for emotions, feelings. The messy business of being human.

Everything he'd built for himself, the way he lived; it would all change if he married Loredana. Those walls he'd erected around himself... she'd bulldoze through them all, the way she'd already demolished so many.

And what if she didn't like what she found when she breached the last one?

Antonio busied himself at the liquor cabinet in the corner, glasses and bottles clinking, while Ruggero took a seat at one of the two wingback chairs in front of the blazing fireplace. The heat felt good, and he held his hands toward it.

How was he going to do this? His gut was tight, as if he were about to go into a firefight.

"Here." Antonio handed him a glass filled with two fingers of Galliano. Its vanilla scent teased his nose, reminding him of the woman waiting for him in the drawing room, the woman he wanted to seek out, to take into his arms, to hold close. But how could he inflict something as permanent as marriage on her?

"Thanks," Ruggero said, taking a gulp from the glass, the liquor warming his throat as it went down, but it did nothing to loosen that knot in his stomach.

"To the future," Antonio said, holding out his drink.

If I have one. Ruggero tapped his glass to Tonio's.

They each took a swallow, then Antonio leaned forward, cradling his drink between his knees. "You look like a man going to the gallows. And that's not what she needs to see."

"So you're giving me advice along with this drink."

Tonio smiled, his eyes on the fire. "Which one of us is married?"

"For all of three weeks, oh wise one."

"That's three weeks longer than you. And I seem to recall you giving me a lecture not too long ago about Bianca. About how I shouldn't break her heart. About how I needed to stop fucking around."

He might as well say it. "I can't do this to her."

"Do you want this? Really want it?"

Ruggero shrugged. "What can I offer her?"

"You're not just a guard anymore."

With a snort, Ruggero took a swig from his glass. "Weren't you listening? I barely escaped with my skin just now, and I still might end up at the bottom of the lake. I fucked up. Don Lucchesi isn't going to reward me for that."

"He's upset. But you're still his friend."

"Some friend. I betrayed him. For a fuck."

"That's not what she is to you."

"Doesn't matter. That's how he sees it."

"That's what he *says*, not what he thinks. You stood by him when he needed help to save Kate. If you hadn't, you think the others would have followed him into that house? He'll never forget that."

Ruggero met Tonio's gaze. "He killed Dom."

197

"He had no choice."

"I haven't given him much of one either."

Antonio tapped a fingernail against the rim of his glass and turned his gaze to the fire. "I hate to say it, but if she's the only one who knows, the problem is easy to solve."

The knot in Ruggero's gut twisted. "That's what I'm afraid of. If I can't convince her, then…" His pulse raced and his fingers tightened on the glass. Was this what it felt like? Was this what Enrico and Antonio had faced, that moment when the women they loved were on the brink of death?

Cristo. He was a coward. A fucking coward. He had to save her, and if that meant marrying her, then marrying her was what he had to do. He had to make her understand. And Tonio was right; he needed to put a better face on it. Surely marriage was a whole lot better than death. *Oh yes, you're quite the salesman, Vela.*

Tonio interrupted his thoughts. "You haven't answered my question."

"What question?"

"The one I asked earlier. Do you *want* this? Do you want to marry her?"

He almost shrugged again, but stopped himself. A shrug was his all-purpose, noncommittal response to everything. Anytime he didn't want to answer, to put himself on the line. Anytime he didn't want to admit a truth.

A shrug was so easy, the truth damn hard.

He stared into his glass, a lump filling his throat. What *did* he want?

He wanted her.

He wanted the house, the kids.

He wanted everything.

His voice hoarse, tight, he forced out the words. "I do." He met Antonio's gaze. "I want this."

Tonio grinned. "Good. You're being honest. Now you have to be honest with her."

"That's the problem. This marriage isn't good for her, but she'll agree because she doesn't have a choice." Ruggero shook his head. "I can't do that to her."

"So give her a choice."

"So, marry me or die?" *Still knocking 'em dead on the sales floor.*

Tonio chuckled. "You know I'm your friend, yes?"

"*Sì.*"

"And I'm *capo di società*, with access to any number of resources. I could help her. I could help you both."

"You'd defy Enrico?"

"He's my father now. Not just my *capo*. And yes, I would. Because I want you to be happy." He held Ruggero's eyes. "You've taken care of me, trained me, protected me. Helped me. Let me help you."

The knot in his gut loosened slightly. "You're a good kid, Tonio."

Antonio shook his head. "No. I'm an awesome *friend.* And don't forget it."

They tapped glasses again, and Ruggero drained the last of the Galliano. Time to see if he could sell Loredana something he could barely imagine.

A future, and a life together.

———— ✦ ————

When Ruggero went back to the drawing room for Loredana, he was surprised to find the women chatting easily. Kate met his eye when he stepped inside, and he gave her a grateful nod. So she'd been responsible for it. He should've known. As an outsider not so long ago herself, Kate would take pity on Loredana.

He approached the sofa where Loredana was sitting, her back to him. Elena caught his eye and smiled. He knew that look—*I told you so.* He wasn't going to give her the satisfaction of pouncing. He leaned over and spoke in Loredana's ear. "We need to talk."

She practically jumped up. So she wasn't quite as comfortable as she'd seemed. But of course not—how could she be?

He retrieved their coats for the walk to Dom's. Antonio had given him the keys. He ought to stop thinking of it as Dom's. It belonged to Francesca now, and she, Bianca, Antonio, and Luca would have been living there if it weren't safer for them to be at Enrico's.

He'd told Tommaso that he wanted privacy for the rest of the day. Guards would patrol the perimeter, but none of them would be in the house itself. In case she reacted badly, he didn't want any witnesses to how he would react in turn.

He'd never been so terrified in his life. Could he do this? Could he ask her?

And what if she said no? What then?

He could use another drink. And a whole pack of cigarettes. Why had he ever agreed to quit?

They left Enrico's villa by the side gate, one of the ones concealed in the hedge that surrounded the estate, and made their way through the barren remnants of the garden that sloped down from Francesca's house to the lake. Were it summer, they wouldn't be able to see the house yet.

"Where are we going?" Loredana asked.

"Francesca's place."

"I thought she lived with Enrico."

"She does. For now. It's safer to have everyone in one house."

"You're that worried?"

"There was an attack last fall."

"The one Nick Clarkston was involved in."

How did she know that name? She saw his look. "I read the files on Enrico Lucchesi. All the suspicious 'incidents' he was involved in. Supposedly Signor Clarkston was working undercover for Interpol, and he got mixed up in some business with a group of Russians."

Ruggero nodded. "They attacked."

"Except that's not really what happened. Because he's part of this family."

Ruggero let out a breath. "He's Enrico's illegitimate son."

"And he's still in Interpol."

Ruggero nodded, and she laughed. "Oh, you people are slicker than I gave you credit for."

"What do you mean?"

"Well, you've got an Interpol agent working for you… and now a judge."

"No comment."

"I assume Delfina is some distant Lucchesi cousin?"

"Not exactly. She's Enrico's niece by marriage. She's actually an Andretti."

Loredana stopped walking. "An Andretti?"

"Enrico's first wife was the granddaughter of Lorenzo Andretti. Delfina is the daughter of Enrico's former brother-in-law."

"And she just happened to marry his son?"

Ruggero sighed. "It's complicated."

They started walking again, then Loredana stopped him. "Is she related to the boy who was killed at the bank? Cristoforo?"

"Yes. He was her brother. Her father blames Enrico for it."

"Why?"

"That is something I'll have to tell you later."

"Later?"

"It's not one of the things you can know right now."

"Okay."

"I've already said too much. About Nick."

She tapped her temple. "I'm not stupid. I'd have to be blind not to realize his involvement. Especially when he went off with all of you. Speaking of which, who was that other man? The tall slender one?"

"My nephew. Orlando."

"Elena's boy?"

"Yes."

"Any other siblings you've hardly mentioned?"

"No. My mother died having me. Elena had to raise me."

"I don't think she minded."

"She was twelve when I was born. Who wants to be saddled with a kid that young?"

"She loves you, very much."

"I wasn't always so sure."

"What do you mean?"

"Elena and her husband came north with us. But after Papà died, she left."

"She left?"

His throat grew tight. "All these years I thought she blamed me, that she hated me." He swallowed hard. "But she said it wasn't that at all."

"What, then?"

"She said she didn't want to see the same thing happen to me."

"Who looked after you?"

"I was sixteen. I took care of myself."

"Sounds lonely."

He shrugged. Why was he telling her all this? "I had food in my mouth and a roof over my head."

They'd reached the back door of the house, and he let them inside. The interior was chilly, the air stale. A light coating of dust covered the furniture. How little time it took for things to change. For a home to become just a house.

He started flipping on lights and adjusting the thermostats. When he finished, Loredana touched his arm. "Ruggero, I'm sorry."

"Sorry for what?"

"Everything that happened to you."

He shook his head. "Sometimes I think I'm cursed. A bad seed."

She touched his cheek. "Don't say that."

"My mother died having me. Right from birth I was killing people." He paced away from her, went to the closed drapes in the living room and opened them.

She followed close behind. "What is wrong with you? You've been acting strange since we got here. Is he opposed to my plan?"

He couldn't put it off any longer, could he? Yet he didn't want to sit in this airless, cheerless house. Because if she said no, he didn't want to be staring at these walls.

He took her hand. "Let's take a walk. We have something to discuss."

They circled back to the barren garden, taking the path all the way to the lake, then out onto the boat dock. The wind whipped at their faces, and Loredana shivered. He removed his scarf and wound it around her neck.

"Thank you."

He took her gloved hands in his and chafed them, still not sure how to start, what to say.

"Tell me what's bothering you," she said.

He couldn't look at her. "I've ruined your life. And I'm about to make it worse."

She let out a breath, and the icy air turned it into a cloud. "He said no. And you have to follow his lead."

"Not exactly. There is a way."

"I can't quit the Baldassare trial. Not yet."

"Before you say anything else, I need to say something." He brought her hands up to his mouth and kissed the backs of them, his heart racing, his mouth dry. "I don't know how to do this."

She looked up at him, and he swore his heart was going to hammer out of his chest. Could he ask her this? Could he?

"Ruggero, just tell me."

"I have nothing to offer you. Nothing but my honor, and my oath to you. I will protect you with my body and my life, until I take my last breath."

She inhaled deeply, studying him. "That sounds a lot like a marriage vow."

"If it was, would you accept?"

"Are you asking me to marry you?"

"It's the condition of his protection and his cooperation. You must become part of the family." *Fuck.* He was supposed to be selling her on this. He was supposed to be giving her a choice. "But if that's not what you want, I can arrange protection for you. You'd probably have to leave the country, but I can keep you safe. I can get you a new identity, a new life. Marrying me would be easier, but I understand—"

How much worse could he be at this? "I mean it would be better. Marrying me would be better. I swear."

She gave him a tight smile, and his stomach turned over. She was going to say no. "That's all very nice, but it's not what I want to know. I'm asking if *you* are asking me to marry you."

"I know it's not romantic, I know it's not what you want—"

She held up a hand. "Are *you* asking me to marry you? You, not your boss, not the circumstances. But you."

His heart sank. He never should have brought her here. "You deserve so much better than me. I *can't* ask you."

"You can."

A spark lit in his chest. "I can?"

"You're a man worth having. Even if you don't believe that."

A lump rose in his throat. "Fuck."

She laughed, and he looked at her, searching her face. "You mean that?" He waited as if his whole life depended on her answer. And maybe it did.

"I do."

He closed his eyes for a moment. So he wasn't a fool for doing this. He wasn't a fool for trusting her. He opened his eyes and gazed down at her, this woman who meant everything, who owned him already, without another word being said, without vows being exchanged.

His heart was pounding harder than it ever had. He'd been calmer in the midst of shootouts. All he had to do was open his mouth, admit the truth. Bare his heart to her mercy. Such a small thing, but everything rode on her response. He tried to inhale, but his lungs were locked. Forcing in a breath, he took the leap.

"Then yes, it's me asking. Me, not my boss. But I meant what I said. This isn't your only choice."

Her brow wrinkled as she looked up at him. "Why would I choose anything else?"

"*Davvero?*"

"*Davvero.*"

Dio, he didn't deserve her.

He twisted the signet ring off the little finger of his right hand. She deserved a better ring than this, but it would have to do for now. He dropped to one knee. This, at least, he could do properly. His voice shook when he spoke. "Loredana Montisi, will you do me the eternal honor of being my wife?"

Her cheeks were red from the cold, her eyes glistening with unshed tears. "As crazy as this all is, I will."

He'd done it. He hadn't even had to sell her on it.

She'd given him everything. Everything he'd ever wanted, but had never dreamt of having.

She took off her glove and he slid the ring onto her finger, then he rose and pressed his lips to hers, pouring all his feelings into the kiss.

By some miracle, she'd said yes. The god he didn't believe in had answered his prayers.

When they parted, he took her ungloved hand in his and rubbed his thumb over the ring. "This belonged to my father, so it means a lot to me. But I'll get you another ring as soon as I can. The thing is, we're going to have to marry soon. Probably tomorrow. And without your family."

"We'd have to do it without them anyway. Without my mother, at the very least."

She looked so sad. And it was all his fault. Did she already regret her decision? He didn't want to ask, but he had to. He wouldn't force her into this life. "Are you certain about this?"

———— ◆ ————

Loredana looked up at Ruggero. The wind whipped at his coal-black hair, and the color had risen in his cheeks. He'd never looked so handsome. Or so worried.

She touched his scar. "I made my choice the day I kissed you." Then she shook her head. "That's not quite true. I made it back at the courthouse, that day you intervened when Andretti's man threatened me. I should've reported our encounter, I should have recused myself from the case. But I didn't."

Not long ago he'd been a stranger. Now she couldn't imagine him not being in her life. "I crossed a line back then, and I knew I was crossing it. And since then, it's been one step after another, moving further away from everything I've ever known. But always toward you. I wouldn't undo a single second of what's happened between us."

"I still don't know why fortune has smiled on me."

"Because you deserve it."

He shrugged. "If you say so."

"I'm going to keep saying it until you believe it." Loredana pulled him down into a kiss, a tender, gentle kiss, to show him she didn't regret anything. Especially not saying yes.

Marrying him—marrying a Mafioso—it was utterly insane. But somehow, somehow this man was the right one for her. The one she'd been seeking. The one she could trust her heart to.

"Let's go back to the house," she whispered.

He smiled and took her bottom lip gently between his teeth before releasing it. "You need warming up?"

"Hours of it, I think."

"Hours?" he said, taking her hand, rubbing his fingers over the ring that felt so heavy on her finger, and yet so right.

"Hours." She gave him a teasing smile.

"I'm going to need to start hitting the gym again. Get my stamina up."

She laughed and tugged on his hand. "Race you back?"

"That eager?"

"Oh yes." She loved the way he was smiling at her, the skin around his eyes crinkling, his teeth showing, so unguarded for once. Letting go of his hand, she started for the house at an easy jog, only putting on speed when she heard him follow.

He didn't try to overtake her, though she was certain he could have. They soon reached the back door of the house, and she turned to him, panting, her breath coming out in great clouds. "Such the gentleman. Letting me win."

He waggled his brows and stepped close. "I was too busy enjoying the view." For emphasis, he placed both hands on her buttocks and pulled her close, his hands kneading her flesh. "*Dio*, you're beautiful."

Her breath caught at the look in his eyes—that mix of lust, love, and a bit of wonder, as if he didn't believe his good fortune. He loved her, he truly did. Even if he hadn't said it. Even if he never did. She knew it, as surely as she knew the sun would rise tomorrow.

And she loved him, this complicated, tortured man. This man who'd won her heart with his goodness, who'd stolen it from her the first time he'd smiled at her—that real smile, the one he was afraid to show.

Except to her. A lump clogged her throat. He was hers, would be hers for the rest of their lives, however short or long that would be.

She'd never regret the choice she'd made. The life she was choosing, the life she was leaving behind.

She had to hope that Papà would understand, wherever he was now. Ruggero was a good man, a good man who did bad things. But a better man than so many others. A stronger, truer man than she'd ever known.

Loredana followed Ruggero into the house and down the hallway. He looked in several rooms, finally choosing a large one with a four-poster bed and a fireplace. He went to the fireplace and loaded several logs in it, along with some kindling. Once he had a blaze going, he brushed off his hands and turned to her. "Hungry?" he asked.

She shook her head, suddenly nervous. Despite how she'd taken charge the night before, what she really wanted was a repeat of their night at the hotel. But it was hard for her to admit. Should she just come out and say it? Ask him to tie her up and do wicked things to her?

He studied her for a moment. "What's wrong?"

"Nothing."

"Something's on your mind. Is this all too fast?"

She stepped closer to him, reached up and smoothed a hand over that thick, springy hair, black as a raven's wing. "Too fast, and yet, not fast enough."

"Still cold?" His voice was a low growl as he crowded into her space, pulling her flush against him.

"That's part of it," she said. How to say the rest?

"And the other part?"

She took a deep breath. "I'd like to do what we did at the hotel. When you had me at your mercy."

His eyes darkened. "You sure?"

She nodded, because she didn't think she could speak. Finally she found her voice. "You liked it too."

"I don't want you doing this because I like it."

"I think you missed the 'too' part."

"You really want that? After last night—"

"Last night was about you. About me taking care of you. Sometimes I'm going to want that too."

"But now…"

"Now I want something else."

He frowned. "I'm not sure that's how a man should treat his wife."

"Don't give me that Madonna/whore crap. I love sex. Really love it. And I love what we did the other night."

"You're just saying that because you think it's what I want."

"You should know by now I'm not the sort of woman who does things *just* to please her man. Sometimes I will, yes, but I also want to please myself." She reached down and cupped his balls. "And what you do to me really, really pleases me."

He took a deep breath, then nodded. "On your knees then." His voice was raspy, excited, and it sent a thrill through her.

She got down on her knees, facing away from the fireplace, heat from the flames seeping into her back. She hadn't even taken off her coat. But she waited for the next command.

"Take out my cock."

With trembling fingers, she unzipped him, then plunged her hands inside his trousers, finding his hard sex straining against the material of his boxer briefs. She pulled it out through the opening, its large head already beaded with pre-ejaculate at the tip. She started to lean forward, to take him in her mouth, but she stopped and looked up at him instead.

Holding her eyes, he pulled his black leather belt from its loops, then held it in his hands, staring at her as if trying to make up his mind what to do with it. "Take off everything above the waist, and put your hands behind your back."

He crossed behind her while she complied, then he wrapped the belt around her wrists, cinching them tight together. The sensation of being restrained, helpless, made her sex go wet. She squirmed a bit, spreading her legs, and he chuckled. "Later, *bambina*."

He tossed his coat on the chair, then stood before her, his erect cock in hand. "You want this?"

"Yes." The answer came out low, her voice husky with excitement.

He stroked himself, his fist squeezing as he did so, the veins standing out on the back of his hand and along his cock. "I'm not sure you should have it."

She almost smiled. He was enjoying himself. Letting go. "Please," she said, not having to pretend she wanted it. Wanted him.

"I don't know." He circled her, his eyes dipping down to her breasts, then back up to her face, lingering on her mouth. "Do you deserve it?"

Now she did smile. "Maybe I can show you?"

His eyes narrowed. "You'll have to impress me."

"I will."

He stepped closer, jerking his cock right in her face, his hand sliding roughly along the shaft. "I've been with experts, you know. Think you can do better?"

She looked up and licked her lips. "I know I can."

Cupping the back of her head with one hand, he used the other to guide his cock to her mouth. "Show me." His voice was hoarse, urgent. Raw.

She took him in, swirling her tongue around him as he invaded her mouth, going almost too far before pulling back. He let go of his cock, then used both his hands to guide her the way he wanted, gasping when she increased the suction, when she played little tricks with her tongue and her lips, teasing him, before she leaned up and forward, actively taking him in, pushing the pace faster than he had.

Her pussy throbbed, wanting to be filled, and she sucked him harder. His breath came in great gusts, and he cursed between them, muttering to himself, then saying, "*Cristo*, you're beautiful," before he came with a shout.

She swallowed and swallowed, enjoying the shudders, the way his hands clutched her head, his groans, the muttered "Fuck," as he slipped from her mouth.

His eyes were closed, his cock deep red and still half-hard. And though she was tied and at his feet, she felt like the one with the power.

Because she'd convinced him to do what he wanted. Because he'd listened to her. Because he'd let go.

He finally opened his eyes and looked at her. "So, am I deserving?" she asked.

"Fuck yes." He reached out and pinched her nipples, making her cry out and push them into his hands. She was so wet, she was sure her panties were soaked.

He helped her to her feet and proceeded to remove her boots and slacks. He chuckled when he touched the damp fabric between her legs. "You *do* like this." He pulled off her panties and stuffed them in one of his trouser pockets. He still hadn't undressed, and she could see he didn't mean to.

He walked her over to the upholstered chair by the fire and the ottoman in front of it. He sat down on the ottoman, then tugged her in front of him. He was already growing hard again. He touched her lightly between the legs, and she shivered, though he hadn't done more than pass his fingers over her neatly trimmed hair. "Open your legs," he said.

She widened her stance, her nipples growing stiffer if that was possible. She kept her hands clasped together, her breasts pushed out, hoping he'd touch her, wanting it, ready to beg if need be.

He lightly caressed her thighs, his hands moving so close, but not touching her pussy, and she moaned in frustration. He huffed in amusement and pulled her closer, both hands on her ass, his fingers playing along the crack. Was he going to try *that* while she was bound?

But no. Instead he took one of her nipples in his mouth, his teeth grazing it as he sucked in hard. She moaned, her legs spreading further, wondering if he'd object to her straddling him. She started to do it, but he stopped her.

"Not yet, *bambina*. Just wait."

"I can't," she said, her voice almost a wail.

"You can." The edge of command in his voice reminded her that he was in control. He was running the show. And she was his plaything.

He went back to sucking her breasts, his hands kneading her ass, his fingers dancing closer to where she wanted them, but not close enough. Why had she pushed him into this?

But she knew. He turned her around so her back was to him. "Have you been good enough?" he asked, as if he wasn't sure.

"Please, Ruggero." Her *figa* pulsed, aching, empty. "*Per favore.*"

He took hold of her hips and guided her down until she hovered just above him, the tip of his cock nudging her entrance. "Please," she pleaded.

He moved her back and forth along his hardening cock, using her juices to coat himself. Then he stopped and stood her up. "Just a second."

"Ruggero!"

He felt around in his pockets, then pulled out a condom. "I can't forget this," he said. Then he looked at her. "Can I?"

She thought about it for a second. She wasn't on birth control. "Not yet."

He put it on, then turned her back around so she faced away from him again. "Please," she said again as he resumed his slow teasing of her. She tried to push herself onto him, but when he laughed and held her in place, she realized how strong he was, a strength he'd half hidden from her.

She truly was at his mercy. "Touch me," she begged.

He kissed her between the shoulder blades. "When you're ready."

"I'm more than ready."

He rubbed his cock between her labia, just grazing her clit, and she moaned. She was so slick now, so ready. "You're torturing me."

"And you like it."

"Yes."

"You love it."

"Yes."

"You want it."

"Yes." Did she ever.

With a sudden movement, he impaled her on his cock, and she cried out, the invasion exactly what she wanted, and yet not quite. Her *grilletto* throbbed and swelled, needing his touch.

She unclasped her hands and struggled against her bonds. If only she could touch herself...

He held her hips tight, but didn't touch her arms. "Stop." That one word, so sharp, so firm. "Stop, or I do."

"Then please touch me!"

"Hands together."

She complied, almost holding her breath, waiting for him to start again. *Hoping* he'd start again.

Eventually he resumed guiding her up and down his cock, and she almost felt like crying. It was so good, the feeling of him inside her, stretching her, and yet it wasn't enough.

She tightened her internal muscles, hoping to intensify the sensation, to ease her ache for release, but all it did was make them both groan. "I need it," she said.

"You do." He let go of her hips, and with one hand on her throat and the other between her legs, he thrust up into her at the same time he stroked her *grilletto*.

She came in a sudden explosion, so intense that she shuddered and cried out, riding his cock and his hand as she came.

"*Troppo bella*," he murmured when she stopped convulsing. He was still inside her, still hard, and he said, "Ready for more?"

She mumbled something half coherent, then felt him buck into her at the same time he pulled her down. He was so deep within her. She spread her legs wider and leaned forward a bit, using her legs to aid him, to push down against him.

His fingers worked between her legs as he started to moan himself, his words a muttered string of endearments mixed with curses.

Finally they both came again. He pressed another kiss to her back, then he murmured, "What are you doing to me?"

She laughed. "What am *I* doing to *you?*" She looked at him over her shoulder.

"Yes, *bella*. You somehow get me to do things I never thought I'd do."

A lump rose in her throat. "Like get married?"

"Like that." He unbuckled the belt, freeing her, then shifted her around in his arms. "You've *changed* me. I don't know if you understand that."

She touched his cheek, that lump still in her throat. Maybe he'd never say he loved her, but this was close enough. "You've changed me too."

CHAPTER 23

Ruggero woke near dawn. For several minutes, he watched Loredana sleep. She'd agreed to be his wife, a fact he couldn't yet believe. Sooner or later, she'd come to her senses and tell him no.

And yet, after last night, he didn't see how he could bear it. The way she'd surrendered herself, the way she'd responded, the way she'd shuddered in his arms... How could he ever live without her?

Sighing, he eased out of bed, reluctant to disturb her despite the raging hard-on between his legs. Would he ever get enough of her? He didn't see how.

She stirred, and he caught his breath, waiting for her to either wake or go back to sleep. She put out a hand, as if reaching for him, and his gold signet ring caught the early light coming through the curtains. He needed to get her a proper ring, and soon.

And he knew just where to get it.

Dressing hurriedly, he left Loredana asleep under the watchful eye of the two guards stationed outside the house.

The morning was crisp, the air biting as he walked over to Enrico's villa next door. If his sister was anything like she'd been when he was a child, she'd be up, already coiffed, at this hour.

Sure enough, he found her having breakfast with Maddalena and Nonna Drina, the maid and the cook the only others besides the exterior guards who seemed to be up and about.

Maddalena rose when he entered and offered him something for breakfast. He refused, but Elena ordered him to sit and eat. He almost refused again, but she added such a charming "*per favore*," that he couldn't say no to her.

He accepted a plate of cold cuts and pastries from Maddalena and a steaming cappuccino. "Can you make up a plate that I can take back to Loredana?" he asked.

"Of course," Maddalena said, and she and Nonna Drina left the room.

"So," Elena said. "How did it go?"

"How did what go?"

"Antonio told Bianca what was happening."

Ruggero took a sip of his cappuccino. "A house full of women, and he's the biggest gossip."

Elena laughed. "You might be right." She raised her cup to her lips, then looked at him over the rim. "So?"

He blew out and picked at a pastry. "She said yes."

Elena put her hand over his and squeezed. "I *knew* it."

He shook his head. "I had no idea what she'd say. And I still think she's going to change her mind any minute."

"She won't. She loves you, fool that she is."

He chuckled. "I should be angry about that comment, but I can't be." He ate a piece of prosciutto. "I know I'm a fucking bastard sometimes."

Elena choked on her cappuccino and sputtered with laughter. When she sobered, she smiled at him. "I've missed you so much."

His throat tightened. "Me too." There was a time when Elena and Papà had been the center of his world. It had been too many years since he'd spent any real time with her. "Thank you, for everything."

"You mean for not strangling you when you kept me up night after night when you were an infant?"

"For that, and for so many things." He placed his hand over hers, unable to say everything in his heart. *For being there, even though I stole Mamma from you.*

"Anytime, you know that." She took another sip of her cappuccino. "Have you thought about the ring?"

"I have." He cleared his throat and looked her full in the eyes. "I thought, if you still have it, of Mamma's ring."

Elena beamed. "Of course I still have it. I've been holding onto it for just this purpose, though I was beginning to think Orlando might end up with it instead."

"If you'd rather save it for him—"

"No. Mamma and Papà would have wanted you to have it."

"*Grazie.*" He took another sip of cappuccino. "So, does Orlando have his eye on anyone?"

Elena shrugged. "Not that I know."

"And you?"

She didn't meet his gaze. "What do you mean?" she asked.

"Tommaso."

Her cheeks took on a lovely pink cast. "I don't know."

"You like him?"

"I do. But..."

"But what?"

"What will Orlando think?"

Ruggero placed his hand over hers. "You've spent the last ten years nursing a dying husband. I think Orlando will understand."

"I'm not sure he will."

"Let me do this for you. I'll have a talk with him."

She frowned. "A talk, not a 'talk,' mind you."

He laughed. "A friendly chat."

"As if you're capable."

He spread his hands. "And what is this?" When she smiled, he leaned forward. "So, Tommaso. If he asks…"

Elena pursed her lips and gave him a speculative look. "He's already spoken to you about me. Asked your permission."

Ruggero nodded, waiting. When she said nothing, he motioned for her to go on. "What's bothering you?"

Her lips twitched and she looked away. "What does he want with me? I doubt I could give him children."

"I doubt he'd be after you if that mattered. There are other things."

She nodded. "There are." After a moment, she looked him in the eye. "You love her?"

He crossed his arms and took a deep breath, something foreign fluttering in his belly. "All I know is I can't imagine giving her up. Is that love?"

Elena nodded, tears shimmering in her eyes. "Oh you've been bitten hard. I never thought I'd see the day."

Was she right? Was this giddy, unsteady feeling in his gut love? Was his constant desire for Loredana, to touch her, to be with her, to never let her go—was that love?

"I'm not sure what happened to me, or when," he half said to himself.

"It has a way of creeping up on you." Elena set down her cappuccino. "Wait here. I'll be right back with the ring."

He busied himself with eating, hoping to leave before the others made an appearance. He wanted a few more hours alone with his bride-to-be before everything took on a life of its own—the ceremony, the vows, and figuring out what to do about her plan to take down Baldassare.

Elena came back into the airy dining room and held out the ring to him. It was a modest thing, its diamond on the small side, but its worth was far more than monetary. By all accounts, his parents had been happy, a happiness he wanted to have with Loredana.

He slipped the ring into his pocket. "Thanks for keeping it safe."

"Always." Elena took her seat at the table. "When will it be?"

"As soon as Enrico can arrange the priest. He wants it done before she comes to live here."

"Then we need to get her a dress—"

A sharp blast of machine-gun fire cut Elena off mid-sentence. The windows behind her were pummeled with shots, but the glass didn't break. Enrico had had the house reinforced in dozens of ways since the Russians had attacked Dario Andretti's place during Nick and Delfina's engagement party. Bulletproof glass and thick steel doors had been installed, and even an underground tunnel had been started.

But Dom's house—the one Loredana was in—hadn't yet been upgraded.

Ruggero bolted out of his chair and grabbed Elena, pushing her under the table. "Don't move. Stay down until the shooting stops."

She nodded at him, her face tight. This was the reason she'd stayed away from him and his life, but he didn't have time to reassure her.

He needed a bigger gun than his Beretta, and he needed it now. Racing into the kitchen and then to the ample pantry, he hit the button that opened one of the small armories hidden in the house. He grabbed a mini Uzi and a bag loaded with spare magazines.

Who the hell was shooting at them? And did they know about Loredana?

He looped the bag's strap across his chest and back, then pulled out his phone as he headed to the side entrance of the house. He hit Loredana's number. No answer. His pulse quickened and he called it again as he reached the door and looked through the peephole. Clear.

Opening the door, he made sure it would lock behind him as he stepped outside. The phone rang and rang, then went to voicemail again. Damn it.

He scanned the area, alert for the intruders, but saw no one. Where the hell were they?

Cursing, he dialed Enrico. The call went through. "What's going on?" Enrico asked.

"Don't know, but they got behind the house. I'm on my way back to Loredana."

"I'll send Tommaso and some others."

"*Grazie.*" He hung up and pocketed the phone, then dashed for the hedges, heading toward the gate between the properties.

More gunfire—this time from Dom's house, and his heart jumped into his throat. Fuck. Whoever it was, they *did* know Loredana was here—and they had her surrounded.

He'd left her alone, with only two guards. How could he have been so careless?

Lorenzo Andretti had to be at the bottom of this. He'd been trying for weeks now to bend Loredana, then to kill her. And now, thanks to Ruggero, the old vulture might succeed.

Ruggero punched in the gate code and slipped through, making sure to close it behind him.

More gunfire on an otherwise still morning. Keeping low, he circled along the evergreen hedges that still provided some cover. Had it been spring or summer, he could have approached the house easily. Now, he had to be careful.

He made his way toward the house's lake side, and finally saw the men who'd dared attack them. There were three of them, spraying the back wall with bullets. Chunks of stone and stucco went flying. The glass was long gone, and one of the two guards he'd left was dead, sprawled on the ground in a pool of blood.

A noise behind him made him whirl around, only to see Beppe approach with Tommaso at his heels.

"Go around front," Ruggero said. "There's return fire from inside, so one of the guards is still alive."

Beppe nodded, then split off from Ruggero and Tommaso. Finding some bit of cover behind a large stump and a half-barren hedge, Ruggero and Tommaso settled in and took aim. "Start on the left, then sweep right. I'll meet you," Ruggero said. Tommaso nodded, his Uzi at the ready. Ruggero signaled, then opened fire, sweeping in from the sides to the center, neatly mowing down the men whose backs were to them.

Ruggero looked behind him in time to see four other intruders come running from Enrico's estate. How had they breached the fence? He tapped Tommaso's shoulder and they used the same technique to cut down the assailants before they got off more than a few shots.

Rising from his crouch, Ruggero went to check on the men they'd just gunned down. A couple of them stirred, and that's when he realized—they were wearing body armor. "Head shots!" he called to Tommaso and gestured toward the house. No doubt some of the men they'd hit earlier were still alive.

He took aim at the men on the ground, a few of them trying to raise their weapons. Then he pressed the trigger, squinting against the shells being ejected in a fierce spray as he swept the Uzi's muzzle back and forth. Soon the men weren't moving, the frosty ground steaming with blood pouring from their heads.

He had time enough to look at the skin exposed on one man's neck. The tattoos he saw there made his blood run cold. The Russians.

They were out to avenge Ilya Vilanovich and his drug-dealing sons. All three had died at the hand of Enrico's son Nick.

Fuck, fuck. And double fuck.

Heart pounding, he took off for the front of Dom's house. Had Beppe figured out that they were wearing armor? Ruggero hoped so. Or else Beppe might become the next victim.

Frozen grass crunched beneath his shoes as he sprinted toward his goal. He glanced at Tommaso, saw him double-checking the bodies lying on the back terrace, then he focused on his target. He stopped short when he reached the front corner and glanced around it, trying to see what was happening in between bursts of automatic weapons fire.

Beppe was pinned behind a large tree, while the two Russians in front of the house stood back to back, one aiming at Beppe, the other firing at the house. The front door had been blasted nearly in half lengthwise, and the only reason it still stood at all was because someone inside was returning fire.

Per favore, Dio, *let her be okay*. Ruggero slapped a fresh magazine into the Uzi and took aim. Letting out a breath, he narrowed his focus to one man's head and pressed the trigger. The big blond Russian jerked and spun, blood arcing from his neck.

His companion whirled around and Ruggero hit him high in the forehead, the man dead before he met the ground.

Signaling to Beppe, Ruggero silently approached the house. When they were getting near the splintered door, he called out.

The man who answered seemed more than a little relieved. When they stepped inside, they found him—Mauro, one of the guards sent by Don Battista. He was bleeding from a wound in his abdomen. "Where's Loredana?" Ruggero asked.

Mauro shook his head. "Don't know."

Ruggero raced down the hallway and burst into the bedroom he'd shared with her, his heart galloping. If she'd been standing by the window—

"Loredana?" he called, unable to keep the worry out of his tone.

"I'm here," she said, her voice muffled. The bedcovers twitched and she poked her head out from beneath the box spring. "Is it over?"

He released the breath he'd been holding and motioned for her to stay put. Pulling out his phone, he called Enrico. "We've secured Dom's place. You?"

"The same. But I'm getting reports of shootings all over Como and Bellagio. Though not our businesses."

"Then whose?"

"Dario's."

What the hell? Then Ruggero realized. *Of course.* If Lorenzo wanted the North, he needed to make sure Dario and Enrico stayed at odds. Attacking only Dario's businesses would make it look like Enrico was behind it.

Clever bastard.

"They're Russians," Ruggero said. "And I bet some of them are Vilanoviches."

"Bring everyone to the house."

"Mauro is hurt. He'll need surgery."

"I've already called Beltrami; he's on the way. Anyone else?"

"We have one dead here. I'm sure there are more. No one came to assist, other than Tommaso and Beppe."

"Damn."

Damn was right. They could ill-afford to lose a single man.

Ruggero helped Loredana out from under the bed. She was wearing the blouse she'd left on the ottoman last night, that was all. "Get dressed, *bambina.*"

"Where are we going?"

"Next door. Where it's safer."

"Safer?" Her hands were trembling, and that trembling made him want to break something. Instead, he took her hands and pulled her close. She shivered in his arms and he closed his jacket around her. "How did they know anyone was here?"

It was a damn good question, one that had him craving a cigarette. Lorenzo must have spies at the lake.

Or they'd been followed from Milan.

———————— ✦ ————————

Only hours after they'd nearly been killed, Loredana stood beside Ruggero in the same drawing room she'd been in the night before. Someone had rearranged the furniture to form a semicircle around the fireplace, where she, Ruggero, and the priest stood.

Bianca had loaned her a wedding dress that fit surprisingly well, though Elena had quickly taken it in around the bust and waist. The woman was a marvel; all the women were, quickly transforming her into something out of a fairy tale. Elena had fussed over her hair and makeup, sighing at one point over the fact that they had nothing green to pick up the shade of Loredana's eyes. Elena's obvious desire to make this wedding special had made Loredana's eyes well. She'd reached up to wipe them, and Elena had stopped her, carefully dabbing at her tears with a folded tissue. "No more of that," she'd said.

"Thank you. Truly." She wished Allegra and Gisella were there. Maybe even Mamma too… except Nora would never look on Ruggero with anything other than contempt. And that he didn't deserve.

"We'll do this again, for your family," Elena said, as if reading her mind. "Today's for Enrico. You understand?"

"*Sì.*" She understood his reasons. Even though the marriage wouldn't be legal until a civil ceremony was performed—and that couldn't happen until after she'd dealt with the Lucchesi-Battista case—the ceremony would still be binding, as far as Enrico and Ruggero were concerned.

Her too. She couldn't stand here, pledge herself to this man, then turn her back on her vows. She was a woman of her word. And if somehow things went awry, she was fairly certain the law would find that she'd entered into a good-faith agreement regarding the marriage—and therefore, couldn't testify against her husband.

Not that she wanted to. Not that she ever would. But if Enrico needed assurances, both spiritual and legal, she'd give them to him.

And to the man standing beside her.

She'd nearly been killed again today, and Ruggero had risked his own life, once again, to make sure that didn't happen. Even if he never said he loved her, it didn't matter. He'd said it again and again with his actions. He didn't have to put it into words; she knew it was there, locked under layers of reserve and self-protection.

He was thawing, ever so slowly, like a glacier, an iceberg. She just had to be patient. Someday, perhaps, he'd feel comfortable putting a name to what he felt. And if it wasn't love?

She could love him enough for the both of them.

They reached the part of the ceremony where they were due to exchange rings and vows.

Ruggero was wearing a light gray suit, the color echoing those wolf's eyes, making them stand out as he looked into her own. When he took her hand and slid the ring onto it, his own shook ever so slightly, the tremor so faint she almost didn't feel it. But it was there.

She squeezed his fingers, and he smiled, that shy little boy's smile she'd seen only once before. When he'd asked her, and she'd said yes.

Suddenly the priest was asking her if she'd take Ruggero as her husband. Loredana tried to focus on the words to make them real, but all she could do was stare at Ruggero. He was her future now, her world, and soon she'd be leaving the law for him, was in effect, leaving it right now.

Surprisingly, she felt little remorse.

She'd studied and enforced the law with zeal, always picturing what her father would think, how proud he'd be of her.

He wouldn't be proud of her today. She knew that.

But she hoped he could be happy for her, wherever he was. She took a deep breath and started to slide the ring onto Ruggero's finger, the words she was saying taking on a sudden clarity. "I, Loredana, take you, Ruggero, as my husband and promise to be faithful to you always, in joy and in pain, in health and in sickness, and to love you and every day honor you, for the rest of my life."

The ring she put on Ruggero's finger was a simple gold band, a gift from Enrico and Kate. A jeweler, a friend of the family, had brought over a selection of rings that she'd chosen from. She'd been assured that the ring would fit, and it did. Perfectly.

She looked up at Ruggero, and the emotion in his gaze almost bowled her over. Elena was right; he loved her, and he loved her fiercely.

That was all that mattered.

The priest pronounced them husband and wife, and Ruggero was kissing her when a commotion started outside. Someone was shouting.

Ruggero broke the kiss. "What's going on?" she asked. He shook his head, then suddenly he grew still and his gaze flicked to Enrico's. There was a moment of silent communication, and then Ruggero said, "I'm sorry, *bambina*, but there's something I have to handle."

At first she didn't recognize the tall, handsome, dark-haired man who burst into the room with Tommaso at his heels. He crossed the floor, heading straight for Delfina and Nick, and then Loredana realized who he was—Dario Andretti.

And he was furious.

CHAPTER 24

As if she were a ragdoll, Dario yanked Delfina off the sofa, and Ruggero stiffened. When Nick tried to stop him, Dario tackled him around the neck, and that's when Ruggero realized what Dario was going to do. But it was too late—the gun was out and pressed against Nick's temple before anyone could take more than a step.

Dario wheeled himself and Nick around to face Enrico. "You dare attack me? You *dare*? After I've lost everything?"

"Papà!" Delfina screamed and lunged for his arm. Dario blocked her with his body. "Sit," he snarled. "Or I pull the trigger."

"Papà, you can't!"

Ruggero saw his opportunity while Dario was distracted. His heart pounding, Ruggero circled behind Dario, hoping Delfina wouldn't accidentally betray him by gazing at him, but either she was oblivious to his presence, or she understood the need to keep Dario occupied.

When Ruggero was in striking distance, he reached in, grabbing Dario's wrist and directing the gun at the ceiling, his other arm around Dario's neck. As soon as the gun was away from his temple, Nick elbowed Dario hard in the solar plexus, and it was all over: Ruggero had the gun, and Nick was free. Dario sputtered and gasped for air, but Ruggero kept a tight hold on him as he handed the gun off to Tommaso.

He placed his mouth beside Dario's ear. "It wasn't us. It was the fucking Russians."

Dario wheezed in air and shook his head. "Don't believe you."

"I can prove it."

Dario took in two more breaths, his face losing its purple hue. "Doesn't benefit them."

"It does if Lorenzo's working with them."

Dario stilled, then he shook his head again. "Listen to me," Ruggero said. "I can show you. We have several of them next door." He gestured to the scarred but still intact windows of the drawing room. "If you haven't noticed, they hit us too."

217

"Could be a trick."

Enrico approached and Dario squared his shoulders, as if he were planning to punch him. Which he probably was.

Ruggero put up a hand to stop Enrico. "Let me handle this."

Enrico hesitated, then he nodded. Good. Dario would struggle—and possibly fail—to see the truth if Enrico were around; some habits died hard, and Dario's mistrust and hatred of Enrico were deeply ingrained. There'd been a thawing, a too-brief period where they'd almost been friends. Then Lorenzo had used Enrico's godson, Sandro, to kill Cristoforo, and Dario had been immune to reason ever since.

But somehow, some way, Ruggero had to get him to see the truth, to acknowledge that Lorenzo was the villain behind the curtain, the one who'd pulled the strings and ordered Cris's death. They couldn't fight Dario and Lorenzo at the same time.

Dario could be a vital ally in the war against Lorenzo. Ruggero had to try, and he wouldn't get anywhere with Enrico involved.

This was the thing Don Battista had tasked him with—saving the *cosca*. Doing the things Enrico wasn't able to do.

With a hand on Dario's shoulder, Ruggero escorted him outside, sparing Loredana—his *wife*, of all things—a quick glance on the way. He should be kissing her now, holding her, instead of handling Dario, but so be it. This was the life he'd chosen, even if at sixteen he hadn't necessarily understood all the sacrifices he'd have to make.

Business first, family second. That was how it was, how it had always been. How it would always be.

And now he'd brought Loredana into this world. He hoped she wouldn't come to regret it.

He directed Dario out through the villa's side entrance, and the frigid outside air hit him like a slap. He hadn't stopped to get an overcoat, and he wasn't about to turn around and get one either. Dario needed to understand the situation as soon as possible. Lorenzo could be preparing another attack any minute, and the less time they spent squabbling between themselves the better.

"Where are you taking me?" Dario asked, suspicion tingeing his voice.

"The boathouse next door."

"Boathouse?"

"We have a disposal job, come dark."

Sudden understanding lit Dario's gaze, and he said no more until they entered the building.

The bodies—ten in total—had been rolled into canvas tarps and wrapped with heavy chains and weights. They were stacked up beside Dom's motorboat, a sleek craft, nearly as nice as Enrico's Riva Aquarama next door. They'd be using both boats tonight, loading them up and dumping the bodies in the center of the lake, under the cover of darkness.

No one would ever find these men, just as they'd never find Sergio Grantini or any of the Lucchesis' enemies who'd been disposed of in such a fashion. Ruggero had no idea how many skeletons littered the lake's floor, and he didn't care. Every man who'd ended up there had deserved it.

Just as these men had. He flicked on the weak overhead lighting and motioned Dario forward, onto the enclosed dock. Their footsteps echoed on the heavy wood, the sound adding to the slap of water on the pilings, the hollow thuds of the boat thumping into the floats that lined the dock and kept the wood from marring the hull.

The lake was choppy today; a heavy wind had come up since breakfast, and it howled through the barren trees and across the water.

The boathouse's walls cut the wind, but drafts whistled through chinks in the boards and around the windows. Ruggero barely suppressed a shiver. He'd need to get inside soon, but not until he was sure Dario understood.

Ruggero crouched beside one of the bodies and pulled back the tarp covering the man's face. Dario squatted on the other side of the corpse, studying the face Ruggero revealed.

The man had died hard, features tight with pain, and Ruggero turned the man's head to the side with difficulty. Rigor had set in. But he was able to show Dario the tattoos on the man's neck, the ones on his hands.

Dario sat back, his face stony. "Another."

Ruggero had half-expected this. He moved to a second body, and this time unwrapped the chains from around the torso. This one was big and bulky. Ruggero pulled open the man's jacket and shirt, revealing the tattoos on his chest, the stars at his shoulders.

"Another."

Were they going to have to look at them all before Dario was satisfied? So be it.

Ruggero repeated the process with the next man. This one he knew was a Vilanovich from the passport they'd found on him. This time, Ruggero slit the man's trousers open at the knees to reveal the star tattoos there. He'd been a captain. Those stars meant he knelt for no man.

Normally a captain wouldn't have been on such a mission, but Ruggero understood why he'd been there. Vengeance. Vilanovich blood had been spilled here, primarily by the Lucchesis. And so the Vilanoviches had sought to even the score.

They hadn't counted on Enrico Lucchesi's ingenuity, however. He'd learned a lesson from the attempted massacre at Nick and Delfina's engagement party.

The house had been well fortified, and the guards hadn't been compromised this time. The Russians had been foolhardy.

"Satisfied?" Ruggero asked. He motioned to the other bodies. "We can look at them all, if you'd like."

Dario sat down on the wood, his arms resting on his knees. "What I'd like is my son back." He said the words with such defeat, a hollowness that Ruggero felt in his bones. There was no comfort for this kind of grief, no solace. A man should never have to bury his child.

Ruggero busied himself with covering the bodies again and securing the chains around them. When he finished, Dario was still sitting where he'd been, staring at the water lapping at the boat's hull.

Ruggero studied him for a moment. He'd never much liked Dario, but he'd lost a son, a fine boy, one any man would have been proud of. "I can't give you your boy back. But I can help you get justice."

Dario's dark eyes met his. "You'd never cross your *capo*."

Ruggero shook his head the barest bit and held back a sigh. The man was the epitome of stubborn. "You know exactly who screwed around with the bank, and you know Enrico didn't order Sandro to shoot your son. You know who did."

"I don't *know* a damn thing. Antonio and Bianca would say anything to protect Enrico."

"Sandro was her brother."

"He was a sack of shit."

"True. But she loved him." He jammed his frozen hands in his suit pockets and suppressed another shiver.

"Sandro was mine to kill." Dario clenched his hands together. "I didn't even get that satisfaction."

Ruggero crouched down across from him. "I know you've been spying on Sal. What have you learned about Lorenzo's plans?"

Surprise flickered through Dario's eyes, then he nodded. "Delfi told you."

Ruggero nodded. "I assume you've learned nothing concrete."

"*Sì*. Lorenzo doesn't like the telephone, so I've learned little that way. Nothing definitive. Nothing that confirms it *wasn't* Enrico."

"Answer me this: Why would Enrico kill Cristoforo? Cris had helped Enrico with his biggest problem. He'd saved him from standing before La Provincia and having to explain how he'd been betrayed by his family and how he'd been merciful where he should have been ruthless."

"And Cris paid for that mercy."

"Because that's what Lorenzo wanted. To teach Cris a lesson and to weaken you and destroy the alliance between our families."

"Enrico would benefit by weakening me."

"You think he'd order the death of one boy, when he couldn't order the death of three others?"

"They were *his* blood. Cris was not."

"Enrico is not your father. Or your grandfather. He's not a monster."

Dario rubbed a hand over his face. "He's taken everything from me. My sister, my son. Even my daughter."

"She spends more time with you than she ever does us."

"The house is like a tomb when she's gone."

"You need to set aside this hatred. It's weakening you, and us."

"I'm not sure I can. My head tells me you're right, but my heart...."

Ruggero took a deep breath. "You need certain proof of Lorenzo's involvement? I can give you it."

"How?"

"I'll take a direct approach with Sal."

Dario snorted. "If anyone can take a beating, it's Sal. All those years he spent in prison for my grandfather, he never said a word. He'll never tell you anything."

A plan had formed and solidified in Ruggero's mind. It had worked before and it would work again. "He will. There's one thing every man prizes above all. And that's what I'll use to get the truth."

———— ♦ ————

The arrangements hadn't taken Ruggero more than a couple hours, and with Dario's help, abducting Sal had been a simple matter. The three of them had driven a short way out of Cernobbio, to an abandoned glassworks that Enrico owned.

When they arrived, Ruggero hauled Sal out of the Fiat by his cuffed wrists. Sal looked around, taking in the scraggly, overgrown grounds, the grimy windows of the building before them, and shook his head. "I'm not a rat."

Ruggero pushed him forward. The main entrance was still unlocked from Beppe and Tommaso's earlier trip, so he directed Sal through the doorway, Dario following behind. They entered a large room, the central factory floor, where Ruggero saw that his instructions had been followed perfectly. A man-sized slab of ice had been dragged into the center of the room.

Sal and Dario exchanged a puzzled look, then they both looked to Ruggero. He motioned to Sal. "Strip. Then lie facedown on the ice block."

Sal laughed. "I told you. I'm no rat."

"Maybe you're a bird," Ruggero said. "And birds sing." He pointed his gun at Sal. "Do it."

"Fine. You think a little ice is going to bother me?"

Ruggero said nothing. He uncuffed Sal, then walked over to the wall, where a heating coil and a bucket of water sat next to an electrical outlet. He plugged in the coil and set it in the bucket.

Sal stripped down and laid himself on the block of ice. Crossing his arms, Dario watched, a dubious look on his face.

Ruggero found a chair and pulled it up to the wall beside the outlet. "I can do this all day," Sal said.

Crossing his legs at the ankle, Ruggero leaned back in the chair. "Maybe you can. But your *cazzo* can't. In an hour, it will be frostbitten beyond saving. Eventually, it will turn black and fall off." He pocketed his gun and pulled out a knife, which he used to clean his nails.

Wind whistled through broken panes that let in the waning light of late afternoon. Ruggero flipped up the collar of his jacket. Dario found another chair and pulled it up beside him. "So we just wait? That's it?" Dario asked in an undertone.

"That's it." They passed the time in silence, the only sound the breeze singing through the factory and an occasional curse from Sal. After thirty minutes, Ruggero made a show of checking his watch. "You have less than half an hour before it's too late."

"Fuck you," Sal said.

Ruggero shrugged. Another ten minutes passed, and he said, "Can you still feel it?"

Sal shifted on the ice, then cried out. "I'm stuck!"

"Probably losing the top layers of skin already."

After a minute, Sal said, "What do you want?"

Ruggero kept the smile off his face. It always worked. "Who ordered the hit on Cristoforo?"

"Lucchesi."

Ruggero *tsk*ed at him. "If you value your *cazzo*, you'll stop insulting me."

Another minute passed. Sal writhed uncomfortably on the ice and winced. "Okay. It was Lorenzo. Happy?"

Dario rose from his chair, fists clenched, and Ruggero grabbed his wrist. "Let go," Dario growled.

"There's still more we need to know." Dario reluctantly took his seat.

"What is Lorenzo planning with the Russians?" Ruggero asked.

"Let me up and I'll tell you."

"Give me the answer and I'll let you up."

"*Vaffanculo!*"

Ruggero made another show of checking his watch. "I figure you've got ten, maybe fifteen, minutes before your *cazzo* is beyond saving."

Sal smacked his forehead into the ice, his growl of frustration audible. "Fuck you. Just fuck you."

"The clock is ticking."

The room was silent for a long time. Then Sal said, "I don't know all of it, but they were supposed to attack Dario's businesses today and make it look like the Lucchesis were responsible."

"And?" Ruggero prompted him.

"There's a meeting, tomorrow, with Lorenzo, the Russians, and Baldassare in San Luca, in the crypt. Baldassare is going to take the vows and join La Santa."

"Bullshit," Ruggero said. No one of Baldassare's caliber would risk joining the secret society at the heart of the 'Ndrangheta.

"It's true," Sal said, bobbing his head earnestly. "And then Baldassare will help Marcello become mayor of Reggio Calabria."

"That's not possible."

"It is. Lorenzo's been careful with Marcello. He's kept him out of any direct business deals or killings. His record is spotless." Sal shivered, his voice wobbling.

"Baldassare would never risk going to San Luca, much less getting caught making a deal with Lorenzo."

"He's going on a 'fact-finding' tour," Sal said. "He's meeting with anti-Mafia officials in Calabria, lending them his support. It's his excuse for being there. He's officially showing he's not afraid of the Mafia; he'll be staying overnight in San Luca. The plan is that he'll slip off at night to meet Lorenzo and the Russians."

"What else?"

Sal shook his head. "I don't know anything else. Just that the meeting is set for after midnight." Sal was visibly shaking from the cold, his teeth chattering. "I'm supposed to be there."

"*Bene*. You'll be useful then. We're done," Ruggero said.

Sal tried to push himself up from the ice, but he winced and cried out. "I'm really stuck."

Ruggero unplugged the heating coil and picked up the bucket. The water was hot, steam rising off it. He took it over to Sal and poured it over his waist.

"*Cristo!* You trying to boil me?" Sal said.

"Can you move now?"

Sal rose from the ice, his movements stiff, jerky, his limbs shaking, his skin a raw, ugly red on his chest, belly, and thighs. Ruggero let him take a step toward his discarded clothes, then he slipped behind Sal and put him in a headlock. With a savage twist, he snapped Sal's neck.

"Hey!" Dario yelled. "You said I could—"

Ruggero pinned him with a look. "He's not the one you want."

He lowered Sal to the ice, then retrieved his clothes and dressed him hurriedly.

Dario stood by and watched. "I've never heard of this… strategy."

"It's my own invention."

"But why bother with the bucket?"

"That way there's no blood, no fuss, very little DNA mess to clean up. And it works every time. It's almost effortless."

Dario shook his head. "Remind me never to get on your bad side."

"Who said you weren't on it already?" Ruggero grinned.

"You need me," Dario said, meeting his eyes. "Or we wouldn't be here now."

He waited a beat, then nodded. "I have a proposition for you. You want justice for your son, yes?"

"Of course."

"Then help us kill Lorenzo."

"You expect me to forget what Enrico has done to me?"

Ruggero sighed. Enrico wasn't going to like him doing so, but it was time to say it. "He may never tell you this, but he's shed tears for your son."

"He has?" Brows raised, Dario held his eyes.

"Yes. He never meant for any of this to happen. Tell me, in his shoes, what would you have done? Would you have killed three boys you considered sons?"

Dario's face darkened. "That's just it. He never dealt with those boys. *I* dealt with Fedele. Antonio dealt with Sandro. Enrico, he can't even deal with Matteo."

Ruggero's neck prickled with alarm. He'd known that fake funeral would come back to haunt them. "What do you mean?"

Dario crossed his arms and gave him an assessing look. "I've heard there's a boy in Toronto who looks exactly like Matteo Lucchesi."

Fuck. There was nothing for it but the truth. "Matteo was nineteen, the same as Cris. His mother had already lost her husband and two sons."

Dario said nothing, just stared. Ruggero pressed on. "You and your son should have died at Enrico's hand after what Carlo did. But he spared you."

Dario remained silent, his chest heaving. He paced away, then came back. "What do you want me to say?"

"Will you trust me? Will you trust him?"

Dario ran both hands over his face and scrubbed them through his hair. When he looked at Ruggero, his eyes were glistening. "I know what Cris would tell me to do."

Ruggero nodded. Here it was. The opening, the chance. "Will you do it?"

Dario closed his eyes and opened them. "I'll try."

It wasn't quite what Ruggero had hoped for. But it was a start.

CHAPTER 25

Loredana paced around the bedroom Kate had shown her to after the wedding. She was officially part of the family now; she and Ruggero would no longer be exiled to Francesca's house.

Where *was* he? Ruggero hadn't told her what he was doing or where he was going with Dario Andretti. Just that he'd return in a few hours.

Was it always going to be like this? Him off on some nefarious mission while she waited at home?

She stopped at the bedroom window and looked out. Dusk was settling over the grounds, and Bianca was rounding up Luca and Cocco after one last romp in the garden.

Sighing, Loredana turned away. She'd known what she was signing up for. It was too late for buyer's remorse. She'd made a decision; she needed to honor it.

Her mobile phone vibrated in her hand, startling her. Glancing at the display, she saw with a pang that it was an unknown number. Not Ruggero. But then she remembered: he could be using a burner phone. She took the call.

"I have your answer." The mystery caller was Silvio Fuente.

Loredana took a deep breath. "What did they say?"

"They will meet with you. But you must come to Calabria. Alone."

"You're going to accompany me."

"Me?" Fuente asked. "Why?"

Loredana's heart sped up. She hoped her gamble would work. "Why did you join the *carabinieri* in the first place?"

Fuente was quiet for a few beats too long. "Why do you ask?"

Loredana said a silent prayer. "Because I think that once upon a time, you were a different man. A man who cared about justice. But I know how the system works. You were a man with no connections, someone who was never going to rise above a certain level, no matter how diligently you worked." She paused. "Am I right so far?"

"*Sì.*"

"And that had to rankle you, a man with a large family. You found a way to get ahead, to beat the system." She waited to see what he'd say.

Finally he spoke. "Perhaps there is some truth to what you're saying."

She smiled. Maybe she'd taken the right tack. "I can help you rise even higher, turn you into a national hero. If you help me bring them down."

"Bring them down?"

"Yes. I'll say you came to me, told me you'd perjured yourself regarding the gun in the Lucchesi case and that you'd planted it in the vault because Andretti had taken your son. But the guilt ate at you, and you couldn't bear the thought that he'd get away with it. After I was attacked, you realized he was going to kill me, and you couldn't let that happen either."

Fuente chuckled. "I'm flattered. I sound so... noble in your version of events. But..." He trailed off, obviously waiting for more.

"There will be a huge promotion in it for you."

"Only if I'm not dead." He paused. "I cannot help you."

Porca miseria! "What if you had some assurances?"

"What do you mean?"

"I think we need to talk. All of us. Come to Como."

"I knew they'd win you over."

"There was no 'winning' me. But if you don't come, you'll be the one who loses."

This time Fuente laughed. "We'll see, *signora*. We'll see."

"You'll come?"

"I shall."

Loredana ended the call. So far, so good. Now she had to get everyone else on board with her plan. Ruggero would be the hardest—and possibly the one she couldn't convince.

———◆———

After disposing of Sal's body—he'd stripped him of ID and hid him in an alley in Cernobbio so that he would be found relatively soon, but not immediately—Ruggero had washed his hands a dozen times, it seemed. He didn't want to touch Loredana after what he'd done.

Strange. He'd never felt this way before. But now she was his wife. And that changed everything.

When he returned, Loredana didn't ask what he'd been doing; instead, she had news of her own: Fuente had arranged a meeting for her in Calabria with Baldassare and Lorenzo Andretti. The same meeting that Sal would no longer be attending.

She'd also somehow persuaded Fuente to help her—or at least to consider it. He was coming up to the lake to talk things over.

"I don't want him involved," Ruggero said. "Or you. I know when and where the meeting is. I'll take some men and ambush it. Problem solved."

She gave him a grave look. "You promised me you'd help me do this. Are you saying you're not a man of your word?"

"Fuck." He *had* promised her.

She smiled at him, her expression saying she damn well knew his weak spot.

"Doesn't mean I can't try to talk you out of it."

She touched his cheek, the triumph leaving her face. "I know the risks. But if I'm leaving the law, I'm doing it with a bang."

If this was what she needed to feel good about upending her life for him, then he had to make her plan work. Somehow.

"Dario Andretti is coming with us, and he wants his vengeance on Lorenzo for killing his son."

"That's not what we agreed to."

"If Andretti lives, he'll be a threat to us forever, *bambina*. You know this."

She sighed. "But Baldassare goes to jail."

"We'll see what happens. Andretti and the Russians won't go easy."

Crossing her arms, Loredana stared at him. "So this is going to be a bloodbath."

"You just told me you knew the risks. We aren't busting up a tea party."

She held his eyes for a moment longer, then she nodded. "Thank you for backing me up on this."

He was an idiot, and if he got his wife killed, he had no one else to blame. But if he went back on his word to her she'd never trust him again.

And that would be worse.

—————•—————

Fuente arrived well after dark, for once calling on the house in civilian clothes. The group of them involved in the plan—Enrico, Fuente, Ruggero, Loredana, and Antonio—gathered in Enrico's study, drinks in hand. Though the mood was far from convivial.

Prior to Fuente's arrival, Ruggero had convinced the others to mention nothing about Dario's role. The less the weasel knew, the better. And the weasel needed to understand his part, and understand it well. Ruggero had already accepted the necessity of Fuente's involvement, but Fuente didn't need to know that. "Why shouldn't I shoot you?" Ruggero asked him.

Fuente smiled and sipped his sambuca. He looked away from Ruggero and directed his reply to Enrico. "You understand that he had my boy. I had no choice."

Ruggero started to respond, but Enrico raised his hand. "I understand... but I also know that you'd tried—and failed—to get leverage over Lorenzo. *You* got yourself in trouble."

Fuente gave a sheepish nod, as if he were actually capable of shame. "And now you're getting me out of it. I won't forget that." He passed his eyes over them all, coming to a stop on Ruggero. "And trust me, Signor Vela, I know which master I'd rather have."

Ruggero leaned forward. "If *anything* happens to Loredana, the only person you'll have to worry about is me."

Fuente raised his glass in acknowledgment. "So, how will we get the evidence that will turn me into a hero?"

Ruggero looked at Loredana and she nodded. They'd talked it over during dinner, and had agreed that they'd hold back another key piece of information—their back-up plan.

She placed her drink on the table. "They'll scan me of course. But not you. So you're going to wear the bug."

Fuente raised a brow. "I'm not sure they trust me so much."

"I am. Why else would they have agreed to the meeting?"

"Perhaps to kill you, my dear judge."

She nodded. "Perhaps. That's a risk I'm willing to take. But I do believe I can convince them they'd be much better off with a well-placed judge in their pockets. Wouldn't you agree?"

"It might work. It might not."

Loredana shrugged. "What's life without adventure?"

Fuente shook his head. "I only like adventures when I know the outcome."

"You're more of a gambler than that, Sottotenente."

With a smile, Fuente leaned back in his chair. "But I try to make sure the odds are in my favor."

"If this works, you'll be free of Andretti, and you'll have made your career." She paused. "And if it doesn't work, you won't know the difference."

Fuente laughed and spread his hands. "When you put it that way, how can I refuse?"

"*Bene*," Enrico said. "We are agreed."

They briefly discussed the plan for meeting up in Calabria. Ruggero and several of the guards would swoop in at the appropriate moment and assist in "subduing" Andretti and the Russians, as Fuente put it.

"We'll do what's necessary," Ruggero said.

Fuente stroked his mustache. "When the shooting starts, just remember I'm on your side."

"I'll try."

Fuente laughed. "A charmer as always."

After Fuente had been shown out, the four of them reconvened. Enrico spoke first.

"I must go down to Calabria with you. Depending on what happens, there could be chaos, and I'll need to be there to restore order. With Don Battista in the hospital and Sal dead, Lorenzo and I are the only active *mandamento* heads left. And by the end of the night, there will be only me."

Ruggero didn't like it, but what Enrico said made sense. Ruggero looked at Loredana, who seemed a bit taken aback. Then she spoke. "It'll work, as long as we can keep you out of sight of the *carabinieri*. But how do we explain Dario's presence? He's not one of the guards. We can't say that he's part of the 'undercover' team."

"We can convince Fuente not to mention him," Ruggero said.

"And what if Dario gets shot?" Loredana asked.

"We'll just have to make sure he doesn't."

"Not good enough."

She was right. "We'll bring some bleach. And a doctor."

Loredana grimaced; perhaps he'd been a bit too matter of fact about it, but if she was going to be there, she needed to be prepared.

Finally she nodded. "Okay." She turned to Enrico. "With the recording from the bug and the other evidence you have from the bank, it will be enough to put Baldassare behind bars."

Enrico nodded. "It will be more than enough. And by providing this evidence to the court, my name will be cleared at the FIU as well."

"And I'll dismiss the case against you and Signor Battista."

Antonio laughed. "If you told me we'd ever be having this conversation…" He let the words trail off as the others chuckled.

Loredana smiled. "No one is more surprised than I am." She took Ruggero's hand and squeezed it. "I never thought this would happen, but I've realized that sometimes you have to break the law to do the right thing."

Ruggero swallowed hard as he looked at her. His bride. His wife. The woman he wanted to spend the rest of his life with.

But would her life be cut short tomorrow?

There was one more thing he could do to up the odds of her survival. And then all he could do was pray.

———— ◆ ————

Today was the day; they'd be boarding Enrico's private jet for Calabria that evening. And then Loredana's plan would unfold, and Ruggero could only hope she wasn't killed.

At least he could give her a fighting chance. He took her up into the hills beyond the villa and set up some bottles and cans for her to shoot at.

"This really isn't necessary," she said as he handed her a 9 mm Beretta.

"It is. We have no way of knowing what's going to happen tonight."

"Either way, I'll still barely know what I'm doing with this." She held up the gun.

"I know." Ruggero met her eyes, trying not to betray the concern that had his stomach tied up in knots.

She chuckled. "Yeah, you're still *so* good with the reassurances."

He shrugged, then let her have a hint of a grin. He tapped her hand that held the gun. "Show me what you know about this." She pursed her lips, a shadow crossing her face. "Stop thinking about him," he said.

She tried on a smile, but it didn't reach her eyes. "You know, the whole time I was at the range with Stefano, I kept wondering what the same lesson would be like from you."

"And?"

"Well, there's a lot less touching."

His fingers curled into fists. That scum had touched her, kissed her… Good thing he was already dead.

She glanced at his hands. "I mean, he was more hands-on, showing me things."

"Right," Ruggero said, though he was sure she was minimizing it for his benefit. He shouldn't care; that was before she'd been his, but he couldn't help it. He took the gun from her, walked her through the parts of it, demonstrated how to rack it, how to sight it. He mowed down a few cans, then stopped and set them up for her.

"Those are much smaller than the targets at the range," she said.

"Just aim for the center. You'll learn faster this way." He demonstrated how to hold the gun, then gave it back to her, correcting her grip and stance. "Now run through a magazine."

She gave him a dubious look, then focused on the first target. She missed. Same with the next. And the next. She blew out hard and shook her head. "I can't do this."

"Pay attention to what you're doing."

"I *am*." There was an edge to her voice, and he took a deep breath, trying to calm himself. It was stupid to be sending her into the crypt alone. Anything could happen, and Fuente was far from trustworthy.

She aimed again. Another miss. Then another. "You're jerking the gun to the right when you pull the trigger," he said.

"I am?"

"Like I said, pay attention." He clenched his teeth together, not allowing himself to say more. He walked over to her and wrapped his arms around her, using his hands to steady hers. "Watch what happens, *bambina*."

She pulled the trigger, and he countered her jerk to the right. The bullet hit the can a bit off-center, but it was a solid hit. "I did it," she said.

"Now try it on your own."

A miss. Another one. Another. She raised the gun again. "Keep your wrists locked."

Two more misses. She shook her head. "I suck at this."

"I taught Antonio this way. Just try harder."

She aimed again, and again she flinched when the gun went off, her wrists jerking to the right.

"Are you even listening to me?"

"Yes!" she hissed. "What is wrong with you? I thought you'd be more patient than this, but you're not. I've barely handled a gun, and you expect me to be a sniper already."

He paced around in a small circle. Then he admitted the truth. "I don't want to lose you."

"You won't."

"You can't know that."

She touched his cheek. "It's going to be okay."

"I just—" He cut himself off. She didn't need to hear all this.

"You just what?"

"Never mind."

She cocked her head to the side, those green eyes of hers drilling into him. "You just what?"

He looked away from her. "I just found you, and you've been mine for what feels like half a minute, and it could all be over in a few hours." He closed his eyes and groaned. "I sound like a little girl."

"Well, I feel like one," she said, her eyes glancing at him, then darting away. "I'm scared too."

"I'll be there, ready to rush in, and I'll hear everything."

She set the gun on a rock and put her arms around him. "I'm not sure I could do this without you."

"Oh, you'd find a way." He shook his head and chuckled. "The last time I was this nervous, I was best man at Antonio's wedding. I sweated and sweated over my speech, and I never got to give it. You know what bit of profundity I was going to say?"

"Tell me." She smiled up at him.

"It wasn't much, just, 'Be thankful, every day, that somehow you found each other.'"

Her smile broadened. "I am thankful to have found you. More than you'll ever know."

He took her hand and kissed the back of it. "You can't be more grateful than I am." He kissed her lightly on the lips, pulling away before he grew tempted to push for more. He retrieved the Beretta and wrapped her hands around the gun. "Now let's try again." He held her in her stance for the first three shots, but didn't try to correct her, other than tapping her wrists after each shot. All three went astray. The fourth one connected, with a metallic *thunk*.

"I did it!" she yelled, and he couldn't stop smiling at her.

"I knew you could. Now again."

She took aim and fired again, again hitting the target.

Maybe, maybe, she had a prayer of escaping alive. Ruggero winced when she missed the next can.

He looked skyward. *If you're up there, and I know I don't deserve it, let her come out of this alive.*

CHAPTER 26

The problem with meeting in the crypt of an ancient church was the lack of heating in the winter. In the summer, when it was hot, the crypt was cool, refreshing. But now, at the tail-end of winter, it had a damp chill that seeped into Lorenzo's bones and made the arthritis gnaw on his joints. Still, he'd made it there under his own power, though he'd almost accepted the assistance offered by Eusebio, one of his guards. Growing old was no job for the weak.

He took a seat on the dais, waiting for Baldassare and the others to show. Tonight, he'd finally get two of the things he badly wanted: Baldassare under his heel, and Loredana Montisi dead. Once the judge was gone, Baldassare would owe him indefinitely, Lucchesi would go back to jail and to a swift death, and the way would be paved for Marcello's rise in politics and Lorenzo's total dominion over La Provincia. The Russians would be appeased by Lucchesi's death, and what was left of Lucchesi's fortune would be Lorenzo's for the taking. With Vittorio Battista still in the hospital and on trial, there was no one to oppose his plans.

The only thing that nagged at him was Sal. The man seemed to have disappeared, and it wasn't like him. Lorenzo even called Dario to see if he knew where Sal was, and all Lorenzo had received for his trouble was an earful of Dario's complaints about Sal not being around to help him strike back at Lucchesi over the attack on his businesses. He even had the nerve to swear at Lorenzo: "What the fuck help are the two of you in a crisis?"

Lorenzo had quieted him, assuring him that Lucchesi would be dealt with.

And then so would Dario. He'd finally get the ass-kicking he deserved. And then Dario would either lick Lorenzo's boots or take a bullet. Lorenzo preferred the former; he'd rather take advantage of Dario's network up north.

But fuck Lombardy if anybody tried to get in his way. Fuck all those rich bastards who looked down their noses at the people of the South. They'd soon know who was truly in charge. When a man had a gun shoved in his face, he learned damn quick.

Someone was coming down the stairs; at least three men to judge from their voices and the sound of their footsteps.

Soon the newcomers rounded the final turn of the stone stairway, and Italo Baldassare stepped into the long, low room, followed by four Russians, one of whom was Alexei Vilanovich himself. The Russians crowded around Baldassare, and Lorenzo smiled. So they had their claws in him too. All the better. Baldassare would soon be asking Lorenzo for mercy.

Lorenzo rose without the aid of his cane, ignoring the grinding in his knee. "Italo, so good to see you," he said, before greeting Vilanovich. The slight had been deliberate, though Lorenzo knew which of the two wielded the true power. But it was best not to let Vilanovich get too cocky.

"Enzo," Vilanovich said, his arctic blue eyes meeting Lorenzo's. He was a tall, lean man, his voice low and deep. His blond hair heavily streaked with gray, he bore a strong resemblance to his brother Ilya, who'd been killed by Enrico Lucchesi's son the prior year. Yet Alexei was clean-shaven and sinewy, not a huge Russian bear like Ilya, and even though he neared fifty, he looked capable of handing out any measure of violence he felt necessary.

If the rumors were true, Alexei was just as ruthless as his older brother, but shrewder. And less likely to make mistakes. Lorenzo would have to watch him closely.

Baldassare and Vilanovich took the two chairs to Lorenzo's right; the guards that had accompanied them retreated to the wall beside the four men Lorenzo had brought. Two more waited outside.

It wasn't like Sal to disappear, and Lorenzo was taking no chances.

Rubbing his hands together and blowing on them, Baldassare addressed Lorenzo. "Why haven't you run some power down here?"

Lorenzo smiled. "Because real men don't need creature comforts."

Baldassare barked with laughter and exchanged a look with Vilanovich. "Doesn't bother you, does it? You Russians have ice in your veins. But a Sicilian like me, no. I'm like the lizard: cold-blooded. I need the heat."

Lorenzo rolled his eyes; the man was impossible. "You grew up in fucking Rome. You're as Sicilian as Vilanovich is. Less, maybe. He at least understands how to fight."

Baldassare's eyes twinkled and he nudged Lorenzo. "Of course I grew up in Rome. You can't let a man make a joke?"

Lorenzo stared at him. "The louder the laugh, the emptier the head."

"You may be right, Enzo. But nothing you say is going to bother me tonight. Tonight, we get that fucking cunt out of my hair."

"Who would've thought she'd be so difficult? And *now* she wants to deal with us?" Lorenzo said.

Baldassare nodded and laughed. "A little late for that, yes?"

"*Sì.*" Lorenzo held up a hand for quiet; yes, he was right. Two people were coming down the stairs, one a woman in fancy shoes to judge by the clacking they made on the stones. He smiled. Loredana Montisi, the incorruptible anti-Mafia judge, was going to regret she'd ever changed her mind and asked for a deal.

Lorenzo had a deal for her all right. She'd never leave this room alive.

———◆———

Everyone in Italian law enforcement had heard about the infamous meetings in Calabria at the Our Lady of Polsi monastery in San Luca. Yet as far as Loredana knew, few had ever set foot in the crypt. As she and Silvio Fuente reached the bottom of the stairway, she heard the faint sound of several male voices, then silence.

Her heart was already pounding; that sudden silence sent it into a gallop. What was she doing?

Fuente, clad in his *carabinieri* uniform, touched her arm and looked at her with questioning eyes. She realized then that she'd frozen on the bottom stair.

She swallowed hard and looked away from him. *Remember the plan.*

She had the back-up bug between the first two fingers of her right hand. Painted gray to match the stonework, it would wirelessly transmit their discussion outside, where Ruggero, Tommaso, Beppe, Enrico, and Dario waited. All she needed to do was stick it to the wall somewhere or under a piece of furniture.

It was a spread-spectrum bug, meaning that it rapidly switched transmission frequencies. A normal RF detector wouldn't pick it up. As long as Andretti hadn't brought a spectrum analyzer, she'd be in the clear.

Well, assuming she planted the damn thing before they searched her.

Taking a deep breath, she turned the corner and walked into the crypt. Arched columns defined the space. Candles had been lit in the area she was in, but the low-ceilinged room stretched off into darkness. A wooden table lined the wall nearest her.

Several chairs had been placed facing a dais, on which sat Italo Baldassare, beside an old man with thinning hair who she guessed was Lorenzo Andretti, and a pale, blond man around fifty who stared at her with piercing blue eyes. Clearly a foreigner, and sporting distinctive Bratva tattoos on his fingers, he must be Alexei Vilanovich, the Russian mobster Enrico and Ruggero had told her was connected to Baldassare and Andretti.

Glancing to her right, she saw several guards peeling themselves from the wall. One of the Italian ones approached, a bug detector in his hand.

Shit! She faked a stumble and grabbed onto the table lining the wall. Desperate, she wrapped her fingers around the top, pressing hard, hoping the bug would stick and be out of sight. The room's dim lighting was to her advantage, but she couldn't check her work. She had to pray as she quickly righted herself.

"Nervous?" Baldassare asked.

She ignored his gleeful tone and turned her attention to the approaching guard. He passed the wand over her body, front and back, then nodded to Andretti. He didn't search Fuente. Excellent. So they had two bugs in the room. They were sure to get a good recording.

Taking a deep breath, she faced the men who wanted her dead. Her plan was going to work, and by this time tomorrow, they'd all be in jail.

She opened her mouth to speak, but Fuente held up a hand. "One moment, Giudice Montisi." He stepped forward and reached up to his lapel and removed something from it—the bug that had been disguised as a button. What the—?

She hadn't even fully formed the thought before her stomach hit the floor and Fuente handed the bug to Lorenzo Andretti. "As promised," he said.

The old man took the bug and looked it over, an avid gleam in his eye. Then he dropped the device and crushed it with the tip of a black cane adorned with a silver wolf's head. Staring at Loredana, he laughed at her expression.

"You fucking worm," she spat at Fuente.

He shrugged. "I always pick the winning side."

"What did they promise you?"

"I'm to take the vows tonight, along with our illustrious prime minister."

"The vows? Bullshit. You can't join the 'Ndrangheta."

"Not the 'Ndrangheta per se. La Santa."

Now it made sense. La Santa was the clandestine heart of an already secretive group—the place where highly ranked members of the 'Ndrangheta conducted their business with politicians and others who'd allied with them but could never, for various reasons, be direct members. She played dumb, stalling for time, hoping the bug she'd planted was transmitting. "La Santa? I'm not familiar with that."

Fuente, as she'd guessed, was only too happy to explain, and she took the time to study her options. If the bug she'd planted wasn't transmitting, her only hope was talking her way out of this mess. Or possibly taking the gun holstered on Fuente's hip beside her.

When Fuente finished talking, she took a deep breath, trying to slow her heart. It was tapping her ribs as if it wanted to escape. Which would have been the wise choice.

She looked up at the three men before her, all too aware of the seven at her back and the traitor beside her. She'd gambled on Fuente and lost. Pointing to the mangled bug, she plastered on a rueful smile. "You can't blame me for trying to get some insurance. You know, in case things *don't* go my way."

Andretti laughed, revealing large, yellowing teeth. "I almost like you, Giudice Montisi. You have balls for a woman, I'll give you that." He placed both hands on the head of his cane and leaned forward. "Too bad that's not going to be enough to keep you alive."

———◆———

Ruggero was about to burst out of the van that he, Beppe, Tommaso, Enrico, Dottor Beltrami, and Dario were in, listening to the transmission from the bug Loredana had planted. He was going to wring that bastard Fuente's neck if it was the last thing he ever did. But Enrico was telling him not to move.

"I told you we couldn't trust that weasel," Ruggero said. "And now I'm supposed to just sit here?"

Enrico's grip tightened on Ruggero's arm. "I'm not sure what Fuente is up to."

"Are you serious?"

"Let's see how this plays out."

"I'm not trusting her life to him."

Enrico held his eyes. "I'm not asking you to. I'm asking you to be patient."

"What the fuck for?" He regretted the words the minute they flew out of his mouth. Beppe and Tommaso gave him scandalized looks; even Dario grimaced.

Enrico just stared at Ruggero, as if the profanity hadn't registered. But it had. "You helped me once when I desperately needed it, and because I've been where you are, I'll excuse that. Once."

Ruggero swallowed and nodded. "Forgive me, *capo.*"

He was forgetting his place, forgetting his vows. If Enrico told him to let Loredana die, he was supposed to let her die. Business came first, always.

But if he had to stand there and listen to her death, it would be the end of him.

Loredana's voice came through the speakers, and what she was saying turned his blood to ice. Now Enrico might very well *want* her dead.

———— ✦ ————

Loredana stared into Lorenzo Andretti's coal-black eyes. They were flat and expressionless, like a snake's. She didn't dare blink, didn't dare reveal the sick, shaky feeling that had taken over her gut and chest, the sensation that she was going to vomit or faint. Or both.

He's just another thug. Nothing more than shit on my shoes.

She opened her mouth, willing every ounce of authority she'd ever possessed into her voice. "A well-placed judge, such as myself, one who's incorruptible, as far as the press and the people know—such a person could be very useful to you, yes?"

Andretti smiled, but it wasn't warm. "So *now* you want to cooperate?"

"I always knew you were a fraud," Baldassare said. "So high and mighty, but here you are, licking our boots and begging for scraps."

She shrugged with a nonchalance she didn't feel. "Let's just say I've seen the light." Loredana swallowed, trying to moisten her parched mouth and throat. What she said next could turn Enrico against her. But she had to gamble on Ruggero. "I know you want Lucchesi out of the way. You've been working with Corvi and Zambrotta, the co-judge, the whole time, yes?"

Andretti nodded. "Of course."

"What if I worked with Corvi to make the FIU case stick?"

"After he accused you of collusion in open court?"

"What better way to prove I'm not guilty, than if I put Lucchesi away?"

Andretti snorted. "Why would I trust you now?"

Here goes. "I realized who's the real power here, especially now that I see the company you keep. You, Lorenzo Andretti, are the power behind the throne. The king maker, one might say."

Baldassare leaned forward. "I don't trust the bitch."

Andretti turned to him. "I wasn't asking your opinion."

Baldassare and Vilanovich exchanged a glance, and Loredana's blood froze. Both men had pulled guns, and she heard a scuffle behind her. She turned to see the Russian guards subduing Andretti's men.

Andretti's brow creased. "What joke is this?"

Baldassare smiled and rose, every millimeter the smug, arrogant ass he'd always been. "It's no joke, *Signor* Andretti." He stressed the *signor* to make a point.

"*You* want to master me." He motioned to Vilanovich. "*He* just wants territory and money, and frankly, I'm happy to let him have it. We have mutual interests that don't involve you." He pointed the gun at Loredana, and she raised a hand to her throat, unable to hide her fear any longer. "Or her," Baldassare said.

Andretti started to rise, but Vilanovich put a hand on his shoulder, pressing him into his seat. "I have a deal with the Vilanoviches. It's ironclad," Andretti said. He stared at Alexei Vilanovich as if willing the man to agree. But Vilanovich did nothing, except rest that hand on Andretti's shoulder.

Baldassare laughed. "You promised the Vilanoviches vengeance and a slice of the pie. But I made them a better deal: vengeance, and the entire pie."

Then he turned to Loredana and smiled. "You should've taken the deal I offered you, Giudice Montisi. Unfortunately, that deal has expired."

Silvio Fuente's hands closed on her upper arms. She was going to die.

———————— ♦ ————————

Getting into the church hadn't been as easy as Ruggero had hoped. They'd encountered two of Andretti's men outside, and after a quick, intense scuffle, had managed to kill them both without attracting attention. They'd dragged the bodies inside the church, leaving them just within the main doors. It wasn't ideal, but they didn't have a lot of choice.

And every second they wasted was another second during which Loredana could die.

Ruggero and Dario carefully descended the main stairs to the crypt, taking care to make no noise. After their fight with the guards, Ruggero had decided to split their force and had sent Tommaso and Beppe in through the rear entrance, in case Andretti had more men posted there.

Adrenaline dumped into Ruggero's system without mercy, and he tightened his grip on the Beretta he carried. A mini Uzi was slung across his back, but until he knew the situation, it was best to have a more precise weapon in hand.

All he wanted to do was race down the stone steps and grab Loredana, but that strategy would surely get her killed.

Had they shot her yet? The last thing he'd heard through the bug was Baldassare saying he didn't trust Loredana. He hoped like hell that he wasn't too late as he reached the bottom stair.

He halted there, Dario right behind him. Listening, he tried to get a sense of how many people were in the room. A sharp, feminine cry stabbed him in the gut, and he nodded at Dario. They charged into the crypt.

Fuente was holding onto Loredana from behind. Italo Baldassare stood on the dais before them, a gun pointed at her. Alexei Vilanovich had a gun pointed at Lorenzo Andretti beside him. What the fuck was going on?

Glancing to his left, Ruggero saw three Russians holding guns on Andretti's four guards.

He couldn't risk shooting Fuente, because the bullet could hit Loredana too, so Ruggero took the shot he had left: Baldassare.

Two bullets, nicely placed midchest, took Baldassare down. Alexei Vilanovich took advantage of Ruggero's distraction to grab Andretti, using him as a shield, and pointed his gun at Loredana's head.

Shots erupted from Ruggero's left, and he realized he'd made a mistake—they were caught in the open with no cover, enemies in front and behind.

But Dario had reached that conclusion before Ruggero had. Dario upended the thick wooden table lining the wall, and the two of them dived behind it.

Bullets slammed into the tabletop shielding them. It was an old piece; thickly hewn, the wood like iron, but it wouldn't last forever.

The only advantage they had was control of the exit behind them. But Vilanovich and Fuente had Loredana.

Vilanovich edged off the dais, taking Andretti with him, Fuente following with Loredana as his shield. They retreated along the far wall, while two of Vilanovich's men grappled with Andretti's guards, and the other, armed with a machine gun, kept Ruggero and Dario pinned.

They had to be headed to the other exit. Ruggero had once wandered the length of the crypt. A number of niches branched off the main space, holding the tombs and sarcophagi of men of faded import. There were lots of places to hide back there, places to hole up. He had to count on Tommaso and Beppe to keep them from escaping.

Somehow he had to get to Loredana.

He pocketed the Beretta and grabbed the Uzi. The Russian with the machine gun—an AK of some sort, most likely—had taken refuge behind one of the arched stone columns that supported the church above. The man kept up a steady barrage of suppressive fire. Every time Ruggero tried to look above the tabletop's rim, he risked getting shot. He was going to have to wait for the man to run low on ammunition, but even then, he'd get only seconds before the Russian had a fresh magazine in place. He prayed the table would hold up until then. Chunks of wood splintered off it with every burst of automatic fire.

Dario turned to him. "What's your plan?"

"When he reloads, I'll take out as many as I can, and give you cover fire. You run to the other side, try to get behind the one with the AK and take him out. I'll follow when I'm done here."

He received a sharp nod in return. Dario carried several handguns, but no heavy weapons. He told Ruggero he'd fired an Uzi before, out of necessity when the Russians had attacked during Nick and Delfina's engagement party, but he said he was no expert and didn't feel comfortable with the weapon. His honesty had surprised Ruggero; he'd encountered more than one guard who'd claimed he had heavy arms experience when he clearly didn't.

Apparently Dario's ego wasn't fragile. And that was good; hubris had gotten more men killed than caution ever had.

There was a break in the machine-gun fire; this was their opportunity.

Ruggero popped his head over the tabletop. He opened up the Uzi on the guards to their left—the two Russians and Andretti's four men, killing at least one—and then focused on the spot where the one with the machine gun was. Shards of stone flew from the column. So far, there was no return fire. Had the Russian's gun jammed or overheated?

Dario left the cover of the table and ran forward, crouching low, Ruggero careful to aim over his head. Dario was nearly to the column across from the machine gunner when someone shot him. He clutched his left side, blood running over his fingers.

"Fuck!" Ruggero muttered. Where had the shot come from? Had they missed someone? He looked over his shoulder just in time to see Italo Baldassare taking aim at him. What the hell?

Ruggero spun and aimed at Baldassare, who jumped off the dais and took shelter behind a nearby column. Bullets pinged off the column, but Ruggero doubted he'd hit him.

Body armor. That was the only explanation for Baldassare's resurrection. Otherwise the man would be dead. No doubt the Russians were wearing it too.

The Uzi ran dry, and Ruggero quickly slapped in a fresh magazine. He had one left. How many did the Russian have? From the way he was spraying bullets, the answer seemed to be well north of Ruggero's meager supply.

Shots rang out deeper in the crypt. Tommaso and Beppe must have encountered Vilanovich and Fuente. It was dark back there; hopefully they wouldn't hit Loredana.

Cradling the Uzi, Ruggero left the safety of the table and headed straight for the cluster of men fighting each other to his left; until they were gone, he and Dario were trapped between two sets of enemies. He had to hope that Dario could cope with Baldassare, or at least evade him.

His boots pounded on the hard stone below his feet, the rhythm echoing his harsh breathing, his mind screaming "Find her!"

He reached the nearest column and discovered a dead Russian behind it. One of Andretti's men clutched at a wound in his abdomen. Ruggero didn't hesitate; a quick trigger pull made sure the man wouldn't be able to shoot Ruggero in the back.

He was going to have to ration the Uzi, or it would soon be useless.

He had guns holstered under each arm, and he pulled them both, flinging the Uzi over his back. Andretti's remaining two men were still holding off one of the Russians. Ruggero peeked around the column. A burst of automatic gunfire tore into the column Ruggero was hiding behind.

The Russian still had plenty of ammo.

Fuck. He was pinned.

And from the sounds of it, Tommaso and Beppe might be in the same situation. Or worse.

CHAPTER 27

Vilanovich fired at someone approaching them from the rear of the church, and Loredana's heart leapt. It had to be Ruggero or one of the men with him. Answering fire burst out; there were two men. She caught glimpses of their faces in the muzzle flashes from their guns. Tommaso and Beppe. That meant Ruggero and Dario were back where all the shooting was taking place. Was Ruggero still alive?

She stumbled in the near darkness, Silvio Fuente's fingers digging into her arms, his hot breath harsh in her ear. He hadn't unholstered his gun. If she could just reach it...

"In here," Vilanovich said, his thick Russian accent coloring his words as he manhandled Andretti into a small side room crowded with furniture and other items. A small window, maybe sixty centimeters by sixty centimeters, let in a beam of moonlight. Loredana's right shin connected with the sharp corner of something, and she let out a sound. "Shut it," Vilanovich grumbled.

"This isn't getting us out of here," Andretti panted.

"You shut it too," Vilanovich said.

Not one for conversation, apparently. What was the Russian intending to do?

Fuente crowded her into the space, and she took advantage of their maneuvering to reach back with her right hand. Her fingertips found the holster, then the butt of the gun. All she had to do was grab it—

She closed her fingers around the grip and tugged, but it wouldn't come free. Fuente's hand closed over hers. "No, I do not think so, my pretty judge." He shoved her against the wall, then unsnapped the top of the holster and palmed the gun, pointing it at her belly.

Damn it! She'd forgotten the snap.

"You'd make a miserable pickpocket," Fuente murmured.

"Unfortunately."

The man had the audacity to smile, as if this were a friendly joke between them, nothing more. "Traitor," she hissed.

He sobered a bit. "Did you actually expect any different?"

"You know in your heart, Silvio, what is right."

"In this world, it doesn't pay to have a heart."

"What do you have? A tarnished badge and a collar around your neck? That's a lot to be proud of."

"Don't forget the pile of dirty money. That's my favorite part."

"Pig."

He shrugged. "At least I get to walk out of here."

"If you're lucky."

Fuente grinned, his white teeth flashing at her in the moonlight. "I'm always lucky, Giudice." He pressed his mouth to her ear. "And I know you didn't trip when we walked in. You're as bad an actress as you are a pickpocket."

Her heart started pounding. Did that mean he knew about the other bug? Was he on her side after all?

"What are you say—"

"Shut it!" Vilanovich barked. He was returning fire with Beppe and Tommaso, his left arm firmly locked around Andretti's neck. The old man still had hold of his cane. He seemed calm and said little. No doubt he was looking for a chance to escape as well. That, however didn't make him her friend. She was in this alone.

"What will you do now that Baldassare is dead?" Andretti asked Vilanovich.

"He's not dead," the Russian said and tapped his chest. "He has the Kevlar."

Had Ruggero been the one to shoot Baldassare? She hadn't been able to see; her back had been facing the men who'd interrupted them. It could've been Dario, but she'd bet it was Ruggero.

Again he'd saved her life. But now—another burst of gunfire erupted from the crypt. She had to help him. Somehow.

Vilanovich dragged Andretti with him and peered out from their niche. Bullets whizzed off the stones near his head. He returned fire, then the gun in his hand clicked empty. He'd need two hands to reload. Maybe—

As soon as he let go of Andretti, the old man jabbed the silver wolf's head atop his cane into Vilanovich's jaw, slamming the man's head against the wall. Dazed, Vilanovich blinked, and Andretti swung the cane like a club, the heavy silver grip smashing into Vilanovich's temple.

The big Russian crumpled, and Andretti grabbed the man's empty gun.

Fuente wheeled and aimed at Andretti. "Drop it."

This was her chance, and she wasn't going to risk it on Fuente. She had to hope Tommaso and Beppe didn't kill her. She shoved Fuente hard in the back, sending him into Andretti.

Then she ran the few steps to the opening in the wall. Arms raised, she cried, "It's me! Don't shoot!" Holding her breath, she plunged out of their hiding space.

A man rushed toward her. "Giudice," Tommaso called, and she let him take her arm and pull her behind a column. He pointed to her left. "The exit is back there. Just run along the wall. You can't miss it."

"I'm not leaving. Give me a gun," she said.

"No."

"Tommaso, please. Ruggero needs help."

"I know, but—"

"Vilanovich is knocked out, and Fuente is fighting with Andretti. One of them will start shooting again soon. Now's our chance."

"Fine." Tommaso pulled a gun from a pocket in his overcoat and thrust it at her. "You've got a full magazine. Make it count."

"Where is Ruggero?"

Tommaso shrugged and pointed to the far wall. "One of them is over there, the other over here," he said, pointing down along the wall they were closest to. "I'm not sure which."

A heavy burst of automatic gunfire came from the near wall. She had no chance against that. "I'll take the other side."

Tommaso nodded and wished her luck.

She kicked off her noisy shoes and started across the cold stone floor in her stocking feet, heading for a far column where someone was sitting against its base.

Was the man alive or dead? Friend or foe?

She'd find out soon enough.

———◆———

Dio, with the adrenaline flowing through his veins, Lorenzo felt twenty years younger. Smashing that Russian fucker had been all too satisfying.

But as he squared off with Silvio Fuente over possession of Fuente's gun, Lorenzo calculated his odds and found them wanting. Fuente was half his age, fit, and expecting Lorenzo to fight.

And the person who could guarantee them both safe passage had just run out into the main crypt.

Lorenzo abruptly let go of Fuente's Beretta and put up his hands. "You win."

The *carabiniere* smiled and withdrew out of arm's reach, keeping his weapon trained on Lorenzo. "What do you want?"

"What you want. To get out of this alive."

"Agreed."

"We need the judge. There is no other way we'll get out of here. I'm sure that Lucchesi has us surrounded."

"Perhaps. You have men you could summon?"

"If my mobile worked down here, yes."

"You have anyone outside?"

"Two, but my guess is they're dead, since they aren't here already." He spat on the floor. "Fucking Lucchesi. Fucking Baldassare." He kicked Vilanovich. "Fucking Russians."

"Yes," Fuente said dryly. "Well, now we're both fucked."

Lorenzo turned to Vilanovich's body crumpled on the floor. "We need more guns and ammunition."

Fuente eyed Lorenzo's cane. "I'm not falling for that."

Lorenzo laughed. So Fuente wasn't as stupid as he looked. He tossed the cane to Fuente. "Satisfied?"

"Hardly." Fuente motioned with the gun. "In the corner."

Lorenzo complied, his knee aching with every step. *Idiot.*

Fuente searched Vilanovich quickly, but he made the mistake of turning his back on Lorenzo.

Grabbing a decorative metal crucifix shoved into the corner, Lorenzo crept within a few steps of Fuente. Vilanovich was a large man, and Fuente was struggling to lift him off the bag he carried, the one with the extra ammunition. With a lunge and a swipe of the crucifix, Lorenzo dealt Fuente a heavy blow to the head. Maybe even hard enough to kill him.

Fuente slumped over Vilanovich. Fuck. Now he couldn't get at the bag himself. With a sigh, Lorenzo retrieved his cane and took Fuente's Beretta. It was better than nothing.

He moved to the niche's opening and poked his head out. A bullet pinged off the stone near his left eye. Damn it.

He needed the judge. But first he had to get out of this fucking hole. Pocketing the gun, he raised his arms and called out, "I surrender!"

Then he stepped out, and two of Lucchesi's men came forward. One of them smiled. "We've got him," he said.

Palming the cane, Lorenzo grinned. Of the two, the smiling fool would be the one who wouldn't see it coming.

———— ◆ ————

Loredana couldn't make out much in the gloom in the back of the crypt. She headed toward the man slumped by the column. He was moving slowly. Her heart pounded erratically. *Dio*, was it Ruggero? Had he been hit?

She nearly reached the man when someone started shooting at her. Ducking behind a large column, she tried to see where the shooter was. Bullets pinged off her column and she took a deep breath.

How had Ruggero survived in this world for so long? The injured man stirred, struggling to raise his gun. What should she do? Shoot, or hope he wasn't an enemy?

A barrage of gunfire erupted on the other side of the crypt. She used it as cover, deciding to run toward the injured man. As she reached him, she realized who he was. Dario Andretti.

He let the gun fall down and looked at her with tired eyes. "How bad are you hurt?" she asked, crouching beside him.

"Bad enough." He touched his side and she pulled at his shirt, baring the wound. Blood oozed from it and she had to swallow hard, a sudden memory paralyzing her: her mother, face ashen and bloodied, her father lying too still in a pool of crimson.

Dario grabbed her wrist and winced, dragging her into the present. "I think a rib is broken."

She nodded, trying to focus. "It hurts when you breathe?"

"Yes. Or move." He laughed weakly, then winced again. "Or laugh."

She asked the question plaguing her. "Where is Ruggero?"

He motioned to the other side of the crypt. "Keeping them busy."

Cristo. She should've known. "I have to help him."

"He seems to have things under control." A sharp burst of fire punctuated his words. "Or maybe not."

She'd been staring at that side of the crypt, and she thought she had a good bead on where Ruggero was. Shifting her weight to her toes, she readied herself to sprint out from her hiding place. Dario grabbed her wrist again. "You have only that?" he asked, his eyes indicating the Beretta.

"*Sì.*"

He shook his head. "Then stay here."

"I can help."

"Not unless you circle behind the Russians and take them out. But that is not a job for you."

"I can do it."

"You looked like you wanted to vomit when you saw my injury."

She shrugged. "Doesn't matter."

"It does." His fingers dug into her wrist. "You won't be able to shoot, and you'll get yourself killed. And then Ruggero will kill me for letting you go."

He was probably right. But she had to do something. "I can't just sit here."

Something hard pressed against her head. "Well then, I have the answer to your prayers." She turned and looked up. Italo Baldassare put out a hand for her gun. "No games."

The next thing she knew, Dario had his gun jammed against Baldassare's left kneecap. "Get that gun off her, or you'll never walk right again."

Baldassare lifted the gun away from her head. "I see we have a misunderstanding," he said.

"I'm in no mood," Dario said. "Go, now, before I change my mind."

Loredana couldn't let Baldassare leave. Without thinking, she jabbed her gun in the prime minister's crotch. "You belong to me now," she said and motioned for his gun.

Dario laughed at Baldassare's expression. He handed her the gun without protest.

"*Grazie,*" she said. Now what? The man was a prisoner, but she had no way to restrain him. And Dario didn't look good.

More gunfire erupted across the crypt. She glanced that way, and Baldassare, clearly no fool, took off for the rear exit from the crypt. She scrambled up after him. He couldn't leave; she wasn't sure if the bug had worked. She could barely see Baldassare as she chased after him in the dark. He was running along the far wall, nearly to the niche where she'd been held captive.

She almost managed to grab hold of Baldassare's jacket when someone snagged her arm. She wheeled around and realized who her captor was: Lorenzo Andretti. His fingers dug into the flesh just above her elbow, and he had a pistol pointed at her. "Drop them," he said, motioning to the two guns she carried.

She hesitated, and Andretti barked at her. "Do it. Now."

Damn it, damn it, damn it. Her hands shook as she extended the guns from her sides and dropped them.

Andretti smiled, and she'd never seen a less-reassuring sight. "Compliant at last," he said.

"What do you want?"

"To escape this place alive, for one."

"And?"

He yanked her close. "To see you beg for your life before I take it."

His words were cold, hard, and without mercy. Loredana shivered. This was the end. The end Ruggero had fought so hard against, the end even he couldn't prevent. Tears welled in her eyes. He'd blame himself; self-forgiveness wasn't in his vocabulary. She managed one word, one word she choked on: "Please."

With a laugh, Andretti tightened his grip. "You had your chance to walk away, and you didn't take it." The next words he whispered in her ear: "Now scream for him. Scream for your lover."

She shook her head. If she did that, she'd get him killed.

Andretti jammed his gun against her left hand, the muzzle pressed to the base of her thumb. "You'll never use this hand again."

She closed her eyes. "Do it," she said.

Andretti snarled in disgust and pinched her arm all the harder. "You think you're tough?" Her foot nudged something on the ground and she realized it was Andretti's cane. Which knee had he favored? The one closest to her. *Dio mio*, she whispered, before driving her heel into Andretti's knee.

His gun went off, and a searing pain tore through her hand. She opened her mouth and screamed.

———— ◆ ————

A woman's scream—Loredana's scream—cut through the roar of gunfire and tore a hole in Ruggero's gut. The pure agony in the sound meant she'd been hurt terribly. He called her name and peered out from his hiding place, trying to see her. Bullets flew off his column and he ducked back.

She screamed again, the cry deep and unbridled. Who was hurting her?

It had to be either Vilanovich or Andretti. Baldassare and Fuente wouldn't have the stomach for whatever was being done to her.

He called for her again, choking on her name, not caring how weak he sounded.

No answer. Was she dead?

The Uzi was near empty, and he was out of fresh magazines. Both handguns were now useless. He'd even used up the gun he kept strapped to his ankle. He'd taken a Glock off one of Andretti's fallen men, but it too was low on bullets.

There was no way he could get to her.

He'd failed to keep her safe. He'd failed her.

He'd promised her, made a vow to her. And he'd failed yet again.

Closing his eyes, he slumped against the column. Loredana was dead. The woman he loved, the one who'd made him live again, was dead.

A heavy weight filled his chest and stomach, and his eyes burned.

Bullets struck his column again, startling him. He looked down at the Uzi in his hands. Should he charge the Russian with the machine gun, and hope his suicide mission helped the others escape?

No. She deserved to be avenged. Whoever had killed her was going to die at Ruggero's hands, and it wouldn't be quick.

———— ◆ ————

Loredana didn't dare look at her hand, couldn't bear to see what Andretti had done to it. She wrenched away, kicking out again, and Andretti went down. Clenching her hand to her belly, she turned and grabbed for Andretti's gun.

He caught a fistful of her hair and yanked, and she came down hard on her injured hand, crying out again, the pain excruciating. She struggled against a surge of nausea. Andretti was not going to win.

And Ruggero was not going to die.

Andretti wound his fingers in her hair, trying to grab her skull, and she knew what he planned next—to smash her head into the stones.

Ignoring the pain as hair tore from her scalp, she clawed at Andretti's eyes with the remaining fingers of her injured hand and grabbed again for the gun. This time she got hold of it and wrenched it free.

Ruggero called her name again, his voice raw with emotion. She got to her feet and ran to where the last two Russians were. They were still firing, and she willed them to continue, each flash from their gun muzzles giving her vital clues. She had to be fast.

One, two. One, two. She whispered the words to herself, her voice wavering, the sound of it a bit crazy, but it focused her. One shot, another shot. That's all she had to do.

Blood spilled from her injured hand, running warm and thick over her fingers, and she swallowed hard, trying not to think about it. She'd have to shoot one-handed and she'd have to be close. Very close.

The Russians were turned away from her. She approached at a low crouch, her breath coming in ragged gasps, her body so juiced on adrenaline, she felt poised between freezing in place and charging at them, screaming.

One, two, one, two, she whispered as she crept up to the men crouched behind the column. Raising the gun, she took aim at the nearest one's head, let out a breath, then pulled the trigger.

The man jerked and slumped over, his companion starting to turn toward her. She could see his left eye, the side of his cheek, and Dario's warning came to her. She pulled the trigger again, the bullet striking the man just below the temple. He shuddered and collapsed on top of the man beside him, and Loredana fell to her knees and retched. She'd done it. She'd saved Ruggero. But Baldassare and Andretti were still alive, and if they got free…

Ruggero aimed a burst of gunfire at the column she now crouched behind. "Ruggero, stop! It's me!" she cried.

"Loredana?" The relief in his voice was palpable.

He rushed over to her, his face hard as granite when he saw her clutching her hand. "Loredana, what have they done to you?" He fell to his knees beside her.

She shook her head, trying to clear it. "Andretti. He shot me. I can't look at it." Closing her eyes, she extended her hand toward him. "Is my thumb… is it gone?"

"No. The bullet went through your palm."

Grazie a Dio. Still, she didn't want to see the damage. "Andretti and Baldassare, they're back there…" She gestured behind her.

Ruggero caught her up in his arms and pressed a kiss to her lips. *"Bambina,* I thought I'd lost you."

A lump filled her throat and she couldn't speak. She just shook her head.

"I want you to know something," he said. She pressed against him, tears running down her cheeks. Gunfire rang out somewhere behind them. Who was shooting at who?

"You are my life, Loredana."

She looked up at him. Nothing like a brush with death to make one brave. "Are you trying to tell me you love me?"

"Yes, but I'm not getting it right."

She started to laugh. "Still afraid to say the word, after all these bullets?"

He tilted her chin up so that she was looking at him, his eyes dark and intense. "Mine," he said.

He touched her cheek, his hands smelling of gunpowder. She put her uninjured hand over his, her throat clamped shut.

"Yours," she finally managed. Then she pushed him. "Get Andretti and Baldassare." When he didn't move, she pushed him again. "Go. Please."

He swiftly kissed her undamaged palm, then grabbed his Uzi and left. She leaned back against the wall and cradled her injured hand against her belly. She couldn't stop shaking. Taking a breath, she said a prayer for Ruggero, then she closed her eyes and rested her head on her knees. She was done, and she could do no more.

CHAPTER 28

If Ruggero's calculations were correct, the only people he had to worry about were Andretti, Baldassare, Fuente, and Alexei Vilanovich.

Where were Tommaso and Beppe? Dario was somewhere off to his right, possibly dead from Baldassare's bullet.

Gunfire came from a niche in the wall, and someone returned it. Looked like Tommaso. Who was shooting at who?

Something heavy and hard hit his right knee savagely and he went down, spinning to see his attacker. He swung the gun around, ready to pull the trigger, when he realized who it was: Lorenzo Andretti. This man he owed a slow death for what he'd done to Loredana.

But she was still alive, and the image of Cris Andretti in his coffin rose in Ruggero's mind.

There was someone else whose vengeance mattered more than his own.

Andretti held his cane like a club, poised to hit Ruggero again, but the sight of the Uzi stopped him. It had to be all but empty, but no matter: Andretti didn't know that, and all it would take was one bullet. "Drop it," Ruggero said.

The old man smiled and let go of the weapon. "Did you find your pretty judge?"

"She's fine."

"She betrayed you."

Ruggero smiled. "Never." She'd walked through fire for him, astonishing him with her bravery, her determination. But he should've known all along.

Ruggero motioned Andretti to his feet. Ignoring the gunfire to his left, he directed Lorenzo across the crypt, to where Dario was, hopefully still alive.

Ruggero had promised Dario justice, and he was going to get it.

———— ◆ ————

Someone was approaching; two someones, one of them limping badly. Dario raised his gun, his hand wavering. He tightened his grip, peering through the

247

gloom, his heart speeding up, clearing some of the fog from his mind.

"It's me," Ruggero said. "And I've brought you a present."

The person with Ruggero stumbled forward, his face catching beams of moonlight from the windows high in the crypt walls. Lorenzo.

Ruggero placed a hand on Lorenzo's shoulder. "On your knees."

"I'll die on my feet like a man."

"You'll die like the miserable worm you are." Ruggero forced Lorenzo down, and the old man winced as his knees hit the stone floor.

Dario studied Ruggero. The cold, dispassionate killer of the day before was gone. Lorenzo had done something. "Loredana?" he asked. He'd heard her screams.

Ruggero prodded Lorenzo with the Uzi. "She's alive. No thanks to him."

"I'm glad she's okay."

Eyes narrowed, Lorenzo stared at Dario. "You're still the weak little boy who lost his finger to a Lucchesi. And now you lick the hand that crippled yours."

Dario had the strangest urge to smile. "And you're just an old, tired man."

Lorenzo chuckled. "Old? Tired?" He tapped his chest. "This whole thing—this whole plan—was my doing. *I* engineered it. Within a few years, Marcello will be prime minister. Our family will soon run this entire country."

"You won't be alive to see it."

"There's plenty of my blood to go on. That's all that matters."

"My son is dead. He was the best of us. The one who should have been leading us into the future."

A glint came into Lorenzo's eye. "The best? He was licking Lucchesi's boots. But I put an end to that."

A chill slid through Dario; it was just as Sal and Antonio had said. "Sandro Lucchesi was your lapdog. You ordered him to kill Cris."

Lorenzo's chin jutted upward, his eyes hard. "I brought you all into this world. And I can take you out of it."

Dario shook his head. "There's something broken in you. You killed two sons, and a great-grandson, and you'd kill me too."

"Remo was the first to defy me, and he should have been the last. But some of you just can't learn your lesson."

So many deaths, so much loss. For what? "Why Cris? Why *any* of this?" Tears pricked Dario's eyes, and his throat threatened to close up.

"You've never been poor. You don't know what it's like to miss even one meal. I did what I had to do to make a future for myself and my blood. Your life has been a good one, full of plenty, not that you'll ever thank me for it."

"We Andrettis have been at each other's throats for years. *That's* the future you've bequeathed us."

Lorenzo smiled, baring his teeth. "The strongest of us will survive."

"And that's not you." Dario raised his gun, but he couldn't hold it still. Lorenzo laughed.

Crouching down, Ruggero pulled a gun and pressed it to the side of Lorenzo's head, then motioned for Dario to try again. Dario lifted the gun and Ruggero took his wrist, steadying it, pressing the muzzle against Lorenzo's chest.

Lorenzo laughed again. "Weaklings. It takes two of you to kill an old man?"

Ruggero nodded to Dario. "Do it."

Dario drew in a breath. He was so tired. So weak. So finished. But Cris... He owed this to Cris for a life of promise cut short. For all the things Cris would never do—marry, have a child, run a *cosca* of his own. All things he should have had, that Lorenzo had stolen from him.

Lorenzo leaned forward, pressing against the gun. "You. Are. Weak."

Dario pulled the trigger, and Lorenzo collapsed with a shudder. Dario dropped the gun. He was so tired. He was so tired of everything. He let his eyes close, and he lay back against the column that had sheltered him.

Ruggero shook him. "Hold on."

"I've done what I needed to do."

"You have a hell of a lot more to do. Grandchildren to spoil. Your daughter will never forgive me if I don't bring you home."

Dario could picture Delfi scolding Ruggero. She'd lost so much. Her beloved brother. And Ilaria too, she'd lost Cris, just as he had...

Would Cris want him to give up? To let Lorenzo win?

No. Cris would want him to fight.

Dario looked at Ruggero and nodded. "Okay," he managed.

For them, he'd try. And if he survived, he'd try to live again, instead of just putting one foot in front of the other.

———◆———

Ruggero checked the pulse at Lorenzo's neck before he left Dario. The old bastard was dead, and good riddance. *For you, Loredana*, he whispered to himself. He hadn't pulled the trigger, but close enough.

Someone—Tommaso or Beppe, maybe both—was still exchanging shots with a person holed up along the far wall. Ruggero carefully made his way over to them, identifying himself before he got too close. Both Beppe and Tommaso were alive, though Tommaso had a nasty gash above his right eye.

"Who's in there?" Ruggero asked.

"Baldassare, we think. Loredana said Vilanovich was unconscious. Not sure about Fuente."

A shot not aimed at them rang out and curses came from the niche. After the sounds of a brief scuffle, Baldassare came out, his hands behind his back, someone following him. "Don't shoot," Fuente said, and poked his head around Baldassare's shoulder. "He's cuffed." Fuente motioned with his head to indicate Baldassare.

So *now* Fuente was going to play the hero?

Not. Fucking. Happening.

Ruggero charged forward, elbowing Baldassare out of the way and grabbing Fuente by the lapels. "You *figlio di puttana*—"

"Ruggero, wait," Loredana called.

He turned to look, saw her rise unsteadily.

"What?" he asked, barely leashing his impatience.

"He knew about the other bug. He saw me plant it."

He looked at Fuente, the man's face millimeters from his own. "*Davvero?*"

Fuente, looking disheveled for once, pushed his hair out of his face. "I gave my word." Ruggero snorted. "You wound me," Fuente said.

Tightening his grip on Fuente's jacket, Ruggero hauled him closer. "You will *never* cross my family again. *Capisci?*"

"I've learned my lesson."

"Make sure you have. You do it again, and I will make sure you die slowly."

Ruggero released Fuente with a shove and went over to Loredana. Her face was pale, and she seemed dazed. "It's over?" she asked.

He helped her to her feet. "It's over. We have Baldassare. And Lorenzo is dead."

He escorted Loredana over to Fuente and Baldassare, who scowled at them. Fuente gave Loredana a little bow. "What should I do with him?"

She looked at Ruggero. "The bug worked? You have him recorded?"

Ruggero nodded. "We have everything."

Loredana's smile lit up Ruggero's chest. She turned to Fuente. "Sottotenente, take Signor Baldassare into custody on charges of attempted bribery, attempted murder, and Mafia collusion."

Fuente tipped an imaginary cap at her; apparently he'd lost his somewhere during the firefight. "With pleasure, Giudice Montisi."

———◆———

They had to move quickly. Dario had lost considerable blood. Fuente raised an eyebrow when he saw Dario, and Ruggero intervened. "He was never here. *Capisci?*"

"You do like to live dangerously. I assume you brought some bleach?" Fuente asked. When Ruggero nodded, Fuente said, "I'll do what I can to keep the crime-scene techs away from there."

Fuente took Baldassare out of sight, while Enrico and Beltrami came in and retrieved Dario. Ruggero scrubbed down the area around the column with bleach. It would have to do.

And he'd have to hope Fuente could work some magic.

———◆———

Enrico drove as quickly as he could, navigating the narrow streets of the town, eyes peeled for the clinic run by Beltrami's cousin. He finally found the place, and they took Dario inside.

Dario looked gray, and he was barely conscious. As the two doctors prepared to operate, Dario turned to Enrico and motioned him forward. He grabbed Enrico's wrist when he was within reach. "If I don't survive, promise me you'll watch over Delfina."

"Of course. She's part of my family now."

"And Ilaria. Lorenzo's gone, but his grandsons might try to stake a claim, and you know what they'll do."

"I'll make sure nothing happens to her."

"I ruined her life." Dario's fingers tightened on Enrico's wrist.

Shaking his head, Enrico put a hand over Dario's. "Cris wasn't your fault."

"But he was yours. And this is the payment I ask of you."

Enrico wasn't about to argue. "I will take care of her. I swear it."

"*Bene.*" Dario released his wrist, and Beltrami put a mask over his face. Within seconds, Dario was unconscious.

Now all Enrico could do was pray.

———◆———

After everyone had been patched up, questioning from the *carabinieri* had started. Ruggero chafed at the intrusion, when all he wanted was to hold his wife. To his credit, Fuente shouldered most of the burden, making clear to his colleagues that his and Loredana's "daring undercover operation" had been his own brainchild, undertaken with her approval and cooperation.

His bosses seemed to swallow it all wholesale, their glee at seeing the untouchable Baldassare go down out of all proportion. Repeatedly, Baldassare had promised to do more to attack Mafia corruption, while mysteriously not quite managing to fund most of the anti-Mafia initiatives the *carabinieri* and DIA had requested. Both organizations were more than happy to hold one of their own up as a hero, and Fuente seemed born to play the part.

Loredana had certainly called that right.

After more than an hour of questioning, Fuente eventually shooed his fellow officers out of Loredana's hospital room, ostensibly to let her get some rest. However, he didn't leave himself, waiting until the others had filed out. Then he approached Loredana's bedside and took her uninjured hand in his. "Giudice, it has been an honor." He leaned closer, speaking so only she and Ruggero could hear. "You freed me from that bastard Andretti. I owe you an immense debt."

Loredana smiled. "And don't forget it." There was humor in her tone, but steel beneath it.

"I think all of us have learned a lesson about loyalty and unity. Yes?" Fuente looked from Loredana to Ruggero, who had to shake his head.

"Have you?" Ruggero asked. "*Davvero?*"

"*Davvero,*" Fuente said. And for once there wasn't a trace of amusement, sarcasm, or irony in the man's tone. He was dead serious. And then he grinned. "But let's keep this our secret, yes?"

Ruggero almost smiled. Fuente was Fuente, after all. Hopefully he understood that Ruggero meant what he'd said. There'd be no more second chances.

Right after Fuente left, Ruggero's phone buzzed; it was Enrico. Dario was out of surgery. They'd removed the bullet. Though he was stable, he'd have to stay in Calabria for a while, since Beltrami didn't think it safe to move him yet.

Enrico had contacted several of the elder *capi* in Reggio Calabria, the ones Don Battista had sounded out for their support. Once Enrico had explained the situation, they'd agreed to maintain order until a meeting of La Provincia could be called.

It seemed there'd be few mourners at Sal's and Lorenzo's funerals.

Their mission was over. Lorenzo Andretti was dead, Baldassare was in custody, and at least for now, the Russians had been thwarted.

It was time to go home.

Alone at last, Ruggero turned to the woman who'd been his wife for only a little over forty-eight hours. He'd almost lost her, his most precious beloved, but by some miracle she'd survived. "You ready? Enrico has the jet waiting."

She put her hand in his and nodded. "More than ready."

She held his eyes, and the memory of her screams crashed over him. He had to look away. "When you screamed, I thought it was over for us," he finally said, his voice cracking.

"But it wasn't."

He looked at her then. "You don't understand. I thought my life was over. I thought about giving up. Just running at them with a nearly empty gun, and hoping Beppe and Tommaso could escape."

Her jaw dropped open. "Why would you think of such a thing?"

Dio mio. If he ever needed a cigarette, it was right now.

He took her injured hand. It was swollen and bandaged and no longer bore his rings. She'd moved them to her right hand temporarily. "I can't imagine going on without you."

She squeezed his fingers weakly, then winced. "Well, you're stuck with me now."

"More like you're stuck with me."

"That's not at all how I feel."

His heart was beating fast. *"Davvero?"*

"Davvero." She pulled herself upright. "Now take me home, please."

Ruggero let out the breath he'd been holding. She seemed to mean it, but now that they'd survived, was she genuinely prepared to accept all the consequences of living in his world?

———◆———

Someone was pounding on the door to their bedroom. Loredana pulled the covers over her head and burrowed into her pillow. Her left hand was throbbing, and the last thing she wanted was to talk to anyone but Ruggero.

He, apparently, was willing to entertain visitors. The mattress shifted under his weight and he was up and at the door in seconds. Was he wearing anything? She couldn't resist checking, and she smiled when she saw the balled-up shirt he'd pressed to his crotch. He opened the door a crack, and Tommaso, three butterfly bandages holding the gash on his forehead together, took that as an invitation to shoulder his way inside.

"I came as soon as I saw it on the news," he said.

"Saw what?" Ruggero asked.

Tommaso gave her a grave look. "It concerns you, Giudice." And then he looked at Ruggero. "And you."

Loredana sat up, clutching the sheets over her naked chest. Her pulse quickened. Had Baldassare managed to weasel his way out of the charges?

Tommaso handed Ruggero a folded-up newspaper and flipped on the flat-screen television mounted on the wall. He scrolled through a few channels until he got to the one he wanted. "You need to see this."

The newscaster, already a serious-looking man, frowned and shook his head before speaking. "Giudice Loredana Montisi, at the heart of the stunning undercover operation that brought down Prime Minister Italo Baldassare yesterday, is herself at the heart of another scandal: she's apparently involved with an associate of accused mob boss Enrico Lucchesi." Loredana's heart started pounding as the pictures Fuente had shown her and Ruggero flashed up on the screen: though the first one, of Loredana and Ruggero kissing in the back of a car, was blurry, it was clear enough, especially in light of the next picture of them kissing on the balcony of the hotel.

Ruggero was right; a camera could be just as bad as a gun, if used by the right person. Her career had been assassinated as surely as if she'd been murdered.

Disgraced or no, Baldassare was getting his revenge.

The newscaster continued. "The question now is: How will Giudice Montisi respond to the charge of Mafia collusion being leveled against her? Stay tuned."

Tommaso cut off the set. "I'm sorry," he said. "Maybe I should've let you sleep, but I figured you'd want to know."

Loredana nodded, and forced a "*Grazie*" from her lips before Tommaso left and shut the door behind him.

Ruggero was busy reading the front page of the *Corriere della Sera*. "What does it say?" she finally asked.

He tossed the balled-up shirt on a chair and came over to the bed, still reading as he sat down beside her. "That fucker Baldassare," he muttered.

She put out her hand, and he hesitated. "Just give it to me."

He sighed and handed it over. When she saw the headline, she understood his reluctance: "Hypocrite Judge Should Resign." Pubblico Ministero Corvi was quoted as saying, "It's always the ones you least suspect. She's probably been dirty all along."

Tears pricked at her eyes. Many times she'd wished her father were still alive, but for once she was glad he was dead and wouldn't have to suffer the shame of seeing the Montisi name dragged through the mud.

"*Bambina.*" Ruggero put an arm around her. "Don't cry. These people know nothing."

She nodded and wiped her eyes. "I know, but... The thing is, it's true. I can't even say that it's unjust or a lie."

He brushed her hair out of her eyes. "If you've changed your mind about anything—"

She cut him off. "I haven't. I have no regrets."

He seemed dubious. She touched his unshaven cheek. "I told you. I made my decision some time ago."

Her phone buzzed on the nightstand, and then her mother's ringtone played. She groaned and reached for it. Nora barely waited for Loredana to answer. "I told you what would happen if you continued to... associate with that man."

Loredana's face and chest flushed with heat. "If that's all you called say, there's no reason for us to talk further."

She was about to end the call when Nora said, "Wait. If you're willing to forgive me, I can forgive you."

Loredana could only shake her head. "So now you think we're on the same level?"

"You can't judge me, Loredana. Not any longer."

"Oh I can, and I will. What you did, you did out of greed. What I did, I did out of love. And I brought a corrupt man to justice. You got Papà killed."

Nora said nothing for a moment. Finally she spoke. "You love that thug?"

Loredana was shaking inside, her gut churning. She was glad her mother wasn't in the same room. Looking straight at Ruggero, who was studying her intently, she said, "Yes. I love him. In fact, I married him. "

"God help you then. Because I can't." Nora ended the call, and Loredana tossed the phone on the bed.

Her hand was aching, throbbing, itching under the gauze, and she felt like vomiting. She pulled her knees up to her chest and rested her forehead on them.

Ruggero touched her hair. "What are you going to do?"

She shifted so that her chin rested on her knees. "Resign. I have to. I had to the minute I married you. But I'm still taking Baldassare down with me."

Ruggero stroked her arm. "The law has been your life."

She took a deep breath and held it for a moment before letting it out. The churning in her gut ceased. "It has, but we both know it's not the life I wanted."

He took her uninjured hand. "But this life—my life—isn't the life you wanted either."

He looked so miserable that she almost lied. But he wasn't a man who'd tolerate such thing. "I'll have to make the best of it, then."

He shook his head. "I never should've kissed you."

"I was the one who started it, remember?"

"*Sì.* But I should've stopped it."

She gave him a coy smile. "I'm irresistible, you know."

He laughed. "I do know."

Leaning forward, she kissed him, softly, gently. He was the one bright spot in all this mess. Then she pulled back and sighed.

There was no delaying the inevitable. "Take me to the courthouse, please."

———— ♦ ————

She'd known the day was coming, but still the shock of it, the sadness, nearly overwhelmed Loredana as she walked up the steps to the courthouse. A swarm of reporters had been waiting for her, but Ruggero, Tommaso, and Beppe kept them at arm's length. At the top of the stairs, she turned to face the mob. "I'll be back here in an hour, and I'll take questions then."

Somehow she managed to keep the trembling out of her voice. Still, Ruggero took her hand when they got inside, and that tiny gesture of support was almost her undoing. She took a deep breath and headed to her office, the guards in tow.

Stepping inside that room, which for so long had been her private space and which would soon belong to someone else, Loredana breathed in the scent of her leather-bound law journals and the lingering aroma of the last espresso she'd had, half of it still filling the cup on her desk.

"What do you want to take with you?" Ruggero asked.

She looked around at the furnishings. "There are a few things in the desk, the rest can stay." She was entitled to take the law journals; she'd purchased them. But what good would they be to her now?

She circled the desk, sat once more in her chair and picked up the phone. There was one person she had to talk to before she typed up her letter of resignation: the prosecutor on the Baldassare case.

Fantoni answered when she called. "Can you come to my office?" she asked. "Right now?"

The man stumbled over himself to answer yes. She hung up and looked at Ruggero. "You have the copy of the recording?"

He patted his chest pocket, then retrieved the USB drive with the recording and handed it to her. "We edited out what was said before you placed the bug."

"*Bene.*" She took the recording and sat back in the chair. Once she handed this recording over, her work in law enforcement was done. Oh, she'd no doubt have to testify against Baldassare as a witness, but her days in the judge's chair were over.

Her eyes fell to the picture of her parents on the desk, both of them in their judicial robes, smiling and holding hands on the steps of this very courthouse. She reached out and stroked her father's face. *Poor Papà. Betrayed by his wife, and now his daughter.*

Ruggero came to stand behind her, and he squeezed her shoulder. "He'd understand, I think."

She shook her head. "I doubt it. But thanks for saying so."

He put a finger under her chin and tilted her head to face him. "*Bambina*, don't be so hard on yourself."

He meant well, but nothing he said was going to make this any easier.

Pubblico Ministero Martino Fantoni knocked on her door and Tommaso let him in. He looked from Tommaso, to Beppe, to Ruggero. "You wanted to see me?" he asked.

She motioned for him to take a seat in one of the chairs before her desk. Leaning forward, she extended the recording to him. "You should eventually get a copy of this from the *carabinieri*, but just in case, I thought you should have it from me."

"What is it?" he asked as he accepted the drive.

"It's a recording of a meeting between Italo Baldassare, Lorenzo Andretti, Alexei Vilanovich, Sottotenente Silvio Fuente of the *carabinieri*, and myself. You will hear Baldassare and Andretti attempting to bribe me and also hear that they colluded with Pubblico Ministero Corvi and Giudice Paolo Zambrotta, the co-judge on the Lucchesi-Battista case. Lorenzo Andretti's links to the 'Ndrangheta are also revealed, as well as the plan to induct both Baldassare and Fuente into La Santa, and thus make them official associates of the 'Ndrangheta."

Fantoni turned the recording over and over in his hands. "So what I've been hearing on the news, it's all true?"

She nodded. "Most of it."

He looked at Ruggero, then back at her. "You realize that your position is no longer unassailable."

She swallowed down the lump in her throat. "I do. However, the allegations against Enrico Lucchesi and Vittorio Battista have not been proved, and Sottotenente Fuente will testify to how he was coerced into producing the so-called 'evidence' against Signor Lucchesi due to the kidnapping and torture of his son. He will also testify that he approached me with his idea to conduct an undercover operation against Baldassare and Andretti, an investigation that neither he nor I could mention to anyone else for fear of the plan being leaked."

She loosely clasped her hands together, suppressing a wince. "Sottotenente Fuente knew that I was being targeted, especially after the shooting. He also knew that he could not trust Corvi with this information."

The prosecutor pocketed the recording. "*Mille grazie.*" Glancing at her bandaged hand, he said, "I realize you risked your life to get this." He looked around the office. "And yet, they'll hound you until you step down."

She shrugged. "I can live with that, as long as I see justice done when it comes to Baldassare. He was planning to let in the Russian *Mafiya*, to partner with them to run this country."

Fantoni shook his head. "*Davvero?*" When she nodded, he ran a hand over his hair. "You've given me much to work with." He placed a hand on her desk. "I want you to know that I've always admired you. And I know, in my heart, that you've always worked in the best interests of the Italian people."

She smiled, hoping to hide the tears his words provoked, and offered him her hand across the desk. "I will of course testify and provide whatever assistance you require."

He clasped her hand. "I am counting on that."

After Fantoni left, she went through the drawers of her desk and filled up a small box with her things, placing the picture of her parents on top.

Then she clumsily typed out a brief letter of resignation, and a letter of recommendation for her clerk, leaving both sitting on her desk. She took one last look around. It was finished, this part of her life.

Ruggero sent Beppe and Tommaso outside with her things. "We need a moment," he said to them, then turned her. "You're certain, *bambina*? You're ready to leave all this for good?"

She met his eyes, studied his grave face. When, exactly, had it happened? When had she fallen in love? And was her heart leading her in the right direction?

He didn't move toward her, didn't try to touch her, just watched her with that steady gaze, his face betraying nothing of his thoughts, acting as if she had a choice in the matter, as if she could leave, walk out the door without him, go on with her life and forget she ever knew him.

But there was no choice. Not anymore. Not after her heart had chosen for her. "I love you," she said, her voice cracking. "And yes, I'm certain."

For just a moment, his reserve wavered, and something flickered across his face—relief, perhaps?—before he covered it with a nod. Then he closed the gap between them and took her in his arms.

He held her tight, saying nothing, stroking her hair. After a moment, he stepped back and looked at her. "You honor me."

There was such feeling in his eyes, a weight to the words that she would never forget. He was telling her he loved her, the only way he knew how. She touched his cheek, then pressed a soft kiss to his lips. "Time to face the wolves," she said.

They walked outside and met the crowd of reporters waiting for her. Ruggero stepped back a bit, but she remained aware of his reassuring presence at her back.

The reporters circled around her, shoving microphones in her face, hurling questions at her. She raised her hands and waited for silence. Then she spoke. "Although I am resigning my position today, I tell you now that I have always loved the law. I have bent it recently, however, but only because there are forces at work that cannot be confronted in an entirely legal manner."

"Will you continue fighting the Mafia?" a woman asked.

Loredana made sure she was looking into the camera behind the reporter. "I will always stand on the side of justice. I will fight evil however I can."

"If that's true," the reporter asked, "how can you be sleeping with a Mafioso?"

Loredana's gut burned, but she kept her voice even. "No Mafia association has been proved regarding Signor Vela or Signor Lucchesi."

Questions came at her, relentless, too many to answer, and besides, she'd said what she wanted. She waved her good hand in the air. "Those are all the questions I'm going to take."

Ruggero, Tommaso, and Beppe started pushing forward, parting the crowd as flashes went off and the reporters continued to pepper her with questions. "If you've done nothing wrong, why are you resigning?"

"Have you broken the law?"

"It appears Pubblico Ministero Corvi's allegations against you were true. What do you have to say for yourself?"

And worst of all: "What would your father say about what you've done?"

She'd thought she was strong enough, but she was trembling by the time they reached the car and Ruggero whisked her inside. He waited until they'd pulled away from the curb, then he took her hand and pressed the button to raise the partition.

"You were so brave out there."

She tried to smile, but she couldn't keep up the front anymore, and she let the tears fall. "I shamed my father today. I shamed the Montisi name."

He squeezed her hand. "You brought justice to an unjust situation. No one else may ever know the truth, but I know it. My *capo* knows it. And you know it." He paused. "But I understand if you want to walk away from me."

She shook her head. "We're married."

"It's not legal, yet. And it's not like we gave you any choice in marrying me."

She touched his cheek. Would he ever believe that she loved him, really, truly believe it? "Listen to me, Ruggero. I had a choice, and I made it freely. I chose you." She drew in a breath. "And yes, I'm feeling a little miserable now. But I also feel free. For the first time in my life, *I'm* choosing my path. Not my mother. Not my beliefs about my father's expectations. But *me*."

He studied her face, searching for something. "How do I know this is real? That you're not just reacting to all the craziness of these last few weeks, of being in danger, almost getting killed more times than I want to count?"

"It's real. I know it. I'm not going to change my mind in a few weeks. Or ever. I can't imagine my life without you in it."

He pressed his forehead to hers. When he spoke, there was a huskiness to his voice that she hadn't heard before. "You mean the world to me. And it kills me that you've almost died several times because of the world I live in." He took her hand and pressed it to his chest. "You feel my heart, how it's pounding? I should just walk away from you and let you live your life. But I can't." He took her hand and kissed her palm. "Loredana, *ti amo.*"

She'd never thought she'd hear it, and she wondered for a moment if she'd imagined it, then he whispered it again.

"*Ti amo,*" she repeated. "My place is here with you. And don't you forget it."

He smiled then, that smile that felt like a secret meant only for her.

Her heart had chosen, and it had chosen well.

CHAPTER 29

The crime-scene tape had been removed only days before, and the crypt had been thoroughly swept for recording devices, but they could wait no longer to call La Provincia together. As Enrico descended the stone stairs to the crypt below the Our Lady of Polsi monastery with Don Battista at his side, he knew what he was going to say to all assembled. It was time for change, a change he'd long hoped for but had almost despaired of coming. But fortune favored the bold, and bold he must be if he ever hoped to see his father's vision for the 'Ndrangheta come true.

There would be no election this time. Don Battista had consulted with a few of the older *capi*, and they'd agreed. Though Lorenzo Andretti and Salvatore Ruscino were dead, there were still those who would have followed them. They could not be allowed to prevail. The recording of what had transpired had circulated among the bosses, as they'd meant it to do, and Lorenzo and Sal's treachery had been apparent.

Once everyone had taken their seats, Enrico, Don Battista, and Gianluca d'Imperio took the dais. Don Battista rose and addressed those assembled. "I will be brief. In light of what transpired here just days ago, it is clear that we must remain united, and loyal to each other. Though Lorenzo Andretti and Salvatore Ruscino are gone, we must be certain their influence isn't still being felt. Therefore, I will step into the role of *capo di tutti capi* and take over the *mandamento* of Reggio Calabria; Enrico Lucchesi will be second in charge and will maintain his position as *capo* of the Lombardy *mandamento*; Dario Andretti will take the Tyrrhenian *mandamento* from me; and Gianluca d'Imperio will take the Ionic *mandamento*."

A flurry of talk rose up and Don Battista motioned for quiet. Then he asked, "Are there any objections?"

Several men rose; two of them were Salvatore's nephews, Pietro and Severino Andretti. "There should be an election," Severino said.

"And there will be," Don Battista said, "when the current terms are up, in about four years."

"We never agreed to appointments to fill open positions."

"And we never *didn't* agree to it," Don Battista said. "As Lorenzo's successor, I have chosen to handle the situation as I see fit. And at this time, I believe an election would be counterproductive."

"You mean you couldn't control the outcome," Severino sneered.

"No. I mean that there are times to invoke special powers, and this is one. We are at war with the Russians. Twice now they have tried to stake claims here. Twice they have been repulsed. But don't mistake that for a defeat. They will rise again, and they will try again. Now is not the time for petty squabbles and divisions. The *mandamenti* heads have agreed on the vision going forward, at least for the next four years." He looked at Enrico. "I'm turning the floor over to Don Lucchesi, who will speak to our future."

Pietro started to protest again, but his cousin Marcello put a hand on his arm. "Enough, Pietro."

It appeared Marcello Andretti would be the voice of reason in that branch of the family. But he couldn't count on appearances.

Enrico took a last look at Pietro and Severino. Those two would be trouble if they weren't dealt with. He'd learned his lesson from Sandro.

He'd send a man or two down, and he'd have them leave the bodies in a public place, somewhere highly visible. Their deaths would be a clear message to anyone else who thought he was going to be weak.

There'd be no loose ends this time. It was kneel, or die.

Rising to his feet, Enrico took a deep breath. What he was going to say wasn't going to be popular, and many would resist it. And yet, it needed to be said, and said with conviction. If more of these men had to die, so be it. He looked out at the *capi* assembled before him. Some looked at him with curiosity, some with open hostility.

He hadn't prepared a speech, but what he planned to say were words he'd often rehearsed in his head. And now was his chance to set them free, to let them loose in the world. To see them do some good perhaps. Hopefully a great deal of it.

"We provide a service, you and I. We keep order in our communities. Businesses thrive, people get educations, everyone wins. A government—even a shadow one, such as ours—works only if it contains lawlessness. We do that. And thus, we, the men of the Honored Society, have thrived as well."

He saw a few nods. "You can go to any of the towns I control and find buildings with my family name on them. Schools, hospitals, churches, orphanages. I *help* people. I give back some of what I take. And I know I am not alone in this; at the same time, such largesse needs to become the norm among us. Or else we become leeches that the people would wish to destroy."

His pulse kicked up a notch. "Today marks a new day for the Honored Society. We will both uphold the codes established by our ancestors while forging new paths in the twenty-first century. We will phase out our operations in drugs, prostitution, and pornography. We will not kill civilians."

A murmuring broke out and he raised a hand to quell it. "There are those who distrust these ideas, who believe without the threat of death, we will lose our power. Perhaps. However, I have found the occasional broken bone or kidnapping incentive enough to deter those who would oppose us.

"There are those who will say that without the vast wealth created by the sale of drugs, we will be powerless. Perhaps. However, there are growing movements around the globe to legalize drugs. If enough countries follow suit, we'd lose our main source of revenue in an instant." He snapped his fingers for emphasis. "There are many other avenues open to us, avenues that don't destroy our communities the way drugs do. Insider trading, gambling, the provision of protection, the loaning of money, the trade in corporate secrets, the hacking of financial networks, the global trade in arms—these are but a sample. Moreover, these are areas the Russians are already proficient in, and we do not want to be at their mercy.

"Together, we will forge a new future. We will rebuild the South, bring in more businesses, do the rebuilding and reinvestment that the government won't. And thus we will be stronger than ever, and we will once again be embraced by the people.

"The Mafias—Cosa Nostra, La Camorra, the 'Ndrangheta—we were born in a time of chaos. We were born to protect the people against a corrupt, failed state that sought only to tax and plunder this land of ours. We rose up and helped throw off a foreign invader. And now it's time for us to fulfill our promise. To rule this country, to bring back justice and peace. To keep our people safe against those who would invade us. To bring honor upon ourselves, not mere wealth, not mere power. But honor. We call ourselves the Honored Society, and yet we have lost our way. We have forgotten our origins, the crucible in which we were born, the vows we've sworn to uphold.

"We pledge ourselves to our brethren, and yet we forget that every person in this land is our brethren as well. We forget, and we take. And so we become what we pledged to overthrow.

"This situation cannot stand. The people are rising against us. The Pope is calling for us to be excommunicated and overthrown. Once we lose the people, we lose our honor. We lose our reason for being. Is the pursuit of money the legacy our forebears sought to leave us? Is it the legacy we want to leave our children?

"I think not. I, for one, want my sons to be honorable." He paused, surveying the faces of the men before him. "Who among you is with me?"

Don Battista and Gianluca d'Imperio rose behind him, and after a moment, men started to rise in front of him. Not everyone, but enough. Enough to give him hope. Even Marcello Andretti stood up. Rico looked heavenward and crossed himself. *Papà, this is for you.*

He looked out and caught Antonio's gaze. His son was standing in the front and started clapping. Enrico smiled, and a lump rose in his throat. *This is for you, Tonio, most of all.*

Others joined in the clapping as he left the dais. This was the first step of many he'd have to take to see his vision come true.

And he still had at least two more things to do before he could focus fully on his mission.

The first would be the easiest; the second depended on the power of forgiveness.

———◆———

They'd just returned from the meeting in Calabria when Enrico summoned

Ruggero and Tommaso to his study. Ruggero wasn't sure why Enrico wanted them, but they needed to talk about the future, whether that was Enrico's purpose or not. Ruggero wasn't particularly interested in being an underboss, but if that was the plan, he'd make the best of it. He just hoped Loredana could live with it.

The two of them had spoken some about her future, but she'd made no decisions, beyond the notion that she might work on legal reform or work on behalf of the poor and help them with legal representation.

She'd called her former clerk at the courthouse and requested her legal journals be boxed up and delivered. Ruggero took that as a good sign.

When Ruggero and Tommaso stepped inside Enrico's study, he asked Tommaso to close the door, then motioned for them to take seats in front of his desk. He addressed Tommaso first. "I understand that congratulations are in order. Elena has accepted your proposal?"

Tommaso nodded and broke out into a broad smile. "*Sì.*"

Ruggero put a hand on Tommaso's shoulder and gave it a good squeeze. Elena looked more carefree than she had in years, and Orlando had taken the news well. Ruggero could hardly ask for a better brother-in-law.

"Do you have a date?" Enrico asked.

"She wants at least a month to plan. She was thinking, perhaps, that Ruggero and Loredana might want to make their wedding official at the same time."

Ruggero chuckled. Of course, Elena would be sly about it. "I see no reason not to."

"*Bene,*" Enrico said. "I'm glad that's settled. I called you both here to discuss your futures."

Ruggero's gut tightened. Loredana said she had accepted his life. But it was one thing to be a guard. Another entirely to be the *capo* of his own *cosca*. How would she feel about that?

"As you know, the ranks of our fighting men, our soldiers, have been severely depleted over the last year or so. We have temporary reinforcements from Don Battista, but we cannot keep those men forever. I'd like you two to address that, to train up the next generation of *soldati.*"

He looked directly at Ruggero. "I realized that perhaps you'd rather be an underboss, and if that is your wish, I will grant it. However, I thought that Loredana might like it more if you were out of the line of fire and taking more of a behind-the-scenes role in our operations."

Ruggero grinned. This was better than he'd expected. "*Mille grazie.*" Tommaso joined in with his thanks.

"The two of you have served the Lucchesi family very well and for many years. I personally owe you both a debt for saving my life and the lives of my family members many times. As a token of my gratitude, I am in the process of buying you each homes on the lake."

A house? That was far more than Ruggero could accept. "Don Lucchesi, I'm not sure—"

The don raised a hand. "I'm sure you do not mean to insult me by rejecting my wedding gift."

"Well—"

Enrico leaned forward. "Ruggero, your father died in service to mine. You yourself saved my father's life, and you have served me faithfully and diligently. Let me give you your due."

Ruggero swallowed and stared at his hands. "My due? After all the mistakes I've made, after Loredana—"

"You did the one thing I couldn't, and that was getting Dario's help to defeat Lorenzo. I put you in a tough position with Loredana. And you supported me with Kate, when I was at the very lowest point of my life. None of us is perfect, and any mistakes you made are no more severe than my own. You followed your heart, and I can hardly chastise you for that when I jeopardized this *cosca* to follow mine. I was angry, yes, at first, but Tonio reminded me that I was wrong to hold you to a higher standard than I hold myself."

Something lodged in Ruggero's throat. He nodded, buying time before he spoke. "I thank you for your forgiveness and your generosity."

Enrico sat back and clapped his hands together. "*Bene*. I look forward to seeing you both wed." He rose and poured them all drinks. "*Salute*," he said, tapping his glass to Tommaso's then Ruggero's. "May you both have all the happiness in the world."

Ruggero smiled and sipped at his drink. He had everything a man could ask for. But what about Loredana? Could she make a happy future for herself in his world?

———— ✦ ————

Ruggero found Loredana out on the back terrace, playing with Luca and Cocco. There'd been a freak snowstorm earlier in the day, and though the snow was melting fast, she and Luca were making snowballs and throwing them for Cocco, and occasionally throwing them at each other.

He watched them for a few minutes, until Luca tossed a slushy snowball his way. It caught him square in the chest. Laughing, Ruggero returned fire, and soon the three of them were chasing each other around the back garden, Cocco barking and running circles around them all as they slipped and slid in the snow.

Finally, Luca threw himself on the ground and started making a snow angel. Loredana lay down beside him, making one of her own. Ruggero watched her, how her eyes sparkled, and it hit him then: she *was* happy. At least for now. And maybe that would be enough to build on.

She motioned to him. "Come on, you make one too."

He huffed with laughter and shook his head.

"Please, Zio Ruggero?" Luca said. "It's fun!"

"You can't let him down," Loredana chimed in.

Ruggero rolled his eyes, but he got down on the ground, feeling like a fool as the wet snow seeped through the fabric of his trousers. He was a grown man, he needed to watch out for them, and he didn't have time for such foolishness...

Except he wasn't a guard anymore. He didn't have to be on alert. He could actually relax. And if he wanted to make a snow angel to please a little boy, then he could.

Ruggero arced his arms and legs back and forth, then rose with Loredana and Luca to inspect their handiwork.

"Look!" Luca said. "A daddy angel, a mommy angel, and a little boy angel."

Ruggero put a hand on his shoulder. "Want to go get your *mamma* and *papà* and show them?"

"Yes!" Luca ran off to the house, Cocco racing beside him.

Loredana shook her head. "I was giving them a break, you know."

Ruggero shrugged. "I wanted a minute with you." He took her in his arms. "Enrico gave me a job. Tommaso and I are in charge of training new guards. I won't be involved in the day-to-day operations anymore."

She beamed at him. "I can't tell you how relieved that makes me."

He kissed her forehead. "There's more."

"More?" Her forehead crinkled in the most adorable way.

"Enrico is giving us a house, here on the lake."

"A house?" Her jaw dropped open. "But we can't accept."

"He insists. It's a gift for our wedding, which will be in a month—the same day Elena and Tommaso are marrying."

She laughed. "Oh! So *that's* why Elena was asking what kind of flowers I like. She's sneaky, that sister of yours." She sobered. "We still can't accept a house, Ruggero."

He kissed the palm of her hand. "That's what I said, *bambina*. Then he reminded me of all I'd done for him, and he said he'd be insulted if I didn't accept."

She stared at him for a second, then she burst into laughter. "He made you an offer you couldn't refuse?"

Ruggero chuckled. "You could say that."

She shook her head. "I don't know when I'll get used to all this."

He touched her cheek. "*Can* you get used to it? Can you be happy? I feel like I came into your life and destroyed it—"

She pressed a finger to his lips. "That's exactly what you did. And I'm glad. Maybe it's not the life I dreamt of as a little girl, but I have everything I need to be happy. And I can do anything now, *be* anything."

"Except a judge."

She waved her hand in the air. "Except that. But I've done that, and it's time to do something else."

"Have you made a decision?"

She nodded. "I'm going to provide pro bono defense work for those who can't afford a lawyer."

"*Bene.*"

"But first I wanted to work on another project."

"Legal reform? Are you sure you want to do that now?"

"That can wait." She touched her belly. "I was thinking… It's not like you and I are getting any younger. I'd like to start a family—if you're ready."

A little thrill ran through him. Then he shook his head. "I'm not sure I'd make a good father."

"You will. You're very patient with Luca and Cocco."

A family? *Dio mio*, he needed a cigarette. "I just never pictured myself with any of this. A wife, a child…"

She touched his cheek. "You deserve it. You deserve all the happiness in the world. All the happiness you never had."

His voice was rough when he spoke. "If you say so."

"I do."

He cleared his throat and pulled her close, then pressed his lips to hers, the spark between them lighting up the way it always did. "There aren't words to tell you how I feel. What you mean to me."

A tear spilled down her cheek. "I know."

He pressed his forehead to hers. "I made you a vow, and I intend to keep it. Always."

A smile overtook her lips, spread across her face, stole into her eyes. "Mine."

"Yours." He kissed her one more time, then swooped her up in his arms just as Luca and Cocco came barreling across the garden, Antonio and Bianca in tow.

Tonio and Bianca laughed. "About to cart your bride off for some private time?" Tonio asked.

Ruggero grinned, but his answer was for Loredana alone. "I thought we could get started on Loredana's new project."

"Which is?"

"Something that will keep us both occupied for a very long time."

She giggled in his arms, this woman he loved more than anything else, and the sound made him happier than anything else ever could.

CHAPTER 30

Enrico couldn't put it off any longer. Delfina had insisted that everyone come over to her parents' house for a party to celebrate Dario's first day back on his feet.

They took three cars—he and Kate in one; Antonio, Bianca, and Luca in another; Ruggero and Loredana in a third. They brought along a couple guards, but that was only a token precaution. Now that Lorenzo was dead, they had peace at last.

At least Enrico hoped so. He swallowed down a flutter in his belly. Would Dario be receptive to Enrico's proposal? Or would he react with anger?

They all met in the drawing room, no traces visible of the would-be massacre during Nick and Delfina's engagement party, other than entirely new furnishings. All of them, except Loredana, had nearly met their deaths in this room, so perhaps that was the reason for Enrico's persistent nerves. But it was more than that. How to raise the subject?

The maids brought in food and drinks, and they all settled onto the furniture in a loose circle, Luca enthusiastically petting the two Rottweilers lying by the fireplace. Cris's and Delfi's dogs, the ones that had helped save their lives.

A lump rose in Enrico's throat. *Cris.* If he had it to do all over again... He took a sip of his sambuca. He should have taken care of Sandro, certainly after he'd shot at Antonio. And yet, he'd held out hope for his godson.

A foolish hope that had cost Cris Andretti his life.

Delfina interrupted his thoughts. She took Nick's hand and rose. "I have an announcement to make. I was saving it until Papà was better."

Dario looked up and smiled. "What is it, *cara?*"

A wide smile broke out across her face. "Nick and I are going to have a baby!"

Enrico squeezed Kate's hand. He was going to be a grandfather again. A year ago, that was something he'd thought would never happen. Kate leaned over and kissed his cheek. "I'm so happy for you, Rico."

Dario looked confused. "But this is not news..." He looked around at the others, at the smiles on their faces. Then he shook a finger at Delfina. "I should be angry

266

with you."

She went over to her father, bending down to kiss him on the cheek. "You should be, but you won't."

He shook his head and laughed. Then he looked at Ilaria, and took her hand. "Your mother and I have an announcement of our own. You're going to have a new brother or sister."

Delfina's hand flew to her mouth. "*Davvero?*"

He nodded. "We were going to wait a while longer to tell everyone, but we might as well do it now."

She kissed both parents and everyone broke into applause. Kate wiped away tears, and Enrico kissed her cheek. They were about to have a population explosion, and it couldn't come at a better time.

Still that lump of sorrow remained lodged in his throat. Would he ever be able to let it go? He met Dario's eyes, and Dario gave him a nod, as if he could read Enrico's mind. Yes, it was time to talk. After the shootout in Calabria, they'd had a brief discussion regarding La Provincia, but they'd discussed nothing else, and the ice between them had seemed as thick as ever.

But now, perhaps... Enrico took a deep breath. Yes. It was time. He crossed the room to Dario. "I'd like a word, if I may."

Dario nodded. Enrico needed witnesses for what he was going to do. He motioned Ruggero, Nick, and Antonio over, and he followed Dario into his study.

Dario moved stiffly but steadily, and Enrico's heart quickened as they took seats around a low table and set down their drinks.

He turned to Dario and opened his mouth to talk, but Dario held up a hand. "Before you say anything, Enrico, I'd like to speak."

Dario turned to Ruggero. "I never thought I'd say this, but I owe you my life. You have my undying gratitude for helping me in Calabria. That is a debt I will never be able to repay."

Ruggero nodded, but said nothing. Dario focused on Enrico. "I should have said this to you earlier. Thank you for agreeing to what I asked of you in Calabria."

"Of course. And my pledge still stands, should anything happen to you. You need not fear for them. Or your child." Enrico hesitated, then took the risk of saying what was on his mind. "We are family, Dario. We have been for most of our lives."

Dario looked down at his hands. "I've had a lot of time to think lately. About how I've been living, and how I want to live going forward. My whole life I've blamed my unhappiness on other people. My father. Your father. You."

He picked up his glass and took a drink. "But that has to stop. Toni told me this a million times, but I never listened. Cris told me too. And I didn't listen then, either." He tilted his head toward Ruggero. "And then I heard it again."

Setting down his glass, Dario leaned forward. "This time I'm finally listening." He looked down at his damaged right hand, at the missing finger. "When Cris was shot..." He trailed off, his voice growing thick, and he stared at the floor. "That was not your fault. I can admit that now." He looked up and extended that hand to Enrico. "Please forgive me."

Tears pricked Enrico's eyes. This was not at all what he'd expected, but it made him feel more confident about what he was going to ask of Dario. He took Dario's hand, clasping it firmly. "I will never forgive myself for Cris. I should've taken more care with Sandro—"

Dario cut him off. "No. That was Lorenzo's doing. And now he's dead. And so is the hatred between our families."

Enrico smiled and took a deep breath. It was time to take the leap, to ask Dario for the favor he might be unwilling to grant. He released Dario's hand and stood up. There it was again, that flutter in his belly.

"Our sons made a blood bond once. I would make such a bond with you. I would call you brother, if you'd let me."

Dario looked up at Enrico, realizing after a heartbeat or two that his mouth was open. The *vincolo di sangue*. Never would he have imagined this request coming from Enrico. Never would he have imagined saying yes. But in his gut, the answer was already there.

"Yes, I will call you brother." He rose from his chair, a twinge of pain from his side reminding him to move slowly. "However, if we are to be brothers, there should be no secrets between us."

Enrico's brow wrinkled, and Dario took a deep breath. He held up his right hand. "For years, I hated your father for what he did to me. I was a boy, not a man, and I shouldn't have paid for my father's crime, no matter how horrible it was."

"True," Enrico said. "And I'm sorry."

Dario forced himself to look Enrico in the eye as he made his confession. "My hatred for your father consumed me. And when I saw my chance for revenge, I didn't hesitate."

It took Enrico a second, then the shock registered on his face. "It was *you?*"

Dario shook his head. "How he died—it was my idea. Part of it anyway. My father—well, you know how Carlo was. He always took everything too far."

Enrico pressed a fist to his mouth and Dario had to look away. He could only imagine what Enrico was seeing—his father's head in a box, his mangled hands beside it—and he shook his head. What Rinaldo had done—yes, it had been cruel. But what had been done to Rinaldo? It had been monstrous.

And it was Dario's biggest regret. His voice was hoarse when he spoke. "Do you still wish to make the bond?"

Enrico didn't move, didn't react. Had he heard the question? Dario was about to repeat it when Enrico nodded. "Too many years, we have blamed each other for our fathers' savagery. That ends now."

Dario exhaled in relief. "*Mille grazie.*"

Ruggero came forward and extended a knife to Enrico, who took it and made a long shallow cut across his right palm, then handed the knife to Dario. He did the same, then they clasped hands, letting their blood mingle. "Blood of my blood," Enrico said, and Dario repeated the words. It wasn't the usual ceremony, but it felt right, this change.

Ruggero took back the knife and addressed them both. "From now on, you are brothers. The blood of one is in the other. Only more blood or an infamous action may untie this bond." Dario squeezed Enrico's hand and nodded, then they let go. For a moment, the echo of the ceremony between Cris and Nick came to mind, and Dario blinked away tears. His son, his wonderful son, was gone. But the man who'd ordered his death was dead. "Cris would have wanted this," Dario said.

Enrico nodded and took out a handkerchief. He pressed it to his own wound, then offered it to Dario. He wrapped it around his hand, his eyes going to the missing little finger. He no longer blamed Enrico for it, and a lightness filled his chest.

Enrico followed his gaze, and Dario held up his bandaged, blood-stained hand. "Ilaria will be pissed to see this. We'll never hear the end of it. She'll probably order the doctor to give me another transfusion."

Enrico smiled and laughed, finally seeming at ease. "I have one more favor to ask," he said. "Ruggero tells me you discovered my ruse regarding Matteo. May I bring him home to his mother?"

Dario pursed his lips, but the anger was gone. "I feel for Francesca, losing two boys. She shouldn't have to be without him."

"Thank you. And I apologize, but—"

Dario stopped him. "I understand. I do." He touched Enrico's shoulder. "So, what are we going to name our first grandchild?"

Enrico looked at Nick and grinned. "Well, you're assuming Delfina is going to give us any say."

Nick laughed. "You're right about that. I'll be lucky if *I* get any say."

"But," Enrico continued, "I think we're both agreed that if it's a boy, it won't be Carlo or Lorenzo."

Dario laughed. "Agreed. What about Cosimo, after your grandfather?"

Enrico shook his head. "The best choice would be Cristoforo." Tears shimmered in his eyes, and Dario embraced him, then stepped back and nodded.

"Agreed."

Nick clapped them both on the back. "I'm quite sure Delfina will have no objection."

Dario laughed. "She'd better not. I've been too easy on that girl." Then he looked up at the ceiling, wondering if Cris was looking down on them. Dario hoped so. And he hoped one day, many years from now, to see his son again.

AUTHOR'S NOTE

Due to the high level of secrecy maintained by the 'Ndrangheta (the Calabrian Mafia) and the relative scarcity of former members turned state's witnesses, there are few resources detailing the inner workings of the society. Therefore, I have used artistic license in portraying certain aspects of the 'Ndrangheta, particularly as regards La Provincia.

Until July 2010, it was widely believed that there was no overarching body in charge of the 'Ndrangheta. However, with the arrest of several prominent 'Ndranghetisti, it is now believed that there is a *capo di tutti capi* (boss of all bosses) who oversees a commission (La Provincia) with direct power over the individual families. The prior books deal with the formation of such a central organization; however, for dramatic purposes, I have simplified the structure somewhat and haven't enumerated all the various real-world constituents of it, such as those located in Liguria (Genoa) or Toronto, Canada.

Additionally, to make this series easier to read for American readers, I have used the term *cosca* rather than *'ndrine* to indicate an individual crime family. I have also greatly simplified the organization of individual crime families and have chosen to name crime families after their *capo*'s blood family; in real life, a *cosca*'s name may consist of a region or place, or a hyphenated combination of the names of the two or three primary blood families that control the *cosca*.

In Italy, women typically don't take their husband's last name; for simplicity's sake, I have chosen to reflect the traditional American practice of taking the husband's last name upon marriage.

I have also used some artistic license in portraying the workings of the Financial Intelligence Unit (FIU) at the Banca d'Italia, Italy's central bank and financial regulatory authority.

Because the Italian legal system is extremely complex and notoriously slow-moving (trials can, and typically do, take many years and involve multiple appeals—Amanda Knox's trial was not exceptional in this sense), I have greatly simplified the workings of this system, while attempting to retain the essence of both how it works and how it differs from the legal system in the United States. For example, there is no bail available to defendants, and there is no jury of one's peers. Prosecutors have significantly more power and control over the police and investigations, and judges have expanded powers. Typically, a defendant (*imputato*) is notified in advance that he or she is under investigation; however, for dramatic purposes, I've chosen to eliminate many of the preliminaries to an Italian legal proceeding, and I have combined aspects of the typical trial phase with the fast-track trial option, so that I could both speed up the action and yet still allow for a trial in the normal sense.

Note that all persons mentioned in this series are fictional; no resemblance to actual people, living or dead, is intended. The family names used in this series were deliberately chosen not to reflect names of actual crime families.

ABOUT THE AUTHOR

Dana Delamar is the author of erotic romance, LGBTQ romance, and the "Blood and Honor" Mafia romance series, which is set in Italy among the Calabrian Mafia. Her first book, *Revenge*, received 4 stars from *RT Book Reviews*, was a Top Pick at The Romance Reviews, and was a double-finalist for Best First Book and Best Romantic Suspense in the 2013 Booksellers Best Awards.

Her second book, *Retribution*, received 4 stars from *RT Book Reviews* and was a semi-finalist in the Kindle Book Review's 2013 Best Indie Book Awards. Her book *Malavita* was a quarter-finalist in the 2014 Amazon Breakthrough Novel Awards, and her book *Redemption* was a finalist in the 2014 Maggie Awards and a semi-finalist in the Kindle Book Review's 2014 Best Kindle Book Awards.

Dana is also an editor with over thirty years of editing experience in both fiction and nonfiction and has worked with everyone from newbie writers to experienced pros. The books she's edited have won numerous awards and critical acclaim, including two Top Picks from *RT Book Reviews*.

danadelamar.com

MORE BY THIS AUTHOR

Thank you for reading *Reckoning*. I hope I have entertained you.

Writing a book is a rather crazy endeavor, similar to trying to put together a thousand-piece puzzle with no picture to guide you. When I started this series, it was going to be only one book. Then two. Then four. Now it's grown to five with more books in the "Blood and Honor" world on the way. I'm in the midst of planning a second series involving many of the characters from the "Blood and Honor" series. The first book will be about Giovanna d'Imperio. I'm looking forward to seeing her find happiness.

If you enjoyed *Reckoning*, please consider writing a review to help others learn about the book. Every recommendation truly helps, and I appreciate anyone who takes the time to share their love of books and reading with others. (And feel free to friend me on Goodreads—I love seeing what everyone is reading!)

To hear about my new releases (including the new "Blood and Honor" books!), you can sign up for my VIP Readers List at www.danadelamar.com.

In case you missed it, you may want to read *Malavita*, the prequel to the "Blood and Honor" Mafia romance series. After *Revenge* and *Retribution* came out, many readers asked for more background about the origins of the feud between the Lucchesis and the Andrettis, so the idea for *Malavita* was born. *Malavita* tells the story of how Enrico Lucchesi came to love Antonella Andretti, the daughter of the man who killed his family. Because the leads of *Malavita* are teens, this story is more of a sexual slow burn than you may be used to with these books, but many readers enjoy this story, which I think of as a cross between *The Godfather* and *Romeo and Juliet*. I really enjoyed traveling back to Enrico's teenage years, and I hope you do too.

Keep reading for a special preview of *Malavita*.

A SPECIAL PREVIEW OF *MALAVITA*
(Blood and Honor Prequel)

Quarter-finalist for the 2014 Amazon Breakthrough Novel Awards!

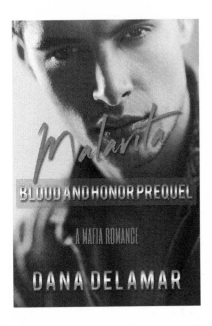

A son determined to avenge his family.
A daughter desperate for peace.
Two fathers intent on destruction...

Enrico Lucchesi never wanted anything to do with the Mafia. But when his brothers were murdered, he accepted that he would someday be the next don. However, he doesn't accept that he must marry the daughter of the man who killed them. Enrico will never trust an Andretti, never mind love one. The Andrettis are up to something with their so-called "truce"—and Enrico must avenge his siblings. But will his dark secret spell the end of his vengeance—and possibly the Lucchesis?

After Antonella Andretti's father tries to destroy the Lucchesis, she persuades him that an alliance—achieved by her marriage to Enrico, the "golden boy" she's loved from afar—would be in everyone's best interests. As her wedding day approaches, people close to her father start dying, and her fiancé's behavior is suspect. When she learns Enrico's true feelings about her—and what her father's actual plans are—will Antonella damn their families to eternal war, or will she broker a peace that might destroy her heart?

---◆---

1982
Cernobbio, Lake Como, Italy

The phone call, when it came, shattered Enrico Lucchesi's world. His mother, his brothers, all dead. Gunned down in the street by order of Carlo Andretti, *capo* of the Andretti family.

He still couldn't believe it was only him and Papà left. Enrico couldn't cry, couldn't speak past the *bocce* ball lodged in his throat. All he could do was stare dry-eyed at his father, who'd done nothing for the last ten minutes but sob, great shuddering wails that shook Enrico to the core. His father never cried. He'd always told his sons a *capo* had to be stronger, braver, tougher than other men.

But here he was, the great Rinaldo Lucchesi, weeping as if he'd never stop.

Enrico finally found his voice. "Papà," he croaked, reaching across the kitchen table for his father's hand. When there was no answer, he tried again. "Papà."

The slight rebuke in his tone—after all, how many times had his father berated Enrico for softness?—caused his father to look up, to notice him at last. Papà took a shaky breath and wiped his eyes with the handkerchief he always carried. He ignored the hand Enrico had stretched toward him, and Enrico pulled it back, all the way to his lap.

In the wake of those sobs, the kitchen seemed deadly quiet, filled only with the sounds of their breathing. His, his father's, and Dario's. Enrico glanced at the Andretti boy, who'd sat mute and wide-eyed this entire time.

That glance seemed to remind his father of Dario's presence, and a murderous glint came into his eyes. He snatched the boy out of his chair, scattering their playing cards to the floor. Dario let out a yelp of surprise. "*Per favore*, it's not my fault!"

For the past three days, ever since he'd taken Dario hostage in an effort to get Carlo Andretti to negotiate, to end the feud between their families, Papà had insisted on treating Dario as a guest. A guest who couldn't leave the house, but a guest nevertheless. Because that's how civilized men handled things. With honor, with respect.

All that courtesy seemed forgotten now as his father wrestled Dario to the butcher block in the corner and mashed Dario's slender body against the counter. When he pinned the boy's arm to the cutting board, bile rose in Enrico's throat. Dario was only fourteen, tall and gangly, all bones. He was no match for Rinaldo Lucchesi, a bull of a man in his prime.

Enrico was no match for him either, but he had to try. He sprang from his chair, his eyes glued to Dario's wrist, thin as kindling under his father's meaty hand. Papà grabbed the cleaver from the knife block and swung it up in the air. Enrico grabbed his father's arm at the top of its downward arc and yanked it back.

Gritting his teeth, Enrico strained to stop his father. *Dio*, Papà seemed stronger than that marlin Enrico had hooked two years ago on a sport-fishing trip. He'd been Dario's age then, too weak to hold out against the enormously powerful fish for long, but he'd put on muscle since. Not enough though. He was still only sixteen, and his father had to outweigh him by close to seventy pounds.

They seemed to struggle forever, his father grunting curses under his breath, Dario's thin reedy voice whimpering "*per favore, per favore*" in the background.

At last his father said something intelligible, his voice a rusty rasp. "I am your *capo*. Do not interfere."

"You always said we aren't savages."

"Savagery is all Carlo Andretti understands!"

Papà gave him a hard shove, weakening Enrico's hold. Catching a whiff of his father's cologne, Enrico flashed back to a time when his father had carried him up to bed as a boy, cradling him in his arms. Somehow he had to reach that part of his father. Somehow he had to make him see reason.

Enrico's lungs burned and his arms shook, his father's muscles hard as granite underneath his hands. "I want Don Andretti dead too. But crippling Dario isn't going to bring Mamma and Primo and Mario back."

His father let out an inarticulate cry of rage and stilled, no longer fighting. "I must do something. I must show Carlo I can hurt him."

"Not the whole hand. The Lucchesis aren't cruel. You always say that."

"The little finger then."

Enrico swallowed against the acid surging at the back of his tongue. Now that Primo was dead, everything had changed. Someday, when he became *capo*, he'd have to make harder decisions than this. Decisions that meant life or death. Decisions he'd never wanted to make, had never pictured himself making. But Carlo Andretti had killed his brothers, had taken any other future away from him.

He could no longer think like a boy, act like a boy. He had to be a man now.

Enrico nodded and released his father's arm, then stepped away and closed his eyes. He tried not to hear the thunk as the cleaver bit into bone and wood, tried not to hear Dario's cries of pain. Tried hard to think of what he'd done as mercy.

———— ◆ ————

Two years later
London, England

Enrico Lucchesi left his infant son howling in his sobbing mother's arms. Because he had to. Because it was his duty. Because he was engaged to marry another.

Antonella Andretti. Carlo Andretti's daughter. A girl he barely knew.

He took one last look at Nico and Veronica. "Rico, don't go!" she called, following him onto the path that led to the gate of the small home he'd paid for, the only thing he'd been able to leave her, aside from a monthly check.

He couldn't marry her. He couldn't raise his son. He couldn't do anything but return to Italy and his fate.

Veronica ran up behind him, her bare feet slapping on the paving stones, Nico letting out another wail. "Rico, please," she sobbed. "Please."

His throat tight, Enrico turned back to her, waving at the waiting driver and holding up a finger to tell the man he would be a while.

Veronica looked like her world was ending, and it was all his fault. He never should've gotten involved with her, no matter how lonely he'd been. Not when he knew he was already promised to someone else. Not when he wasn't free. He'd just wanted *something* for himself. Something—someone—who was *his* choice. At least for a while. But it had all been a horrible mistake. Except for Nico.

Reaching up, he brushed away the blonde strands that had fallen across Veronica's green eyes. Eyes flooded with tears, all because of him. "I am sorry, *cara*. I must."

Her face crumpled. "You can't leave us. What about Nico?"

His fingers drifted across her cheek. Leaving them was going to kill him. "He has you. And I will be back. To visit."

She shook her head, her voice low, urgent. "You can't marry her. Not when you love me."

The lump in his throat grew. "I told you, *cara*. I have no choice."

"I don't understand. How can your father make you marry this girl? You're eighteen. You're a man. You can make your own choices."

He shook his head. She'd never understand. Even if he explained who he really was—that the Enrico Franchetti she knew was a fiction—she'd never understand the life he led, the rules he lived under. The rules of the 'Ndrangheta, the Honored Society. The Calabrian Mafia. They'd considered him a man for two years now. Ever since he'd taken the vows and become the one thing he'd sworn he'd never become: a man of honor. One of *them*. A Mafioso.

But with Primo and Mario dead, he'd had no choice. His father needed him.

And if Enrico didn't marry Antonella Andretti in four weeks, he and his father would be dead shortly after. Carlo Andretti would ensure it.

Leaning forward, he pressed his lips to Veronica's forehead, then both of her cheeks. "I'll be back as often as I can."

She grabbed his collar with her free hand and rose up on her tiptoes, pressing her mouth to his, the kiss desperate, urgent. He didn't return it. Instead, he gently tugged her hand from his shirt. "Veronica, that is over between us."

Anger erupted over her face, and she punched him in the chest. "Go then! Go back to Italy and leave me. Leave your *son*." She held Nico up so he could take one last look.

Nico was fourteen months old now, his green eyes bright, his chestnut hair curling around his plump cheeks. He waved a chubby fist at Enrico. "Papà," Nico burbled, and tears pricked Enrico's eyes. He kissed his son's fist, kissed his cheeks, and let him go.

Veronica snatched their son to her chest and glared at him, her pale cheeks flooding with color. "You go, Enrico Franchetti. You go, and don't darken my door again."

"I will be back, Veronica." He said the words wearily. At first he'd loved her volatility, her fire. But there was a frantic, histrionic edge to it that had worn thin over time. She'd changed so much from when they'd first met. Had he really known her at all, or had he been too young to see her clearly? Maybe with him gone for a while, she'd calm down, relax. Find someone new.

Though the thought of another man raising his son made his gut twist. Nico was his. *His* son. *His* child.

But Nico was safe here. He'd grow up far away from the 'Ndrangheta. And if Enrico was careful, Nico would never know that world, would never have to fear for his life. Would never know a man like Carlo Andretti.

Carlo Andretti. The one man Enrico desperately wanted to kill.

"You can't leave me like this, Rico," Veronica sobbed. "You can't."

"I do not want to." He raised a hand to touch her cheek, to touch Nico again.

"You have to do something. You have to come back."

He hated seeing her like this. Hated the desperate look in her eyes, hated the quaver in her voice. He'd done this to her with his omissions, his wishful thinking. He owed her and Nico something more. "I will try. Perhaps there is a way out of this marriage."

Her mouth curved into a grateful smile, and his stomach contracted into a ball. Had he just lied to her again?

He sincerely hoped not.

There had to be a way to win his freedom. There had to be a way to keep his son.

---·---

Two days later
Blevio, Lake Como, Italy

Since returning home, Enrico had dreaded this moment. He turned to his father as the driver pulled onto the road that led to the Andretti estate. Papà looked drawn, pale. Thin. The sight made Enrico burn. Carlo Andretti had ruined the man Enrico had always admired. "Why are we doing this? All he wants is to rub our noses in shit. Like his damn dogs."

"Rico, control yourself. Don't let him rile you."

Enrico's blood pressure skyrocketed. "Don't let him *rile* me? After what he's done? After Mamma and Primo and Mario? After forcing me to leave—"

Rinaldo raised a finger for silence. "We are the only ones who know about that."

Enrico flicked his eyes at the driver and his father's bodyguard, Livio, in the front seat.

"You don't trust them?" he whispered.

Rinaldo leaned closer. "I do. But men can't speak of what they don't know. Yes?"

His father was right. The fewer people who knew, the better. If Carlo Andretti ever learned of Nico's existence, the boy would be dead, and Enrico and Rinaldo along with him.

"You need to meet the girl. It's customary," Rinaldo said.

"It's also customary that I can refuse her." Before his father could speak, Enrico added, "Oh that's right—I *can't*. I marry her, or Carlo hunts us down like rabbits. Frightened fucking rabbits. Have I got that right?"

Enrico didn't have time to do more than recoil from the slap to his cheek. "Stop it. Now." His father's voice was like iron. "I'm doing this for *you*. So you'll have a future. Instead of a grave. You think I like this any more than you do?"

The car pulled to a stop, and Rinaldo slammed out before Enrico could answer. He rubbed his stinging cheek, shame overwhelming him. His father had always been a proud man who'd never bowed to anyone. And certainly never to Carlo fucking Andretti. But that was before everything that had happened during the last two years. "I'm sorry, Papà," Enrico whispered to himself as he got out of the car and followed his father and Livio inside. The four guards who'd accompanied them in another car brought up the rear. Their weapons weren't drawn, but their alertness spoke volumes. They were in enemy territory.

Carlo's villa wasn't nearly as grand as the Lucchesis' own, but it was well-furnished, as Enrico recalled from the last time he'd visited. Four years ago, before all the trouble had started between his father and Carlo.

They'd come for a wedding—some cousin of Carlo's had wanted to be married on the lake. It was the first time Enrico had met Antonella Andretti. He'd been fourteen, she twelve. A gawky slip of a girl, all large dark eyes and a mass of black hair. Nothing special. He'd barely taken notice of her. And there'd been that one time at school when some very stupid boys had been harassing her and her twin brother Dario. Enrico had stepped in and stopped it. She'd tried to thank him, but he'd brushed her off. He couldn't even remember what her voice sounded like.

He'd find out soon enough.

They were shown around back to a large terrace beneath a huge plane tree, its silver-gray bark peeling. Sunlight filtered through the thick green foliage, dappling the figure of Carlo Andretti, who was sitting at a table and sipping from a steaming cappuccino. Breakfast dishes had been set out for six. Carlo's family, plus Rinaldo and Enrico.

The guards fanned out and took positions around the table. Carlo watched them, but didn't comment beyond the amusement in his eyes.

He rose when Rinaldo and Enrico approached, a smug smile spreading across his face. "*Prego*," he said, motioning them to take chairs at the table, playing the gracious host. Enrico wanted to strangle him. A bitter taste rose in his mouth and his stomach churned. How could he be expected to just *sit* there and have breakfast with the man who'd killed his mother, his brothers?

Enrico placed a hand on the back of a chair, but didn't sit. He was gripping the painted metal so hard his fingers hurt. His emotions must have shown on his face because Carlo's grin widened. He looked at Rinaldo and said, "So your pup thinks he's a wolf, yes? He thinks he will challenge me?"

Enrico looked at his father. "Papà, *per favore*—"

"Sit," Rinaldo said between gritted teeth.

Holding Carlo's gaze, Enrico took a seat. Carlo chuckled and leaned across the table. "You'll live longer if you learn to be more like your father. Accept your losses and move on."

Enrico took a deep breath and looked away. Someday, somehow he'd make Carlo Andretti pay. What he didn't quite understand was why his father was just *taking* this treatment. Sure, things were bad, but they couldn't be *this* bad, could they? Something had happened. Something Papà hadn't told him.

Carlo smoothed a hand over his coal-black hair and took another sip of his cappuccino, motioning for a maid to pour espresso for Enrico and Rinaldo. Nodding at Enrico, he said, "You've grown. So where has your father kept you stashed these last two years?"

Enrico looked at his father, who nodded. "England. Boarding school."

"Did you enjoy their bland food?"

"Would you?"

Carlo laughed. He addressed Rinaldo. "I like your pup."

"Does that mean you won't shoot me too?" Enrico asked.

Carlo laughed harder and slapped the table. Rinaldo glared at Enrico, but Enrico didn't apologize. "You could teach my boy a thing or two about balls," Carlo said.

The double doors in the back of the house opened, and Enrico turned, his heart speeding up. What did Antonella look like now?

Dario stepped out first. He'd filled out some since Enrico had seen him last. He was followed by his mother, Romola, who stopped just outside the doorway and spoke to someone still inside. Her voice was pitched low, and he couldn't hear what she said.

Was something wrong? Did Antonella not like this idea either? If so, maybe she'd refuse him, and he and his father could make some other arrangement with Carlo to end the feud.

And Enrico could go back to England and his son.

Finally Signora Andretti walked toward them, and her daughter stepped outside. Antonella's head was down, her eyes staring at her feet, her mass of black hair shielding her face. She was wearing a light, flowery sundress with simple sandals. She was quite tan, her legs and arms shapely, her body willowy. Not much in the way of breasts, but that was all right—

She looked up and straight at him, her eyes locking with his.

A pang of disappointment hit him. She was plain, so plain. And she had the "Andretti beak." That overlarge nose that looked fine on the males, but that overwhelmed the faces of the women. Perhaps "plain" was being kind.

Her step faltered. *Merda*. She'd seen what he was thinking. He forced a smile, but she looked away and stalked to the other end of the table where she wouldn't have to talk to him.

He wanted to crawl under his chair. He was a worm. An insect. He'd just upset this poor girl. She'd been teased plenty at school—the taunts had reached even his ears. He'd been among the popular crowd, but despite their wealth, the Andretti twins had been outcasts. As far as he knew, Antonella had ignored the taunts and Dario had remained silent, speaking to no one but his sister.

Well, she'd apparently *pretended* to ignore the insults. Obviously they'd made their mark.

And here he'd gone and made her feel them all over again.

The only good thing was that she was sure to reject him now. And then he'd be free.

Breakfast—an assortment of cold cuts, fruit, and pastries—was served, no one chatting much. Dario kept his right hand in his lap, eating awkwardly with his left. Had Carlo told him to do that, or was the boy ashamed? Enrico's cheeks heated. Here was another Andretti he'd wronged. He should've argued harder with his father. Maybe he could've spared Dario that pain.

But maybe—if he was honest—maybe he hadn't wanted to.

Maybe he'd wanted his vengeance. And maybe he'd taken it in the wrong place.

He pushed his plate away, suddenly not hungry. Perhaps his father was right, and he needed to get a better handle on his feelings. At least when it came to the Andrettis. He couldn't seem to do anything right when it came to them.

His throat clogged, an apology lodged in it. But how could words ever make up for what he'd done to Dario?

"May I be excused?" Antonella asked. Her voice was a lovely, husky contralto, and Enrico found the courage to meet her gaze.

"You may," Carlo said.

She tossed her napkin down and rose, heading up the hill toward the olive grove.

"I'd like to talk to her. If I may," Enrico said, not stopping to second-guess himself. He was going to apologize for something today. Carlo nodded, and Enrico sprang up from his chair, loping after her. She was surprisingly fast, and he had to put in a little effort to catch her. "Antonella," he called as he came up behind her.

"Spare me," she said, not looking at him. He placed a hand on her shoulder and she shrugged away. "Don't touch me."

"*Per favore*—"

"I should've known better. To think I thought you were nice!"

His steps faltered, but hers continued. She split off her present course and veered for the hedge maze to their right.

For a moment, he stared after her. Maybe he ought to leave her be, let her reject him—

But he couldn't stomach the idea of her thinking that he hated how she looked. That he was rejecting her.

Even though he had.

His face hot with shame, he trailed her into the maze, and she broke into a run, sprinting away from him. He charged after her, following her around turn after turn, soon utterly disoriented.

Exasperated, he put on some speed and grabbed her left arm. She stopped and whirled on him, her eyes blazing. "I told you not to touch me!"

The tremble in her voice signaled how close to the edge she was. "Antonella, *per favore*. I just want to apologize."

"For *what?*" she asked, stepping closer to him, her arms crossed over her chest.

His cheeks flamed hotter. What could he say that wouldn't make her feel worse? "For my behavior."

She stepped closer. "For what *exactly?*" she asked.

Oh *Dio*. She was going to make him say it aloud. He couldn't do that.

"I'm sorry," he stammered.

"Sorry for *what?*" Her voice could cut glass. He took a step back as she advanced. "Afraid to say what you were thinking?" she asked, motioning to her face.

"No, I—"

She snorted. "Go ahead, *lie*. Because you're too *kind* to say what you were thinking. How disappoin—" Her voice grew thick and she turned away.

He placed a hand on her shoulder. "I'm sorry I caused you pain. Truly."

"Papà says I'm beautiful. But I know the truth." She wiped her eyes and sniffed, still not looking at him.

"You have beautiful eyes, and your voice—"

"Stop. Just *stop*." She rounded on him. "Life's been easy for you, Enrico Lucchesi. Have you ever even had a pimple?"

He scratched his chin. "A few."

She laughed. "And how long did that phase last? A week?" She gestured up and down his body. "You've always been a god. You don't know what it's like to realize you have a face only a parent could love."

He didn't know why he did it, but he reached out and tweaked her nose. Her mouth dropped open in rage. "What are you *doing*?" she yelled.

"Making you stop feeling sorry for yourself. Your being angry at me is better."

She placed her hands on her hips. "You need me, Enrico Lucchesi, whether you realize it or not."

"I don't need you."

"Ask your father. I did this for *you*. For Dario. For my own father."

"You sound like this was your idea."

She crossed her arms again. "It was the perfect solution." After a moment she added, "It *was*."

"What do you mean?"

"My father wouldn't stop the *faida* until your family was ground to dust. But he didn't realize what this war was costing him. The men were weary, the merchants were sick of being caught in the crossfire, and the *carabinieri* wouldn't keep looking the other way, no matter how much money he threw at them. The war had to be stopped, and in a way that let both sides save face."

She honestly thought she'd stopped the feud? "Wait a minute. Your father took advice from you? A girl?"

She nodded. "I suggested it, and he listened."

"But… why?"

Her face darkened. "Because he loves me. I was afraid for Dario. Especially after we got his finger in a box."

"*Madonna*," Enrico murmured. What must that have been like for her? "I'm sorry about that too."

"You might tell Dario that."

"I don't think he wants to hear it."

She shrugged. "Maybe not."

They stood there in silence, both of them looking anywhere but at each other. Finally he said, "Can we start over?"

Her eyes snapped to his. "I will *never* forget the look on your face."

He groaned. "I was caught off guard."

"No. It was an honest reaction. The last thing I want from you now is lies."

He threw his hands in the air. "*Basta!*" Enrico wheeled away from her and tried to retrace his steps but ended up in a dead end. Even though the mid-May day was just pleasantly warm, he was broiling in his suit jacket, so he whipped it off. Then he surveyed his surroundings, searching for anything that looked familiar. Turning around, he saw her standing a few feet away. She'd trailed him, probably having a good laugh at his expense.

"Follow me," she said. They'd gone a few meters before she stopped. "You honestly want another chance?" she asked, her voice low, her eyes darting toward him then away.

Strangely, he did. "Yes."

She smiled. When she wasn't scowling, her face lit up, and her curved lips caught his eye. They were soft, kissable. Plump. She was... passable. Even almost cute. "That's the first honest thing you've said to me today."

How had they gotten to this point? She'd been ready to reject him—she'd been ready to do what he'd *wanted*—and he'd begged her to reconsider?

The smile left her face then, and she pressed a palm into the center of his chest. "But I want to be clear—I'm no pushover, Enrico Lucchesi."

He nodded, letting a hint of a grin touch his lips. "Believe me, I've figured that much out."

They returned to the table in silence, Carlo's eyes on them. "All is well?" he asked, his eyes sliding from Enrico to Antonella. She nodded, but all Enrico could think about was how miserable his father looked. Just what had Carlo been saying to him while they were gone?

This wasn't how it was going to end. He—they—weren't just going to roll over for Carlo. Not if Enrico had his way. His family needed to be avenged.

There was only one problem. Carlo Andretti was a nearly impossible target.

Then a crazy thought struck him: perhaps the men who'd pulled the triggers weren't.

END OF SPECIAL PREVIEW

Print and Ebook

www.danadelamar.com

Continue reading for a special preview of Kristine Cayne's third Deadly Vices novel

DEADLY BETRAYAL

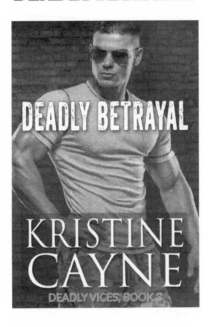

An Afghan women's rights activist with a dark secret.

Azita Seraj, doctor and women's rights activist in Afghanistan, is horrified to learn that her late husband's brother, Khalid Mullazai, is giving his eleven-year-old niece to a militant warlord. Desperate to save the girl, she reaches out to the only hope she has: an American soldier she treated several years earlier for a near-fatal gunshot wound. A wound he received in an ambush she'd unwittingly initiated. Can she enlist his aid and still keep secret her betrayal?

An American soldier searching for answers.

Kaden Christiansen never forgot the beautiful Afghan doctor who saved his life, and when he receives her cry for help, he doesn't hesitate. He relishes the opportunity to see Azita again, and being in-country will give him a chance to hunt down the person responsible for the ambush that left one of his men dead.

A deadly conspiracy that threatens them both...

Pursued by Mullazai and the warlord's fighters as they travel across the country disguised and posing as a married couple, Kaden and Azita begin to fall for their own act and for each other. But Kaden senses that Azita is holding back. Is the reason their cultural differences, or something darker?

Praise for Kristine Cayne's *Deadly Betrayal*

"Kristine also did a great job putting a hopeful love story against, what at times felt like a hopeless background, a country or world that had lost most of its hope. The contrast there was remarkable. Between the action scenes, the several OMG suspenseful plot twists, and my own personal love and devotion for the main character (have loved [him] in all the previous books), I believe this book should be what everyone picks up!" – *Xavier's Book Reviews*

An excerpt from *Deadly Betrayal*

With his fingertips, Kaden lightly traced her cheekbones, her jaw, the length of her throat. Azita's eyelids dropped. Was she embarrassed?

"Open your eyes, honey. Watch how I'm touching you. Look at my face." He tilted her chin so their gazes met. "See how much I'm enjoying it."

Whatever she saw in his eyes caused her skin to turn a very pretty shade of pink. Her nipples on the other hand, turned a deep copper, like an old penny. Forcing himself to be patient, he stroked lightly over her shoulders, her collarbones. When he trailed a finger down the valley between her breasts, she shuddered. Goose bumps covered her arms, and he swore the blue of her eyes darkened.

"Watch my hands," he said. When she broke eye contact, he allowed his fingers to circle her breasts, to feather their sensitive undersides. His cock strained as need flashed over him, leaving him breathless. His tongue ached to follow the path of his fingers, to suckle the swollen peaks. *Soon,* he promised himself.

Print and Ebook

www.kristinecayne.com